THE GOLDEN VOID

Copyright © 2020 Louis Mulvenna

Louis Mulvenna, traveller, author, dreamer, currently lives on Planet Bristol. Grateful thanks are due to all my long-suffering friends and family on whom I dumped this book, demanding feedback.

To get in touch, please write to louismulvenna@gmail.com.

THE GOLDEN VOID

Louis Mulvenna

To Annie, my champion

Chapter 1 | Mumbai

Arrival is a nightmare. A sequence of nightmares. How could it be worse? A cascade of misfortunes. But overriding and undermining the actual events – the incidents and mishaps and accidents and follies – even without those essential components of the nightmare, if the occurrences had not occurred, it would still be a nightmare. For a start there is the background noise, a kind of steady scream or siren, pitched far too high, making it hard to think. It is grating, disorientating, like static, skewering all perception. That's the underlying layer. On top there is the foreground noise: the shouting, the yelping, the random crashing, the motorised din, the clinking and clanking – a complex cacophony that is ubiquitous, inescapable and excruciating.

And that's just the audible part. Visually, too, nothing computes. Everything is happening at once. There is no logic. And anyway, the airport lights are too bright, blurring outlines, clouding vision, deflecting thought. And then there is the heat, a dense weight imbuing everything, suffocating sensation, garbling judgement. It's extreme and absurd. At this hour – past midnight local time – it makes no sense for anything to be this hot.

This is the context of their arrival. So it stands to reason that things will descend further into chaos as soon as they are past the myriad passport and security checks. How could it be otherwise?

Stumbling out of the terminal's confusion, weighed down by heavy backpacks, they have to make sense of a new outside world that snags their attention in every direction. They negotiate their way past a disorderly parade of hyper-active men offering all kinds of services, their ears ringing with the shouted inducements, and eventually find themselves warily following a turbaned figure in dun-coloured shirt and trousers to a vehicle parked under a street-lamp in whose sodium glow seethe multitudes of insects. It is a cumbrous yellow and black Ambassador, big and bulky, into which the man unceremoniously ushers them after receiving their instructions on where to go and pocketing the fare which, he insists, must be pre-paid.

It is fiendishly uncomfortable, even more so when the vehicle lurches into motion, the tight-lipped driver manoeuvring at speed through the wayward night-time traffic like a disturbingly calm, homicidal demon. To left and right they catch sight of bodies deposited at random, as if they have been spat out of the sky, abandoned where they have fallen in the dimly lit streets. Even with all the taxi windows open it is hard to breathe; the air is damp, sucking the energy out of them, and doesn't seem to contain enough oxygen. By the time the Ambassador deposits them in front of the hotel they have previously pulled from the internet, they are still drenched with sweat, but now in a semi-delirious state, simultaneously listless and feverish. The street is reeking with the acid stench of urine, there are mice running around their feet, and there follows a complicated dispute with the suddenly loquacious driver concerning an excess fare which, for obscure reasons, he is obliged to charge them. In the end, after a series of non-sequiturs and leaps of logic, Dougie fishes from his wallet a wad of notes that he knows is way too much and thrusts it into his hand. Profanities are exchanged instead of tips or thanks, and the Ambassador speeds off in a black blast of exhaust.

From the outside the hotel appears far seedier than it appeared on the booking site and more squalid than the dubious online reviews suggested. On one side of the neon-lit entrance there is a boy who looks about nine years old, hunched over a steaming cauldron suspended over a gas flame. On the other side, sprawled on a sheet of cardboard on the ground, is a man without legs, whose beseeching hands and eyes the two westerners manage to avoid but who nonetheless succeeds in instilling in them a guilty terror.

Inside, the reception area has what look like shit stains on the blue walls. A ceiling fan turns sluggishly and mosquitoes whine around their faces. A TV with over-saturated colour shouts from one corner of the room, in front of which an obese man in a vest is reclining on a tattered sofa. He turns to contemplate them with sleepy, scornful eyes, then, cutting across Dougie's introduction, demands their passports, his attention already back on the screen.

And that's when the shocking truth hits Jules, a lightning bolt that turns his insides to water. His bum-bag, containing cash, cards, phone and passport, is no longer around his waist. Stupidly he keeps feeling for it, unable to believe its absence, dumbly patting his pockets as if it might somehow be in one of those. But there is no denying: it is gone.

The two gape at each other in panic. Jules flies out of the reception to make doubly sure the taxi is departed. Of course it is nowhere to be seen. The beggar's hands reach for him and pleading noises are uttered, the nine-year-old is grinning and gloating. It is gone. The taxi is gone and his bum-bag is gone.

Jules scrutinises the two hotel sentinels, trying to identify his possessions among the small heaps of rags around them. The bag could be in the midst of those rags – how can he know? Then, out of nowhere, a motorised three-wheeler pulls up beside him, a voice jabbering. Jules frowns uncomprehendingly, part of him thinking that the solution to his problems has miraculously arrived, then he realises that the voice is demanding to know where he wants to go. It is an autorickshaw. He shoos away his tormentor and re-enters the hotel, his pace now slow and leaden, his knees trembling. He turns despairing eyes to Dougie, who looks blue-skinned under the neon light but somehow manages to engage his reason. 'We'll deal with it later,' he says. 'The guy's got my passport. That's all he needs for now.'

But the man, now stationed behind a chipped reception desk, isn't finished with them. He pushes two sheafs of paper at them: two lots of booking forms separated with carbon paper, and two pens which don't appear to write. They run their eyes over the faded print in a daze. Name, address, birth date, arrival date, departure date, last place visited, onward destination, flight number, passport number, visa number, room number and signature in triplicate. Jules doesn't know his passport or visa numbers so he makes them up. The fan seems to make no difference to the heat in the room, rivers of sweat stream off their faces and onto the forms, blinding their eyes, while the mosquitoes keep droning and biting. Then they are instructed to stare at the man's phone while he takes a photograph of each one of them. He examines the results, grunts, then indicates for the process to be repeated, this time with their heads tilted slightly upward. The two westerners demand to see the results: Jules, normally so neat and self-possessed, with hair cut short around his ears and growing to a longer, floppy-but-groomed style on top, looks wild, panicked and desperate; Dougie, who is shorter and stockier, his scalp clipped smooth as snooker felt, appears equally deranged, with startled eyes and yellow-blue skin.

Finally it is over. The fat man hands them a key, gestures upstairs, and slouches back to his sofa in front of the blaring TV. Shouldering their bags, they stagger up narrow stairs and along a short corridor, searching for their room number in the weak light emitting from a buzzing fluorescent tube. Locating their door, they find a flimsy padlock fastened around the latch, which, after a few fumbled attempts, yields to their key, and they let themselves in. An exhalation of odorous hot air greets them. They find the light switch, and quickly take in the cramped room, the pale green walls smudged black around the two single beds where bodies have leaned, with a deeper black above the yellowed pillows. There is a cracked basin in the corner with a single tap. On the ceiling, a fan whirrs into life when another switch is flicked, swaying precariously on its slender stalk. There is no window. A door leads into a tiled bathroom across whose floor half a dozen cockroaches scatter when they switch on the light to peer in. The bathroom contains a ceramic squat toilet and another single tap sticking out of the wall above a grimy red bucket. None of this bears the slightest resemblance to the photos on the website.

'I don't believe this,' Dougie mutters, his mild Scottish accent sounding grim and exhausted.

'Let's check out now,' Jules says.

'And go where? It's night-time. And what if the taxi-driver comes back with your money-belt? And where are we anyway?'

'We'll check out tomorrow.'

'And what about your passport? And money?'

'Tomorrow. I'm famished. We've got to eat. Now'

'And drink.'

But they remember the hostile night outside, and the daunting heat, and the legless beggar, and decide to stay put. Jules secures two bottles of water from the fat man in the vest and they lock themselves into their room with the fan turned on full and sit on their beds wondering why the hell they are here.

Chapter 2 | Chennai

Cynthia stares hard at the Shiva Nataraja. It is mad, with four flailing arms, each engaged in a different activity: two pointed up and down and two bearing what seem to be a flame and a drum. One leg is raised and lithely bent, the other pressing down on some wretched creature – a dog or a demon perhaps. Shiva is the Creator, the Preserver and the Destroyer all in one. How neat. The god wears an inscrutably beatific expression on its face and is adorned with earrings, pendant, chain and some kind of tall headwear. All within a flaming circle. It is the dance of life that he dances, and he is the lord of the dance. That is the meaning of 'nataraja', her guidebook tells her – lord or king of the dance. It is this never-ending jig that keeps the universe turning. She could look at it for hours, here in this dusty, ill-lit hall, once part of a sultan's palace, now a museum of Chola sculpture. Sinuous and dynamic, it commands attention. The last time she was so absorbed in a piece of Asian statuary, it was an image of the Buddha, or rather, many of them, as seen on a visit to Burma ten or fifteen years ago. Is it called Myanmar now? But the experience then was so different. The plump, contented Buddhas she saw there exuded serenity and stillness, suggesting simplicity and wisdom; this, on the other hand, is slim, spry and nonchalant, brimming with vital energy, charged with potential.

Oliver, she notices, seems equally intrigued, giving the image his full attention for several minutes before moving on to study a stout Ganesh and a buxom Parvati. He doesn't comment, but releases one of his explosive grunts that sounds like he is clearing his throat but is in fact an annoying tic – one that he seems quite unconscious of. He usually has something to say when viewing art (or rather, as he puts it, 'art') in Cynthia's company, but this time he merely drinks it in. Whether he is admiring or mystified or neither, Cynthia can't tell, and she's happy not to ask. She finds the mystery of Oliver one of his most attractive qualities, and feels vaguely afraid of pulling away the veil. Experience has told her that it's usually best not to know what lies beneath.

For now she is living in the moment. On this, her first visit to India, she is continually struck anew by the smallest details: the sudden billowing of a sari, the smooth curve of a rocky bluff, the multiple trailing columns of a banyan tree, the creviced face of an old woman, the simple poise of a child – all these fill her with wonder. Every new perspective, every turn of the head, imparts a novel sensation. The colour combinations alone make her dizzy: a salmon seascape under a lavender sky; bright white teeth in a dark brown face; a shawl of black and tangerine, or jade and violet, or saffron and turquoise. Yes, it is probably the colours more than anything that she finds most rapturous, but she can also be captivated by sound – the rhythmic tapping of a distant woodpecker, the melody of an unseen flute, or the squealing of a flight of parakeets. Odours, too – pungent waves of jasmine and vanilla and ginger and nutmeg wafting over her without warning. And then there are the flavours: coconut and citrus and mustard-seed and coriander, all in the same dish. She even finds the spicy tea, masala chai, perplexing, cloyingly sweet yet curiously satisfying.

This morning they joined a group of tourists to view Chennai's most famous sights. There was Fort George, full of pompous portraits of British royalty and governor-generals. Then there was the Hindu temple, where, to Oliver's evident disapproval, Cynthia was persuaded to sample some truly disgusting 'holy water' (fearful of causing offence, she forced herself to retain it in her mouth until leaving the temple precincts when she was able to spit it out discreetly). At a museum dedicated to Gandhi, where, as the only white-skinned members of the group, she and Oliver nonchalantly tried to avoid the accusatory eyes of the other members of the group – all Bengali, for some reason – as they listened to horrific tales of British iniquity and shameful colonial crimes. They also visited a 'snake park', where snakes were in short supply but whose other inhabitants, including a large group of crocodiles, all appeared to be asleep. Engrossing as all of these things were to Cynthia and Oliver, the sight that most warmed their hearts were the gaggles of smiling schoolchildren that were also present at each of these stops, neatly attired in *churidar* tunics and scarves of magenta or saffron. With their plaits and satchels, they filed hand in hand up and down the steps and in and out of the enclosures, expertly shepherded by bespectacled women teachers wrapped in saris. Oliver marveled at how polite and groomed and impeccably behaved they all were.

But it is all rather tiring too. On more than one occasion, Cynthia has felt a sense of overload, as if her brain is already replete and ready to close down, just for a spell. And right now, there is no better place for decelerating, for digesting and absorbing and reflecting, than right here in this hall of static statuary, so still yet containing so much energy. It is the perfect opportunity to study the cosmic dance – perhaps even learn a few steps – from a stationery standpoint.

Oliver's abrasive bark suddenly jolts her back to dull reality. She glances at her watch: they must move on. Rousing herself, she leaves the hard museum bench, feeling her knees creak and crack, and totters off to join him. Things to do, appointments to keep. This is their last day of sightseeing before heading west to join the others. Duty calls. Oh, ghastly! How anomalous that word sounds in this here and now!

*   *   *   *   *   *   *   *   *   *

Later that afternoon, while Oliver dozes, Cynthia sits on the balcony of their hotel room, sipping tea and staring into the clear blue sky. After a full day, she is happy that their crowded itinerary is done. She doesn't have to listen to anyone now, or view anything, or admire or learn or form an opinion about anything. Idly, her eyes focus on two tiny black squares in the distance, dancing above a horizon of square apartment blocks with washing strung across every roof: they are kites, struggling restlessly against the wind. She wonders about the little girls or boys down on the ground below them, at the other end of the tethering strings, and remembers how she too once stood at the end of a string, exhilarated, watching her own yellow diamond riding the wind, trailing its tail of streamers. She was a little girl herself then, with a whole lifetime in front of her. She can recall the excitement as if it were yesterday.

Nearer to hand, she now sees another kite, this one snagged irretrievably on the branches of a tree. That must have caused some little girl or boy a deal of heartbreak. She remembers the sharp pain she once felt in her own distant youth when her carefree pleasures were also dashed, as must happen to every child. For some reason this makes her think of the reason she and Oliver are here at all, in India. Sightseeing is just a sidetrip, after all, a diversion from more serious business. But no, she won't let herself dwell on that now. She wants to be here, in this moment, for as long as possible, while she can.

Leaning back in her chair, Cynthia allows her lids to close, resting her eyes from the waning afternoon light. She does not sleep, though. Instead, her ears become attuned to the sonic drama being played out around her. India, she reflects, is the noisiest place she has ever been in. Her systematic brain sifts and sorts through the layers. Most melodious is the melange of birdsong: the cawing of crows, the twittering of smaller birds, and the resonant hoots of others, all unseen. More gratingly, there is the insistent racket of vehicles – horns honked, engines revved, the roar of buses and trucks. And all is interspersed with random human voices – the laughter and musical gabble of children, the eruptions of men shouting, women calling, a megaphone crackling – and animal notes, the yelping of a puppy and the salvo of a larger dog's bark. Also in the mix are diverse bangs, crashes and minor explosions, a grinding, a drilling, a hammering, while closer at hand, on the street just below, someone is hawking and spitting. Nearest of all, from the other side of the bedroom door, there intrude irregular scurrying noises within the hotel itself – buckets banged on floors, abrupt commands and the electronic squawk of a TV set.

Cynthia is rather overwhelmed by it all. Sometimes she thinks it is too much for her, the plenitude of it. She is too old for this unending tumult. She is alarmed by India's hectic multiplicity, by the sheer challenge it presents to each one of her senses. Her only previous experience that comes close to this constant confusion were her brief visits to Hong Kong and Bangkok, many years back, but even in those swarming places she cannot recall the same degree of simultaneity – of everything happening at once, all the time. Then, there was Malaysia, of which her abiding impression was a more peaceful harmony, of smiling faces, of mostly friendly and considerate people. Memory, of course, is selective, and there must have been plenty of underlying currents there that she was not aware of, but she does not remember the same levels of tension and ceaseless striving that she senses here – not so much spitting or begging or staring or signs of disease and malnutrition. Of course Malaysia didn't reveal the same rich depths that she finds here, and, like Hong Kong, it was over-westernised, but at least travelling there was relatively easy and stress-free. She isn't even sure whether she actually *enjoys* being here, in India. How can one enjoy something so muddled, so consuming? Fascinating, of course, but likeable?

The words of Forster – Cynthia's preferred member of the Bloomsburies – come back to her, as his various wise insights have done repeatedly since their arrival in India: *I like mysteries, but I rather dislike muddles.*

She must remember to buy some postcards tonight, must remember to check her emails and charge her camera. Travelling is so much easier nowadays, and so much more complicated. She hears Oliver's benign low snore behind her and chuckles to herself, eyes still closed. The tired old woman listens and reflects, the enigmatic old man snoozes and dreams, the spry dancer dances eternally and smiles mysteriously. All sharing this moment, all separate but also, on one level, intrinsically connected. Strange life. Strange and happily inexplicable.

Chapter 3 | On the move

Ensconced at the back of a rusty, roaring, smoke-belching bus, scarf wound loosely around her hair and face, Esme has found the anonymity she craves. Only the occasional glance turns in her direction, and she is impervious behind her thick black sunglasses. Wearing white leggings and a knee-length kurta of dark crimson, she has left only her hands and ankles uncovered. Unless one were to notice these, a casual look might well identify her as an Indian tourist, not a westerner. The scarf encasing her face is partly a protection against the vile fumes and polluted air, but it also makes a good disguise. Since her first arrival in India she has not been able to accustom herself to being the object of people's attention. Somehow, people feel they have a right not only to stare but to fire inane questions at her, to attempt to trap her into pointless conversation, to define and reduce her. She has learned to mistrust every advance, and though at first she attempted to be polite, she soon became surly and unresponsive, and all the time hating herself for her rudeness, for seeming to fulfil every stereotype of the haughty foreigner lacking basic manners. It just wasn't her.

At least now it's easier. As she makes her way to the airport, ready to begin the next phase of this Indian adventure, she feels hardened, and better armed. She is on her way to join the family. Not her family, but the Daniel-Johnson clan. She will need her armour there. She won't be the only non-family member, but she will still be very much the outsider.

At least she will have dealt with the culture shock, or a large part of it, by the time she joins them. She won't have to cope with the hurdle of engaging with this crazy, complicated, unpredictable country in a virgin state, fresh off the plane, while having to face up to the crazy, complicated, unpredictable family that will undoubtedly encompass and overwhelm her attention over the following days. That would be too much at once.

Esme planned it all. She gave herself three weeks to acclimatize, to do her own thing, prior to her two weeks with the clan. Looking ahead, she had anticipated that the negotiations, the tactical give and take, and the forbearance and compromise awaiting her would be gruelling. And since she has sacrificed precious time to be here, she knew she had to mine this preliminary experience for everything it could offer.

True, she was ready for a break from home. India would not have been her first choice for unwinding and gathering herself, but all the same, she reasoned, there was a lot to recommend it too. Number one: she hadn't previously visited the country: she could cross it off the bucket list. Number two: it would mean some kind of closure in her personal life. Three: India was immensely ... challenging. That much was clear from the start – from the arrangement of her visa and the organisation of vaccinations and medications to her passage through immigration and security on arrival, every step of the way has been fraught with unforeseen obstacles and frustrations. But that has simply fired her, hardened her, and infused her with a determination not to be beaten, to get through it and triumph. Life, for Esme, is most real when it's a test, and she enjoys a challenge so long as there is a good prospect of overcoming it.

Lastly, of course, India is the mythic home of yoga. What started as a flirtation five years ago has grown to be a passion for her. She practises yoga every day, and when she isn't practising, she tries to live by it. She isn't a preacher, but she is a believer. From the long-sustained poses of yin and the satisfying precisions of iyengar, through the flowing movements of dru and vinyassa and the meditative depths of nidra, not to mention the propulsive exertions of ashtanga, jivamukti and kundalini – she has become a convert to the whole package.

So it was that Esme's first destination after the claustrophobia of Mumbai was the nearby city of Pune, where a taxi transported her to a quiet neighbourhood in the city's outskirts, home to the Chaya Ashram, to spend a week in the company of like-minded yogis. The pre-dawn rises, the constant exercises, the communal singing, the shared vegan meals – all of this has topped up her reserves of spiritual calm, so that by the end of it, when Esme boarded a night train – huge, monstrously long – heading north for a fortnight of intensive sightseeing, she was in a heightened state of receptivity and calm.

It didn't last. India took over – and it was incredible. At first she found herself mesmerised, her brain going into a kind of paralysis when confronted with the chaos and the sheer endless mass of humanity in all its forms wherever she looked. It was all too overwhelming – unmanageable, un-navigable, un-processable. Then she found the right method for dealing with it, primarily by joining the flow and putting herself in motion – by travelling. She found a quiet contentment in observing the land and its people from a succession of train and bus windows, traversing the subcontinent's infinite flatness, crossing broad rivers, passing sudden elevations and precipitous dips, watching it all through the perpetual, filtering haze of bleached light. She found herself sucked into the passing drama, the continuous parade of water buffalos on river banks or wallowing in lakes, of brilliant blue peacocks in immense grassy expanses, of gangs of monkeys infiltrating stations with criminal stealth, and of gracefully erect women in brilliant saris, expertly balancing tall bundles on their heads as they weaved in single file though densely-planted fields of maize. She glimpsed jaunty groups of boys and girls playing cricket in woodland clearings, dusty labourers and hobbling pilgrims, not to mention the numerous people nonchalantly defecating by the rail tracks. Quite possibly they were also dreaming or composing poetry while they were thus engaged.

She wrote it all down in a travel blog, detailing her kaleidoscopic observations and including numerous photos. Everything was recorded, not omitting India's more repellent aspects, such as the mountains and rivers of discarded plastic strewn along the train tracks and outside every town and village, sometimes picked over by cows and crows and dogs and goats but often neglected even by these otherwise undiscriminating scavengers. In the crowded corridors of the trains, where she tried to turn a blind eye to the roaches and mice scurrying across the carriage floor, there were horribly mutilated beggars, blind or limbless or with ravaged faces, part of a procession that included chai-wallahs, peanut sellers and fortune-telling transvestites.

It was impossible to maintain her objective eye in the face of this constant spectacle, but she thirstily drank it all in anyway. She came to enjoy the travelling more than the actual destinations of her various bus and train journeys – the dutiful stops where she performed all the prescribed tourist rituals. In Ajanta and Ellora she clambered in and out of caves filled with ancient sculptures. In Agra she joined thousands of camera-toting Indian, Chinese, Japanese and Western tourists for the slow traipse around the Taj Mahal. In Jaipur she toured palaces, silk emporia and backstreet bazaars. Sometimes, fellow sightseers, mostly Indian, would stop her and ask her to pose with them in their photos in front of a temple, mosque or fort. She never queried why they wanted her, a complete stranger, to appear on their social pages, but she posed anyway, planting a smile on her face which immediately vanished when they released her to pass onto the next photo op.

It was all hard work, and every day the battle was renewed.

Every morning, she hoisted her unwieldy rucksack onto her shoulders, donned her scarf and dark glasses and geared up for the next challenge. She learned fast: first and foremost she learned not to be drawn into any social interaction with any of the local people in any tourist environment. Just to answer any of the endlessly repeated questions (more like demands) – 'Which country?' 'What is your name?' 'Madam, where are you going?' – even to respond to a 'Hallo!' from a stranger on the street was to initiate a long, formulaic, ultimately meaningless exchange that more often than not led to an invitation to make a monetary transaction. Even to meet someone's eye was to solicit an unwanted proposition, even to rest one's eye for a second too long on anything from a tourist trinket to a pile of fruit was to encourage a plea to buy, buy, buy. Once she understood how it worked, the rules were simple: never accept a favour, never take anything at face value, never allow your eyes to linger.

Her antidote to the daily hassles and palaver was, of course, yoga, which she practised morning and evening. While she was doing it she was able to rise above the daily troughs and stresses, though serenity's spell never lasted long. Stepping forth from her air-conditioned hotel she was soon coated with soupy sweat and subjected to the usual intrusive stares and brazen inquisitions. Her exertions quickly drained her, reducing her to a dull lethargy. Browbeaten and intimidated, wrapped in her protective shell and reluctant to enter into conversation, she met few people until, in Rajasthan, she made the acquaintance of a Swiss chef on her second day in Pushkar, with whom, to her complete surprise, she formed an unlikely alliance. Twenty years her senior, Marcus was revisiting the country after a gap of three decades. He joined her for dinner at the hotel where they were both staying after the neighbourhood generator failed and they agreed to share their candle-light. With no air-con and no ceiling fan to shift the sweltering air, they stewed in their sweat, batting away insects as they ate, but she found herself responding to Marcus's easygoing enthusiasm. She laughed at his accounts of the mishaps and misfortunes that had befallen him on his journeys, and came to see the funny side of her own experiences too. What had she been thinking, trying to see India in a fortnight? What had the local people made of her, all trussed up in queenly seclusion as she performed her brisk gallop across the subcontinent? It was absurd; India was absurd and so was she.

Afterwards it had seemed natural to join Marcus in his room, and they stayed together for the next three days, her schedule discarded. It felt good to have stopped travelling. With no itinerary or timetable, she had space simply to soak up the local flavour, enjoying the mountain backdrop, the fiery Rajasthani colours and the dry air. She never mentioned the reason why she was in India – as far as Marcus was concerned she was simply a tourist vagrant like so many others – and she enjoyed listening to his rambling talk of his culinary career, his ambition to set up a course of Indian cookery in Zurich, his family. At night they lay under a mosquito net together, mingling their sweat and achieving a slippery, grimy but also deeply satisfying union.

Now the time has come for Esme to embark on the first leg of her convoluted journey to the rendez-vous in distant Kerala, and she feels once more uneasy. She experienced a fleeting sadness at saying farewell to Marcus, who was travelling on to Udaipur and Gujarat, but she savoured even this wistful sensation, the feeling of temporariness that accompanies every journey. They did not pretend that they would ever meet again or stay in touch, and there was no regret. Regret forms no part of Esme's persona – she takes no pleasure in looking back. Which is why the next stage of the adventure would be the greatest trial of all: from now on, it would be a journey into her past, an evisceration of a time that she once

17

dearly hoped to have left behind. But if all goes well, it will be an exorcism too. That is the reason for her journey.

Chapter 4 | Fort Kochi

Miranda and Simon stroll lazily past boutiques overflowing with silky, vaguely hippy scarves and blouses, past upmarket craft shops and galleries piled with luxuriantly moustachio-ed heads – characters from the local Kathakali theatre – past cafés from which the authentic aromas of freshly-ground coffee waft enticingly, past bookshops and jewellery stores, and they can almost imagine they are in Europe. The biggest giveaway, apart from the perennial tropical heat overlaying everything, is the presence of autorickshaw drivers stationed at the end of every street, coaxing, cajoling, insisting that the callow westerners take a ride in their black and yellow insect-like pods.

'India-lite' was how Baby Jesus sniffily labelled Fort Kochi on his rare but wildly hallucinogenic letters home – even then, twelve years back, before the neighbourhood had found a place in the weekend travel supplements. But for these two novices it is the perfect entry point to the subcontinent. Not too crowded, or chaotic, or noisy, or shocking, not too anything. It is diluted, possibly, yet to them still rich with culture and history. And it has such romantic resonance – Kochi was Cochin, on the Malabar coast, not so far from the Cardamom Hills. It was the first great terminus of the spice trade, settled by Persians and Arabs, colonised by Portuguese and Dutch, appropriated by the East India Company, absorbed into the British Empire, and now part of communist Kerala and destination of choice for well-heeled and stylish tourists of a certain sophistication – people like them. It even has a biennale.

The 'homestay' they have booked into – a kind of luxury B&B – was an old merchant's house, built by the Dutch or Portuguese (the manager, Matthew – a Christian – said both at different times), with lofty ceilings and a stately dining-room. The guestrooms are former storerooms and have air-conditioning. It has a walled garden where hibiscus, bougainvillea and other delicate purple and scarlet flowers bloom, tended by quiet women who smile at them as they pass. Geckos splay motionlessly on the clean white walls. At breakfast, where they are served mangoes and melons with fresh croissants, they meet Irish and Canadian fellow-travellers clutching Lonely Planets, eager to share their travelling experiences. Outside the homestay, on the dusty, partially lawned Parade Ground, boys play cricket beneath huge, overarching raintrees with thick brown limbs. It is just a short stroll from here to the seafront, where the promenading crowds pause to watch the wobbly red sun disintegrate into the sea every evening, and where they have posed for pictures in front of the gantry-like Chinese fishing nets where rows of egrets and cormorants perch as they wait for the nets to be raised with their loads of flapping fish.

Unfortunately, the two of them must leave all this in two days' time, when they are scheduled to make their way to a small place some forty miles south down the coast, somewhere that few of their fellow guests have heard of, where they are to meet up with the other family members.

'When are we going to eat?' Simon wants to know. It has been a couple of hours since their last mango lassi and he is feeling irritable at the prospect of leaving this comfortable haven and moving on.

'Whenever you like,' his sister replies, eyeing a brilliant, crimson-patterned shawl hanging outside a shop.

'How about now?'

'Okay.'

'What do you fancy? Italian, Greek?' he asks.

'What about Indian?' Miranda proposes. They have been four

days in the country, and still haven't had a proper curry, worried about the effects it might have on their western stomachs. 'We could try the *Dal Roti*.' Matthew has suggested they try this place, located a few streets from where they now are.

After some further browsing they turn their steps towards the restaurant, a ten-minute walk. Outside it are a cluster of people – mainly young, smartly dressed Indians – milling and idly swiping phones. The restaurant, when they enter, is spacious and cool, with small wooden tables surrounded by fashionably distressed white walls. They are immediately met by a genial-looking man, bald but with a thick and well-tended beard, who listens to their request for a table for two with the gravely attentive air of one listening to instructions on a complex surgical technique. He nods, and still with his grave demeanour informs them that they must wait outside with everyone else. He will let them know when a table becomes available.

They glance around at the other diners – prosperous-looking men and women, mostly in their twenties, all chattering animatedly or tapping at their phones, often both at the same time. Miranda nods and says they will wait to be called.

Outside again, Simon contemplates the formless crowd. 'So this is a queue.' He shrugs and pulls out a beedi, the aromatic, leaf-rolled cigarette that he has seen huddled rickshaw drivers sucking on after dark.

Miranda returns her younger brother's frown with an encouraging smile. 'Hey! We're in India. We've arrived! Lighten up!'

'Right, right.'

'Don't look so worried. Maybe it'll all be fine. You never know.'

'At the *hostel*?' Simon utters the word disdainfully as he fires up the beedi. The very word hardly evokes any notion of pleasure or fun, certainly little in the way of comfort compared to their present lodgings. 'Hmm...'

'If it's okay for Dad, it'll be fine for us.'

A rickshaw driver across the road catches Miranda's eye as she says this, and smarmily smiles, pointing at his gleaming three-wheeler. She turns away, and when she looks back he is already importuning someone else, a lone tourist in baggy white shorts and a floppy hat ('Sir? I've been waiting for you. Where you like to go?').

'You have to keep telling yourself that it's for a good cause,' she says.

'Just don't tell me it's for Baby Jesus.'

'And it's for Baby Jesus...'

Simon scowls, blowing a smoke-ring into the air. 'Like he ever gave a shit.'

Miranda grunts noncommitally, returning her gaze to the lolling rickshaw driver, then quickly tearing it away as, lightning fast, he latches onto her eye once more.

'Excuse me.' A bushy-bearded Indian hipster of around thirty with thick-rimmed glasses and a turquoise tie-dyed tee-shirt is addressing Simon, who whirls round, startled. 'I beg your pardon. But smoking is not allowed here.'

'Not allowed?'

'Smoking in public places is not allowed in India.' The man smiles apologetically.

'You're joking!'

'No.' The man shakes his head and Simon, embarrassed, immediately grinds his beedi into the road.

'Right. Thanks. Sorry,' he mutters grimly. The hipster nods and rejoins his group.

'Can you believe that!' Simon says to Miranda. 'Here! In India!'

'It does seem quite draconian,' she agrees, 'when so much else is permitted.'

She contemplates her glowering brother as, face averted, he wordlessly fulminates. Like her, he has soft, almond-shaped brown eyes, full lips that are always slightly open, and a serious, no-nonsense expression, but the resemblances do not go much further. His long, straight hair tied back into a neat pony-tail, his wispy beard and round, Lennon-esque spectacles lend him a somewhat clinical and humourless air, sometimes almost supercilious – for instance now, as he regards the modern murals daubed on the restaurant wall. His querulous underlying dissatisfaction with the world makes her wonder – not for the first time – if this is their mother's influence manifesting itself. It's certainly not their dad's characteristic trait. So placatory, their father, so eager to appease and resolve – somewhat like Miranda herself. How like their father she is, and how little like him he is!

Whatever psychological attributes they might share, however, physically Miranda has as little in common with their father as she has with her brother. She has thick, slightly frizzy brown hair, centre-parted and usually gathered at the back by a clip, and unlike her father and brother she wears contact lenses rather than glasses. Slightly below average height, with a slightly stocky figure and an aversion to make up, Miranda can exert a striking physical appeal if she chooses, but her body language usually negates any suggestion of striving for effect, as does her plain garb. Right now, she is wearing loose, cream-coloured cotton trousers and a simple, pale blue collared shirt, her only adornment a thin silver chain around her neck. Her dress sense seems calculated to make her invisible. It's not as if her clothes choices not carefully considered, however; she would neither wear tight-fitting trousers that could draw attention to what she perceives as her thick thighs, nor baggy tops that might make her appear fat. Every item undergoes a meticulous process of selection.

Nonetheless, Miranda is not given to self-reflection. For her it is not even an indulgence – it is boring. Other people hold far more interest for her, and she is still meditating on aspects of her brother's personality when the bald waiter emerges and gestures to them. Simon switches his attention from his phone and they re-enter the restaurant. The waiter allocates a small table by the wall for them, and they request water and scrutinize the menu. As ever, Simon defers to his older sister's greater knowledge of the various dishes, asking her to explain the unfamiliar items, but willing too to make his own investigations, consulting his phone when she can't supply an answer. By the time a jug of filtered water arrives they are ready to make their order: fish curry, kati rolls, naan bread.

Their food arrives with a flourish. This waiter is a pro, Simon can see that, though he is also a ham. And, he concedes, there is nothing wrong with that. Everything here is theatre after all, and he instinctively approves of theatre. He begins to feel more comfortable, and his mood lifts further as they savour the various dishes, each one fiery but tasty and stimulating too.

'You know,' he tells his sister after a few bites, 'there are compensations for fulfilling a duty.'

'That's what I've been trying to tell you. Relax, bro. Everything will work out fine.'

In managing the moods of her disconsolate younger brother, Miranda is conscious of falling into an old habit. It has been her designated task ever since she can remember, though much less in recent years as the vagaries of adult life have set them on separate paths. She enjoys the role, for all its onerousness, and is confident that she performs it well. The sense of responsibility that goes with it means that she has no wish to share with Simon her niggling scepticism about this quirky place they have landed in – which is entertaining enough, sure, but also, she suspects, commercial, slick and inauthentic – let alone her wider reservations about their entire mission plan. It is easy enough to refrain for now from voicing any premature judgements on Fort Kochi, but she is more careful to hide from Simon her suspicions and sense of foreboding about coming here in the first place, even if it is evident that he too harbours doubts on that score.

For now, though, she is content to set aside that critical, over-analytical, sometimes conflicted part of her and focus instead on the present task, which consists of getting reacquainted with her younger brother. Now there's a subject she can unreservedly and full-heartedly throw herself into – everything else can take a back seat, for now.

Chapter 5 | Getting it together

Everything doesn't look much better in daylight, in fact most things look considerably worse. Gradually, however, as the day progresses, Dougie and Jules manage to restore a degree of order to their Indian holiday. Horribly jet-lagged, and feeling edgy and demoralised after too few hours' sleep, they emerge early from the hotel onto the now sun-baked and traffic-ridden thoroughfare and go searching for breakfast. To their surprise, on turning into a quieter street nearby they chance upon a café/restaurant selling Western-type food, including French toast and fruit muesli. Tucking in, sipping at ludicrously sweet but still comforting glasses of tea, they feel revived enough to discuss their plight and the obstacles stacked up in front of them.

'Sounds like you fellas are having a hard time!' They look round to see a tall, crop-haired man in a sleeveless waistcoat at the next table He is wearing a large silver ring on one ear and leather bands around his wrists, and is generously tattooed. 'Just arrived?' The voice is friendly, the accent Australian.

They nod, and briefly outline their predicament. The man blows through his teeth and shakes his head. 'That's sounds like a heap of tough shit. Mind if I join you?'

He climbs around and installs himself at their table. Normally they would mind the intrusion, but now they are clutching at straws, and the man, whose name is Terry, turns out to be a trove of useful advice.

'The first thing you've got to do is get yourself a fixer. A facilitator. You'll never get by without one. Ask one of the taxi guys at the end of the street, one who speaks decent English. He'll set you straight. Hire him for the day. It'll cost you a couple of thousand, but it'll be worth it.' Then he enumerates their priorities, taking out his phone to show them a map of the city with the rough locations of the police station and the various offices they'll have to visit.

'You'll need a police report. You'll need a new visa. Get yourself a local sim card, it's much cheaper. Get yourself a bunch of ID photos too. You'll need those. And you'll need to think about your onward journey. Get yourselves out of Mumbai as quick as you can. Where are you headed?'

'We were thinking of spending a few days in Goa.'

'That's an overnight job. 11pm on the Konkan Express. You need to book train tickets as early as you can, though. In fact they'll be booked up weeks in advance, but you can usually get on the emergency list. You pay a bit more but that's what you've got to do. Go to the Tourist Ticketing Facility upstairs at the Reservation Office at Victoria Terminus – the main station. CST they call it now. But do all your other stuff first. You've got a tough day or two in front of you, but it's all possible. You'll get through it.'

'You make it all sound relatively straightforward,' Jules says, gratefully.

Terry snorts. 'Straightforward? Nothing in India is straightforward, mate. But it's do-able. It's all do-able. Everything in India is possible.'

'Where there's a will there's a way,' Dougie says.

'Not really, mate. Just wanting something doesn't get you anywhere. Where there's a demand there's a supply – that's the rule here. You can get everything you want in India. Satisfy every appetite, feed every craving, it's all possible. It's your choice. You just have to set the limits. But you need money. Without money you're fucked. That's what I'm doing in this shithole. Waiting for money. Only reason to come to Mumbai.'

He leaves them soon after, bound for the local Western Union office. Under the soothing gusts provided by the restaurant's ceiling fan, bolstered by more glasses of tea, calls are made on Dougie's phone to banks in the UK to block Jules's bank cards. Then the two go in search of a taxi-driver who speaks good English and quickly enter into negotiations with an ebullient Sikh called Raj, with whom they strike a deal for the day. In his shiny white Merc, Raj first taxis them to a cash machine, where Dougie is able to extract a ridiculously large wad of banknotes – necessary for the various transactions that must be undertaken – then to a photographic studio where more passport-size photos are taken on a mobile phone and printed. The next stop is the British consulate, where, after numerous phone calls and a long wait during which first Dougie and then Jules falls asleep, a clerk grudgingly agrees to issue Jules with a temporary passport which will be available to collect in two days. Armed with an official statement attesting to this, they drive to the local police station to report the loss. After another long wait, interviews take place, statements are made and numerous forms are laboriously compiled. Then they have to visit a government building across town in order to obtain a new tourist visa for Jules, where, after yet another lengthy wait, several more forms are filled. Multiple photos of specific dimensions are required, which are once more provided at a nearby photo studio and taken back to the government building with signatures attached. Another long wait ensues, at the end of which Jules is unceremoniously issued with a new tourist visa, allowing him a sojourn of not more than thirty days. No question about it, they are making progress.

Each time that Jules and Dougie emerge into the street, the perspiration starts flowing off them as if a tap has been turned. It gathers on their faces and arms and drenches their shirts. Combined with the sweat, the crowds and heat immediately set their heads ringing, which, on top of their jet-lag, induces a state that somehow combines both semi-hysteria and mind-numbing torpor.

Raj, ever cheerful, drives them to CST, depositing them outside the Reservation Office. They take a numbered ticket and await their turn, and are eventually seen by a deeply bored-looking official who barks commands at them for filling out the booking forms correctly, after which he is able to put them on the emergency list for two berths on a night train to Goa departing in two days' time. They just need to report back to the office at 10.30am of that day for confirmation. No problem.

Elated, the two stumble into the non-air-conditioned streets of the city and, back in their taxi, instruct Raj to take them to a phone shop in the neighbourhood in order to acquire a local sim card for Dougie's phone. Raj tells them he knows the best place, drives for a quarter of an hour past several dozen other phone shops, and finally leads them into a darkened store piled high with boxes of trainers. Here, he introduces them to a friend of his, Raval Pathak, who, with a surprising show of formality, bows to each of them with hands joined and informs them that he can provide anything they desire. Raj swiftly summarises what it is that they desire and Raval nods reassuringly. 'Of course! Straightaway! Tea?' He bids them sit on two stools, switches up the speed of the fan on the counter, and orders four glasses of tea from a barefoot scamp outside the shop. As they sip the tea he explains to them that photocopies of Dougie's passport and visa will be needed, which may be obtained nearby, establishes what kind of phone contract Dougie requires and tells him what the overall cost will be. When their glasses are drained, Raj leads them across the street and into a fly-blown alley where, in a musty shop advertising Xerox, the taxi-driver rapidly negotiates with the shopkeeper. Armed with the photocopies, he accompanies them to yet another photo studio where he again negotiates a price. This time Dougie and Jules insist on a dozen prints each of their respective mugshots, which, on examination, somehow show them looking even more crazed than the ones taken last night at the hotel.

Raj hurries them back to Raval Pathak's shoe shop, where the tortuous procedure of acquiring the sim card is finally completed, the card acquired and the bill paid. But then, feeling almost reluctant to leave the comforting breeze supplied by the fan on the counter, Jules casually asks shopkeeper where he might obtain a cheap cell phone. Raval beams his reassuring smile once more and, without dropping a beat, pulls open a drawerful of second-hand phones, throws them on the counter and begins to list models and specifications in a rapid, mainly incomprehensible commentary. Noticing Jules's increasingly vacant expression, Raval produces another handful from behind his counter, then rummages in a filing cabinet to show him several more. Overwhelmed, and panicked at the prospect of another round of hectic transactions, Jules grabs a phone, examines it without really seeing it and makes a gesture of bargaining down the price. He achieves a small reduction, also a gesture on the part of Raval Pathak, and quickly pays using Dougie's wad of cash. And then the process of acquiring an Indian sim with the requisite passport and visa photocopies is initiated once more.

At last the business is complete and they escape, back into the oven of the streets. The late afternoon sun has lost none of its vigour. Drained of energy but feeling triumphant and even heroic, Dougie and Jules climb back into the taxi and speed back to their seedy hotel, promising themselves to find alternative accommodation on the following day. They even feel they are beginning to get used to Mumbai's migrainous buzz and swelter, the tinnitus of traffic and the throbbing sensations of tension and threat. They hand over a bundle of banknotes to Raj, who counts them carefully, then counts them again before stuffing them into his trousers. Then, as they are about to enter the hotel entrance, giving a wide berth to the legless beggar and juvenile tea-seller, he calls after them and asks what they have planned for tomorrow.

They hesitate. They can't remember what they've got planned for tomorrow.

'So you must take a sightseeing excursion, good sirs! It is essential. I will drive you, and show you the unforgettable sights. You cannot leave Mumbai without this.'

Dougie and Jules exchange a befuddled glance. They are wilting with fatigue.

Dougie shrugs. 'Go on, then. How much?'

'To you, just two thousand rupees. It is magnificent, you know, you will see places...'

'Fine,' Dougie interrupts. 'What time?'

'I will be here at eight o'clock, sir. Before it gets too hot, you know.'

'Too early.'

'Nine o'clock, sir. I will first show you...'

'Ten o'clock,' Dougie cuts him off him, and they turn listlessly away and shamble into the hotel lobby, where the fat receptionist is talking loudly on his phone without deigning to concede a glance.

Upstairs, seeing the flimsy padlock on their door, Dougie experiences a sudden spasm of fear. He thrusts open the door and crosses immediately to his backpack. Rummaging inside, his hand closes around what he is looking for with a wave of relief.

'Hallelujah,' he cries, flourishing a thick wad of tattered exercise books tied together with string. 'I had an awful premonition it was gone.'

'Why the fuck would anyone take that?' Jules demands.

'I don't fucking know. Why does anyone do anything? But if that's gone we're totally fucked.'

'You're not making any fucking sense...' Jules says wearily as he bolts the door behind them, kicks off his shoes and collapses onto one of the single beds.

'Sorry. I can't think straight,' Dougie says, and he throws himself down next to Jules, planting a kiss on his forehead. Wrapped in each other's arms, they lie inertly beneath the clanging ceiling fan, oblivious to the whining and nipping mosquitoes and the bed bugs that share their mattress, leaving lines of red dots on their skin.

'Second round to us,' Jules murmurs, stroking his partner's close-cropped head. 'I think we're gonna survive India, Doug, I really do.' But Dougie does not answer; he is already unconscious.

Chapter 6 | St Antony's Hostel

In the enclosed garden of St Antony's Hostel, a lone figure in a baggy white suit is seated on the scrubby expanse of green-brown grass. He has an open newspaper on the table in front of him, but is clearly not giving it his full attention as his fingers thrum impatiently on the table and every so often he throws an irritated glance at the open doors of the veranda behind him, tutting.

There is loud birdsong all around, mostly coming from the thick walls of vegetation that line two sides of the garden. Everything is copious and prolific, bursting forth in unruly abundance and jostling for space, from the mango and jackfruit trees from whose mossy limbs thick tresses of creeper trail down, to the dwarfish banana trees with broad, fan-like fronds and the firs with their symmetrical, radial branches terminating in clusters of green spikes. Soaring above them all is a row of palms whose lance-like trunks sway gently in the faintest of breezes.

Inside the building, Thomas is gazing earnestly at his reflection in the mirror pinned on the wall behind the office desk. He smiles. He looks serious. He frowns, listening. He nods sympathetically. He smiles again, this time raising his eyebrows, delighted.

'Good morning!' he ventures. 'How are you today? Are you having a good day? I am well. And how was your journey? I trust you have had a pleasant and trouble-free voyage? Yes, sir. Thank you. May I be helping you with your luggage, madam?'

He furrows his thick eyebrows. Then smiles again. He has a 'lovely' smile. All the foreign guests say so – or at least the female ones do. Whipping out a comb he flicks a loose hair back into place above his ear. Most of his hair is around his ears now, with a thinner area around the back of his head – plus, of course, the thickets actually in his ears and the generous eyebrows. He doesn't mind. Flowery doesn't mind. Gives him more dignity, she says. He dabs at his eyebrows with the comb. Despite the hair loss, his face is unlined. Flowery says he looks younger than his forty-four years. Still handsome. Dashing even.

He walks out of the office and stands behind the tall counter in the lobby. Everything is in order. The booking diary is open on the desk, and he casts his eyes over it. Nine names. All arriving in the space of four days. Staying for ten to fourteen days. It will liven the place up, but it is a great responsibility. At this time of year, May, there are few bookings at the hostel. Pre-monsoon. Too hot. A few clerical visitors, maybe, a couple of family members related to the children. But most people keep away at this time of year.

Francis enters the lobby from the dining room and wordlessly presents Thomas with the chef's weekly menu. Francis is a dull, humourless employee, but he's reliable enough. His wife does an efficient job with the hotel's laundry, though never seems to give the same attention to her husband, whose trousers, Thomas notes, are currently stained.

While they are perusing the sheet, Mr Pereira appears at the doorway, dressed in his usual shapeless white suit.

'Where is my tea?' he demands in English.

Thomas looks up and furrows his brow.

'I ordered tea fifteen minutes ago.'

Thomas exchanges a look with Francis.

'I am sorry, sir,' Francis tells Mr Pereira. 'I will find out the whereabouts of your tea.' Without showing the slightest suggestion of urgency or even haste, Francis walks calmly back into the restaurant, watched by Thomas and Mr Pereira. They exchange a look that might speak volumes or might express nothing at all, then Mr Pereira grunts and shuffles back to his seat on the lawn. He is not a resident but comes in every day, sometimes twice a day, to drink tea as he pores over the Times of India, or sometimes to meet one of his former business colleagues to moan about the economy, Keralan politics or the state of their pensions – often all three.

Thomas turns back to the shopping list, but he is almost immediately disturbed by another interruption. This time it is Shibu, poking his head in at the garden entrance. 'Taxi arriving,' he announces in his native Malayalam, then returns outside into the dazzle of mid-afternoon. The first arrivals. Thomas resists his initial instinct of returning to the mirror in his office, but manually checks his collar and the knot of his tie. He knows that his short-sleeved white shirt is immaculately pressed, that his moustache is neat, his ear hair trimmed, his fingernails scrubbed.

He hears the sound of an engine approaching along the drive, a car pulling up outside, the handbrake applied. The engine idles for a few moments before being stilled, and his eyes narrow as he waits, jaw stiffened, ears cocked. He registers the driver's door opening, then someone opening one of the back doors and feet climbing out. He hears Shibu's voice, its tone correct but his English, as ever, drastically imperfect. Of course it is: he is Hindu. Another door opens and slams shut. Two people. His eyes return to the list in the booking diary as he speculates which of the guests it is to be.

Someone opens the boot of the car, Shibu or the driver, and suitcases are heaved out and onto the ground.

It is time.

Thomas strides smartly out from behind his desk, crosses the lobby and stops at the threshold, shaded by the porch. A smile – the famous smile – takes over his face as he surveys the new arrivals on the drive. An elderly white couple. So must be Mr Oliver Maitland and Mrs Cynthia Braithwaite. He strokes his hands, waiting for them to notice him. The gentleman spots him first and offers a hint of a curt nod, clearly unsure of Thomas's status. Dressed in a loose white linen suit with a striped tie, and a good-quality Panama hat on his grey head, he has a clipped, silvery moustache, an upright, authoritative bearing, and looks around seventy years old though might be much older (it's so difficult to tell with Europeans). The woman, of around the same age, wears a short, light, white jacket and cream-coloured slacks. She hasn't noticed him yet. Rather stick-like, flat-chested, she has a string of thick pearls around her wrinkled neck. Thomas approaches them, the wide smile still pasted on his face, and she looks up from the bags and suitcase she is arranging and smiles thinly back before gesturing to Shibu to proceed with the luggage into the lobby.

'Good morning madam, good morning sir! I trust you have had a pleasant and trouble-free journey? Welcome to St Antony's Hostel.' He stops in front of the couple, clasps his hands together and offers a little bow.

'Good morning,' says the man, his features studiedly neutral.

'Good morning,' says the woman, also rather crisply. 'You must be Mr Gonzalo?'

'Indeed I am, madam. But please call me Thomas. That is my Christian name. And I am speaking to Mrs Braithwaite, correct?'

'That is correct. How do you do?' Although softer and more demonstrative than the man, she is still slightly reserved, a bit tight-lipped, thoroughly English.

'And Mr Maitland?' he turns to the man, who is now fanning his face with the Panama, revealing a shiny, spherical pate. Thomas bows once more to him. 'Good morning, sir. And how was your journey?'

'No problems at all,' Oliver tells him, before loudly clearing his throat. 'Bloody hot, of course. At least the taxi benefits from air-conditioning, but my God, when you get out... It's like drowning in soup.'

'Yes, indeed, sir. It takes a little time to be accustomed.' Thomas turns and speaks in Malayalam to Shibu, who immediately commandeers Oliver's suitcases. The suave smile is back on Thomas's face as he addresses once more the new arrivals: 'It is so much cooler inside. Please...' He gestures for the couple to precede him into the darkened lobby, pausing only to allow Oliver to pay the taxi-driver – tipping him, Thomas notices, with two five hundred-rupee notes.

Flowery is at the porch now, waiting to greet the guests. A short, full-bodied woman with a prominent mole on one cheek, and wearing a bright pink patterned dress and a scarlet blossom in her grey-threaded hair, she smiles warmly.

'My wife, Flowery,' Thomas says.

'What a charming name,' Cynthia exclaims, sounding girlishly delighted.

'A pleasure to meet you,' Oliver tells Flowery with a brief bow.

Flowery gushes and smiles, and, once inside the lobby, she fills two glasses from a jug of iced water on a table and hands them to the guests. Thomas sees Mrs Braithwaite look uncertain, and is quick to reassure her: 'Filtered water, madam. Pure and clean.'

Cynthia smiles briefly and takes a tiny sip from the glass. Oliver downs his in one long, thirsty swig. Flowery immediately refills his glass and tops up Cynthia's by a millimetre, then withdraws through the door behind the counter.

'I will show you to your rooms,' Thomas tells his guests. 'I will require your passports, if you please, when you are ready, which I will return to you afterwards.'

'Rooms?' the woman enquires, arching one pencilled eyebrow.

'Yes, madam. I will show you to your rooms where you may refresh yourselves. Then you may have a snack or a meal in our restaurant as you prefer.'

'The booking is for one room, I believe,' Cynthia informs him.

Thomas frowns. 'One room?'

'One room, thank you.'

Thomas walks round to the reception counter and consults the booking diary.

'Not two rooms?'

'No. One room.'

He raises his head, anguished now. 'Please excuse me, Mrs Braithwaite. An error has occurred. Mr Laurence – Professor Johnson, that is – has booked one room for Mrs Braithwaite, and one room for Mr Maitland.'

'No, no. It should be one room for my husband and me.'

'Of course, madam. Absolutely. Will you be requiring a matrimonial room or twin beds?'

'Matrimonial, of course,' she returns drily. 'Laurence must have made a mistake when he made the booking.'

His brow still furrowed, Thomas turns to a second book, a thick ledger whose pages are densely filled in two hand-written columns. He is checking availability, though this is not strictly necessary, as he knows there are no other rooms booked for the week apart from this party's. He flips over the pages anyway, examining each column.

Finally he looks up and in Malayalam addresses Shibu, still waiting expectantly at the bottom of the stairs amid a heap of bags and suitcases.

'Room twenty-five for both guests.'

Without a murmur, Shibu slings the bags over his shoulders, grasps both cases, and sets off upstairs, staggering slightly under the combined weight.

Once more showing his calm and efficient face, Thomas turns to the two arrivals. 'We have the perfect room for you and your husband, Mrs Braithwaite. I know it will be to your utmost satisfaction. All I require is your passport, and Mr Maitland's passport, which I will return both to you in due course.'

They hand over their passports and Thomas places them delicately in a drawer, a beaming smile once more gracing his features. 'Please,' he says. 'Upstairs.' And he gestures the way Shibu has gone, following a respectful few steps behind the couple as they ascend the curved wooden staircase.

Professional at all times, thinks Thomas to himself. Maximum professionality. Perfect. No problem.

Back at his station in the lobby a few minutes later, he is perusing his ledger when Mr Pereira enters once more, his face unusually animated.

'Who are those people?' he asks as he approaches the desk, flicking his eyes upstairs.

'They are two guests, Mr Pereira, just arrived.'

'I am aware of that, of course. What are their names?'

Thomas reads from the passports in front of him. 'Oliver Maitland and Cynthia Braithwaite, from England. Why do you want to know?'

'Maitland?' Mr Pereira repeats. He looks for a moment completely confused, then nods solemnly and withdraws without any explanation.

Thomas sighs with annoyance. He wouldn't mind the man if he spent a little more at the restaurant. And he can't tolerate the cloak of mystery he throws over everything. What business is it of his, anyway?

He reverts back to the ledger. Professional, Thomas, professional.

Chapter 7 | Awakening

In the hush of the bedroom, where the sharp light of day has not yet penetrated and the net curtains are gently nudged by the whirring ceiling fan, the snoozing air is abruptly shattered by a loud electronic buzz. Oliver jerks awake and opens one eye wide. After a pause, the intrusion is succeeded by another, this time the fuzzy rasp of a throat being cleared. Both his eyes are open now. There follows the unmistakeable and heavily amplified call of the muezzin. It is as if he is in the room.

'Crikey!' Oliver exclaims, sitting up. At the end of a long, lilting phrase suffused with ardour and yearning, there is a low muttering, then a second plangent line resonates through the room. 'For God's sake!'

'Yes,' answers Cynthia beside him. 'Precisely so.' Her eyes are also wide open, though she doesn't otherwise stir from her prone position.

Further orotund phrases issue forth, punctuated by more muttering, more throat-clearing.

'He's certainly got a good voice,' Cynthia observes. Oliver blinks at her, exasperated, then issues his own throat-clearing rasp. Muttering an oath, he lurches out of bed, crosses the room to close both windows, and, huffing, settles back onto the mattress. The closed window doesn't make any discernible difference to the noise level: the voice flows smoothly through the glass and bounces off the walls of the room, every note attentively listened to by the couple in bed – Oliver with his eyes fixed on the ceiling, Cynthia with eyes closed and breathing gently, a faint smile on her lips. Neither of them has noticed a mosque in the vicinity, but it must be quite close, perhaps just the other side of the thick growth of trees at the end of the hostel's garden.

Then, without warning, the quavering appeal is cut off and silence floods back into the room. Oliver lets his breath out slowly and allows his eyes to close. There is the birdsong again, but he can live with that, might even be able to drift back to sleep.

After an immeasurable length of time has elapsed, possibly ten minutes, possibly thirty or forty, Oliver's eyes flick open again as a new disturbance infiltrates his consciousness, this time a sharp metallic clang. A second dull clang follows, then a third, as if an iron saucepan is being irregularly struck with a spoon. After another half-minute or so of this, the clanging is replaced by a voice – a male voice, but not the same one as before. This one is softer and lighter than the muezzin's, more supple and melodic. It is soon joined by a female voice pitched a couple of octaves higher. It is clearly a recording, probably a devotional song, Oliver judges, and most likely Hindu. It must be coming from the small temple just outside the hostel's grounds. They noticed it yesterday: a pink and orange structure within a walled enclosure – little more than an open-sided room topped by a crude pink dome and with a concrete forecourt. Looking over the perimeter wall, they could see within the room the usual lingam and yoni with a top dressing of orange and red blossoms.

There are more metallic clangs, and a new song ripples through the air, sung now by a single male voice accompanied by tabla and flute. Oliver listens, lips pursed, while Cynthia continues to breathe evenly beside him, eyes still closed though she is awake.

How strange, she is thinking, to be in a land of faith. There is the mosque; there is the temple; two or three hundred yards from them, at the end of the lane leading to the hostel, stands the soaring white facade of St Antony's basilica. And just yesterday morning, in Kochi's Jew Town, when she and Oliver were touring some of the city's sights in the couple of hours available to them before their onward rail journey, they visited the city's oldest synagogue, there since the sixteenth century to serve a once flourishing Jewish community. Back outside, they observed a coach disgorge a crowd of turbaned Sikh tourists visiting the nearby Mattancherry Palace, who were afterwards spotted browsing among Tibetan shops that were presumably run by Buddhists. It's all such a jumble.

God is truly everywhere here in India, he is inescapable. Every street holds a temple or shrine of some description, large and small, often two or three. She remembers how, in a stuffy sanctum of one of the vast temple complexes that the couple visited last week in Tamil Nadu, Cynthia was suddenly assailed by waves of nausea. Eventually, they both developed a kind of temple fatigue, with Oliver declaring that he didn't mind if he never saw another temple again. 'Drunk on religion,' was how he described the local people, all following different gods, segregated into different faiths.

But somehow they all jog along together. Yesterday, here in Allapoorha, in the course of a brief exploration of the town in the relative cool of early evening, the two of them peered into the pure-white immensity of St Antony's church where a service was in progress. The building was crammed with the faithful – so different from the sparsely attended church services back home. The congregation seemed to be living the mystery, it was real. Cynthia was impressed and made up her mind to attend a service during their sojourn, to sample the spirituality. Who knows? Some of it might even rub off on her. Sometimes she would like to experience that small candle of faith in her breast again.

She herself was brought up a Catholic in a large, expatriated Irish family, the seventh of eight children, and educated in a convent. When asked, she will still label herself a Catholic, and every few months she might even attend mass. Once a Catholic always a Catholic, they say, but is she really? She doesn't really feel entitled to call herself one any more than she might call herself an Anglican or a Jew. In these climes she might well be Hindu or Jain. It is all in the genius loci. And perhaps in the phase of life you currently occupy. You are supposed to get closer to God as you grow older, whether out of spiritual awakening or fear, but if anything she has grown more pagan. She is a godless Catholic. What is it that Forster puts into the mouth of one of his characters? 'I am a holy man, minus the holiness.' Does that apply to her now? Spiritual but faithless?

As the lilting singing washes over her, half-asleep, Cynthia's thoughts drift back to her life in England. How different are her awakenings there, hearing the cries of seagulls rather than muezzins and temple bells. Since her husband's passing some thirty years ago, Cynthia has lived in Cornwall. She has a Georgian cottage on a narrow street that lies just a few minutes' walk from the centre of Penzance. She has a garden and a small conservatory where she sometimes paints in the afternoon. She volunteers two days a week in a charity shop, and is a member of a swimming club that every Friday, year-round, braves the choppy waters of Mount's Bay. She is now the oldest member of the club. She is dutiful in keeping to the weekly regime, not least because of the alleged health benefits. Swimming keeps your body in trim. It is recommended by every doctor she has ever spoken to. Some say it also keeps your brain in order. Unlike some other members, she might not often voice her opinion on the matter, but this is what she fervently wants to believe. She hasn't seen any tangible evidence in the form of books or research papers to back up the theory, but it sounds very plausible. In a way, it's a question of faith – she chooses to believe it. It is a belief that the club-members share, one that unites them, though she has her moments of doubt, too. What if the opposite were true? Occasionally this heretical thought hovers in front of her. Of her four closest friends at the club, two – one female and one male – are now in varying stages of dementia, and one is in a care home. Part of her mourns their fate, while another part exults that she is not yet a member of that club. So far. But what if it is the swimming in that inhospitable sea itself that somehow predisposes people to losing their minds?

However, if age has taught her anything, it is to control her fears, banish her doubts and steer her feelings into calmer waters. So, while the fear and the heresy are there, she keeps them at bay. It is a sort of cognitive dissonance, and it is part of her modus operandi. That is something she really can believe in – in some ways it defines her. She embraces life and yet she is afraid of it. She laughs at ageing and death while those phantoms also dominate her thoughts. She is ruthlessly uncaring yet at the same time cares deeply.

This convenient disassociation is something that has evolved in the wake of her widowhood. She grieved following Roger's death, of course. When he went, she felt that the foundations of her life had been violently toppled, like a phalanx of skittles in a bowling alley, leaving her scattered and helpless. Then she got herself back on her feet. She would not be defined by a death, or what's the point of staying alive? Life is worth more than that. And so, while she does not run away from the memories, while she frequently dreams of Roger, marking his birthday, keeping in touch with his friends and regularly tidying his grave, she is able to carry on her day-to-day existence unaffected. She has compartmentalized death and loss, and this gives her a certain equilibrium.

Half-consciously, she now applies the same strategy of dissociation to all her worldly interactions, including her newly acquired relationships. Thus, when Oliver first appeared in her life, she mocked him to her friends. An accountant, of all things! How much further could he be from her ideals and values? Yet, a man of contradictions too, for undeniably he has multiple facets. There is a whole dark area within him that she has not begun to penetrate. That's what drew her, partly. And so, while she instinctively rejected him, she also courted his attention, and while she reviled his attitudes and recoiled at his prejudices, a part of her simultaneously relished them. How refreshingly different he was to everyone else in her life! She had to close one eye, of course. That's the secret. But when all is said and done, when the accounts are totted up, it has proved a successful strategy, for it gives her the best of all worlds.

Cynthia is suddenly aware that the singing has stopped, and wonders how long it has been quiet. Not that it's exactly quiet – birdsong seems to have swollen to fill the empty space left by the devotional singing. She looks across to her multi-facetted 'companion' (vile word!) – her temporary husband. He lies on his back, rigid, his nose still pointed towards the ceiling but with his eyes now closed and his breathing regular and deep. What a strange proposition he is, what a perverse creature!

She leans across and kisses him tenderly on the cheek, causing him to twitch.

'Come on, old duffer!' she murmurs. 'Time to rise! Time for tea and breakfast.'

Awake now, he turns his head to her with a wry almost-smile, her favourite expression of his.

'Alright, old girl!' Swinging his legs out from under the sheet, seated upright on the side of the bed, he stares for an instant at the far wall of the room and spontaneously intones:

'For fyry Phebus ryseth up so brighte
That al the orient laugheth of the lighte.'

Then, rising: 'Can't beat Chaucer! Everything else is bollocks. And there we are. On we go and up we get! Yes – onward and upward!'

Chapter 8 | Bedroom issues

'I can't help it. I know it's prudish and desperately old-fashioned. But she's my mother. And she's seventy-eight!'

Laurie contemplates his wife sitting opposite him on their balcony. Although she is showered and changed, with a glass of lime soda to hand, she looks wan, no doubt enervated by disrupted circadian rhythms and the unremitting heat. It is fiendishly hot. Why did Jake have to be born in May?

'That's not so old these days, love!' he says. 'And she's allowed to have relationships.'

'Don't be ridiculous! That's not what I'm saying at all. But with him? He's an accountant!'

He nods, refraining from offering any response. Stef is clearly not in any mood for rational debate.

Stef and Laurie arrived that morning to find Cynthia already installed in the hostel after a week of 'doing the tourist thing' with Oliver. 'What's the point of coming all this way and not seeing a bit of India?' she had declared when the schedule was being finalised. She said it in her loftiest tone. Stef is used to her mother's tones, of course, but the lofty tone ranks as the most irritating by far. Though even if she had used the mildest of tones her declaration would still have been intensely annoying. What vexes Stef most is the assumption that her mother is entitled to a holiday. As she has repeatedly reminded everyone – implicitly if not in so many words – this occasion is absolutely not a holiday, nor should it be an excuse for one. Obviously Cynthia knows this, but she will keep referring to it as if it were just a jaunt, a fun thing to do.

This is not Stef's only grievance. Although she was expecting to find Oliver here, she has still not fully accepted it. His participation in the plan could not be refused, in the end, given the generous and decisive donation he had made to Jake's trust, but since Stef was not originally reckoning on even her mother's participation, the news that her companion would also be present came as a further dispiriting blow. Her first reaction had been to exclaim to Laurie in horror: 'But he's not family!'

'...yet,' Laurie added under his breath, fearful of ratcheting up Stef's overwrought state. More audibly, he reasoned: 'Nor is Dougie, nor his mate. Nor is Esme for that matter.' Stef's expression fleetingly changed as the thought crossed her mind, not for the first time: If only she were. Everything might have been so different.

Laurie saw that his wife was not mollified, but he sensed that she had accepted – for now – his logic, and wasn't about to flare up again. In fact, when she thought about it later, she had to concede that Oliver's presence might not be such a bad thing after all – if he is there to look after her mother, it would be one less thing for her to worry about. He would take responsibility. With his debonair, self-assured manner, his business-like mind-set, Oliver chafes her like a prickly pullover on oversensitive skin, in fact everything about him is peculiarly abrasive – but he might yet have his uses.

Stef's irritability with both Cynthia and Oliver was made acute in the first few seconds of her and Laurie's arrival when the hostel manager informed Stef that her parents had arrived safely yesterday. Her parents? And then, even more galling, if that were possible, was the discovery that her mother and Oliver are sharing a room. The pair had appeared as Stef and Laurie were signing in, uttering words of welcome as they descended the stairs to the lobby. Then, having led them outside into the garden, Cynthia casually announced: 'Our room is over there. The one with the rubber plant on the balcony.' Our room! It was a fait accompli.

Stef blinked and found herself peering up at the white-rendered, two-storey construction and looking for a balcony with a rubber plant on it. In fact she was completely uninterested in which room it was, but she was struggling to compute the fact that her elderly mother was sharing a room with a man. With that man. She struggled to think of something to say, something on a completely separate subject but not so separate as to suggest she was attempting to change the subject. For once, however, words failed her. In the brief, uncomfortable silence, Laurie was sure he detected a hint of a smirk settle on his mother-in-law's features. She was sure to have registered Stef's discomfiture. Time to move the conversation on.

'How are you coping with the temperatures?' he asked.

'There's no air-conditioning,' answered Oliver. 'It's not really that sort of place.'

Laurie nodded, knowing full well that it wasn't that sort of place, having stayed here several times in the past.

'It's not a hotel,' he had explained to all of them, several weeks previously. 'It calls itself a hostel, but it's not really a hostel either. It's connected to the church and the orphanage. It's where visitors to either place stay – churchy types, charity-workers and so on.'

He and Stef had discussed whether they should arrange accommodation for everyone in a proper hotel, but this would have escalated the costs, and anyway, it would have seemed anti-social, snobbish even, to arrange their lodgings anywhere else, in spite of Stef's misgivings.

'Not too monastic, I hope?' Laurie asked Oliver.

'Not at all. In fact it's extremely comfortable. En-suite bathrooms and everything. Hot water. Firm mattresses.'

Laurie glanced at his wife and saw that she was still put out. He knew what she was thinking – They're sharing a room. Are they sharing a bed? – and he knew that she would never ask but would be determined to find out.

'There's a ceiling fan,' Oliver went on. 'That's quite sufficient. And western loos...'

'Thank God for that,' Stef remarked, partially regaining her composure.

'...but with bum guns built into the seats!'

Stef blinked uncomprehendingly, and Cynthia said, 'Oh, please!'

Oliver quickly continued: 'Actually those squat jobs aren't too bad either. Don't mind them at all. Usually considerably more hygienic too.'

'But not for the likes of us,' Cynthia interposed. 'Not at our age.'

The conversation was drifting into unseemly areas again, and Laurie hastened to divert it onto safer ground.

'I assume you have a shower in your en-suite. That's what everyone wanted, except for us. We've got a tub in ours.'

'I must have a bath,' Stef told them. 'Every day at home, without fail.'

'How are you getting on with the food?' Laurie asked.

'Oh, dear!' Cynthia exclaimed, then, continuing in a whisper: 'Breakfast this morning was ghastly...'

'Diabolical!' Oliver agreed, not bothering to keep his voice down. 'Eggs hard-boiled to the point of extinction, or else scrambled and cold. Bland cardboard squares of toasted white bread – cold of course – and gluey jam.'

'The fruit salad was quite nice,' Cynthia interposed.

'Ah, yes,' Oliver continued. 'The water-melon was alright, but the papaya tasted like paper.'

'Breakfast is normally Oliver's favourite meal,' Cynthia explained.

'Anyway, dinner last night was acceptable,' Oliver continued, 'and lunch today was good enough. Everything curried, of course. You can order curry for breakfast if you fancy. Which I might have to do.'

Stef was now desperately weary of this topic and her eyes wandered over the scrubby lawn to the balcony with the rubber plant.

'We ought to get up to our room,' she said. 'The receptionist sent the boy there with our cases.' In a half-whisper she asked her mother: 'Is it safe here?'

'Safe? Safe?' Cynthia repeated, over loudly.

Stef rolled her eyes. 'Do you think our cases are safe?'

'My dear, this is a Christian establishment,' her mother declared grandly.

'And that makes it okay?' Stef enquired.

'Oh, go on,' her mother answered, waving her hand as if to shoo away her daughter's words. 'Stop worrying! It's fine. Everything's fine. Go up and have a wash, I'm sure you need one. I expect we'll be having a cup of tea in an hour or so. Come down when you're ready, and we'll tell you all about our travels. We've had an extremely interesting time.'

Laurie could sense Stef bristle.

'Wait till you taste the tea,' Oliver said. 'It's hilarious. But don't drink the water – we've got purification tablets. We can give you some.'

Stef brandished a plastic bottle from her shoulder bag. 'I'm equipped. We'll see you later for "tea".' To Laurie she said: 'Come on. I'm stressing about our bags.' Donning her wide-brimmed bush-hat, she brushed away invisible clouds of flies and strode across the scrubby lawn without waiting for him.

On their balcony now, washed and relatively refreshed, Laurie rises and, stands behind his seated wife, laying his hands on her shoulders and gently rubbing. He feels her tense up and stops rubbing.

'How are you feeling, old thing?' he asks.

'Like shit, to be honest.'

'I'm a bit jangly too. But glad we've arrived. Everything is going to be alright, you know,' he adds in his most reassuring voice.

'What makes you say that?'

'Because it is. And because we're strong. We're fighters, Stef. We'll get through this together, and we'll be even stronger.'

'And you live in a fool's paradise, Professor Johnson. Always have, always will.'

He wishes he could kiss her shoulder, caress and comfort her, but resists the thought. Better not even to attempt any semblance of affection. Not yet. Early days.

'At least a fool's paradise is a paradise – of sorts,' he says.

'Sure. You keep on believing that,' she tells him. 'I've got no objection to optimism.'

'You were an optimist once,' he reminds her. 'And an idealist, remember?' She says nothing and he continues, aware that he is on dangerous ground. 'You can be again, when all this is over.'

'Yes, Professor.' She pulls back her shoulders, shrugging off his hands in the kind of diversionary tactic he is used to. Well, time will tell. Stef calls him an optimist, but optimism is as good as any other mechanism for getting to the end of the day. She has her own methods, of course. Now, though, he needs to believe in his own words more than ever. It's the last shake of the dice, they both know it, and the stakes are higher than they have ever been.

He glances up and sees her gazing across the lawn with a frown. Oliver is there, seated under a parasol and deep in conversation with an Indian man in a baggy white suit.

'Who's that?' Laurie asks.

'Whoever it is seems to be hanging on his every word,' Stef answers absently. 'I can't imagine what that could be.'

'A man of mystery,' Laurie suggests.

'Oliver, you mean? That's rather an understatement.'

51

Stef has never fully trusted Oliver – from the very beginning, when he first appeared in her mother's life. All of a sudden, he was there, in Penzance, on the scene. When Stef offered to drive down to spend a couple of days with her mother, to accompany her on a hospital visit or help her paint the kitchen, it was, 'Oh no, dear, you don't have to worry at all – Oliver will take me,' or 'Oliver has offered to lend a hand.'

Eventually, Stef decided she had to meet this much-vaunted figure, if only to satisfy herself he wasn't a gold-digger. She suggested as much to Cynthia but she had pooh-pooh-ed the idea. 'Don't be daft, he's very well-off! Much richer than I am.' All the same, Stef had her doubts. When eventually she made her visit to her mother's cottage, however, and met her new companion face to face, she actually found him in the kitchen wearing an apron. There was no question about who was in charge, and any notion of him being a gold-digger was quickly dispelled.

'Where on earth did you find him?' Stef demanded to know, as soon as she was alone with her mother.

'Online dating,' Cynthia told her.

'What!'

But then, the deeper Stef probed, the more of an enigma Oliver turned out to be. For a start, he certainly didn't look or behave like anyone's idea of an accountant. It was hard to pin him down. Here was a man who could be schoolboyish and dufferish almost in the same breath, nor did it take her long to discover all the other awkward contradictions residing in him: snobbish and populist, ribald and highly read, with a stunningly accurate memory able to disgorge lengthy chunks of Chaucer and Milton at the slightest encouragement while the next minute regurgitating exchanges or jokes verbatim from The Godfather or Monty Python. Oliver is sophisticated in his tastes, blunt in his opinions, and conservative with suspiciously liberal leanings. How can one get the measure of a man like that?

'What do you see in him?' Stef asked her mother when they were out walking along the seafront.

Cynthia cocked her head, thinking.

'He's handsome,' she started. 'And he's smart, and witty, and funny. He's financially secure, and he's five years younger than me.'

Stef stared at her severely, struck anew by her mother's capacity to infuriate her.

Not knowing how long Oliver will be in Cynthia's life is another impediment to familiarity. Her mother has had other attachments in the decades since her husband died – platonic, so far as Stef could tell, though one of them lasted a couple of years. If she ever asked about them, Cynthia would bat away her questions with evident annoyance, as if to say 'I don't pry into your marriage. Keep out of my relationships. My business.' Infuriating.

Yes, Oliver is a man of mystery, alright. And abrasive. But now – what can he possibly be telling that man that is so fascinating?

Stef sighs, yawns and gets to her feet. 'It's no good,' she tells Laurie. 'I'll have to lie down. Just for half an hour.'

Laurie gives her a worried look. 'Don't make it much longer. You'll want to sleep tonight...'

'No, Professor. Yes, Professor. Three bags full, Professor.' Entering the room, she slips off her sandals and stretches out on the bed. With her mind full of irritations and anticipations, and her skin tingling, she knows that she will be unable to sleep but closes her eyes anyway. It is the semblance of sleep she seeks, just the show. That's the most she can ever manage these days, and it's usually enough.

Chapter 9 | The tremendous shower

It is five o'clock in the afternoon and the four guests sit in a loose semicircle on the veranda, gazing watchfully over the ragged, green-brown lawn in front. Every so often one of them raises a hand to flap away a fly or a mosquito, or to scratch fretfully at an exposed patch of skin. At the centre of the group is a table on which there is a bamboo tray bearing a chunky white tea-pot, a jug of milk with a piece of gauze covering it and a sugar-bowl, also with a gauze, together with four cups, saucers and spoons. There are two other tables on the lawn, each shaded by a frayed parasol, but they have chosen to sit here, on the covered veranda. The lawn stretches some fifty metres to the thick mesh of trees and vegetation that also provides a barrier on the garden's left-hand side. With an ivy-strewn wall on their right and the hostel building behind them, the four have a sense of being in a select, secluded space, a haven from the havoc that is downtown Allapoorha.

Cynthia, who is rhythmically flicking a small lace fan, rests her eyes on the enclosing dense walls of foliage with their flagpoles of spiring palms. Every few minutes the chemical green evanescence of a parakeet flashes across her vision.

'Well, here we all are, taking tea on the veranda,' Cynthia says, breaking a silence. 'How very civilised.'

'Stands the clock at ten to three, and is there honey still for tea?' Oliver murmurs.

'Don't be so colonial,' Cynthia tells him.

'Colonial, *moi*? I was being literary.' He pronounces the last word with exaggerated clarity, as if speaking to a child.

'I suppose it's difficult not to be colonial, four English sahibs in the subcontinent, sipping tea and discussing the weather,' Laurie says. He looks across to his wife, who, leaning back, appears to be lost in her own thoughts. 'You'd agree with that, Stef? We're reinhabiting defunct colonial roles whether we like it or not.' Aware that someone is addressing her, Stef looks around inquiringly.

'Are you dreaming, dear?' Cynthia demands. 'Laurence is making sociological pronouncements.'

'Really?' is all Stef says, appearing completely unimpressed, and there follows another long pause in the conversation.

Cynthia notices Laurie frowning vacantly at the teapot on the table in front of them with fingers interlaced. Even he seems not entirely present. What is going through his mind, if anything? Laurence, too, can be something of a riddle at times.

With the frequent interpolations of Oliver, Cynthia has been relating some of the sights that have stood out during their tour of Tamil Nadu – the huge rock carvings of muscular gods and emaciated river sprites, the spectacular, vimana temple towers with their carnivalesque sculptures, the imperial palaces – while not omitting all the negative experiences, not least the torrents of traffic, the time Oliver quarrelled with a dishonest taxi-driver, and of course the stomach bugs and sudden, inexplicable rashes.

Laurie seemed politely interested, but Stef's eyes were glazed, her mind elsewhere. She looks aloof, severe and somewhat out of focus – undoubtedly jetlagged, though, as far as Cynthia is concerned, her daughter's precise mental state is usually best left unanalysed. Perhaps she'll be more engaged later, when she is rested.

'Hear that?' Oliver asks suddenly.

The others look up at him.

'What are you referring to?' Cynthia asks.

'That ringing sound. Hear it?'

Each of them listens now for the bell-like rhythm that they have all been aware of but have somehow failed to notice. It's almost metallic – a steady, insistent background beat.

'It sounds like someone hammering,' Cynthia says.

'That's why it's called the coppersmith barbet.' Oliver looks round the group triumphantly. No one responds. 'It's a bird. But it's not hammering. That's the sound of the call it makes in its throat. It also pecks, of course, battering holes in trees.'

'Like a woodpecker?'

'Correct. When creating a nest. But that metallic rhythm comes from its throat.'

'It's very monotonous,' Cynthia says. 'Positively metronomic.'

'I thought it was a machine,' Laurie says.

As they all concentrate on the repetitive clang, their attention widens to take in other elements of the soundscape, the interweaving melodies emanating from the trees and the more distant background of traffic noise from the nearby roads. The birdsong seems to be simply a more musical version of the street noise filtering through – both are emphatic, random and unceasing. In the mix too is a high-pitched vibration of crickets and buzzing insects, and, at the bottom end of the spectrum, a barely perceptible drone, low and throaty, produced perhaps by toads or conceivably even an engine – possibly a generator. Everything is invisible and mysterious, and for a while they sit entranced by the hooting, screeching, tweeting and chirruping.

'It is an intriguing spot,' Cynthia remarks. 'Layers and layers...'

Laurie nods thoughtfully. 'You never really get to the bottom of things here,' he states. 'The old cliché rings true: India is unknowable. And it's its very unknowability that keeps you interested. I'm always expecting the spell to wear off, but it never does.'

'Damn hot, though,' Oliver comments. 'And humid.' Apart from Stef, they all nod in silent agreement, and once more relapse into silence. 'But here we are, anyway,' he continues, as if trying to halt the slide into lethargy. 'More or less in one piece, having overcome all adversities.'

'Half the party is here,' Cynthia corrects him. 'The elders...'

'The who?' Stef demands, suddenly present and alert.

'The elders. Us. The older generation. We've arrived in one piece.'

'Christ, you make us sound like the ancient crones of Mu-Mu.'

'I don't know where Mu-Mu is, dear,' Cynthia says.

'So, who are the youngsters?' Oliver asks.

'I've told you several times already,' Cynthia answers. 'There's Esme. Jake's girlfriend. Such a sensible girl. I only met her once, but even then she struck me as mature for her age.'

'He let her go,' Stef says to no one in particular.

'Yes, that was a pity,' Cynthia responds. She glances at her daughter, and knows what she is thinking: *She may have been wise and sensible, but she couldn't save my Jake!* 'Then there's Simon and Miranda – Laurence's two,' she continues. 'And Jake's friend from university, what's his name?'

'Dougie,' Laurie says.

'He's arriving with a friend, I believe.'

'That's right. We haven't met the friend.'

'Will they all be here for your grand dinner?' Oliver asks Laurie.

Laurie shrugs. 'I hope so. The others will probably be here, but we don't know when exactly Dougie and his friend are arriving. Miranda told me that it might be early next week, so too late for the dinner. Anyway, please don't expect a particularly grand dinner. We just thought it would be an opportunity for us all to get together and exchange notes. Shetty has promised to prepare a Keralan feast.'

'Shetty?'

'Shetty the chef. Have you met him? A big man. And a dab hand at dosas. He's been here for years.'

'Anyway, I'm sure it'll be excellent!' Oliver tells him, before explosively clearing his throat. Cynthia sees Stef bridle at this attention-grabbing compulsion of his. That's understandable. She herself is used to it. Oliver crosses a leg and gazes up at the sky, oblivious to his impact on others, and Stephanie withdraws back into her private world, perhaps still listening to the coppersmith barbet and the other diverse descants and warbles of the bird orchestra secreted within the trees.

To pull her back, Cynthia addresses her: 'So when are you going to the orphanage to meet the nuns?'

Stef appears not to hear, and Laurie answers on her behalf. 'We'll go first thing tomorrow.'

'Do you have an appointment?'

'Yes. Well, no,' Laurie says. 'Sister Mercy didn't reply to our last email.'

'We told her we'd visit tomorrow,' Stef clarifies, back in the conversation. 'She didn't reply, which I thought was rather rude.'

'She probably has a very busy schedule.'

'Hallo,' says Oliver. 'Something's afoot.' He is frowning up at the sky. The others look up to see a swirl of darkness above them. It seems to have appeared out of nowhere, an invasion of cloud suddenly blotting out a significant portion of the featureless blue dome that has covered them until now. The unexpected change is uncanny, and they are suddenly aware of a wind snatching testily at the trees and a greater commotion of birdsong.

'It's all so extreme, isn't it, this climate,' Cynthia says, gazing round in wonder, 'so unambiguous. Such a change from dear old England. Are we in the tropics?' she asks Oliver, but before he can explain where the tropics begin and end there is a deep bass rumble that fills the air as if rising out of the earth itself.

'Gosh,' murmurs Laurie in awe. Then there's a brief spark of lightning in the black cloud and a wind that whips through the leaves of the trees with renewed vigour. Again, the volume of birdsong seems to turn up a notch, and they can feel electricity in the air around them.

'Bit early for monsoon, isn't it?' Oliver observes. 'Something tells me we're in for a bit of a spectacle.' There is a second cannonade of thunder, and small detonations can be heard in the vegetation around them – the first hesitant salvos of rain.

Stef jumps to her feet, leaving the shelter of the veranda to stand on the grass, turning her face up to feel the raindrops on her face.

'Stef!' Laurie warns. 'That's not very wise! Come back in, love.' Another booming groan follows, another flash, and the explosions in the vegetation become louder and more urgent. Within a few seconds the sky has blackened several degrees more and the single drops are turning into a steady downpour. Stef hurries back to the shelter of the veranda, her knees seeming to buckle under her as she falls back into her seat. The rain is now pelting furiously on the roof of their terrace and bouncing around them, causing a mist to rise up from the grass. Upstairs, they can hear doors and windows being banged shut. The trees sing no more, the birds are muted, it is the turn of the sky now, a raging bully, stamping and bellowing and drowning everything else out.

'It's so angry!' Stef exclaims, almost breathlessly. She looks around at the others, and, to her own surprise, feels something like solidarity with her frail fellow humans, cowering together in their vulnerability. Laurie appears dumbstruck, and Cynthia is frozen in her cane chair, gripping the arms as she beholds the performance, her fan now stilled. Even Oliver is silenced by the sudden turn of events. But when a harsh crack sounds above them, followed immediately by another dazzle of lightning, much closer than before, a palpable feeling of alarm infects all four of them, their passive appreciation of the drama replaced by a kind of exultant fear. There is another splenetic crash, another brilliant flare, and they exchange excited glances.

'Dear me, it's all getting rather close,' Cynthia ventures.

Laurie begins to say something: 'It's rather like...' but his words are overwhelmed by yet another tearing thunderclap and a redoubling of the pounding rain.

'I think we should go inside,' Cynthia suggests, her voice edged with urgency now.

'You know, I think that would be very wise,' Oliver agrees, almost shouting as he helps her to her feet.

And as the thunder reverberates around them and the rain pummels on the veranda roof, the four of them abandon their seats and fall into the gloomy, cluttered lounge like frightened children. The power supply has evidently failed and there is thick gloom here, the usual calm of the room shattered by the metallic clatter of rain pellets. Suddenly Thomas is in the room, swiftly and efficiently shifting furniture and slamming shut the veranda doors as, shouting, he tries to make polite conversation with his guests, though none of them can make out his words.

All four of them tacitly dismiss the idea of remaining in the darkened lounge, and without further discussion exit into the hall and file upstairs to the safety of their bedrooms.

'Enough excitement for one afternoon,' Oliver is heard to chirp, his voice in the corridor sounding a little too jolly. 'See you for supper, I hope!'

Stef and Laurie close the door behind them in their room, glad to find that Thomas has been in and bolted shut the doors to the balcony. Stef sits on the bed, looking, Laurie notices, small and a bit twitchy. He senses her thirst, but says nothing. He'd welcome a drink himself, though he has resisted indulging since their arrival. If he is the one to start, she will surely follow.

'My God, what a dramatic turn!' he says, stooping to look

through the shutters at the window. He turns and casts around the room in search of some diversion, then pulls a book from the shelf next to his bed. 'I think this is the right moment, don't you?' he says to Stef, flourishing the book.

She looks up and nods dumbly.

'How about I read aloud?'

She nods again, and he leafs through the pages until he alights on her favourite passage from her favourite book, The Waves, the one she returns to again and again.

"'The cliffs vanish. Rippling small, rippling grey, innumerable waves spread beneath us. I touch nothing. I see nothing. We may sink and settle on the waves. The sea will drum in my ears. The white petals will be darkened with sea water. They will float for a moment and then sink. Rolling over the waves will shoulder me under. Everything falls in a tremendous shower, dissolving me.'"

His voice fills the room, occasionally struggling to make itself heard above the persistent roar of the rain on the balcony and the foliage outside. As his eyes flick from the page to her face, he sees she is watching him, lips slightly parted, the hard lines of her face seemingly softened. The habitual irony is gone. Extraordinary. She looks almost rapt. We can still do it, he is thinking, as he declaims the lines in his most sonorous voice, his mind already racing ahead to select the next passage to recite. With everything still to play for, the future might yet trump the past.

Chapter 10 | The Institute

The next morning, it's as if the storm never happened. The sky's passion has been spent, and life on earth vibrantly reasserts itself. As the day takes form, the tentative, pre-dawn chamber music of the birds swells incrementally to symphonic proportions, resounding from the trees at the bottom of the garden, complete with fugues, glissandos and crescendos. It infiltrates, then subverts Stef's sleep, but she has no wish to wake up. Eventually, she knows she has no choice. Cautiously opening her eyes, she sees a space in the bed beside her. The imprint of Laurie is on the sheets. His absence is as strange and unfamiliar as the presence of his body was earlier. Why isn't he there? He merely stirred and groaned at the first pre-dawn buzz and crackle of the muezzin's call, without emerging from his heavy, jetlag-induced torpor, while Stef's eyes flipped open instantly, simultaneously alert and confused. She listened to every nuance of the summons to prayer and can still recall the shocking silence that followed it, as if time itself was briefly suspended, but at some point she must have drifted back to sleep.

Her head feels thick and heavy, and everything is an effort. She is exhausted, but cannot return to sleep now. Things to do. She decides to postpone her bath and instead aggressively rubs her face with water in the bathroom before pulling on some clothes – pale cotton trousers and a white blouse – and strapping on her sandals. At the mirror, she hurriedly applies make up. It's a big day, one that she has rehearsed in her mind for many months.

She finds Laurie, Cynthia and Oliver seated together over breakfast. They look up at her entrance and she sees Laurie's face wearing its characteristic combination of anxiety and reassurance.

'There you are!' he says, as if merely getting up were a major achievement. He pulls out a seat for her. 'I thought I'd better leave you to sleep, but I was getting worried. We'll need to get going soon, love. Here's some juice, and there's fresh coffee in the pot.'

She pours a cup of coffee without taking her seat.

'How are you feeling, dear?' Cynthia asks.

'Very rough,' Stef replies. 'And not up to small talk.' She walks away, cup in hand.

'Where are you going?' her mother calls after her.

'I'm having my breakfast outside.'

'But you haven't got any breakfast!'

She waves her cigarette packet in the air as she disappears through the veranda door. 'You just carry on...'

Fifteen minutes later, Laurie and Stef are passing through the hostel gates on their way to the Institute, both wearing broad-brimmed hats. Behind her thick black sunglasses, Stef feels less fragile. They turn right into the narrow, traffic-free lane outside, swerving to avoid a dog lying just outside the entrance, stretched out inertly in the dust, its coat horribly eaten by mange. Further on, as they are passing the entrance to the little Hindu temple that neighbours the hostel, they are confronted by a tall, thin and strikingly erect man standing in their path. He is barefoot and almost naked, clothed only in a tattered loin cloth around his middle and ropes of beads hanging from his neck. A coil of matted grey hair is perched on his head like an intricate nest. He is muttering insistently as he holds out his stick-like arm, blocking their way. Stef is startled as much by his near-nakedness and intimidating proximity as by his inexplicably contemptuous eyes. They burn fiercely in his gaunt, hollow-cheeked face with its fragments of teeth, so close to hers. There's a strange discrepancy between his towering crown of grey hair, suggesting great age, and his sleek, youthful brown torso from which his shoulders and elbows jut prominently.

They attempt to move round him, but he smartly sidesteps in unison with them, and does the same when they move to the other side. With his upturned palm thrust under their faces, she can't avoid seeing his fingers, slender and knobbly, with long blackened nails sprouting from them like crows' beaks.

'No,' Laurie tells him. 'Sorry!' The man keeps up his monotonous mumble, drilling into their faces with his hostile eyes. Despite his outstretched hand, there is nothing remotely beseeching in his stance, nothing to indicate he is pleading – rather, a disconcerting suggestion of defiance and lordly prerogative.

'Please go away!' Stef declares, uncomfortably aware of her absurdly high-pitched and imperious-sounding tone. It is an impasse. For a moment she thinks they might have to turn back, humiliatingly, and return to the safety of the hostel, giving up all thoughts of leaving, but then a sharp, cracked exclamation from behind causes her to wheel around. There, crouched by the wall, is a second figure, one that she might have taken for a pile of rags had she spotted it sooner, but it is no doubt another impoverished beggar – whether male or female she cannot immediately tell. A bald head and deeply creased face meet her scrutiny, and out of the toothless mouth another injunction crackles forth, at which the tall man blocking their way ceases his mumbling and steps to one side. He watches impassively as Laurie takes Stef's arm and ushers her past. Stef feels deeply shamed, cowardly even, as she imagines the bitter, undaunted eyes of the two beggars boring into their retreating backs.

At the end of the lane, she is still feeling shaken as they wait for a fleet of bicycles to sail by before they can cross the main road. On the far side, she stares up aghast at the imposing white edifice of St Antony's church that dominates a wide, empty and shadeless expanse of black and white chequerboard paving. The vast facade of the deserted-looking building fills her vision, and seems completely incongruous in the midst of the low and dishevelled buildings all around. Its flamboyance and powerful aura of self-confidence lend it the air of a gigantic folly, an elaborate confection transplanted from Europe. In that sense maybe it does fit here after all.

Hurrying over the black and white paved area, conscious of the heat radiating from it, they cross a road on the far side and follow a stained, pink-painted concrete wall to where a white humped cow is standing stock still in front of a once-grand wrought-iron gate.

'What's it doing?' Stef asks, giving the creature a wide berth.

'There's never any answer to that,' Laurie replies cryptically.

Stef stops to read the lettering above the gate: 'St Antony's Institute for Disadvantaged Minors'. 'So this is it?'

'This is it,' Laurie confirms. 'The Institute.'

She feels a confusion of emotions. It is a place that has filled her thoughts for so long, so many years. She has seen pictures, but nothing has prepared her for this reality – the aged, rather neglected feel of it, the banality.

'Come on,' she growls. 'Let's get it over.' But there is no resolution in her advance through the gates and into the Institute's grounds, closely followed by Laurie. They stop and gaze around them, taking in the chipped and flaking plaster on the tall three-storey building in front, the faded brown of the lower building on the right with its covered passageway alongside, and the ranks of fiercely-coloured flowers planted in cakey red soil. In Stef's mind she momentarily conjures up her son there, ambling past with his customary lazy stride, his light ginger curls bobbing as he walks. Then he evaporates. Close to the wall on one side and in the shade of a giant eucalyptus tree, they notice a couple of static figures watching them. They revert their gaze back to the tall building, from which they can now hear chanting emerging through the open windows – morning assembly, perhaps. Stef turns back to the figures under the tree, and sees one of them hesitantly approaching. It is a woman, barefoot, with a dull blue sari and a red bindi in the centre of her forehead.

'Oh, no,' she mutters. 'More beggars...' But then she isn't so sure. Instead of stretching out her hand, the woman stops a few paces away and simply stands and stares, an expectant expression on her face, almost as if she has recognised them, as if she were waiting for them. Stef now sees that she is wearing a gold ankle-bracelet, a thin gold necklace and a nose-ring. She looks like any number of the local women Stef has observed since their arrival in India. But there is something that marks this woman out: the broad, almost ecstatic smile that lights up her face. It seems directed specifically at Stef. No one has ever smiled at Stef like that before. Like the tall beggar outside the temple, the woman looks ageless, with her shiny, neat hair and smooth skin, though her face appears careworn too. Twenty? Thirty? Forty? Recalling this strange encounter later, back at the hostel, Stef struggles to guess her age. Right now, though, all she is aware of is that intense, expectant smile, as if she is renewing an old acquaintance.

Laurie grunts something to hurry them on, but Stef doesn't move. She is waiting for the woman to say something, to explain herself. Her eyes are a similar shade of brown to those of most other people here, but they are as warm and glittering, as vibrantly alive, as the tall beggar's eyes had been cold and lifeless. Stef frowns at the strange woman, feeling almost mesmerised by her.

'Stef? Come on, love!' Laurie is urging. Stef blinks and catches herself shuddering. 'Let's go, come on!' Laurie once more takes her arm and guides her forward, smiling and nodding at the woman, and mouthing, 'excuse me' as they pass.

'She's obviously a bit touched,' Laurie murmurs to her as they move on. Once more Stef feels dazed, and wonders if this is to be her default condition in this place. She hardly has time to digest or even acknowledge one sensation before being overwhelmed by another, and for the first time the thought occurs to her that possibly she isn't strong enough to cope with India.

Familiar with the layout from previous visits, Laurie leads the way past the flowerbeds towards the arcaded passageway, nodding a cheerful 'Hallo!' at a short, moustachioed man in dun-coloured overalls whom Stef takes to be a doorman or janitor and who offers a shy smile in return. The passageway is lined with official-looking numbered doors, all of them closed apart from one at the end, which they enter.

At first it seems that there is no one inside, but out of the gloom comes an impatient voice: 'Yes? Can I help you?' They have to wait for their eyes to adapt to the dim light before they are able to make out the woman seated at a desk in the middle of the room. Clothed in a light blue and white nun's habit, she regards them severely through round, wire-rimmed glasses.

'Ah, good morning,' Laurie says. 'We are Laurence Johnson and Stephanie Daniel. We are here to see Sister Mercy.'

A troubled frown immediately darkens the nun's smooth visage and she consults something on her desk.

'Do you have an appointment?'

'Not exactly. We emailed Sister Mercy to say we'd come today. She told us that she's always available.'

'Sister Mercy is not here.'

'Is she coming later?' Laurie asks.

'She is no longer here. She is gone.'

Stef and Laurie exchange a glance.

'*Where* has she gone?' Stef demands.

'She is gone to Bangla Desh.'

Neither Laurie nor Stef knows how to respond to this news.

'But we had arranged to meet her,' Laurie says. 'She told us to pass by any time to discuss the memorial. The Jake Daniel Memorial.'

'Show me the email,' the nun demands, arm outstretched.

'I don't have it on me now,' Laurie tells her. He looks around the room, past the suspicious-looking nun to an open door behind her, leading perhaps to another office. 'Is there someone else we can speak to? We need to discuss the memorial ceremony. Due to take place next week.'

'Do you mean the inauguration of the Recreation Centre?'

'Yes. The Recreation Centre was to be inaugurated at the same time. It is named after Jake Daniel. Who worked here.'

The woman creases her brows. 'One moment. What did you say your name is, please?'

'I'm Laurie Johnson, and this is my wife, Stephanie Daniel.'

The woman shakes her head in resignation as she pushes to one side whatever it was she was working at on her desk. 'It is always better to make an appointment, you know...'

'Yes, no, I'm sorry. We can come back later, if it's easier. We just need to discuss a few things.'

'Later?'

'Yes...'

The nun creases her brow, rubs her ear and stares at the sheet in front of her. Finally she says: 'Do you wish to make an appointment?'

'Is there not someone we can speak to right *now*?' Stef demands, losing patience.

The nun leans over the sheet without answering, apparently ignoring her. Finally, she looks up at them, still frowning.

'No.'

'What do you mean, "no"?'

The nun turns back to consult her sheet yet again, pursing her lips and grimly shaking her head.

'Sister Margaret is very busy.'

'Alright,' Laurie says. 'We can come back later. At any time. Only we need to speak to her quite soon. About the inauguration...'

The nun abruptly picks up the phone on the table in front of her and jabs at the keypad. She speaks fast in Malayalam into the receiver, then listens with furrowed brows, nods, speaks some more, listens some more, speaks again, listens again, and finally replaces the receiver.

'Sister Margaret will see you shortly.'

'Oh, marvellous!' Laurie exclaims. 'Thank you so much.'

'Wait outside, please.' She gestures outside the door and turns back to her work without another glance.

'Thank you, thank you,' Laurie says. 'Er – what is your name?'

The nun looks up again, her eyes innocent and austere behind her glasses.

'My name is Grace.'

'Pleased to meet you, Sister Grace. We'll wait outside,' Laurie says, steering Stef out of the room.

'I don't know why you're being so sycophantic,' Stef whispers crossly to Laurie as soon as they are at a safe distance.

'I don't think she likes us...'

'How is that relevant?'

He shrugs. 'It matters in India.'

There is nowhere to sit so they stand in the passageway a few paces from the office. Stef looks past the flowerbeds to see if she can spot the woman who approached them previously, but there is no sign of her.

'Who do you think that was, that woman at the entrance?' she asks.

'Who, the beggar?'

'The one who was smiling. She wasn't a beggar.'

'No idea,' Laurie says. 'A cleaner? Or gardener?'

The moustachioed caretaker shuffles into view, meets Stef's eye and nods and smiles. She tersely returns the nod and directs her gaze to the Institute's buildings, which she studies critically, taking in the dusty red tiles, the lizards skittering on the dry, flaky walls. Once again she imagines Jake here, sitting on the low wall, perhaps smoking a cigarette. He raises his slow, languid gaze to meet hers, their eyes locking, exchanging a knowing, irreverent look. Doubtless he would have had immense fun mimicking the strict tones of the humourless nun in the office. Then he dissolves.

Steps clack along the tiles and a woman of about forty appears: another nun. She also wears a blue and white habit and glasses, but she is without a head scarf and her glasses are thick-rimmed. A mass of black, curly hair spills loosely onto her shoulders. Compared to the woman in the office, she gives the impression of being simultaneously efficient and overwhelmed. She carries a stack of files in her arms and a biro entwined between her fingers. Her gaze is direct and, Stef thinks, inhospitable as she addresses them: 'Mr and Mrs Daniels?'

'Daniel,' answers Stef. 'I am Stephanie Daniel and this is my husband Laurence Johnson.'

'You are the parents of Jack.' This is a statement, not a question.

'Jake. Jake Daniel.'

'I am Sister Margaret. We have not been in communication, I believe?'

'No,' Laurie tells her. 'We have been in communication with Sister Mercy.'

'Sister Mercy is in Bangla Desh.'

'So we understand. Did she not advise you about our visit?'

'I know all about you, Mr Daniels,' she says. 'You are here for the inauguration.'

'Mr Johnson, actually. Laurence Johnson. The inauguration,

yes. Of the Recreation Centre. Next week.'

'Do you want to see it?'

'Yes...' he sounds uncertain. 'Soon, definitely. But I understand you are rather busy right now, Sister. If another time suits you better we can come back later.'

'It is always better to make an appointment.'

'Would you like us to come back later?'

Sister Margaret sternly consults her wristwatch.

'Or tomorrow morning?' Laurie asks, a pleading quality in his voice that adds to Stef's irritation.

'It is better that I will let you know. Where are you staying?'

'You must know where we're staying,' Stef says. 'It was all arranged months ago. Have you seen *any* of the emails that we exchanged with Sister Mercy?'

Sister Margaret contemplates Stef for a moment in silence, then says: 'Sister Mercy is not here, madam. We are trying very hard. It is better that I contact you for our next meeting.'

'We're staying at the hostel,' Laurie says quickly, anxious to defuse any potential confrontation. 'St Antony's Hostel.'

'Of course. Are you having a pleasant stay?'

'It's not a holiday,' Stef briskly informs her. 'We're here for my son.'

Again, the nun mutely appraises her. 'Yes, no doubt. Well, I will contact you regarding your next visit. I will show you some of the good work we are doing here.'

'Right,' Laurie says. 'Thank you, sister. We'll wait to hear from you, then.' And before Stef can remonstrate he stretches out his hand, shakes the nun's hand, and spins round towards the exit, arm lightly pressed on Stef's shoulder to guide her out.

Stef just has time to say 'Goodbye' before being whirled around.

'Why are we leaving now?' she hisses to Laurie as soon as they are out of earshot.

'It's obvious she's not going to give us any time now,' Laurie says. 'She won't budge. It's better to comply. That's the best way here, believe me. In fact, it's the only way. It's futile to get cross. And we don't want to get her back up.'

'We're giving her thousands of bloody pounds and she's treating us like ... like we're interfering!'

'We just have to be patient, love. It's for the best.'

Stef scowls. Maybe he's right. But she's furious.

Back at the entrance to the Institute the smiling woman is not to be seen, but a few minutes later they brace themselves on seeing the two beggars still stationed outside the temple next to the hostel. They are squeezed against the wall to take advantage of the narrowing strip of shade. This time, however, neither of them acknowledges Stef and Laurie as they stride past. In fact it is unclear to Stef whether the mound of rags by the wall is occupied until she spots a bony foot protruding. As for the tall austere one, he has his eyes closed as he squats against the wall alongside his staff.

Once inside the safety of the hostel grounds, Stef immediately rushes upstairs, leaving Laurie to report to Cynthia and Oliver on the veranda. She has no interest in pointless discussion. Tired and empty of resources, she simply requires solitude right now. People are no solution. It has been a fruitless expedition, and she can think of nothing more consoling than to close her eyes in a darkened room. Maybe she'll feel stronger later.

Chapter 11 | Allapoorha

Miranda is perched somewhat uncomfortably on a concrete ledge overlooking the lake, a bottle of water beside her, a guidebook in her hands. She is not reading, for her attention is on a group of children swimming and splashing a short distance from her. They are apparently being ignored by their mothers who are squatting on the bank a few feet away, wielding short paddles which they use to batter the clothes they have brought to wash in the scummy lakewater. The slow thudding of their paddles is dolorous and depressing. *What violence is encoded in this daily task*, she thinks. *What monotonous servitude in being a mother and a wife in this country.* She wonders if the housewives are venting their accumulated frustrations by beating the hell out of their husbands' underwear. She wouldn't blame them one iota.

It is nine o'clock in the morning, she feels like rubbish, and her thoughts are blackly misanthropic. The last couple of days have seen Miranda's tentative cynicism regarding Kerala, India and Indians harden. On the whole, she had found everything to be pretty much as expected on first arrival. There were a few surprises, yes, and some discomforts, but nothing that really shocked her. She was enjoying the experience – a break from her rather high-stress city life and her occasionally gruelling job as a teacher. Fort Kochi was fun, despite its commercial manipulations. But she soon came to realise that Fort Kochi is not 'India'. It isn't the whole story. In retrospect, it was a charmed, insulated illusion which melted away the further Miranda and Simon ventured from the tourist enclave where they were lodging. On their third day there, they wandered away from the seafront and the Parade Ground to delve into the teeming neighbourhoods to the south. Suddenly, inescapably, she was seeing evidence everywhere of misery and destitution. There were vile, odorous open sewers and heaps of debris everywhere, while the 'pavements' resembled demolition sites, randomly scattered with piles of bricks and cement that made them practically unusable. Through gaps in the paving stones they found themselves looking down on the fetid grey fluid of drains. The frequent potholes and trenches all required careful negotiation – this was definitely not a place for the blind or disabled. Since the pavements were not viable, everyone walked on the roads, but these were furious with endlessly flowing traffic, making no concession to the footbound majority. The simple act of walking became a nerve-wracking experience, with eyes and ears constantly alert to the perils of speeding cars and motorbikes. To complicate matters, knotty tangles of lethal-looking black cables hung low from masts, occasionally catching out Simon, who is taller, and once swiping off his cap as, eyes lowered, he picked his way over the uneven surface underfoot. Ancient beggars shuffled after them, clothed in rags and dragging diseased limbs, while children pursued them pleading for a few rupees or a school pen.

Oppressed by their surroundings and stupefied by the sun, Miranda and Simon found refuge in a café-restaurant advertising fresh juices. As they sat in a daze, they became aware of a man at an adjacent table watching them with unconcealed curiosity while dispatching a dosa. He had a red smudge on his forehead and, in his neat, white-collared shirt, was better dressed than the other people in the restaurant. When he had finished his dosa he rinsed his fingers, then called across to them in near-perfect English.

'Are you lost?'

'Not lost,' Simon told him. 'Just out for a wander.'

He raised his eyebrows in wonderment. 'Congratulations! Most foreign visitors go no further than the ghetto. That's what we call the tourist shops and restaurants around Fort Kochi, the ghetto. Foreigners don't see the real India.' He smiled sardonically. 'They have no idea. Fort Kochi is not the real India. Did you even see a temple there?'

'There are lots of churches,' Simon pointed out.

'Churches! That is what I mean. It is full of wealthy Christians! That is why all the tourists love it. But Christians are a small minority in India. They are privileged. The city administration puts all its money into those few streets in order to please the tourists. They are creating a sanitised version of India!'

It emerged that he was a bank clerk on his lunch break, and also a supporter of a Hindu nationalist party. He wasn't personally hostile to Simon and Miranda, but he seemed to be critical of everything they represented. As he spoke, summarising and then lambasting the policies of the left-wing state government, his tone steadily became shriller, more hectoring, until finally Simon nudged Miranda and suggested they should make a move.

They rose, and the clerk, with smouldering eyes, fired a last question at them: 'And what about the test?'

They both looked mystified. 'What test?' Miranda asked, thinking it must be some ideological vetting procedure imposed by the state government.

'Are you not following the test series?'

'I – I didn't know there was a test series.'

'You do not follow the cricket?' He looked disbelieving.

'Sorry.'

He looked crestfallen, and in his disappointment became more sympathetic – apologetic even.

Outside, they hailed a rickshaw and returned to the safe familiarity of Fort Kochi's 'ghetto'. But even here things turned sour. The following day – their last before moving on – brother and sister entered a café tucked away at the southern end of the

Parade Ground. Hot and thirsty, Miranda pulled back a chair and was about to lower herself onto it and rest her aching feet when she felt something squishy under her left sandal, simultaneously hearing a cracking sound. There, under the table, was a large, flattened, headless rat. The weight of her foot had squeezed a slimy-looking sauce of red innards out of its neck, around which there swarmed an army of busy ants. Presumably a cat or dog had wrenched off the head, possibly even eaten it.

'Let's get out of here,' she told Simon, ashen-faced, and without explanation walked quickly out of the café, leaving her confused brother to collect his hat and hurry after her.

Clearly, not even Fort Kochi is immune from reality.

This morning, in the grey light of dawn, she and Simon caught a ferry across to Ernakulam, where they boarded a train for the short journey south to the much smaller town of Allapoorha. Their ridiculously early departure would not have been their first choice, but there was only one train that had seats in the air-conditioned Chair Car class available at short notice. From Allapoorha's station, they took a rickshaw into town, but, as it was still early, they decided to wait an hour or two before travelling on to the hostel where they would be staying. Eight o'clock is too early to arrive, Simon said, no doubt wanting to put off as long as possible the moment of family reunion – and anyway, he was hungry. So they consulted the guidebook and decided to make their way to the shores of Punnamada Lake, at the eastern end of town, where they found a quiet spot and a shack serving food. Having breakfasted on a spicy pav bhaji and tea, Simon then went in search of a bank to pick up some cash, leaving Miranda to watch their bags.

Reading the guidebook with increasing scepticism, Miranda notes that Allapoorha has been dubbed 'the Venice of the East', for, in addition to its lake, it has a network of canals. They passed along some of these on the way here. However, although tree-lined and relatively peaceful, the canals were mostly choked by weeds and drifts of floating plastic, and nothing like the neat and alluring waterways that she was expecting. Away from the canals, the town was ramshackle and nondescript, its noisy streets shabby and littered on every side. Barefoot children played in the gutters and they saw packs of pariah dogs. All further evidence of India's alternative reality. And here, the children frolicking in the grey-green lake-water might be relishing the liberation that water everywhere promises, but they are probably poisoning themselves too.

Miranda hardly slept last night. This morning's air-conditioned Alleppey Express was relatively comfy, but she could not rest on the train either. She has suffered a degree of insomnia for most of her adult life and is used to short nights, but now her fatigue has combined with the early-morning heat to drain her of all enthusiasm, while failing to staunch the stream of negative thoughts that race unceasingly through her brain. She has always had an over-active mind, constantly engaged, whether grappling with issues, tasks and intentions or just turning over memories or making mental audits. Unlike Simon, she is incapable of retreating from the world for long. Of the two siblings, she is the more 'grounded' – a word she likes to use about herself – but also more weighted by doubts and reservations. She sees herself as both more introverted and more socially engaged than her brother. She gets on with things.

She glances at her watch: Simon has been gone over half an hour and she feels uneasy and exposed, the object of casual scrutiny by the washerwomen and passing locals. Above all she wants to shower, to rub all the grit out of her skin and hair. She takes a sip from her bottle and gazes wearily about her. A haze of flies hovers over the malodorous water. Further out, over-sized houseboats file by, disruptive and polluting vessels no doubt catering to wealthy tourists. As in Kochi, the contrast between the insulated privilege of a minority and the material deprivations of the majority is stark and searing. The gulf that separates these wealthy weekenders – and her and her brother for that matter – from the great impoverished mass of the population increasingly troubles her. India, she has found, makes her angry. And though she has made a point of tipping generously, of doling out notes to every beggar that propositions them and willingly overpaying for goods and services, still she can't escape the feeling that she is colluding with the status quo.

Now, jumbled together with the moral ambivalence and indignation, she feels something else, too – a sort of trepidation, fear even. No doubt it has to do with Baby Jesus, with the imminent prospect of arriving at the place where he walked and joked and worked, no doubt exuding his own brand of entitlement and privilege. It is entering a land that has previously only been imagined and will now become frighteningly real. It is his world.

Because she has always been the competent, steadfast one, it fell upon Miranda to see The Project through. Stef has never been more than a detached observer, while Laurie sometimes seems to be merely going through the motions. So, by default, Miranda has become most invested in its smooth running and successful outcome. She has planned and prepared and expended a ton of energy on it. Without her organisational skills, the Jake Daniel Memorial Trust might never have got off the ground, and once launched it would never have achieved this apotheosis, when everything they have worked for will come to fruition and they can finally close the books.

Paradoxically, while Miranda has never allowed life to dictate the terms of her place in it, and while she can be decisive once decisions have been made and opinionated once opinions have been reached, nonetheless she is slow to judge and prone to long reflection. Her teacher's profession has instilled those qualities in her. Her work, at which she is extremely competent, demands that she must listen to all sides and when necessary go with the flow. In fact, this suits her temperament. Like her father she prefers consensus. Which is why, though she has no time for the dubious motives that underpin the whole ethos of The Project, she recognises that it must be seen through to the end, even if a positive outcome is by no means assured. She is ready to ride out present difficulties for the sake of a potential longer-term good.

She herself has raised nearly £8000 over the last five years, making her – until Oliver's late contribution – the largest single donor. She does not have much money of her own but she has plenty of initiative, and while being entirely unathletic herself she has been able to mobilise others in sponsored swims and marathons.

And yet – as The Project nears completion and it is possible, just possible, that their lives might return to something like normal – now more than ever she feels the pangs of anxiety.

'Hey!' Her brother's voice from behind cuts through her reverie, making her spin round.

'You gave me a fright!'

'Are you alright?' he asks. 'You're really pale.'

'Just dead tired. What took you so long?'

'I had to go to three different ATMs. The first two didn't recognise my card.'

'Why is everything so difficult here?' Miranda complains, and is shocked to hear the whining note in her voice.

'Hey! That's not like you, sis. Positive, remember?' He points back to the road. 'I've got us a rickshaw for the ride to the hostel. Negotiated a good price.'

She gets to her feet, feeling foolish as she gathers her bags. *He's right,* she thinks. *This isn't me. I need a shower. And maybe a change of attitude.*

'I'm ready. Let's go.'

Chapter 12 | Delhi

Esme is staring at the sign on the wall of the palace:

1. BEWARE OF PICKPOCKETS
2. DO NOT SPOIL WALLS BY WRITING
3. SMOKING AND CHEWING OF BEATLES PROHIBITED
4. DO NOT INDULGE IN ADULTERY IN THE PALACE
5. OFFENDERS WIILL BE HANDED OVER TO THE POLICE

She cannot imagine anyone either pickpocketing or writing on the walls of this abandoned palace – let alone committing adultery – because there is not another soul to be seen. The man selling tickets had to be sought out, and seemed amazed to see her. The palace had been called an 'undiscovered gem' by Major Omri, the amiable host of the hotel on the outskirts of Delhi where she is staying before her flight south. She found him and another gentleman engrossed in a game of chess when she started out this morning, but they abandoned it to advise her in the most extravagant terms of the charms of this hidden treasure. Esme had other sightseeing plans, but Major Omri, who has short bristly hair and a luxuriant handlebar moustache and speaks in an endearingly old-fashioned style that evokes the manners of a distant era, insisted that she should prioritise this place. He even enlisted on her behalf the services of a rickshaw driver called Jalil, who arrived outside the door in less than five minutes. Jalil has a dyed orange beard and a white skullcap, and has not so far been too pushy apart from a couple of half-hearted attempts to inveigle her into dropping in on a handicrafts shop he knows. He is now waiting outside as she tours this echoey labyrinth of bare rooms, dusty passages and courtyards patrolled by grey, longtailed langur monkeys.

Major Omri was certainly right in calling the palace under-appreciated and unsung, insofar as she seems to be the only tourist here. The absence of other visitors is not altogether surprising, though, since, apart from the building itself and the monkeys, there is nothing actually to see. Most of the doors in the dim corridors are locked, the rooms that are open have ornate plaster mouldings that are swathed in dust and bat droppings, and chandeliers that are draped in cobwebs, and there are birds' nests on the elaborate cornices. It is a shell, but one that resonates with a kind of absence of memories, like a picture album from which the pictures have been removed. Esme is struck anew with the layered secrets of this land, where it is not necessary to venture far off the beaten track to find oneself in another epoch and culture haunted by previous lives. She can fill the hollow spaces with her imaginings.

After an hour of wandering through the deserted corridors and chambers, it is a relief for her to pass through a door hanging off its hinges and emerge into a different world, in the form of a large and surprisingly fecund garden filled with trees and straggling shrubs – roses, jasmine, lantana and hibiscus. The air of neglect is overwhelming, but the fierce light and eruption of colour is delightful after the faded walls of the musty rooms she has been in, with almost a surfeit of objects commanding her attention. Shade is provided by a variety of tall trees, from one of which are suspended what appear to be big black handbags, which on closer inspection turn out to be gigantic fruit bats hanging upside down from the branches. She approaches a thick cluster of apricot-coloured, trumpet-shaped flowers that hang down in messy profusion, and is breathing in their sweet fragrance when she is startled by a voice nearby.

'Be careful, madam! Every part of that plant is poisonous.'

With a sinking heart, she turns to see, seated on a bench a few feet away, an Indian man watching her. He is gripping a cane between his knees and has a large, curved nose and thick tufts of white hair spilling out from a shapeless white fedora. His creased, pale magnolia suit is lent colour by a maroon handkerchief protruding from the top pocket, a red flower in the lapel and his green and yellow striped tie.

'In English it is known as "Angel Trumpet". The seeds and leaves are particularly toxic.'

'Oh... Thank you.'

He regards her with interest through yellowed, rheumy eyes weighed down by deep, wrinkly pouches.

'Would you like to sit down?' With his cane, he gestures another bench opposite him on the overgrown path, and likewise overshadowed by the dense foliage of a tamarind tree.

Against her better instincts, but feeling suddenly fatigued, she takes a seat opposite him.

'Are you enjoying the palace?' His voice has a smooth, caressing quality, almost that of a cat's purring.

'It's very interesting. Quiet.'

'It is rare to find tourists in this far-flung corner of the city. Which country are you from?'

'England.'

'Ah...' he says, as if her answer explains much. After a short pause, he continues: 'I come here often. It is the property of the Indian government now, but it once belonged to my good friend.'

'He must be very wealthy.'

'No, in fact he was extremely straitened, and he is no longer alive.'

'I'm sorry...'

He shrugs. 'Hiram was the last prince of the royal house of Kutch, the son of the Nawab of Kutch, but he lived his last years in abject poverty.'

'I've never heard of the royal house of Kutch,' Esme tells him.

'It is one of the oldest houses in India.'

'Are they Mughals?'

He looks shocked. 'Mughals? Don't talk to me about Mughals – they were vulgar! Savages! The kings of Kutch were one thousand times nobler. They possessed great palaces and estates in Gujarat and Uttar Pradesh, and hosted lavish parties.' He frowns. 'The British, of course, considered them to be irredeemably and unacceptably dissolute, and so deprived them of their estates. The family was left only with this palace and a mountain of debts. The Nawab himself – Hiram's father – resigned himself to a life of dissipation, debauchery and low pursuits, and when his wife complained he expelled her.'

'That's very cruel.'

'He was a proud man. But the Begum was a proud woman, also. She took up residence in the first-class waiting room in Delhi railway station together with three of her bloodhounds, a collection of Persian carpets and a retinue of Nepali liveried servants. When she was unwilling or unable to pay their salaries she went to live in a hotel where she resided in regal isolation. Eventually, after years of depression, she took her own life. According to the rumours, she ground her remaining diamonds into dust and swallowed them.'

'My goodness! And what about the Nawab?'

'He shot himself.'

'What a sad story!' Esme exclaims.

'It is an Indian tragedy,' the man replies. 'After his father's suicide, Hiram continued to live in two of the rooms here, alone. He never forgave his father. Every evening, until the end of his life, he laid a table setting for his mother the Begum, with a plate and a glass of lemon sherbet.'

'Did he have a job?'

'No. In the mornings he wrote letters to the government complaining about the rain that came in through the roof, and the spiders that proliferated in the rooms, and the jackals that howled outside at night. There was no electricity, and a sign on the gates informed potential intruders that they would be shot. Apart from his servant, he was completely alone. He was very lonely, I think, but he refused to consort with those he thought were socially inferior. He considered himself apart from the rest of society, you see. He believed that ordinariness is more than a crime, it is a sin.'

'How did you know him?'

'I knew him at school. Afterwards I came to visit every few months and stay the night. We would have dinner together and play cards. Then, while I was in Kolkata on business, he was not replying to my telephone calls. I grew concerned and contacted the Delhi police to ask them to investigate. The police came and found his body in one of the rooms. The rats had feasted on him.'

'Ugh!' Esme responds. The man turns away to face the glass-less windows of the palace and doesn't address another word to her. It is only when she finally rises to leave that he gets to his feet, a little unsteadily, bows his head, and wishes her a happy and prosperous journey through life. Returning his bow, she sees pearls of moisture glistening in the corners of his sallow eyes.

Esme finds her way back to the entrance and Jalil's rickshaw. At her next stop – a grand Mughal tomb in well-tended parkland, this time well patronised by other tourists – she mulls over the strange tale she has heard and the palace that has been comprehensively stripped of its grandeur, like the family that once inhabited it. She wonders whether Prince Hiram could have been happy if he had not been so convinced of his superiority, or was that his only route to happiness? His hubris and self-defeating pretensions pull her thoughts back to her own past, and the object of her journey. Could

Jake have been accused of hubris? And if so, would he have found a niche here? How was he regarded in this land of enigmas and eccentrics?

Esme heard diverse and usually incoherent stories about Jake's time in India, though he himself hardly ever spoke about it. His mother was always loquacious on the subject whenever Esme went to stay at the family home in Winnersh. 'India changed him,' Stef told her. 'It was a proper education. He learned about the world there. It matured him.' Esme of course had not known Jake pre-India, and couldn't imagine what the 'immature' Jake could have been like, but she was deeply sceptical. There was no particular self-awareness in him that she was able to detect, no empathy or gravitas or wisdom. When she asked him about his Indian experience, all he mentioned was the heat, the sweat, the frustrations, the misunderstandings, the bloody locals. 'Indians!' he lamented. 'No sense of humour!'

That was one of his favourite accusations against anyone who didn't respond to his provocations, as in: 'Where's your sense of humour...?' 'Unspontaneous' was another. When he did something thoughtless or stupid, he put it down to his 'spontaneity'. It was the closest he came to making any kind of apology. He would look you straight in the eye and come out with something like: 'Whoops, what am I like? Being spontaneous again...' But he always overrated the value of spontaneity – it was a poor cover for all manner of misbehaviour. Eventually Esme or Dougie or anyone else who was about would lose their cool and shout, 'For fuck's sake, will you ever fucking grow up!' Whereupon Jake would either shake his head pitifully and say, 'No sense of humour!' or else purse his lips, look away, and cast an air of tragedy about him. If he felt seriously hurt he might look shifty and wounded and sidle out of the room, but the next time you saw him he was his usual nonchalant self, the slight apparently forgiven and forgotten.

As far as Esme could tell, India for Jake had simply been another gap year holiday. He might have been doing anything – diving off the coast of Belize, traversing the Australian outback, being a barista in Joburg – for all the difference it made. As far as she could tell, he didn't even do any of the tourist things, no sightseeing, trekking, beach-lounging – so what *did* he do?

She finds it hard to imagine Jake here. But these days she finds it hard to picture him at all. Her imagination seems to fail her. How strange it is that, though those months with him were probably the most intense of her life, she has so few specific memories of them. She can recall the sense of excitement, yes, and the frustrations, certainly, but few individual experiences or events, happy or otherwise. How could it be that the person who once turned her world around in that formative period of her life, the one who educated her in the shifting limits of possibility as profoundly as her tutors did in the abstruse rules of linguistic theory, is now just a collection of disconnected sensations in her mind? And how strange that, of the memories she retains, she seems to recall the strife much more vividly than the good times. What did they row about, she and Jake? Trivialities, for sure, as she can't now recall any specific issues. Did the exasperations really outweigh the joys?

Jake seemed exiled from reality. Never one to be distracted by forethought or reflection, he was allergic to real life. The palace he constructed for himself was as much a confection of fantasies as Hiram's, a house of dreams where he ruled supreme and alone. Was it this overarching sense of entitlement that lay at the root of their quarrels? Was it this that she finally rebelled against? How he had to have things his own way, and how any opposition or frustration she might express was met with either point-scoring petulance or mute hurt. She shudders to remember the scenes, the sudden hysterias, the sullen silences. He was manipulative and cruel, she knows that now, not to mention exhausting. Each day with him was like renegotiating the relationship from scratch.

What was Jake's fundamental flaw, the one that ran through his whole being, destabilised and finally did for him? Where was the crack? Was it fatherlessness, or having an over-bearing mother? Esme has always believed that it was Stef's obsessive love that turned the path of her son's life into a cul-de-sac – if you can do no wrong, you have to keep on pushing the boundaries, you're condemned to being the bad boy, the scapegoat, until the day comes when you realise that those boundaries are only ever constructs anyway. Where do you go then? However, while psychology might find reasons, it can never fully explain or justify. There are no excuses for abusing others or yourself. And anyway, how can you analyse anyone who is all surface? One of his sayings swims up through the muddy waters of her memory: 'Superficiality is my secret weapon.' And another time: 'My shallowness is my greatest strength.'

And yet, and yet – for all his character defects, he remains a precious part of her identity, of who she was then and who she is now. She is convinced that she would be quite a different person were it not for that mad chapter of her life – and quite possibly a diminished one. Like those old folks endlessly turning over their wartime memories, she has never felt so alive since then, despite everything that happened. Because nothing, then, was predictable.

After a lunch of samosa and curd, Esme's last stop is a museum of musical instruments set in an old, well-to-do house built around a shady courtyard. She is given a personal tour by the curator, whose other job, he says, is coach for a hockey team. He shouts a lot and is clearly an enthusiast, but after a while she feels her attention wandering as he points out yet more display cases of ancient sarods, vinars, citars and tablas, not to mention the shelffulls of photos and trophies. She has had her fill, and is grateful to get back to her hotel, where she finds Major Omri now engaged in a chess game against another soldierly man, this one short and bald but with an equally flamboyant white moustache.

'Well?' her host jovially demands. 'What about it? Are you glad you went?'

'It was intriguing,' Esme tells him. 'What a shame it's so empty.'

'One day it will be a grand hotel,' Major Omri says. 'The property has been purchased by a Chinese company.'

'Oh. That will be sad.'

'Sad? Yes, sad for me perhaps. But in any case I will be retired by the time it opens.'

'It's sad that there will no more memory of the Nawab of Kutch,' Esme says.

'Who is that?'

'The Nawab of Kutch. His family owned it before.'

The Major narrows his eyes. 'Who told you that?'

'A man I met there. He said it was the Nawab's son, Hiram, who lived there before the government took it over. He was the last prince of the royal house.'

Major Omri shakes his head, mystified. 'I don't know who that is,' he says. 'It was a lunatic asylum until eight years ago. And before that it was a factory. A hundred years ago, perhaps, it was owned by a royal personage. But not in my lifetime.'

Esme feels her head spinning. Flies are crawling on her neck, perhaps attracted by her sweating. She's not sure of anything any more. Who was that she met in the garden, a ghost?

'Excuse me, I must have a shower,' she says, taking her leave. She needs a siesta, too – perhaps followed by a yoga session. She has an early flight tomorrow.

Chapter 13 | The Project

Time here is measured not in hours or days but in the slow gyrations of the ceiling fan. Although Stef, in the midst of all the arrangements and preparations back in the UK, worried about the lack of air-con in their accommodation, to the point of suggesting to Laurie that a fully-equipped three-star in Allapoorha might be a more appropriate option, in the event she finds comfort in the old-school ceiling fan. Its regular rhythm forms a hypnotic focus for her brand of abstract meditation, its regular clicks a comforting mathematical corrective to the random, uncontrollable nature of everything else. The fan is perfectly obedient: one turn of the switch and the rhythm increases, two turns and it races, three and it ceases. How satisfying.

Now the fan revolves at just the right pace – rapidly enough to create a mild movement of air against her skin, but slowly enough to be able to make out the individual blades on their endless journey. Following their motion allows her to sink deeper into herself. It is mid-afternoon, and she is lying naked on the bed, having thrown off her clothes and the cotton bed-sheet. Laurie has gone, taking a walk into town, he said. His walks are a regular feature of his day wherever they are – he regularly disappears without any explanation, she does not know where and does not ask. He says that he enjoys the change of air, the mental tonic that exercise brings, which may be true, but she also knows that he needs to get away from her. That is the pattern, their *modus vivendi* over the last few years. The truth is that they each quietly relish their own company more than the company of the other. She is grateful to him for that: he has always given her plenty of space.

This time Laurie muttered something about finding a gift for

Sister Margaret, no doubt some kind of peace offering, but Stef wasn't particularly interested. She bolted the door as soon as he departed – she has no wish to expose herself if there were any chance of him (or anyone else) blundering in. She has no wish to taunt him with something he can't – or won't – have. They have not had sex for three and a half years. She herself feels no desire, and it wouldn't do to resuscitate even the memory of it in him.

Thinking of it now, she retains a cold memory of their physical interactions. Her fingers brush her breasts, press between her thighs – everything is in place, it's just dormant. Currently redundant. She can't imagine ever feeling desire again.

It is hard now to recall the time when Laurie was so right for her. One part of her brain, the rational side, knows that back then he was the right man at the right time, and from the beginning she recognised in him an ally. In the nomenclature adopted by Virginia Woolf – her model, her guiding light – he was the Precious Mongoose to her Mandrill. They were strong together, tight as anything, marching forward with arms linked against the enemy, whether in the streets or in the academic corridors of the university where they both worked. Of course they both knew that it was an unequal alliance. She counted on his ideological rigour and his invaluable support, but she was always the one to set the agenda. He was loyal, that was the main thing, desperately loyal. He would once have followed her anywhere. Now she has drifted into places where not even he can follow.

It all came unstuck of course on that fateful morning, when Jake Daniel flew through the air at an estimated 60 miles per hour, propelling his golden head into the road surface, snapping his neck as his motorbike exploded catastrophically over the East Sussex countryside. Then it was that Stef and Laurie's forward march stumbled and, like Jake's bike, crashed out of control. The campaign was over, the enemy had won.

Grieving, the psychologists say, demands that you live either in a hyper-real remembered past or in the sterile, desert-like expanses of a denuded future. True, Stef inhabits those imaginary places far more than is good for her, but she spends far more time in the here and now, condemned to live in the ruthless minutiae of the present. And there is no payback. She agrees with Emerson: 'I grieve that grief can teach me nothing.'

There was nothing to prepare Stef for the cataclysmic event of her son's death. No words, no warning, no mitigation. How could there have been? And so she disappeared into a sealed chamber, unreachable. She found hidden comforts there, deep inside, and she has never really felt an urge to come out.

Laurie, in contrast, re-entered the currents of his life after just a few days. It was an intellectual decision. There was his work, there were Miranda and Simon to consider, and anyway, he had already known bereavement: his first wife, Charlotte, succumbed to a vicious, late-diagnosed cancer when their children were still small. But Stef's grief was on a different level – depthless, infinite. It was as if her insides had been scooped out and dissolved. First, there was the disbelief, the numbness; then the terror that accompanied the awful, indescribable realisation; then the anger, the frenzy. Her brain was constantly in over-drive. She couldn't sleep, couldn't even close her eyes. The insomnia was due to a series of sleep disorders: night terrors, sleep paralysis, apnoea. That was the instigation for her and Laurie to sleep in different rooms. Other strange symptoms manifested themselves – blinding migraines that forced her to hide in her room for days at a time, and hyperacusis, which made her ultra-sensitive to certain sounds. Everything was suddenly too loud, too discordant. 'I'd be hopeless as a spy,' she told her sister. 'All they'd have to do to get information out of me would be to get a dog to bark for a couple of minutes, or rub a glass the wrong way, or put a clock with the wrong kind of tick within earshot.'

Back then, Laurie and her mother, her sister, her friends and colleagues, even Miranda and Simon, came up with whole menus of possible remedies. They knew better than to utter such hollow phrases as 'moving on', but they did urge her to address her loss, to absorb the reality, to re-focus. Try counselling, psychoanalysis, medication, meditation, they advised. And, for a while, she did follow their advice. The shrinks, whom she despised, told her that she was grieving not just for Jake but for her father and for Jake's father, Michael, too – something she had never allowed herself to do when they too had unceremoniously disappeared from her life. And it was true enough. It was all true, obvious even, but none of it helped. After the first few sessions, Stef couldn't go through with any of it – the meetings, the consultations, the counselling, the cognitive treatments. All therapies have to explain everything, rationalise it, but there is no reason to be found in loss, neither is there any resolution or closure. Her grief is bottomless; she is falling, falling, and does not expect to finish falling until the final obliteration. That is the only closure.

Eventually, inevitably, she alienated her family and her friends, they all drifted away one by one. There was one upside to this: people gave up offering condolences and compassion, gave up discussing her feelings, dissecting her grief. How could they understand? Their lives could move on, but hers was stopped forever.

The drinking started quite soon afterwards. It was one way of getting to sleep, after all. But her daily intake gradually increased. People began to cast significant glances at her, virtue-signalling their worry. It didn't bother her, though. For one thing, drinking runs in her blood – her father was diagnosed with cirrhosis of the liver when she was fourteen, it's a sort of family trait. Secondly – and surprisingly, given her daily intake – Stef finds that she is able to function well enough under the influence. After all, it's not that she has a complicated relationship with the bottle. She has a very straightforward one: they get on very well. But she has a complicated relationship with everyone else on account of her very straightforward relationship with the bottle. They don't get it. They want to 'save' her when she doesn't wish to be saved. She knows she's an embarrassment and a disappointment, and that's too bad, but it can't be helped. They should leave her alone, allow her the indignity of stewing in her juice.

Not that any of them are exactly unflawed. Laurie – he has his own dark secrets that have already fatally undermined him. Her mother? She regards herself as some kind of wise saint though she must bear some responsibility for her husband's recourse to booze. Her sister Rebecca? A slave to convention, forever chasing the illusion of stability. Her step-children? Ungenerous, and somewhat hypocritical. Anyway, that relationship burned out many years ago, her own fault, she acknowledges that, but it's too late to do anything about it now. Frankly, she doesn't respect them enough, or trust them. And they depress her: she finds them inert when compared with Jake, who was constantly moving, questing, breaching boundaries.

That's what he was doing here, of course. She realises that now, for the first time. He was exploring, learning, testing himself in the face of this ruthlessly alien environment. How simultaneously glad and distraught Stef is to see this place finally. It was she who had found the gap-year placement for him, she had pushed and pushed, until finally he relented and allowed her to organise his visa and flights. And it was so gratifying to read his letters and learn of the new worlds that opened up for him in this parallel universe. Here, he had finally learned to give, to feel, to contribute, to immerse himself in a world where everything didn't revolve around himself. It was the missing piece of his education.

This is Stef's first visit – to the Institute, to the hostel, to India. Laurie has been three or four times in the last six years, but she has always refused. She doesn't know why now. Was it because she did not want to be where Jake had been, to be reminded of his presence? Or because it was part of his other life, and nothing to do with her? Or because the whole thing is irrelevant? While it was Stef who steered Jake to India in the first place, this scheme to memorialise his life was Laurie's inspiration. Laurie's allegiance to Jake was at best tenuous, of course, but his devotion to Stef is and always has been absolute. And he – ever the pragmatist, the conciliator, the problem-solver – became convinced that this would be the perfect way to channel her loss into something good, something concrete and productive. Once the idea was planted, he and Miranda masterminded the whole thing. They came to refer to it as 'The Project': a cause they could unite around, working together towards an end that was both positive and poignant. She went along with it, of course, just as she went along with everything, on one level. She would not want to seem ungracious. But in truth her heart was never really in it.

And, she suspects, deep down, neither was Laurie's. He visited and planned and liaised, but for him it was more like an interesting diversion, an exercise. And gradually she has sensed his interest dwindling. She no longer detects in him the enthusiasm that he showed in the early days of The Project, he rarely discusses it nor relays the latest developments and plans as he once did, doesn't share with her the latest events appearing on the Institute's Facebook page. No, his heart isn't in it... Where is his heart now? She has no idea.

Stef's thoughts today and yesterday have been a bewildered swirl of disappointment and frustration, keeping her brain awake far longer than is good for her. Everything has been too fast, too open-ended, too unresolved. Arriving at the hostel and visiting the orphanage should have been a catharsis, when instead it has made her feel insecure and weak, like opening a wound. Being here is like negotiating a precarious route along stepping-stones that cannot be relied upon: some are stable, some are liable to slide away as soon as she rests her weight on them, some are complete illusions. Nothing is as she expected or hoped for. She cannot trust anything anyone says. The heat is disorientating and draining. The hostel is, after all, just a place to stay, not a haven or a retreat. The orphanage is chaotic and bizarre. She did not expect a welcoming committee, but perhaps a tiny sign of recognition? A warm word or a gesture? Instead, they found rudeness and the sensation that she and Laurie were in the way. Everything conspired to accentuate her sense of loss, the finality and borderless extent of it.

What was she expecting? She does not now know. Not a plaque, obviously not, but maybe a photo of her boy on a wall or a shelf (she and Laurie have sent several over the years). No, there was nothing. What she certainly hadn't been expecting was the overwhelming, irrefutable absence of Jake. But why should there be anything? The orphanage existed long before he had ever set foot there, long before he was born, and it continued to exist after he was gone and presumably will continue for the foreseeable future, and on its own narrow terms. What's a year – not even a year, eight months – in the bigger picture, in the life of this institution? What difference has he really made? Is it possible he made none?

What was she hoping for? To find him there. But he simply isn't there. Her mind projected his image, tried to recreate him in that mundane and dreary place, yet he refused. He kept disappearing. She could not, after all, place him there. Had he even been there? Or was it an elaborate hoax? He was quite capable of it.

So why are they here? Is it to ensure that his legacy *will* make a difference? No, that's absurd, because that legacy doesn't matter two hoots. What matters is the book – Jake's book. It surely holds the key.

It was cruel of Jake to absent himself from Stef's orbit in the last months of his life. She could take his multiple rejections, his denials, his mockery even, but she could never accept his shutting her out so completely. Which is why Stef had never felt so relieved – so vindicated – when Esme had mentioned to her that Jake was writing during those crucial last months. It suddenly explained his absence, body and soul, his complete distancing from her. It made so much sense.

But then, when the time came this link, this precious lifeline, to become manifest, there turned out to be nothing there. There was no trace of any book found among his belongings, and Esme was unable to shed any more light on it. It became another elusive phantom, another plank in the mythology that amounted to nothing.

That was the strangest thing, its disappearance.

'I just don't get it,' Stef told Esme, the last time they spoke. That was after the funeral, when she was trying to salvage something, anything, any trace or clue. 'How can it simply vanish?' Esme did not respond, but Stef persevered. 'You know what *I* think? That it's out there somewhere! Somebody's got it. They must have. There's no other explanation. Someone has stolen it!'

'Why would someone do that?' Esme asked.

'That's the crux, the whole mystery. That's what I'm going to find out. I'm determined. And I won't rest until I've seen that book. Touched it. There's so little of him left, you see...'

And Stef didn't rest. She did not stop thinking about it in the intervening years. The book became for her a new absence, and one that seemed to embody the first one – that of Jake himself. It haunted and taunted her.

But now the waiting is almost over, and it is as if a Sisyphean burden has been lifted. Since that email from Dougie, just a week or two ago: 'Do you want me to bring Jake's notebooks?' *Do you want me to bring Jake's notebooks?*

'What notebooks? What are they?'

Dougie didn't know, they looked like scrapbooks, or maybe notes for a project he was working on. Jake had left them in a plastic supermarket bag in Dougie's room shortly before he disappeared all those years ago. Dougie had forgotten about it until just recently when he came across the notebooks in a suitcase, still wrapped in the supermarket bag. Didn't know what they were at first. Then he recognised Jake's scrawl, the unmistakable scribble of his cartoons and doodles, his manic word-play and zany doggerel.

Could they have been his book?

But Dougie didn't know anything about any book. He'd bring the notebooks with him, give them to Stef when he arrives. Maybe she can make something of them...

Yes, yes please, yes! Yes, she could.

The book hadn't perished with him after all.

Stef has no idea how far he had progressed, but she is convinced that reading those notebooks will be the key to unlocking the door – and, perhaps, to setting her mind at rest at last.

She had always known that her son was an artist. He had so much potential, so much latent ability that was forever seeking an outlet. That was what she always championed in him, it was what above all else she could never get others to see. To her his uniqueness, his creativity and his inspiring take on life were obvious – he was a true original, albeit one who never found the right conduit. She was always waiting for him to find the right conduit. Never one to disclose an inner life in any but the most oblique terms, he surely revealed something in those pages that was core, and that would be his greatest gift. She will resurrect it. She can live and die in peace once she has prised open those notebooks. *That* is what matters, not his bloody legacy in this alien and inhospitable spot.

She hasn't mentioned their existence to Laurie, of course, or to anyone else. She can't take the risk – it would be tempting fate to share the knowledge of this potential treasure trove. Let her see them first, assess them for what they are. But she is pretty sure she won't be disappointed. And her life will begin again.

Energised by the thought, Stef abandons the bed and stumbles to the bathroom. It is time to re-enter the day. As she pees, she tries to marshal her thoughts, to make a rational assessment. She has agreed to come, and here she is. It is important. This week marks Jake's thirtieth birthday, a significant landmark. That is important. It is twelve years since he was here – in this place, possibly in this room, in this bed even – and it is eight years since he has gone. It is also Stef's fiftieth birthday (or it will be in three weeks). So it is all falling into place, the moment is right, and she has made this effort, as promised, however futile the ostensible rites and however empty the ceremony itself. Then they will return to England and she will have turned a corner and will proceed to put her life back on track. Having laid her son to rest, she will rejoin the stream of life, re-engage. That is her pact with Laurie.

And the quid pro quo? That she will be allowed to resurrect her son's last and greatest work, the one that will be his and her final vindication. Laurie is unaware of that part of the deal, but it doesn't really matter what Laurie knows, for this is her true Project.

Chapter 14 | Hampi

At Hampi, a sacred town of ruined and semi-ruined temples carved out of the rock above the Tungabhadra River, the boulders glow gold in the evening light. The settlement appears much older than its mere half-millennium of years. Towering gopuras attached to the temples punctuate the landscape, and rice paddies and banana plantations spread for miles along the valley floor. By day, herons stand sentinel in the tranquil pools fed by the river, jade-green woodpeckers cling to telegraph posts and egrets perch on the backs of cattle. In the evening a creaking chorus of frogs rises from the paddy fields, swelling to a rattling crescendo once the sun has set. Right now, the chorus is confined to a few tentative notes, a vocal warm-up before the main performance. Up on the roof terrace of the Funky Monkey restaurant, a few hundred yards from the boulder-strewn riverbank, Dougie and Jules are ensconced on thick embroidered cushions, listening to Spanish rap and pulling on a chillum. They have already been three nights in the town and don't want to leave.

'Thing is,' says Jules, 'we could stay here another two or three nights, then take the bus back to Hospet, then the train to Bangalore and Mysore.'

'Banguluru and Mysuru,' interposes Dougie.

'Yeah. Spend a couple of nights in Mysore, then head south.'

'Or: we could just stay here for a few weeks.'

'Right, dude.' Jules's gaze sweeps across the room to the dozen or so other western travellers similarly engaged. After a pause, he continues: 'So what are we going to do?'

Dougie is staring across the dry saffron landscape at the sinking sun with a troubled frown. Then enlightenment comes.

'Here's a plan,' he tells Jules. 'We'll ask the Sacred Cunt.'

Jules snaps his fingers, points at his partner, and nods sagely. 'Yo, bro, go for it. That sounds like a plan.'

Doug adjusts the scarf wound around his head, shuffles into a cross-legged position and, with hands clasped, turns his eyes skywards.

'Oh Sacred Cunt,' he intones. 'Guide us in our hour of confusion. Show us the way, oh Cunt, in your infinite wisdom. Give us a sign, Cuntish One.'

Jules falls sideways, clapping and laughing, kicking Doug as he goes.

'Yeah, man! Summon that bastard. He owes us! He's the reason we're here!'

'Show us, lord! It's the least you can do,' Dougie pleads through his own suppressed laughter. 'We await your guidance!' He waits, eyes still rolled, then points his middle fingers up. '... Nah. The bastard's let us down again.'

'Wait!' Jules exclaims. 'Something's coming through. Speak, master. We are listening.' He turns his eyes up, poised expectantly. 'He says ... he says ... light another bowl!'

Dougie howls out with laughter, attracting curious, amused looks from the other patrons of the Funky Monkey. He bumps fists with Jules, spluttering, 'Yes! At last he's making sense. Do it, man!'

'He is verily a Cunt,' Jules nods, reaching for the dope.

Despite the profusion of stalls selling trinkets and the relentless pressure to consume, Hampi is a definite improvement on Goa, their previous stop. The beaches there were broad and infinite, and the rural interior was a tranquil relief after Mumbai's urban mayhem (though what wouldn't be a relief?), but the incursions of modern hotel developments on the one hand and the hordes of heavily tattooed Russian and Israeli ex- or would-be ravers on the other made them feel it was no place for them. Away from the hotels and villas, in the scattered beach communities that they gravitated towards, there were smiley faces galore, fluorescent-painted palms and hopeful posters advertising wild all-nighters. Even if they were interested in revisiting the rave scene, the prevailing mood of fake nostalgia for the era of free beach parties made them feel as if they were chasing someone else's dream of something that had probably never existed in the first place.

Still, there was fun to be had. They rented scooters, and experienced the rare freedom of feeling the cooling breeze in their hair as they rode helmetless between grand, palm-sprinkled beaches where there were perhaps half a dozen other people to be seen for a mile on either side. They met some cool characters, too. One, Hamish – tall, with long, blond hair and festooned with jewellery – claimed in a broad Dundonian accent to be seventy-six years old with nineteen grandchildren, and related hair-raising accounts of the various tropical illnesses he had endured.

'So you must have seen a heap of changes over the years, Hamish, in India,' Dougie said.

'Too right, pal,' Hamish eyed them beadily. 'It's fucking unrecognisable.'

'How so?'

'For a start, there's a lot less smoking and spitting and betel-chewing these days. That's good. That's healthy. But there's ten times more traffic on the roads. That's bad. The guys who used to have push-bikes now have scooters, and the guys who used to have scooters now have motorbikes, and the guys who used to have motorbikes now have Suzuki cars, and the poor bastards are all stuck together in an endless traffic jam. That's what they call progress.'

'Well, it sounds like people have got a bit more money.'

'Aye, and a lot more debt. They've all got the latest smart phones, too. But they use them mainly for taking pictures of themselves.'

'Have you got one?'

'Aye,' Hamish replied, tapping his breast pocket. 'But I don't take pictures.'

He raised a forefinger at an old timer rumbling past on a large Enfield bike, grey locks flying behind. The biker, looking weathered but benign, returned his salutation with the hint of a nod. In the opposite direction, a twenty-something tourist buzzed by on a scooter, with aviator glasses and a baseball cap turned back to front. A blond girl in micro-shorts sat behind him, one arm wrapped around his bare chest, the other jabbing at her phone.

'And then there's the twenty-first-century tourism,' observed Hamish sternly, watching at the scooter disappears around the corner. 'Why should India be immune?' He gestured at a waiter at the other end of the bar for another beer.

Another foreigner they met, John – short, bald as a nut, deeply tanned with glistening white teeth – was a cockney who claimed to have been living in a shack on the beach for the last eight years. 'But I occasionally take a few weeks off to see the missus in Bangkok. Got a couple of kids there, too. Can't understand them, though.'

'Younger generation, eh?' Dougie said.

'Nah, it's not that. Can't understand the lingo. Never got my tongue round it.'

'Is your wife Thai, then?'

'Thai, yeah. Twee.'

'Twee?'

'That's her name, yeah. She speaks a bit of English, fortunately. You boys looking for something to smoke?'

They both shook their heads emphatically, but by the end of the evening they'd bought half a tola of charas from John, and a small amount of opium.

'Just eat it, mate,' John told Jules. 'Set a day aside. You'll find it interesting.'

The next morning, on an impulse, they swallowed the opium and spent the next twelve hours in a benumbed, free-falling suspension of time. The vomiting didn't seem to matter – in fact nothing seemed to matter, as they wandered for miles along the sea-shore, occasionally drifting into the warm surf, rolling about in the waves and wondering if they were going to die and what it would be like. Everything was important, and nothing was. They set up skittles made of palm fronds, bowled coconuts along the sand and collected shells that resembled homunculi.

They were still vomiting for two days afterwards, and had no desire to repeat the experience, but they didn't regret it either.

It was a strange departure on the overnight train to Hospet. They left Goa's Vasco da Gama station in a disorientating blackout, the whole area cast into impenetrable darkness due to a power failure, and for once it took them an age to track down a rickshaw. When they eventually found one, the journey to the station took far longer than anticipated. Luckily their train was late, and they still had to wait well over an hour on the platform together with hundreds of other long-suffering passengers and a pair of statuesque cows. When the train finally arrived, well after midnight, they found that the booking for two berths that they had made from the dodgy-looking agent in Vasco da Gama was in fact for one, meaning they had to spend the night with their feet in each other's faces and secure themselves into their third-tier bunk with string. Dougie fell asleep almost immediately, joining the carriage's symphony of snoring, but Jules spent the whole night awake, teetering on the edge of the berth and shivering hard from the air blowing through the compartment's jammed open window. He spent their first day in Hampi in a catatonic stupor.

Rested now, they feel they are beginning to get the hang of travelling in India. Everything takes far longer than it should, everything is far harder, but the rewards go deeper. It's a succession of crushing disappointments and triumphant surprises, in no particular order. As Hamish told them, when asked what kept him in India all these years in spite of his numerous illnesses and setbacks: 'Well, it's never boring!'

In the Funky Monkey, Dougie jerks his head in the direction of the door. 'Christ, here comes William Morris.' Jules looks over to the figure who has just entered the café and giggles. William Morris is the name they have given to one of the café's habitués on account of the rich embroidery of floral tattoos that cover the entire upper part of his torso. 'Wallpaper Man,' Jules commented when they first saw him.

'And not just any wallpaper,' responded Dougie drily. 'It's William Morris unless I'm very much mistaken...'

William Morris acknowledges them with a flick of his chin as he passes, and squats down opposite a couple of other Funky Monkey denizens at the far end of the terrace: a tall, skinny man with bare arms and multiple piercings and an equally thin woman with prominent white teeth and a vivacious laugh. They greet each other in Italian and the newcomer reaches into his frayed purple shoulder bag to produce the various bits and pieces required to assemble a chillum.

'They look pretty hard-core,' Jules comments.

'They've been here since nineteen sixty-eight,' Dougie tells him in his soft Scottish lilt. 'That's what weed does to you. You get stuck in an era and can never leave.'

'Is that what's going to happen to us?'

'Not if we keep moving, bro.'

They bump fists and Jules requests another two chais from the laid-back waiter as he passes.

'So tomorrow, right?'

'Tomorrow it is, bro.' He turns to survey once more the silver ribbon of river beyond the flat-roofed buildings below. 'Or the day after,' he adds.

Chapter 15 | Miranda's mission

Miranda is sitting on a cane chair on the lawn with a bowl of cashews and an open book on the table in front of her. Behind her brown-tinted glasses she is frowning. Beneath the parasol, she is in the shade, but she is still damp with sweat. Her attention flickers compulsively from the open page to a large, black, malicious-looking crow perched on the back of the seat opposite. It is eyeing her, and eyeing her bowl of nuts, tufted head cocked, beak hanging open though not uttering a sound. Several times she has tried to scare it away – waving her arm, or half-rising as if to get up and chase it; at first the crow simply flew to another seat-back, returning a few seconds later, now it doesn't even bother to do that, and Miranda doesn't bother to pretend to chase it away.

She has observed these predators from her window. Rapacious and malevolent, they swoop in and out of the trees, sometimes landing on the grass where they hop mischievously about in twos and threes. They are trouble boys, chancers all, sizing up the situation, seeking opportunities. They feign innocence yet exude guiltiness, ready to pounce on any scrap, however unlikely, from the fragments of a coconut shell to the rusty coil of an eviscerated mattress, then flapping triumphantly away with its beakful of spoils. The opportunistic pilferers increase Miranda's pervasive sense of being oppressed – by the blinding heat, by her sweating, by the airless capsule in which they all now find themselves.

Right now, she is most oppressed by this one crow, by its silent, gaping beak, its watchful eyes waiting for a slip on her part, for any chance to filch a cashew. Once she threw it a nut, which it pounced on, flapping away with it clutched in its beak. Presumably it gobbled the cashew, but then she looked up and it was back on its perch, waiting for more. They eye each other suspiciously. The crow is India; India is the crow.

Underlying this petty annoyance, though, is a more general malaise. She is troubled by something else, something greater, but something that she can't quite identify. She wants to feel positive, reassured, should be feeling hopeful now, but she cannot relax. She wonders how much her father shares this disquiet. Her brother certainly does. Since their arrival in India, Miranda and Simon have hardly mentioned the purpose of their visit – not explicitly anyway – but even without articulating their thoughts, she knows that they think along similar lines: both harbour serious doubts about the whole scheme, the whole concept even. After all, they are both here on sufferance. There was no escaping it – they have known for two years or more that they would find themselves at this point, as surely as the tracks of a train are destined to carry them to a terminal. But while neither of them has much desire to be here, they have both longed for it, too, if only so that it can be in the past rather than in the future.

For far too long The Project has consumed all their lives, Miranda's especially. Though the initiative came from Laurie, once he had outlined his vision to her and Simon, she was the one to take it on. Something to do with being the eldest child, of course. Throughout her childhood Miranda was cursed with the special expectations that come with the role – eager to please and always expected to do so, she was the sensible one, the quiet one who did the homework, got the grades and was the reliable all-rounder. She became skilled at reading situations and coming up with solutions. And, naturally, she was egged on by her father, by his repeated reminders that she should be setting a good example to her younger siblings. And she delivered, uncomplainingly. 'Moderate Miranda', her dad jokingly called her. Consequently she never allowed herself to be too naughty, never went off the rails. Not like

Baby Jesus, who was able to get way with things that were unimaginable for her. How she and her brother envied him!

That was surely another reason for Miranda's model behaviour – it was precisely because Jake was so bad that she felt it incumbent on herself to be so good. Not that she completely resented his waywardness. While he was with them, Miranda and Simon regarded Jake as a kind of exotic specimen. He clearly didn't fit into the family. He was one of life's vagrants, ever seeking, never settled. He was always in love with someone. As a child he had serial obsessions: first with TV celebrities, then film or pop stars, then with fellow students or his friends' sisters – it could be anyone, young or old, however inappropriate. Even when he was with Esme, he would mention to Miranda his flirtations with other women, or how other women were besotted with him. She had no idea how much of it was true. In the end he stuck with Esme because she stuck with him.

Maybe he was an artist, as his mother liked to believe, doing things on his own terms; more likely he was just acting the part. Sometimes Miranda actually believed he was some kind of a genius, at other times she saw him as a hopeless loser, a sort of lost child. He wound people up, no question, but there was something vulnerable about him too, something Miranda could respond to despite everything. He trusted people too much, and he was always being ripped off (something he attributed to dark, malevolent forces out to get him). He was born without any armour, and for this Miranda could begin to understand the fierce, protective devotion that Stef heaped upon him in compensation. Of course, it suffocated him in the process.

Steps approach, and she looks up to see her father. Laurie is wearing loose, cream-coloured cotton trousers and shirt and a jungle hat of the same pale shade, and looks a little as if he is about to embark on a trek through hostile territory. His face displays his usual blend of calm optimism and gnawing unease.

She smiles. 'Morning, Dad.'

'Hallo, love. What're you doing?'

She holds up the book as he settles down beside her.

He snorts. '*Siddhartha*! God, that takes me back. How are you finding it?'

She shrugs. 'I can't get into it. Probably too mystical for me. Not enough meat. And anyway, there are too many distractions.'

'Like me?'

'No,' she laughs, giving his arm an affectionate rub. 'I didn't mean you! I mean everything else. It's nice to see you. It's *always* nice to see you.'

He seems to lap up her warmth. 'We haven't really had a chance to chat since you got here,' he says. 'How's it going?'

She shrugs again. 'You know…'

He thinks he does, but, removing his jungle hat, he waits patiently for her to elaborate as her eyes travel across the garden. She is looking for her tormentor, the crow, who is now nowhere to be seen.

'It's weird being here. For Jake. Being where he was, after all this time.' She turns her gaze to him. 'But he isn't here. I can't … *feel* him.'

Laurie nods understandingly. He feels that he has always understood his daughter instinctively, even when they have been apart.

'We've waited so long for this,' she says. 'And now I feel almost nothing.'

He looks beyond her into the trees.

'I know. But we're not really here for Jake.'

'No…' she says.

He turns to her, hesitates, clears his throat. 'You know, this is so important for Stef, this trip.'

'I know it is,' she says.

'And I think it's just possible that it might be a milestone for her. It might even be a kind of cure. And it could make all the difference – to her and to me...'

Miranda nods. She has half-known this already. Time to steer the conversation away from Stef.

'So how's the sabbatical? Surviving all that lovely free time?'

Laurie seems to come back to earth. He shrugs, looking a bit embarrassed. 'Well,' he says, 'I'm getting on with things, you know...'

'What things?'

'You know... Catching up. Once all this is over I'll be able to settle down a bit more – concentrate.'

Miranda eyes her father critically from behind her tinted glasses. Not for the first time it occurs to her that as her father ages, as he declines, it will fall to her to be the main carer. She sees this clearly, has done so all her adult life. Stef doesn't come into it.

In the pause that follows they both become aware of meandering flute music floating gently in the air about them. They look round but see no obvious source.

'It must be coming from the temple,' Laurie suggests. 'There's always something going on there.' They both listen to the melody, simultaneously serene and restless. It has a soothing effect, like a balm seeping into their skin, loosening muscle and easing the blood. Neither of them wants to interrupt the spell, and as the meditative pause lengthens their thoughts begin to unmoor, flowing and eddying with the wavering notes of the flute. Dimly, Miranda begins to sense the possibility of a contentment that has until now evaded her. She doesn't feel it, but she is aware of it, some place just beyond her reach, and for the first time, she wonders if it is something that she has been unconsciously craving. And why shouldn't she have it? She is here, with her father and brother, in this vibrantly rich and exuberant place. Despite the heat and discomfort, the injustice and inequality, something valuable is here that she might grasp.

Laurie, for his part, is smiling, the gates of his heart opened to yet another of India's delightful tricks. He is almost used to them now, though each time they still manage to ambush him. Observing his enchanted expression, Miranda feels a surge of sorrow for him. There before her is revealed a lifetime of dashed hopes, of unfulfilment. His eyes are earnest behind his brown-rimmed spectacles, and above his creased brow a thinly-sewn dome of grey has replaced what used to be a thicket of luxuriant, wavy brown hair. Out of nowhere a memory comes to her from years ago, an image of him with hair over his ears and strumming a guitar. What happened to that? He would play old '60s and '70s protest songs – never in public, of course, it was always a private performance for them, the kids. They loved it, those rare times when his usual parental role gave away to something subversive, almost transgressive. As he played and sang, Stef would cast stern, condescending looks but never pause from whatever it was she was doing. In fact, her participation would have spoiled the moment.

Sometimes, listening to records, he even used to throw his arms around and dance, to the delight of his children. They joined in the mayhem, giggling manically. Not Jake, of course – though he would probably snigger afterwards, making some cynical comment or snide dig. Once, she remembers, when Laurie was out of the room, Jake picked up the guitar and banged out some Dylan-like chords, spontaneously stringing together a bricolage of disconnected lyrics and bellowing them out in a high, strangled voice, eyes screwed shut as he gave his all. It was a ruthless piss-take, and provoked hoots of laughter from Miranda and Simon, soon joined by Stef egging him on with her throaty, coughing convulsions of mirth. Miranda felt bad about it afterwards, of course, nagged inside by little worms of guilt. It wasn't really fair. Laurie didn't have such a bad voice – certainly nothing like the grotesque whine that Jake attributed to him. But it was funny too, the mimicry. Baby Jesus was undeniably a brilliant caricaturist.

When did Laurie stop singing and dancing and playing guitar? She can't remember. He did, and then he didn't. She suddenly misses it, and, contemplating her father now, lost as he is in the moment, she is tempted to ask him why he stopped. Maybe one day he could be persuaded to do it again, for old times' sake – but she immediately dismisses such a crazy notion. What is she thinking? It would all be far too embarrassing, and he might even think he was being mocked again. You can't go back. Looking back is bad enough, but don't ever think you can return there.

The flute stops without warning, in mid-phrase, and Laurie blinks, jerked out of his semi-rapture back into the present. He exchanges a surprised look with his daughter and a dreamy smile.

'Feel like some tea?' he asks.

She nods and closes her book. 'That would be dandy.'

'I'll go and find someone to cook up a pot of hot, disgustingly sweet, nauseatingly milky tea.'

'Just the ticket,' Miranda laughs, and Laurie disappears into the building.

Miranda isn't someone who flaunts her emotions. Her mother died when she was six, but she was always able to compartmentalise this huge loss. Her pain was private, it was her affair. That's why, when she regards Stef, she is able to pity her, to offer mute sympathy, but never to empathise or justify. How could her step-mother bear to make her grief so public? Didn't that make Jake's death public property? Wasn't that a theft from yourself? True, Stef would never actually discuss it, never complain or show a smidgeon of self-pity, nor even bring up the subject voluntarily – but that very omission makes her desolation a suffocating, silent presence, a proverbial elephant in the house. The thought often occurs to Miranda that Stef is indulging herself, and in the process sucking up everyone's attention. And then she feels callous for thinking that. After all, what does Miranda understand about a mother's love? From what she can gather, it's a sharp, searing fire, irrational, unfathomable and destructive.

As she calls to mind her own orphaned state, an unwelcome memory forces itself onto her – one of the dark instances of Jake's deceitful ways. She must have been around twelve and he was about ten, and he entered her room and announced that he had found out the truth about her mother.

What truth? She hadn't been aware there was anything to discover.

'I've been looking in your dad's things,' Jake said. That alone shocked her. Did he mean looking in his desk, in his drawers, rummaging around in his personal stuff? 'I found lots of old letters. And photos. And I found out your mum was a lesbian.' She frowned. 'Don't you know what a lesbian is?' he said. 'A woman who hates men. Who only likes women.'

'No she wasn't,' Miranda told him.

'She was.'

'Show me.'

'I haven't got them. They're in your dad's desk. They're in a folder that says "Charlotte".'

Turning back to her drawing, she asked, 'How could she hate men if she married Daddy?'

He shrugged. 'I dunno. Maybe she wasn't a lesbian then. Anyway, she left him.'

'No, she didn't. She died.'

'She died after she left him. She went to live with her girlfriend.'

'That's not true!' she finally looked up.

'And I found something else,' Jake persisted.

She didn't say anything, pretending to concentrate on her drawing.

'Your dad looks at pictures of girls.'

'No he doesn't,'

'He does. They're on his computer.'

She looked up, amazed. 'Have you been on his computer?'

Jake nodded, pleased to have commanded her full attention at last. 'He's got loads of pictures on there.'

'I'm telling that you've been looking in his computer,' she said, scribbling harder now.

He just looked at her, smirking. 'Your dad's a weirdo,' he said. 'And your mum.'

'No they're NOT!' Miranda cried angrily, at which point Jake cackled and left her room.

She didn't believe him, but she was troubled, and a few days later, when no one was about, she sneaked into Laurie's study and pulled open his desk drawers. She didn't dare look at his computer, wouldn't know how to anyway, but she could easily take a quick peek in his desk. She didn't see any folder labelled 'Charlotte' in there, but she wasn't able to look very far because her father suddenly appeared in the doorway. She froze, immediately turning bright red.

'What are you doing, Mirrie?' he asked quietly, not angry.

She said nothing, just felt her cheeks burning.

'Why are you looking in my desk?' She kept silent.

'Were you looking for something?' She stared at the floor.

He looked mystified. 'You only have to ask if you're looking for something, Mirrie.'

She nodded and fled past her father out of his room, feeling his questioning look on her retreating back. She knew what he was thinking: why is a good girl like Miranda looking so guilty? How could Miranda ever be naughty? She shut herself in her room and cried hard.

Though Miranda never found anything to support what Jake had said, it bothered her for a long time afterwards. Of course she never mentioned any of it to Simon or to anyone else. Eventually, she dismissed Jake's wild claims from her mind, and when she was older and thought back on the episode, she decided it was just Jake being Jake. He grew up fatherless and wanted everyone with a father to feel bad. That was the rationale they often used to explain his errant behaviour. After a while the rationale grew somewhat frayed, but that was the one they used. Jake was bad news, Miranda knew that now. He was a mischief-maker, and they were all his victims. And yet ... yet for some reason, they all still loved him. It didn't make much sense.

And being here is like being once more in one of his mind games. In his head.

Laurie returns with a tray bearing a pot of tea.

'Success!' he announces. Miranda smiles up at him.

Now, above all, her mission is to save her father. She feels overwhelmingly protective towards Laurie. She has watched him for years closing up, withdrawing further into himself as his relationship with Stef unravels, as Stef herself unravels. It doesn't take a genius to perceive that his long subservience is a hollow, corrosive thing, effectively a sham. And yet Laurie clearly does not see that. He does not seem to understand that his naive allegiance to Stef was never much more than an infatuation, and even if it was once meaningful Stef herself has ensured that it has degraded into something base, almost sordid, a relationship of exploitation, and one so pernicious that the only humane course is to kill it. It would be an act of mercy. Stef is probably too far gone to be redeemed, Miranda thinks, but Laurie could still be saved.

He believes they are all here for Stef, but they are really here for Laurie. To save him. That's Miranda's mission now.

Chapter 16| In church

Sunday has arrived and Cynthia decides to sample the local brand of Christianity at the afternoon service in St Antony's basilica. She is intrigued by the vast edifice. She might have expected to see this triumphant baroque style in, say, Madeira or Mexico, but not here, not in this land of perfumed temples and austere mosques. Yet Christianity, she has learned, is a well-established and still flourishing faith in these parts. She does not know what to expect of a service at this remote, exotic outpost of her native creed, but her hopes are high.

Arriving a few minutes before the five-thirty service, she slips into a pew half a dozen rows from the back and watches the congregation file into the echoing space. They are an even mix of men and women, all ages, but fewer children than she anticipated. All appear well dressed, well-fed, comfortably off. She spots Flowery near the front, who beams and waves at her. Several low-hung ceiling fans revolve at a stately pace above their heads, and there are also long, shallow sheets slung laterally across the nave, moving back and forth by means of a complicated system of pulleys. Cynthia looks around for a punkah-walla, but decides it must all be operated electrically. Bare red lightbulbs attached to the columns of the building impart a faint crimson glow, perhaps representing blood, and there are numerous images of Jesus, fair-haired and pale-skinned, though surprisingly few of Mary and the saints.

After a few minutes, Cynthia becomes aware of a small procession of shawled women moving up the aisle, each carrying a posy of flowers. Voices quieten, the congregation rises and the women disperse into the front rows as a priest appears behind the altar, resplendent in emerald-green vestments. He is dark, quite dashing, with a neat goatee beard. Taking his place behind the altar table, he speaks into a microphone, his voice booming around the nave. Cynthia finds his thick English accent hard to understand but she thinks she hears him introduce himself as Monsignor Vincent Price. He speaks for a few minutes, the congregation still standing, then he raises his arms and music fills the church. Cynthia frowns. With its guitar and drums accompaniment, it sounds to her improbably like a country and western tune, and the woman's voice singing the main part also seems to come from that musical genre. She casts her eyes around the building but can see no sign of singers or musicians, so she assumes it is a recording. For the most part the worshippers don't seem to be joining in, though Cynthia sees a few mouthing soundlessly along.

Oliver declined Cynthia's offer to join her for this appointment with God. He calls himself an unrepentant agnostic, but he is undoubtedly a pagan. When they have discussed religion, he answers glibly when she points out the good works of the teachers and nurses that the Church provides locally. But how can one fault them and their good works? If faith has any tangible value, here it is, plain to see. He simply retorts: 'If they can build a big, imposing church like that, why do they need donations?'

'You do talk tosh!' she tells him. But she lets it go. The truth is that people in the west don't bother much over belief and disbelief these days. Oliver certainly doesn't. Fortunately, it doesn't trouble her in the least that she and he have such divergent views about this and most other things. In fact, the gulf between their backgrounds and values amuses her. He is a staunch conservative, while Cynthia is proud of her sporadically radical past, including a brief stint many years before at Greenham in the company of her daughters Stephanie and Rebecca. She hasn't told Oliver about that.

Two of the shawled women have ascended onto the platform, one positioning herself to one side as the other begins a reading – in English – from Isaiah. Then they switch places as the other reads from Corinthians. After a while Cynthia gives up attempting to follow them, her thoughts settling instead on her daughters. They were good girls and they had a good childhood, in the sense that they felt comfortable and blessed. Even with their father dying young, at least they knew they were cherished. They did, didn't they? And yet, later on, it felt as if her elder daughter, Stephanie, was no longer blessed. God seemed to have abandoned her, regardless of whether she was good or not. Was her God uncaring because Stephanie herself didn't care for her God? That's unanswerable, but the fact was that they seemed to have fallen out. Stephanie was buffeted in life, tossed around and pulled hither and thither, just like those flimsy kites that caught Cynthia's attention in Chennai. After the death of Roger, she was messed around by Michael, her dodgy 'partner' (vile word!), and, worst of all, suffered the loss of her son. Like her icon, Virginia Woolf, Stephanie has been beset by loss and death. She can't be blamed for those things, of course. But she never really helped herself either. Cynthia feels she could have helped her once, but her relationship with her elder daughter was sabotaged years ago when Stephanie made her complicit in her mad lie about Michael. Thinking it would help to bring them together, Cynthia acquiesced, but instead of bringing them together it drove a wedge between them, as if her daughter resented her for being a party to the deception. And the resentment lives on. Somehow Stephanie has never accepted that her mother has some kind of a hold over her. Cynthia recognises this, but is powerless to alter it.

Cynthia's relationship with her eldest daughter is, in many ways, the embodiment of the paradoxical impulses that have shaped much of her life. Stephanie is a being she both cleaves to and is repelled by, one she admires yet pities, whom she understands so well but who is a distant stranger. Stephanie is herself a contradiction, for she is apparently immersed in grief though to all appearances her life seems rather to be consumed – or possibly sustained – by rage. And of course she is the reason they find themselves in this unintelligible place, though she herself seems to have no wish to be here. They are ostensibly gathered here to support her, and she rejects all notions of support.

Was it her father's early death that propelled Stephanie to choose the harder road? It affected her badly. The two of them, father and elder daughter, were as close as anything. Roger was close to his sons, of course, and to Rebecca, but he had a special bond with Stephanie. He wouldn't allow the boys to bully her, or even exclude her from their games. He stood up for her. And Stephanie adored him. In some ways, his drift into alcoholism was hardest for her. Cynthia could handle the downward spiral, mainly by ignoring it. When he was on one of his binges, she would bar him from the children's activities, even banish him from the house, and just get on with things. Stephanie, aged ten or twelve, understood that her daddy was ill but she treated his illness as some kind of temporary misfortune, like measles or 'flu. She never blamed him – if anything she seemed to blame her mother, hating her for the laws she laid down, for refusing to allow Roger to eat with them or making him sleep in the spare room – but she seemed to accept the situation. Daddy was ill, and he would get better.

He didn't, of course. The cirrhosis, at the end, was swift and deadly. Roger became bloated, incontinent and completely irrational in those terrible last months. Stephanie remained as calm as anything, calm when he went into the final coma, calm when he died. She was there to hear his death rattle, but still she was calm. It was only later that the effects manifested themselves, when the quirky fourteen-year-old transmuted into a snarling, rebellious adolescent, plunging headlong into an extended period of revolt and fury with the world. The determined, independent-minded child became a possessed and dogmatic warrior. To an extent, these were typically adolescent dramas, the others went through similar changes – but Stephanie's rage was on a different level.

Once, after a particularly ferocious row in which she screamed abuse before flouncing theatrically out of the house, Cynthia, in desperation, searched her room, thinking she might find drugs or some other explanation for her volatility. There was nothing there except for a half-empty bottle of vodka pushed behind the mattress. Then, at the back of her cupboard, she discovered a hoard of exercise books. They were her diaries, chronicling in extravagantly untidy handwriting, rich with crossings-out, ornate decorations and grotesque illustrations, her tumultuous inner life over the last two-and-a-half years. There were numerous scraps of poetry, mainly dark stuff by Sylvia Plath: *I inhabit/The wax image of myself, a doll's body./Sickness begins here.* Some of these seemed to refer to Cynthia herself: *Mother of beetles, only unclench your hand ... Give me back my shape.* That was only to be expected, she supposed.

But Cynthia's horror increased as she went deeper, reading accounts of how atrociously unfair she was, seeing cartoons of herself as a mad, bug-eyed witch. It was completely unfair. Feeling rather sick, she was about to close the journals when she turned to the first page of the first book: 'Daddy died.' Cynthia hesitated, then read on: 'He's left me. I hate him. You do not do, you do not do. Never again. Daddy, I have had to kill you. You died before I had time. Never again....' And thus it went on, lines from Plath interspersed with accusations of betrayal and hatred directed at her, Cynthia. Yes, the pain was acute, far intenser than the fourteen-year-old girl had ever let on. The scars ran deep. But what had Cynthia herself done to deserve this bile?

She closed the book, put it back in the cupboard, and never went to find it again. Grief and passion she could understand, but not these screeds of hate and violence. Stephanie was clearly blaming both herself and her mother for her father's death. Absurd.

From then on, Cynthia held her eldest daughter at arm's length. She would continue to love her, of course, always love her, but there was always that knowledge there, lurking, that memory of vitriol and venom. You can't erase that. From that time on, Stephanie was a special case.

The contrast with Rebecca was stark. Rebecca was certainly less affected by Roger's death, but of course she was younger. And with the passing of years, it became increasingly evident that she was the more stable of the two – less passionate, less judgmental, and more self-contained. She has always been reconciled to the world in a way that Stephanie never was. She certainly didn't share Stephanie's devotion to radical causes – she had opinions, of course, and she had boyfriends, but she was not in continual pursuit of the unattainable. Eventually she settled down in an uncomplicated relationship with the most sensible of the boyfriends and went to set up a new home in Canada, where they had three children in quick succession. Her womb was fecund, while Stephanie managed to squeeze out just one offspring. As far as Cynthia knows, there was no physical reason why Stephanie didn't produce more children. She could have done with Laurence, but must have chosen not to. Well, perhaps it wasn't such a surprise, Jake being such a handful.

Over the years, Cynthia has watched and stood to one side as Stephanie slid further out of reach. It pains her to think that her daughter is lost to her, and that she is in danger of losing those remaining pillars of her life – her husband, her family, her profession, her self-respect. Yet Cynthia won't allow herself to mourn. Stephanie herself has not allowed her to. Not that that prevents the periodic waves of guilt that come crashing down when least expected; then she has to remind herself that it's not the mother's fault that her daughter is inconsolable.

So it was almost with Stephanie's connivance that Cynthia resolved years ago not to agonise over her daughter's predicament. At the risk of appearing hard and unfeeling, she determined not to enter the murky pool of pity. What would be the good of that? Who would gain?

On the platform, the reader stumbles, pauses. She seems to have lost her place. Then, to Cynthia's delight, she restarts: 'I am lost, Lord...'

As the voice drones on, Cynthia sinks back into her musings. When younger, Stephanie formed intense attachments to her female friends. They would form tight-knit conspiracies, exclusive clubs, and devote themselves to projects – writing scripts together, performing sketches. Once, Cynthia caught her and her current best friend rehearsing a funeral. Death, again.

It's not as if Stephanie doesn't have a solid network of support. Laurence is a decent man – ineffectual, but decent. He is not perfect, he is just a man, but he is a valuable prop and a reliable shelter. His children, Miranda and Simon, are also decent human beings. There is a structure there, a safety-net. But despite everything, Stephanie, too, is lost, Lord. Her daughter is loved, but she is adrift.

Also like Virginia, Stephanie has her priggish side. Cynthia has to admit the frisson of pleasure it gave her to see her daughter, normally so acerbic, dumbfounded when she learned that her mother is sharing a room with Oliver. Cynthia knew exactly what was going through her mind. It was a moment to savour.

Sometimes, Cynthia suspects that Stephanie's youthful worship of Virginia Woolf somehow allowed that writer's life to leak into her own, not excluding her desperate mental fragility – but again, this is an unproductive line of inquiry, best left unexplored. During her episodes, Virginia would hear the birds chirping in Greek.

On the other hand, if one does not worry, how is one to understand?

Just as Cynthia has clashing views of Stephanie, so her attitude towards her unfortunate grandson, Jake, was similarly tangled. In life, as he is in death, he was a conundrum. What in God's name was he up to, who did he think he was, and where did he belong? He surely inherited his father's mischievous ambiguity. Yet when he was small he was a sweet little thing, a rascally urchin with light ginger ringlets and tireless energy. He had a thing about copying everyone. Almost compulsively, he mimicked people's gaits, their facial expressions, their tics and verbal mannerisms. Where did he get *that* from? You could have a conversation with him and be amazed at his fluency and maturity, until it dawned on you that he was simply aping you, or worse, making fun of you. He was utterly convincing.

So, just as Stephanie became a stranger to her own mother, Jake grew from innocence to something darker, more knowing. Cynthia, who had once marvelled at his precocity, now felt daunted by it. His energy became hyperactivity – he was forever climbing, shouting, demanding attention. And then there was that unpleasant screaming phase he went through, when he squealed from morning to night. Just to annoy you, it seemed. Eventually, he repelled everyone who had previously mollycoddled him. Apart from Stephanie, of course. Stephanie would forgive him anything.

As he got older, Cynthia became increasingly unsettled by Stephanie's almost unnatural championing of her son. A mother's devotion she could understand – Cynthia's own maternal instincts were almost Victorian in comparison, but she can grasp the strength of it in others. Stephanie's relationship with her son, however, was something else. Even when they were at war with each other, during Jake's own stormy adolescence, she was obsessed by him. She couldn't let him go. When she had had enough, she would send him to stay with Cynthia in Cornwall, but even then she would call every day – not to speak to him, but to speak to Cynthia about him. Those were ghastly times, living with Jake in Cynthia's small cottage. He was a constant source of mischief, disappearing for hours, going to pubs, bringing tramps back for tea.

Cynthia sighs inwardly. Why doesn't she have any good memories? Where did it all go wrong? How did it happen? Was it she herself who must bear the blame, or her difficult daughter, or her impossible grandson? But it is futile to pursue that line. She prefers to let it all be. What else is there to do? It is her old strategy, her method. Head high, eyes directed straight ahead, even if they are sometimes half closed – and even occasionally winking. It isn't particularly admirable, as philosophies go, indeed it is rather selfish, but for the most part, with occasional compromises and concessions, it seems to work.

The last piece of advice Cynthia gave to Stephanie, years and years ago, took the form of a little homily, a well-worn cliché which causes her to wince whenever she recalls it: 'It isn't what life throws at you that matters; it's what you do with it.' She knew as soon as she uttered the words that it was a colossal misjudgment, and she can still see the look of revulsion on her stricken daughter's face before she stormed out of the room. She couldn't blame her, and she never offered any such cut-price gems again.

Now, though, she will make amends. Stephanie never wanted her mother on this expedition, never asked her – Cynthia had to demand to be included. She saw it as her chance to repair bridges, to attempt to heal those deep wounds. Now is the time to take responsibility. Her mind flies back to those hateful diaries. She must forgive her daughter. She, Cynthia, the mother, must, if not be accountable for her daughter's adolescent passions, at least transcend them. And once this mourning for Jake is over, there is every possibility that Stephanie will forgive *her*. She can pull through, be more receptive to her mother's silent support and forgive her. Whatever it was that needs forgiving. For that is the only reason for Cynthia to be here – for mutual forgiveness, and to be available when her daughter finally emerges into the bright light of a new day. It has been Jake himself who held them apart, and with this final farewell, a new beginning is possible. For that is His commandment: that ye love one another. And that is her prayer.

The congregation is standing once more, now, as schmaltzy music again washes over them. This time, surreally, new words have apparently been put to 'Spanish Eyes'. Cynthia stands with the rest, but cannot quell her disdain. More than that, she is deeply bored. During the lengthy sermon that follows, she watches a lizard or gecko climb the white wall behind the immobile, emerald-clad priest, and then a pigeon that flies the length of the nave and settles on a high beam. She kneels with the rest, contributes fifty rupees to the passed basket, and turns to shake the hands of her neighbours on either side in the salutation. But she is disappointed. She was hoping for something new and different, but the service has turned out to be merely a restatement of tired old European tropes with an overlay of modern pop gospel. She sought something rarefied and recondite but has only found banality. There is no veil here.

As members of the congregation line up for communion she takes the opportunity to shuffle out of her row, half-genuflect and cross herself in the aisle, and walk quickly out of the church.

Later, she describes the experience to Oliver as interesting but not very enlightening. He harrumphs, clearing his throat, and nods in modest triumph. 'Always worth a go,' he condescends. 'Good to get it first-hand. Now you know.'

'But you knew without experiencing it,' she challenges him.

'Ah, yes. I have an instinct.'

'Smug git...' she mutters.

'What's that?'

'Nothing, nothing,' she sings. 'God may forgive you, I suppose. Eventually...'

Chapter 17 | Encounters

There is something of the loner in Esme. She doesn't know whether she was born that way, or whether it comes with being thirty and single. There's also the factor of her work circumstances: her job as a freelance translator does not bring her into much contact with people, though it suits her well enough. Her independent disposition may also explain why she is drawn to this mode of travel – she could never, ever go on a group holiday. She prefers the freelance state, unhindered, on the fly. Often, during her numerous train rides in India, she has regarded her fellow female travellers with pity. They are rarely on their own – mostly they are surrounded by children and elderly people, most likely parents or parents-in-law. Nonetheless, there is something about their poised composure as they sit compactly cross-legged on their few inches of seat that is upright and strong, denoting an independence of spirit. In the midst of their families, of the bonds that tie them down, they emanate an aura of invincibility. They might have no financial or political power, but they appear to preserve a cool inner strength. If Esme were ever to be corralled into having her own family, she would take these proud Indian women as her paradigm.

Strangely, her very affinity with solitude is one reason that she responded to Jake, all those years ago. Despite his addiction to other people, to making fresh acquaintances (and then letting them go), there was something detached behind it all – she thought she recognised a singular, impermeable spirit of independence beneath the studied nonchalance.

Toiling now under the weight of her rucksack on the last leg of her journey to the hostel, phone in hand to guide her, she frowns, shakes off her line of thought as she finds her mind reverting once more to Jake. It was inevitable that the person whom she believed she had left behind all those years ago should come back to fill her thoughts now – she was expecting it, for this is indeed a journey into her past – but all the same it is disconcerting. And she certainly hasn't reckoned on the intrusion of his family into her consciousness too. Just last night, as she slumbered in the transit lounge of the airport waiting for her connection, his mother, of all people, made an unwelcome appearance in her dreams. A bent and cowled figure was following a few paces behind her along a dusty Indian street. It was twilight, and the muezzin was calling. Esme turned round and the figure halted, then brusquely swept aside the cowl to reveal Stef. She was wearing sunglasses. Wordlessly, she extended an arm, palm held open. She was begging alms in the way that Esme has seen so many beggars do in India. Esme walked on, but the woman followed, and when she called out her voice was that of an old Indian woman, cracked and pleading: 'Please... give me...' Esme stopped again, reached into her pocket and handed her coins, whereupon Stef removed her sunglasses to display two black holes instead of eyes, and in her normal voice shouted, 'No! I want the book. Give me the book...' 'You should be grateful,' Esme reprimanded her, moving away, but the figure reached out a bony hand, clamping it on her shoulder and squeezing. Then Esme woke with a start to find a tea-vendor shaking her awake, offering her tea.

She enters the grounds of St Antony's Hostel and follows the drive alongside a mottled lawn, shuddering as she recalls the horrible vision. She tries to focus on the present but it is not easy. Bells are crashing discordantly from somewhere nearby. It is mid-morning and the air shimmers with heat. Besieged by the noise, the building itself appears still and calm. There is no movement, not a soul to be seen. She enters to find herself in a darkened reception area where a large ceiling fan provides instant succour. As her eyes adjust to the interior dimness she sees two figures at the back of the lobby seemingly engaged in a shouting match as they strive to make their voices heard above the clamorous bells. There is a simple wooden crucifix on the wall above the counter separating them. At first neither of the figures notices her entrance, then the one behind the counter, a tall, thin man, whips his head up and instantly replaces his perplexed expression with one of benevolent welcome.

'Good afternoon, madam! May I assist you?' he hollers.

The other figure turns to face her, and Esme's heart receives a violent jolt as last night's dream comes to life – it is Stef. Her antagonistic stance is instantly transformed into naked delight as she exclaims Esme's name with wild joy, then rushes across and throws her arms around the newcomer. Esme is taken aback at the barrage of enthusiasm, by Stef's exultation in seeing her, but before she can respond Stef is heaving off Esme's rucksack, dropping it to the floor and whisking her back outside and onto the veranda. Thankfully, that is the moment when the din of the bells suddenly diminishes until, after a couple of exhausted clangs, they cease altogether.

'Thank Christ for that!' Stef gasps. 'Here, sit here with me. You must be worn out, poor thing.' And she is fussing over her, pulling chairs into position and rubbing her sweaty shoulders. 'Where have you come from? It's so good to see you! Tell me all about it. Thomas! Thomas, can we have a jug of lemonade, please. Thank you. No ice!'

As Stef interrogates her on everything she has done since arriving in India, often not waiting for an answer, Esme has a chance to examine her more closely. She looks thinner, her face more lined, her eyes more deep-set, since the last time the two met seven or eight years back. And her voice sounds shriller than she remembers. Esme humours her by supplying brief answers to each of the rapid-fire questions, all the time telling herself not to appear patronising or stiff, but constantly aware of Stef's nervous energy, her exaggerated attempt to appear interested in Esme's responses before firing off another question. Is her hand trembling as she pours the lemonade?

'It is *so* shockingly hot,' she is saying. 'Everything is full-on here. To be quite frank, darling, I've had a raging headache since we stepped off the plane. But you'll find a bit of peace here, you really will, it's a perfect spot for yoga, too. Apart from the millions of insects – ugh!'

After the previous hours spent only in her own company, Esme finds the exchange uncomfortably intense, and she eventually summons the courage to excuse herself, promising to meet Stef later to continue their 'catch-up'.

'Of course, of course, darling!' Stef insists, lighting a cigarette. 'Off you go up to your room. Have a good, long rest, and I expect you'll appreciate a nice wash. Though the water's not too hot! In fact it's only ever tepid. But it's too baking here for hot water anyway. A cold bath is my recipe. Such a relief. Alright, darling, we'll see you later!'

As Esme re-enters the lobby, the gaunt receptionist is still there at his counter as if time for him has been suspended since her arrival, or as if her previous entrance was a false start, for he puts his hands together and makes a little bow. 'Madam, welcome to our hostel. I trust you have had a pleasant journey.'

She makes the same modest bow, palms joined, and politely smiles.

'And what is your lovely name?'

Cheered by his choice of words, she tells him: 'Esme Simmons.'

'Welcome, Miss Simmons. My name is Thomas and I am here to attend to your every need. Please let me know in what ways I can be of assistance.'

She starts to thank him, but he has already turned away. 'Shibu! Shibu! Please take Miss Simmons's bag to her room.' The young, tousle-headed man who previously brought a jug of lemonade to the guests on the veranda now reappears from an adjacent room and effortlessly shoulders Esme's grimy bag. She protests, saying she can carry it, but Thomas will have none of it. 'Shibu is here to serve you, madam. You will please deliver your passport to me when you are rested. For the registration.' He hands the boy a key, barks a room number, and turns his attention to his densely inscribed register as Shibu leaps ahead of Esme up the polished wooden stairs.

She follows him along a corridor to a door which he throws open with a flourish. Depositing her rucksack on a low table, he exits from the room with a wide smile and a minimum of fuss, all without uttering a word.

Unsure whether she should have tipped him, Esme shuts and locks the door with a deep sigh of relief. She lets her eyes wander over what will be her home for the next eight days, taking in the room's clean, cool but fairly Spartan appearance, the only decoration a silver, embossed image of Jesus, one hand raised in benediction, the other pulling open his garment to reveal a flaming sacred heart. There is an attached bathroom with a shower, and a sliding insect mesh and louvre doors that open onto a balcony where two chairs overlook the expanse of lawn. She sits down on one of the chairs and after a few minutes decides that she likes the feel of the place. To her surprise, she welcomes the safe, institutional setting, a world away from some of the raggedy places she has stayed in and a cool relief from the bustle and stress of the last twenty-four hours spent on taxis, buses, trains and planes. The thin, dry lawn reassures her, as does the barricade of trees at its far end from which an invisible avian chorus rings forth. There is also a background rumble of traffic and the buzz of machinery from a construction site someplace nearby, but there is still no one in sight, just a glimpse of a striped squirrel scurrying nervously up a trunk before being swallowed up by the tangle of greenery.

The thought of seeing Stef again fills Esme with dread. As in the dream, she is sure to bring up the subject of Jake's book. The last time she saw her she seemed acutely interested in finding out about it, taking Esme by surprise as she herself had largely erased it from her memory. In fact, the book was once a subject of interest to her too – now it's the object of her revulsion.

With a sigh she rises from her seat on the balcony, extracts her washing accoutrements from her bag, and showers. After drying herself, she performs a few yoga stretches and pulls on some clean clothes.

Descending the stairs, she is relieved to find no trace of Stef, though Thomas appears, emerging from his back room at the sound of her steps.

'Mrs Daniel and Professor Johnson are in their room, madam,' he tells her. 'Probably resting.'

Esme relaxes. That's fine by her.

'I will be needing your documentation, madam.'

'Passport?'

He nods. She has anticipated this and hands it over.

'And I will need some information, madam. For the registration.'

Esme is impatient to get out before Stef shows up, but submits to the inevitable inquisition.

'Place of residence?'

'My address? Manchester.'

'Street, madam? House number? Postal code?'

'Let me,' Esme says, and she swivels round the book, grabbing Thomas's pen to scribble in the details.

Thomas, with a haughtily aggrieved expression, rotates the book back to scrutinise the additions, eventually waggling his head in grudging satisfaction.

'Thank you, madam, most kind,' he mutters, and keeps a firm grasp of the book and his pen for the remaining information required, only relinquishing the latter for her signature in three places.

Finally, Esme is able to escape from the gloomy lobby and step out into the sharp noon light. The deserted feel of the place, the lack of the frenetic movement that she has become accustomed to everywhere else on her travels, is almost eerie. It is refreshing, too, though she cannot enjoy it now, intent as she is on avoiding any encounter with Stef or anyone else. Slipping on her sunglasses, she walks along the dusty drive, keeping within the shade of the jungly trees, and turns onto the secluded lane that leads back to the busy road.

Turning left here, she takes the route that she followed when she arrived at the hostel two hours earlier, the noise and traffic increasing as she nears the town centre. Intimidating buses and snarling motorbikes converge on her, and, on an impulse, she turns off the main road and soon finds herself in Allapoorha's market district. Here the air is pungent with a blend of tangy fruit (mango, melon, papaya) and earthy vegetables (ginger, onion, garlic), all larded with India's ubiquitous odours of dung and urine. The main thoroughfare is teeming with men and women of all ages, plus dogs, goats, cows and pigs. It is too narrow for cars, but there are plenty of motorbikes in evidence, aggressively ridden by men with their hands permanently on their horns, confident that the noise alone will scatter all before them – which it invariably does. Only the cows are completely safe.

Feeling her equilibrium restored by the busy throng, Esme pauses to photograph a barrow piled high with chilli peppers. When she looks up, she is shocked to see at a nearby stall two familiar figures in the process of buying grapes. For some reason the vendor, squatting on the ground beneath an open umbrella with heaps of dark purple bunches on either side, is cackling with laughter.

'Hey, you two! Hallo there!'

Miranda and Simon spin round and evidently experience the same momentary confusion of finding someone familiar so far outside their normal context.

'My God, Esme!' Miranda says, rushing up to wrap her arms around her. 'You're here!'

Simon and Esme also embrace, then they all stand and stare at each other in wonder.

'This is a very weird,' Simon says.

'Totally odd,' Esme agrees. 'The last time I saw you was at the funeral.'

'When did you arrive?' Miranda asks.

'Just now. A couple of hours ago. I flew in to Kochi yesterday.'

'We were there a couple of days ago,' Miranda says. 'Dad and Stef are already here...'

'Yes, I saw Stef.'

'And Cynthia and her companion are here.'

'Companion?'

'Her new fling,' Simon says. 'Oliver.'

'Not so new,' Miranda adds. 'They've been together for a few months. Hey, come on,' she beckons them away from the hubbub. 'Let's find somewhere quieter. It's too busy here.' She completes her transaction with the grape-vendor, then leads the way behind the stalls into a narrow alley where there is a chai shop – just a couple of benches around a kettle and a cauldron of milk on a flame. 'Tea all round?' The other two nod and she orders three teas, which are quickly handed to them in flimsy plastic cups.

Although Esme and Miranda have exchanged emails in the last

few months, they have not met for many years. Esme has never had a close relationship with either of the siblings, but she welcomes their presence in this strange business, appreciates their normality.

'What about Dougie?' she asks. 'Is he here? I was surprised to hear he'd be coming.'

'Stef wanted him to be here,' Miranda tells he, 'as a member of Jake's social scene.' *Like me, then*, Esme thinks, *that's my credential too.* 'To be honest, apart from you he was the only one who replied to my emails. But he hasn't got here yet. We don't know where he is or when he's arriving.'

'He's coming with his partner,' Simon adds.

'Oh?'

'He insisted, apparently. It was a sort of condition.'

'Who's his partner?'

'No idea.'

'It was good of you to agree to come, Esme,' Miranda says. 'We know it's a big ask, all the time and expense. We really appreciate it.'

'Well... I couldn't really refuse. And I didn't have much work on.'

'So you've seen Stef?' Miranda asks.

'She was in the reception when I arrived.'

'How did you find her?'

'Fine... I suppose.' Esme hesitates an instant. 'Enthusiastic...'

Brother and sister raise their eyebrows.

'She's kind of all over the place at the moment,' Miranda says.

'Is she still teaching?'

'Not for the last year or two. I'm not sure why. It's possible that she's sort of retired. And Dad's taking a break – he's on a sabbatical. Supposed to be writing a book, not that I've seen much evidence of it.'

'She was a bit ... hyper.'

'She is,' Miranda tells her. 'I suppose it's natural, in the circumstances.'

'She's a one-off, isn't she, your step-mum?'

'Unique, I'd say,' Miranda agrees. 'A bit Jake-ish, in some respects, but still unique.'

Esme is about to speak, but hesitates. Then she ploughs on; somehow, in this noisy, public place, it seems easier to say now what's been bugging her, what needs to be said.

'You know ... I feel I'm here under false pretences, in a way.' Her tone sounds apologetic, and Simon and Miranda look quizzical, waiting for her to continue. 'I mean, why *am* I here?'

They stare at her, still puzzled.

'Because you were his girlfriend?' Simon says.

'But that's just it. I wasn't.'

'Sorry, I'm not with you, Esme.'

'I mean, I *was* his girlfriend. But Jake and I weren't together when he died...'

'You weren't "together"...' Simon repeats, if only to fill the silence.

'Not when he...went. We'd actually split up a few months before. Didn't you know?'

'No, we had no idea,' Miranda says, looking disconcerted. 'He never mentioned it.'

'He didn't mention it? Are you sure?'

They both shake their heads. 'Jake didn't exactly keep us informed of anything to do with his private life,' Simon says.

'To be honest, I spoke to Stef a few times afterwards, but never spelled it out that we weren't an item,' Esme says. 'For some reason it was important for her, she wanted me to be a sort of permanent fixture in Jake's life.'

'She thinks the world of you,' Miranda says. 'She certainly never mentioned to us that you weren't together.'

'So why did you split?' Simon asks.

'Hey, that's really none of our business,' Miranda jumps in.

But Esme replies anyway: 'It's ... complicated. We still saw each other occasionally. We remained fond of each other.' Hearing herself, Esme shakes her head crossly. *Fond* is so not the right word. 'I guess I just got tired,' she adds with more conviction. 'Jake could be extremely bloody awkward. And strange.'

'Strange... yes.' The other two nod in agreement, and there's another pause. Simon pulls out and lights a beedi, cupping it in his hand after the first surreptitious puff.

'So you dumped him?' he asks.

Esme nods vaguely but her mind is elsewhere, following her own train of thought. 'I couldn't tell her. And then I didn't want to bring it up in all the drama that followed. I didn't think she wanted to hear it.'

'She wouldn't want to know that you dumped him, anyway,' Simon says. 'Nobody would be allowed to get away with that. She probably wouldn't have believed you if you *had* told her.'

Miranda drains her cup. 'People believe what they want to believe sometimes,' she remarks.

'Stef especially,' her brother adds. 'Her vision's never been twenty-twenty when it comes to Baby Jesus.'

'Who?' Esme asks.

'That's what we used to call him at home,' Simon says. 'She hated it. But she still believed in his infallibility. I think she almost believes he died to save mankind. But then we're all lying to ourselves most of the time.'

'So anyway – that's why I feel a fraud, being here,' Esme continues. 'I really wasn't part of Jake's life any more, and he wasn't part of mine...'

'But you were an important part of his life once' Miranda tells her. 'That's the point. In fact you were probably his most important relationship. You must know that.'

'Really?' Esme says with evident dismay. This is not what she wishes to hear.

'Yes. Definitely. It's good that you came. Really. Don't worry.'

'I'm sorry that I never said goodbye...'

'None of us did,' Miranda says. 'That's why we're all here, I guess. This is our chance.'

'Is that really why we're here?' Simon asks. The others look puzzled. 'It doesn't really matter what Stef believes or believed, anyway,' he continues. 'What's was it Montaigne said? *The heart has its reasons that reason knows not.*'

'That was Pascal,' Miranda corrects him.

'Whatever. It's the emotional truth that counts. Why should it matter whether Stef thinks you were together or not? For her you were and always will be Jake's partner and her potential daughter-in-law.'

'I don't want to lie any more,' Esme says. 'It's just so bloody awkward.'

'Everything about this situation is awkward,' Simon says. 'I wouldn't even mention it, Esme. It's all a bit delicate, obviously.'

'Actually, honesty is usually the best policy' Miranda says. 'But you're right that we have to be sensitive in this case. Truth can hurt.'

'Okay,' Esme says, more decisively. 'I won't mention anything about it for the time being. But if she brings it up I'll have to be honest. Jake and I were together for nine months nine years ago. Then we went our separate ways and the story was over. History. And I've moved on.'

'That's just the thing,' Miranda says, '*she* hasn't moved on. She carries the past around with her all the time. It's what defines her now.'

The three exchange worried glances, and it occurs to Esme for the first time that the days ahead will be as much an ordeal for Miranda and Simon as they promise to be for her. They are really on the same side. But then she thinks: *If we are on the same side, who or what is on the other side? Stef? 'The Project'? The truth?*

'We'll just have to make it okay for her,' she says, 'and get through this.'

'Agreed!' Miranda says, as if anything has been agreed. She gets to her feet and fans her face with her hat. 'Let's move.'

They pay and leave, each silent now as they negotiate the human, animal and mechanical traffic, feeling daunted by the obstacles to come.

Chapter 18 | The face in the mirror

Laurie regards himself in the mirror and is amazed at what he sees. The face staring back at him belongs to a respectable, thin-bearded, academic-looking type, polite and accommodating, probably innocuous. This is what he has become. He used to believe that the Jungian persona – the one that is adopted to interact with the world – is set in one's late teens or early twenties, when a character is defined and a carapace selected, and that both are fixed more or less in the same form for life. He can see now that this isn't the case. Age and the vicissitudes of life play their part too, possibly the dominant part. He was sure, for instance, that back in his twenties he was an angrier soul – more opinionated, less ponderous, more eager, less predictable, more sociable, more humorous, more … fun. People reacted to him differently then, and they took him more seriously. They respected him. Now strangers smile at him for no reason and he can't lose his temper any more. What's a character worth if it can't lose its rag every now and then?

Actually, he recently found out why people smile at him. The smiles from strangers bothered him for years, in the street, on his bike, complete strangers smiling at him. Were people getting kinder? And then, walking along a shopping street near home, he caught sight of himself in a mirrored shop front – smiling. He mentioned this to Stef, and she confirmed it: 'Didn't you know? You're always smiling. You smile too much.' So that was it. People smiled at him because he himself was smiling at them. They were smiling back – perhaps in case he was someone they knew, or just someone whose cheerfulness deserved acknowledgement. He is pretty sure he doesn't intend to smile, but his almost-smile has somehow become part of him. It's his set expression when out and about. It could be mistaken for a real smile, but it's not.

Alone with himself in the mirror, he tries to shed his social face. Now he is not smiling. The face that returns his scrutiny is a sober one: serious, watchful, wary. It's a cold soul: he sees no humour or bonhomie there. No bitterness either, or anger, just – what? Resignation?

He wonders whether people can detect this chilly underlay of seriousness beneath the good-hearted, well-meaning persona that he presents to the world. He doubts it: people seem to take a liking to him, at least on first encounter, they assume he's a decent sort. Obviously, it's a good strategy to appear likeable – that's how to get by in the world, it oils the way – but has he taken it too far? If he continues on this course, his persona will be, at best, that of a redundant old duffer, cheerful enough, able to get on with most people, harmless, innocent maybe, but not one to merit serious consideration, in fact one who is virtually invisible. At worst they will take him for a smiling simpleton. That's what ageing does to you if you're not careful.

Sometimes he feels as if he is in a large house with many rooms, and he is lost. He can't find his way back to the entrance and that first long corridor he embarked along, the place where he thought he knew where he was going.

He sees a similar process of encroaching invisibility in some of the few friends that he still sees from all those years ago, though in others he sees a greater heft, a stronger grip on the world, they appear more sure of themselves, less accommodating and flexible. Character and age... And life's vicissitudes. These are the variables. Nothing is fixed after all, ever. One's face, and with it one's character, changes. Nothing is forever.

On that wistful note, he turns away from the face in the mirror with a sigh and steps back into the bedroom. The sleeping form of his wife on the bed makes him pause, and for a split second he wonders who she is, and where he is. Stef looks uncharacteristically vulnerable, wearing just her underwear beneath the cotton sheet. He can't remember the last time he saw her in such a helpless state. Her face, though grooved by stress, reveals something akin to innocence. Framed by her thatch of reddish-blond hair threaded with strands of grey, the hard lines, the thin pointed nose, the truculent jaw, are blameless in repose. As his eyes travel slowly over the contours of her body, it occurs to him, not for the first time, that the body is not at all bad for one approaching fifty (five years younger than Laurie himself). Though her skin has a slightly pasty, grey hue, age has been unexpectedly kind to her in other ways. It is hardly surprising that she has maintained a slender figure, since she normally eats little, preferring cigarettes to breakfasts or puddings, but her flesh is still smooth enough, her breasts and thighs firm enough, her legs shapely, her ankles trim. He once delighted in this body, and his blood still feels a residual pull despite everything, but he understands that it's just a stubborn old habit, a Pavlovian response.

He turns his eyes away and creeps across the room. Picking up his current read, he eases open the door, softly pulls it shut behind him and pads along the corridor to the stairs. As ever he feels a conflict of emotions. He likes the idea of sharing a room with Stef, but there are practical problems. There is sadness too, and regret, but most of all there is the difficulty of sharing this intimate space. They only agreed to share a room at the hostel for appearances' sake; at home they long ago took to separate bedrooms. It seemed natural, in the light of their separate lives. Almost the only time of the day that they still share, when their brief interactions take place, is dinner – invariably prepared by him, cleared away and washed up by her.

She is tired now. When she manages to sleep, she could sleep forever. She loves sleeping, perhaps because it is so difficult for her. Given the choice, she might spend the rest of her life asleep. Last night was particularly hard, with the thunder grumbling insistently. He was not aware of any rain, this time, just the disconsolate rolling thunder, and they both lay awake for hours.

'Professor Johnson!' It is Thomas, stationed behind his tall counter in the lobby. He is peering from under his thick eyebrows at the weighty registration book in front of him, a troubled expression on his face. 'There is something for which I need your kind assistance, good sir.'

'Yes?'

Without looking up, he taps a space in the book in front of him with his pen. 'This one. I need to ask what is your wife's occupation?'

'Same as mine. Academic.'

'Academic?' He raises his head to meet Laurie's eyes as if to challenge him.

'Yes. Write "professor", or "teacher". She doesn't do much teaching now, though. Better write "lecturer".'

'Lecturer...'

Laurie nods. 'Yes.'

Thomas slowly nods back. 'Is she not a professor?' he asks finally.

'Yes. She is.'

'So – Professor Daniel?'

'If you like. Professor Daniel.'

Thomas hesitates, then makes a note in his ledger.

'Is that it?' Laurie asks. Through the open door across the hall, he spots Cynthia and Oliver sitting in the lounge, she absorbed in a book, he sucking on a pencil and staring at his newspaper.

'There is something else...' Thomas taps another part of the form. 'What is the place of her residence?'

'You need to know her address?'

Thomas nods.

'It's the same as mine.'

'Thank you, Professor.'

Laurie starts to move away when he is stopped by another enquiry.

'And what is the place of her birth?'

'Where was my wife born? Lewisham.'

'Sorry?'

'London. Put London.'

'London?' Thomas looks doubtful, then looks up at Laurie with narrowed eyes.

'London,' Laurie repeats.

Thomas raises his eyebrows with a resigned expression, exhales slowly, and begins writing in tiny letters. Before he can be detained any further, Laurie quickly crosses the hall to the front door and squints out at the afternoon's glare. To his left, under a parasol on the lawn, two Indians are sipping demurely from cups of tea, one of them dressed in a capacious, European-style, pale suit, his hair pressed back and brutally parted on one side of his head, the other in a neatly laundered white dhoti and a paisley-patterned, tunic-like top, with a Nehru cap perched on his clipped white hair. The two men look up at him and they exchange nods and smiles. He has noticed the first of these, the suited one, previously, talking to Oliver on the day of their arrival. Looking to his right, Laurie sees his son seated at one of the low, wicker tables on the covered veranda, sitting opposite a figure whose back is turned to Laurie. Simon looks up as Laurie approaches and his interlocutor half turns.

'Esme!' Laurie exclaims, 'Gosh! What a surprise! Lovely to see you. How are you?'

She rises and they exchange a brief embrace.

'Don't tell me you weren't expecting me!' she says.

'Well, of course I was. Stef told me you were here, I was just ... distracted. But you look marvellous – how was your journey?'

She nods. 'Interesting... I was telling Simon about a rat temple I visited in Rajasthan.'

'A rat temple!'

'Full of rats. Running all over the place. Holy rats.'

'Good grief!'

As Esme resumes her description, Laurie watches her but is hardly listening. It has been several years since they last met, though they have exchanged emails during the preparations for The Project. She is as trimly petite as he remembers her, her straight, dark hair tied back in the same style, emphasising thin eyebrows finely arched above the clear white and chocolate brown of her eyes and her delicately aquiline nose. She looks older, of course, and a bit ... hardened? weathered? A silver pendant hangs around her neck, she has a bracelet of turquoise stones on her wrist and there is a small blue lizard tattoo on one shoulder.

In response to Simon's questions she is describing some of the other places she has seen on her travels, most of which mean nothing to Laurie. He wonders whether he should sit down with them, but feels intrusive – he has clearly interrupted their reunion.

'What are the stars like down here?' she is asking Simon. 'I bet they're amazing.'

'We've hardly seen any since we arrived.' Simon replies. 'It's cloudy every night. And stormy.'

'Oh?'

'Pre-monsoon. So far it's only storming at night, with occasional downpours, but Thomas says we can expect the odd drenching during the day, too.'

Both of them look up at the sky, which shows not even the

suggestion of a cloud. Laurie considers this a good moment to step in.

'Well, it's terrific to see you, Esme,' he beams. 'Stef is upstairs having a rest right now, but I take it you're around later? And have you heard – we've got a grand dinner planned for tonight. Here at the hostel. A sort of welcome do, so we'll all be there, and we can have a bit of a chinwag. I want to hear about your adventures.'

He waves and sets off from the shelter of the veranda towards the gate. As he leaves he is aware of a smile on his face and quickly erases it for fear of meeting the two beggars outside the adjacent temple – they might infer from it a foolish benevolence. This was an authentic smile, however, as he feels nothing but warmth towards Esme. He has always respected her, always found her thoughtful, original, intriguing. He wonders how he appears to her.

He wasn't intending to leave the hostel when he came down from his room, but planned instead to while away an hour or two of the afternoon on the lawn with his book. That is not an option now, and he wonders where he is going. It doesn't much matter. Here, anywhere is good.

Although he has only seen a tiny fraction of the country, Laurie loves India. He first came to Kerala five years ago, after he and Stef decided to commemorate Jake's life (no, he can hear his wife's angry, exasperated reminder – not *commemorate*, to *celebrate* Jake's life) in the form of a charitable trust based here, at the orphanage where Jake had worked. At the time it seemed the appropriate thing to do, to support a place that Jake had supported, and though he later came to question the decision – all the ramifications, all the ethical dilemmas – he was glad of the opportunities it gave him to immerse himself in this other world, which for him has been a source of continual fascination. For Laurie, every visit has been a leap into an alternative reality, so different from his everyday life that it simultaneously challenges and trivialises everything he has ever known. On the whole, it has been a positive experience; by turning everything upside down, India has revitalised him, for India is a place where nothing can be taken for granted.

And it is India itself that has caused him to question the very premise of The Project. Increasingly, Laurie has come to wonder first what on earth Jake thought he was doing here, and then, inevitably, what on earth they think they are doing here. In both cases, the ostensible answer is charity, or at least charitable intentions, but that is insincere – in fact it makes no sense at all. What right have they to be charitable here anyway? Or anywhere? It seems egregiously presumptuous. Why not just give the dosh to the professionals? It isn't as if the government of India or the state government or the aid organisations aren't capable of doing the job, and could no doubt do it better. So why are they here? It sometimes seems to him a gigantic folly – almost a throwback to colonialism.

But having begun, they were obliged to see it through, above all for Stef's sake. And anyway, India has sucked him in. It was on his second or third visit that Laurie decided that he actually quite enjoyed being here, relished being so far from his daily tasks, his professional quandaries and domestic worries. He even likes the heat, the disorder, the strangeness and the absurdity. He likes the fact that he has known Thomas and his charmingly named wife for five years – granted on a superficial level, but enough time for them to be old acquaintances by now – but actually he doesn't know them at all and they don't know him. He likes that he feels a sense of belonging here, and paradoxically likes the pall of mystery that drapes over everything and everybody. And, of course (though he would never put it in such words), he likes being away from Stef.

In the unlikely event that anyone were to conduct an audit,

Laurie would have to confess that, up till now, whatever business there was that required his attention in Allapoorha could usually have been wrapped up in a couple of days, yet, whenever possible, he extended his stay to a couple of weeks or more. The rest of the time he simply ... *hung out*. Stef wasn't to know that. Not that she would have much cared, but it was better that it wasn't spelled out.

So, yes, it is a holiday and an escape for him, as it was, of course, for Jake, however much it was dressed up. It was Stef who had found Jake the placement, when she was at her wits' end. She would never admit it now, but she was desperate to find somewhere for him to go, somewhere out of the house. She couldn't stand the thought of him spending a year or more waiting aimlessly, making trouble, stirring things up, filling in time before the start of his new life at university. Mother and son were already driving each other doolally, finding new irritations in each other every day. Jake was at his worst – i.e. intolerable – when he had nothing to do. So Stef might have dressed up Jake's time in India as something fine and noble, as education, training, charity, whatever – when in truth she just wanted him out of the house.

Moving from the shade of one tree to another, Laurie saunters along the scrubby lane bordering a sewage channel then turns towards town. Allapoorha's customary hubbub rises in intensity as he progresses: a restless roaring, tooting cacophony. He will have a chai at his favourite chai shop, read a chapter or two of his book, perhaps buy some fruit on the way back. That is all one needs here in terms of a purpose.

An angry horn startles him and he steps back just in time to avoid being struck by a motorbike. They are the very devils here, these bikes, adding an unnecessary extra element of mayhem to India's street-life. Here in India, he reflects, pedestrians are the lowest caste of all. In fact, Laurie has a particular phobia of these motorbike bandits. Well, the whole family has, naturally.

'Ali Baba! Ali Baba!' Laurie's way is suddenly blocked by two little urchins who are pointing at him and laughing.

'No, I am not Ali Baba,' Laurie tells them, determined to play it straight. 'You are mistaken!'

But the boys are stroking their chins and laughing. It's his beard. To them he must resemble a picture in a schoolbook or a character in a cartoon. He walks on, but can hear their chortling as he proceeds up the street.

He arrives at the chai-shop on the edge of the market area – a dim, earth-floored room with rickety wooden tables and air heavy with the scent of cinnamon. There are two other customers, facing each other across a table, hunched over glasses of tea in wordless communion. He orders a masala chai, chooses a table and opens his book. Reading, however, is a strain in the limited light, and his eyes soon unfocus as he sips at his tea, his thoughts reverting to those early days, his life with Stef. Everything comes back to Jake, of course. Without him, he and Stef would probably have never got together, and yet he is the one who has kept them apart. And now he is the dark centre of this whole charade.

And Esme? Not for the first time he wonders how she ever got together with Jake. Chalk and cheese. The attraction of opposites? What did she see in him and what did he want from her? For Jake, every relationship was just another game, just play-acting. He didn't care that people suffered. But Esme never struck Laurie as one to be played with.

Was it as simple as sex?

Thinking of this possibility makes Laurie feel old. For him, the culture of sex is the biggest divide between the generations. The young seem so relaxed about it, in a way that he never was. Seeing Esme earlier, she seemed to emanate a kind of easygoing, freewheeling sensuality. Not that she looks sexy or raunchy or whatever they call it now, she just looks free, unselfconsciously free.

His mind returns to the image of his wife under the sheet in their room. How would she react if he slipped under the sheet with her, naked perhaps? He rolls the thought around, savouring it, then expels it. The idea of physical congress with Stef is, when seriously considered, ridiculous. He might still find her attractive, but while the notion of coupling with most other females is, frankly, a turn-on, Stef is a sexual no no. It would be like starting over, almost like committing adultery. And Laurie is not well versed in the art of seduction. How does one even start? How did he? Now he only ever dreams about it...

After a considerable time immersed in these thoughts, Laurie pulls himself to his feet and pays. Walking back through the bustling market, absorbing the multifarious sensory input on every side, he feels obscurely exhilarated. India does this to him. For no reason that he can identify, it makes him feel stronger. Something within him is energised, potentialised, when he is here. What is it? If he knew, he would bottle it and bring it home in his suitcase. The simplest explanation that he can come up with is the sheer pulsating vibrancy all around, the richness of life. Death is here too, of course, part of it, alongside it. Laurie is not remotely spiritual in England, yet here he catches himself feeling a participant in some kind of universal drama. Being here is like being part of a gigantic work of art, sucked into its rhythm and temporality, a vital component in the whole kaleidoscopic performance. And, best of all, he can choose his role. Here, where everyone plays a part and everyone is an actor, it's no effort to adopt a new persona or even to be a different person. The thought makes him feel absurdly free, liberated from the limitations of time and experience, and anything and everything becomes possible. That must be what they're doing here – extending the limits of possibility. There is a reason after all. So, why not? Let the performance begin!

Chapter 19 | Sketches of Jake

Their eyes linger on Laurie's slightly stooped figure as he lopes across the lawn, watching him pause at the hostel gate, as if unsure of where he is going, then exiting with a more determined step in the direction of town.

'He looks a bit lost,' Esme remarks to Simon.

'A bit of a dreamer, is dad,' he says. 'He told me he dreams better here, whatever that means. I've been dreaming, too, since we arrived.'

Esme nods. 'Yes...'

'Travel does that, doesn't it, feeds your dreams. You must have been dreaming furiously, with all those miles you've covered. It sounds like you've seen India from top to toe.'

'Well... It made no sense to come all this way without seeing some of the place,' Esme explains. 'Then I found out that there's far too much to see. It's all a mish-mash of memories now, and actually I'm quite knackered.'

'Have you been disappointed?'

She looks puzzled, shaking her head. 'Absolutely not. Challenged, maybe. It's not the easiest place to negotiate. But I've learned a lot, and met some interesting people. I'll have lots to tell Amrita. She's one of my closest friends in my yoga group in Manchester, from a Gujarati family but she's never set foot here. I'm putting a lot of stuff on Instagram so she can follow my progress.'

'Well, I hadn't travelled outside Europe before coming here,' he says. 'Kochi was okay, but it's a hell of a long way to come for a curry. And to be honest I think I'd rather be in Spain or Greece.'

'I spent a couple of hours in Kochi – that was enough. It's a bubble. Nothing like the rest of India.'

'So – better or worse?'

'It's just different.' She smiles and looks away, a bit sniffily, Simon thinks. He pulls out his pack of beedis, lights one, and leans back in his seat, blowing out a stream of smoke as he stares into the flat blue sky. He keeps looking for common ground, for ways to relate to Esme, and she keeps pushing him away. There's something cold about her, moralistic even. Yet still he is drawn to her. The more he looks, the more compelling he finds her – not just physically, it goes deeper than that. Her fine, regular features, scrubbed-looking skin and clear eyes combine with her air of composure, equanimity and detachment to produce something like grace. It's a quality he values above all others, but one he rarely encounters.

Annoyingly, though, he can't help but see her through the prism of Jake. He keeps trying to imagine her and Jake together. He saw Jake only intermittently at that time, a period when Jake was at university and Simon was engrossed in his school exams. Esme came to the house once or twice, but he remembers keeping his distance from them. There was one incident that stuck in his mind, however – not even an incident, it was little more than a look. They were at table one evening, Laurie was away somewhere and Stef was in the next room on the phone. Jake made a cutting remark about his mother, Simon can't remember what, something idiotically banal and forgettable – typically Jake – and then Simon saw how Esme looked at him, saw her expression that was an uneasy amalgam of exasperation and fascination, ardour and repulsion, love and hate, almost as if he was a grotesquely misshapen and misbehaving puppy, or a misconceived drawing by a favourite artist. He remembers wondering even then what went on in her mind, what she saw in his brash, lazy, supercilious and smart-talking step-brother. He can see that look even now, eight years later. For the life of him, though, he can't recall exchanging any actual conversation with her. Now he wishes he had taken a greater interest; he is sure they could have been friends.

Both of them are now gazing across the lawn, Simon smoking pensively, enjoying the sweet savour of the beedi and studying the visual details of the trees at the far end, laden with fruit. The bananas, he thinks, are like cradled fingers, the jackfruit like baggy, part-deflated basketballs, and the mangoes are dainty green pendants, like baubles. He wonders how he would draw them. The exuberance of nature that Simon has found in Kerala is a constant source of wonder in him, and once or twice he has unpacked his pad and attempted some visual representation of it. Drawing is something Simon only does on rare occasions, often when he is stressed or preoccupied, and his usual sketches are meticulous, highly detailed portrayals of buildings, formal and intricate. His girlfriend, Jessica, calls them repressed, but they are the natural emanations of his organised, systematic mind. Among his colleagues at work – he is a draughtsman in an architect's studio – he is known for his attention to detail and perfectionism. At the same time there is a part of him too that wants to reject the careful measurements and geometric precision that his profession demands, a sort of hankering for some disorder in his life. He has recently discovered in himself an obscure fascination for the things that refuse to be confined by rules and straight lines, and India, it seems, nurtures it. Something in him responds to the disarray he sees all about him here, that sense of everything teetering on the edge of chaos. At the very least, it tweaks his curiosity. His assertion to Esme that he would prefer Spain or Greece was partly intended as a provocation, in contradiction to his true feelings, for undoubtedly there is something here that attacks his imagination – disturbing, but also new and creative.

Perhaps one day he will return and explore further, but for now he accepts that his experience has been superficial, a mere scratching of the surface. Esme has gone much deeper, though even she seems to relate to India at one step removed, observing and absorbing it as some kind of intellectual exercise. For her, being here, travelling alone, seems to amount to a task or a test. She talks about India as if it were a vast arena – perhaps, obliquely, she had a similar attitude to being with Jake.

Jessica is slim and angular, and, like Simon, a bit arty. She makes jewellery and runs market stalls in North London. They don't live together, preferring to maintain their independence. She has had occasional scenes with other men, which Simon has tolerated, though he has never done that himself. Perhaps he should. One day he might even stray a little, let himself drift to where his inner wildness might lead him. Just a dabble, for a while, in the waters of transgression.

'Where's your sister?' Esme asks.

'Dunno. In her room, I think.'

'What does she make of it all?'

'What all?'

'India.'

'Oh – it makes her cross. The inequality, especially. She's read a couple of books about it. Says the caste system is still very strong and corruption is rife.'

'Is this her first time, too?'

Simon nods. 'But she's much more travelled than me. She lived in Australia for three years, and toured Southeast Asia from there – Thailand and Indonesia and Vietnam. She was better prepared for the climate. I can't get used to it. Sweating from morning to night, and then again in bed – it does me in.'

'It is *seriously* hot,' Esme agrees. 'It's hot in the north, too, but much drier. You should have done this thing in December or January.'

'We had to do it on Jake's birthday. That was the plan.'

'Oh yes, "The Plan". No – what is it? "The Project". Isn't that what you call it?'

'Yeah. It's mainly Miranda's thing. She's the organising genius.'

'Jake always said she was the sensible one in the family.'

'Still is.' He suddenly wants to ask what Jake might have told her about him, but refrains. Wouldn't be cool.

'Has she got a boyfriend?'

'Not that I'm aware of. I don't see that much of her.'

'I can't imagine her with... anyone not sensible. I can't imagine her with a rock and roll drummer.'

Simon chuckles at this as he stubs out the beedi. So they have found some common ground after all: dissecting the character of his sister. 'Maybe she'll surprise us,' he says.

'Hallo! Excuse me?' Esme is hailing Francis, the taciturn waiter who has just appeared at the restaurant's garden entrance. 'Could you bring me a jug of filtered water, please?'

'Yes, madam.'

'Me too,' says Simon. 'No, I'll have a lime soda. A glass. Thanks.'

'Yes, sir. Sweet?'

Simon holds his fingers closely together. 'Just a little bit.'

'Yes, sir.' They go through this ritual every time.

When Francis has brought her jug, Esme pours the water into her flask, screws on the top and gets to her feet. 'I'm going up to my room,' she tells Simon. 'See you later.'

'Right. See you, then.' Simon is slightly nonplussed, feeling suddenly abandoned. Left with his thoughts, he sips his soda and ponders on Esme's surprising revelation this morning in the market that she had given up on Jake. For some reason the thought comforts him, but it is also shocking, and it is odd that the fact has only now emerged. He wonders if Stef knew, if so why she never mentioned it, if not what she will make of it.

On an impulse, he picks up the shoulderbag on the ground next to him, rummages in it, and extracts his drawing pad and pencils. Unthinkingly, he begins to sketch the row of pencil-thin palms at the far end of the garden. Then, just as impulsively, he turns the page and starts to draw from memory Esme's face. After a few minutes he abandons this too, and, on the facing page, starts another sketch, this time of Jake. It is just his head, at three-quarters profile. It doesn't work. He starts again, depicting him instead looking straight out of the page. Then he tries another, this time side-on. He contemplates the three drawings, frowning. None of them works. He has never attempted to capture Jake on paper before. It can't be that hard. He sighs, embarking on yet another: Jake on a motorbike. Ten minutes later, engrossed in this, he slams the sketchbook shut as his sister appears on the veranda and walks over to join him. He decides to continue in his room later. Now he's started, he's determined to get a likeness – even a partial one would do.

Miranda settles down opposite him, takes out her phone and begins to scroll.

'What are you looking at?' Simon asks.

'Instagram.'

'So what's happening on Instagram?'

'Everything,' she says, vaguely.

'Everything and nothing,' he says. 'What's so interesting?'

'What people are looking at. What interests them.'

'Why? It just increases social anxiety.'

'Does it?'

'That's what dad says. It used to be what the neighbours thought, now it's what strangers will think.'

'He's reactionary and so are you.'

Simon regards his sister scrolling, pausing, swiping, and wonders if she is happy. He wonders how she remembers their childhood, and Jake. They have hardly discussed Jake since he died.

'Have you got pictures on there?' he asks her.

'On my phone? Yes, of course.'

'Family pictures?'

'Not really.'

'Pictures of Jake?'

'Definitely not.'

A memory suddenly comes back to Simon of photos in a dustbin.

'Do you remember when Stef threw out all her pictures of Jake?'

Miranda finally looks up.

'God. Yes. That was weird. I'd completely forgotten.' It was after an especially vehement row when Jake was seventeen. Stef and Jake were hurling insults at each other, Jake crashed out of the house, and, in the ensuing silence, Simon came downstairs to find Stef removing all the photos of Jake from the shelves and wall, tearing out images of him from albums, and depositing them all in the bin. What struck him most was her lack of emotion: she wasn't doing it with rage or passion or vindictiveness of any sort, but with a kind of matter-of-fact calm.

'Some of those scenes will stick with me forever,' Miranda says. 'Do you remember when she slapped him?'

'I only heard his version of it. I wasn't there. What happened?'

'She found out that he'd been in her purse and stolen money. She was incandescent.'

'Did you see it?' Simon asks.

'I was a witness. She confronted him, he denied it, and then she presented the evidence. He said something like "So what?" or "It's only money," and she turned round and slapped him on the face. Hard.'

'How did he react?'

'He just stared at her. I saw tears. Then he walked out. That was when he disappeared for a week. He left the next day and sent her a postcard from Skye.'

'That's right. To punish her. She really hated it when he disappeared! She went a bit bonkers.'

'She couldn't stand the thought of losing him,' Miranda muses.

'She never slapped us...'

'Because she didn't love us enough,' Miranda says.

The two look at each other, both shocked at the statement. They have never put such thoughts into words, though the notion has often been there, unspoken. And the logical next postulation, still unspoken: perhaps she never loved them at all. Does it matter now, at this late stage? Yes, for some reason it does. Anyway – it's out there now, unretractable, and it reinforces their bond like a shared secret. It's as if a barrier has been breached, and they are free of something.

An hour later, sitting by the window in his room, instead of drawing, Simon worries about not being able to draw. Or at least being unable to capture certain faces and features. Difficult to believe that that face in particular could elude him so completely when it is so often present in his dreams. What does Jake look like in his dreams? Tantalisingly, he can't now summon him up. Simon has had a very active dream-life in the last few days, and when he's not dreaming he has spent a lot of time trying to recall his dreams and wondering what they mean. For him, they are a direct access to the world of unreason. The other morning, while travelling on the Alleppey Express, he idly made a mental list of the people who turn up in his dreams most often and was disconcerted to conclude that Jake was the one who crops up most, ranking above friends, girlfriends, family members, even his mother – though, annoyingly, even Stef ranks above his mother. Yet now he can't even translate that face onto paper. Maybe that's a good sign. He wonders what Jake would look like now, were he alive. Corpulent, untidy, gone to seed, he imagines. Perhaps if Jake had lived he would long ago have been expelled from Simon's unruly dream-world. And the corollary of that is that, now dead, he's there to stay. His eyes widen at the thought and he has a moment of panic. The idea of sharing his head-space with his dead step-brother for all time fills him with horror. Shaking his head violently as if to expel the notion, he clambers onto his bed. Drawing doesn't work, he'll have a sleep instead – and trust not to dream.

Chapter 20 | On the beach

Moving gently out of her lotus position, Esme rises, stretches and gazes across the garden from her window. She feels revitalised and restored after her afternoon yoga, but restless too. The sense of motion, the rhythms of travel, have not left her. Leaning on the balcony, she inhales the hot air through her nostrils and listens to the birds' clarion chorus disseminating from the trees, wishing that she could identify the individual species. They seem to be striving against each other in their enthusiasm to be heard. Every nuance is represented: inquisitive, insistent, boastful, shy, cheeky, lascivious, nagging, declamatory. All attention-seekers, but reticent too, concealed behind their thick green curtain with only the occasional emergence of a rainbow flash to indicate there is anything more than a soundtrack in the trees.

Detaching herself from the garrulous thrum, Esme re-enters her room and rinses her face at the bathroom sink. Raising her head, she briefly regards herself in the mirror. Her smooth skin and steady gaze express her innate self-confidence. She has never lacked that. Once, when she was still a student, she was offered part-time work to model make-up. She was tempted, the cash would have been useful, but she did not like the idea of pasting her face with cosmetics. She has never needed them herself, only ever used the bare minimum if any. She has been called a natural beauty, and that is the image she has always tried to present – the effortless, unself-conscious allure of the innocent. Sometimes she looks at other, plainer women and wonders how she might have fared without her natural good looks. Perhaps she would have been less solitary.

Slipping on her sandals she goes downstairs to the lobby. It is empty, and she passes into the hostel's stuffy lounge, an over-furnished room with tasselled lampshades, doilies on the occasional tables and an armoury of solid, mid-twentieth-century sofas and armchairs. With the shutters closed, it is dark and at first Esmc thinks the room is deserted. She is about to push open a shuttered door when a croaky voice sounds behind her.

'Oh, don't do that, darling. You'll let all the heat in, and the flies.'

With a quivering heart Esme turns to see the dark profile of Stef seated at one end of a sofa, quite still.

'Oh, I'm so sorry!' Esme says. 'I didn't wake you, did I?'

'I wish,' Stef says. 'Haven't been able to sleep. I tried having a rest upstairs, but it was no good. Thumping headache and everything.'

Esme offers a tight smile. 'Oh...'

'But it's nice to see you, darling. We haven't had a proper natter yet.'

'No...' Esme admits. She feels she has no choice now but to sit down and talk to Stef, and sinks into an over-upholstered armchair opposite her. 'Apart from the headache, how are you feeling?' she asks.

Stef winces at this, her least favourite question.

'Well, if you really want to know, I'm a little bit discombobulated. It's a big thing for us, this business. A very big thing. Momentous, even.'

'You've waited a long time.'

'Very long... But it's so gratifying to come to where Jake gave so much of himself. He loved this place, didn't he?'

Esme nods, though she doesn't remember hearing him give any indication of loving it, or any opinion of it at all. As Stef rests her gaze on her, Esme struggles to maintain a cool, neutral expression. Having adapted to the dim light, she can see that Stef's eyes are a troubled mix of fatigue and edgy watchfulness.

'I'm glad you're here, Esme,' Stef says, her voice softer now.

Esme smiles and nods.

'Jake would be glad. You know, I was so pleased when you and he got together. And now ... now you're a sort of daughter-in-law to me. God, that sounds idiotic. I mean you're the sort of girl who would have been a wonderful daughter-in-law. You're my surviving link, you see, the link to my son – perhaps the strongest I have.' Stef's eyes release Esme's and look away with a frown, as if she is struggling to articulate something. Esme maintains her neutral smile, though she is cringing inside.

'But you know the one thing that's missing? The thing that would make everything complete?'

Esme shakes her head blankly.

'The missing piece of the jigsaw...' Stef's voice is now a hoarse whisper.

Esme stares uncomprehendingly.

'The book!'

Understanding dawns, but it is mixed with horror. 'Oh! The *book...*'

'Yes, Jake's book! The one he was writing. I haven't stopped thinking about it since the first time you mentioned it all those years ago. It was like...like...an *epiphany*. It meant everything to me.'

Esme sighs sadly. 'But I'm afraid it's gone forever, Stef. We've just got to accept that.'

'No, but that's the thing, darling. It's not gone forever. I've found it!'

Stef's eyes are shining brightly, and Esme's heart skips a beat. In the hot, airless atmosphere of the room she feels a sudden chill.

'You've – *found* it?'

'Yes! Isn't it marvellous!'

'Well – yes. Brilliant. Where have you found it? Where is it?'

'Well, I don't have it on me. I haven't even seen it yet. But it exists! That's the wonderful thing. I was beginning to think it was a figment of your imagination, but Dougie's bringing it!'

'Dougie...?'

'Yes! He told me. He's got it, or at least he's got Jake's notes for it, possibly a first draft. He came across it among his things just recently, and now he's bringing it here!'

Esme feels as if she is dreaming again. She is in a land of fantasies and ghosts. It's as if she everything she has ever put her trust in, her very instinct for reality, has been shown to be a pretence. Suddenly she can't trust anything or anybody – least of all herself.

She gets up, she has to get out of this over-heated cave immediately.

'It's unbelievably good news. Fantastic! I'm terribly sorry, I've got to rush now. I'm expecting a call and my phone's in my room...'

'Oh! Alright,' Stef says, clearly put out. But just as Esme is about to leave the room she calls her back. 'Wait!'

Esme halts, turns.

'One thing! Please don't mention it to anyone – the book. I only mentioned it because you're the only one I can say it to.'

'Oh. I see. Right,' Esme says, desperate now to leave the room.

'You're the only one I can trust, darling,' Stef is saying. 'I'll tell everyone eventually, of course. I just need to see it first. It may amount to nothing after all. But I've got a feeling, Esme, a feeling in my bones. This is the real deal!'

'Okay. That's so great. Anyway, must run. I'll catch you later...'

Esme escapes into the lobby. Thomas is there now, bent over a newspaper on his counter. She is about to race past, but a thought strikes her and she stops.

'Excuse me...' He looks up guiltily from the article he is engrossed in, hastily straightening his jacket as he faces her. 'How close are we to the sea?'

'The sea?' Looking mildly relieved, Thomas assumes a thoughtful expression, directing his gaze at the far wall. 'The ocean lies at a distance of approximately six and three-quarters kilometres, madam.'

'Is that all? Are there buses?'

'Yes, there are frequent buses from the bus stand in the centre. Or it is a comfortable walk or bicycle ride.'

'Great! Where can I find a bicycle?'

'The hostel possesses bicycles for our guests' use, madam.'

'That's perfect! Thank you! Can I take one now?'

'Now?'

'In a few minutes. I'll need to fetch a few things from my room.'

Thomas frowns, processing her request, trying to recall the state of the two bicycles in the hostel's possession. He shouts Shibu's name, and the youthful factotum promptly answers the summons, appearing at the door and acknowledging Thomas's instructions with a nod.

'The boy will show you the bicycles, madam. Please accompany him when you are ready.' He hesitates, then fixes Esme squarely in the eye with a stern expression. 'Madam, I would not advise swimming in the Arabian Sea.'

'No?'

'Not at all. It is very dangerous. Unfortunately, it is very poorly named, in fact. The Arabian Sea is not a sea at all – it is an ocean, a mighty ocean, one that has very strong currents and powerful undertows. People have been pulled out to a great distance and never found. It is much better that you do not swim.'

'Oh. Alright. Thank you.'

Thomas's head waggles, still earnest, and it takes Esme a moment to realise that the conversation is ended and he needs to return to his article.

Shame, Esme thinks as she skips upstairs. The prospect of immersing herself in the ocean strongly appealed to her. Maybe she'll chance it. She'll decide when she's there.

Five minutes later she is stepping out of the lobby, flying past the open door to the lounge without looking in. Shibu is outside amid a cloud of dust, energetically sweeping the porch and veranda. He stops his sweeping and smiles reassuringly as she approaches, then beckons for her to follow him round to the back of the building. He stops at a cobwebby brick shed with a corrugated-iron roof, tucked against the wall opposite the kitchen. Producing a key, he unlocks the padlock, pulls open the creaking door and wheels out two dust-covered bikes. He examines each one critically, pinching the tyres and pressing the brakes, before settling on one. Then he dives back into the shed and produces a pump which he uses on the tyres. Not a word has passed his lips. Esme watches, also silent, admiring his painstaking and efficient work and for the first time studying Shibu himself. Tall and slender, with smooth dark brown skin and thick black hair that flops jauntily over his forehead, he might be in his mid-twenties. He has cheap plastic sandals, a pale white dhoti that emphasises his narrow hips, and a purple tee-shirt with the words 'Mogambo Magic Anti-Fouling Paint' emblazoned across the front. A showy silver bracelet watch is fastened loosely around one thin wrist, and there's a leather thong around the other.

After wiping away a coat of dust with a cloth, he presents the bike to Esme with an eager smile and his first words: 'You try?'

She mounts. It seems to be the right height, but when she dismounts he makes a further adjustment to the saddle with his spanner. Finally, he points out the lock built into the back wheel with a key attached.

'Thank you!' she smiles. 'Now – which way is the sea?' Shibu frowns, but after Esme makes a fluttering motion with her hand

and mimics the sound of waves, he seems to understand. 'Ocean? Ocean is … very …' he manages to say, then points along the lane in the opposite direction from the church and the main road into town.

She nods, then stows her bag in the front basket, mounts the saddle and launches herself with a brief wave to Shibu. He waves back, grinning, and is still standing there with his wide grin when she glances back before passing out of the gates.

It is a flat, little-used tarmac road, bordered by drainage ditches beyond which lie neatly tilled fields. People stare at her with interest as she cruises past, but her eyes are fixed on the road surface which is pitted with numerous pot-holes. She does not go fast, but it is still hot work, and by the time the sea shimmers into view forty minutes later her shirt is clinging stickily to her back. Dismounting beneath a stubby palm tree, she parks her bike and takes a deep draught of her water, enjoying the feel of the warm marine breeze on her face. Looking about her, she is struck by how huge everything is, almost overwhelmingly so, and she feels diminished by the great expanse of pale yellow sand and the immensity of the grey-green water beyond. Even the milky blue sky looks grander and more intimidating here.

It takes another fifteen minutes or so to walk to the water-line, where the waves are rearing and thunderously crashing, much bigger than she expected. As soon as a wave draws back, a squad of brave little birds appear, pecking rapidly with their curved beaks into the wet sand before retreating like excited children to escape the next assault. Incongruously, an image occurs to Esme of the beach at Morecambe Bay.

Approaching the surf, Esme removes her sandals, hoists up her skirt and wades in – just a few steps, allowing the water to swirl around her knees. It feels absurdly warm and soupy, so much so that she feels sure that if she were to cup the water and put it to her lips it would taste as cloyingly milky and sweet as chai. Then she feels the strong tug at her ankles and has to brace herself. Thomas was right: the undertow here is scary. It would be foolish to risk anything more than a shallow paddle.

Stepping carefully back through the water, bag held close, she returns to the beach and looks up and down it with her hand shading her eyes, taking in the emptiness. Far away, splashing through the water, a lone rider on a pony is visible on the sand, and she feels the poignant, familiar sensation of being alone – the way she felt before arriving in Allapoorha. It is satisfying and refreshing. Her recent headlong immersion in the swampy milieu of Jake's family has brought uncomfortable echoes of the old claustrophobia that she once felt in the company of Jake himself. True, she is granted a degree of independence by virtue of her slightly detached role, but the deep relief she finds here, at this safe distance, makes her wonder if the unnatural, insulated atmosphere of the hostel is filling her with negative energy.

Her thoughts return to her recent encounter with Stef in that gloomy room, and she feels a resurgence of the panic that gripped her at the news about the book, filling her with an urge to return to the hostel right now, to pack her bag and make a swift, dishonourable withdrawal. But it is too late for that.

Her first instinct, of course, months ago, had been to shun this bizarre valedictory pilgrimage altogether. She had been informed of the existence of the Jake Daniel Trust soon after its inception, some five years back, and had given it her full support, qualified only by her polite refusal to get at all involved in it. She applauded Miranda's many money-raising schemes and even made a modest financial contribution, but would not commit herself to anything more. Then came the email from Miranda inviting her to participate in a macabre mission to commemorate Jake's memory in India. She had almost laughed out loud at the absurdity of it, and was ready to reply immediately with an excuse. But something stopped her, and she told herself to sleep on it, give it a day or two before responding. That night, perhaps triggered by the summons, she dreamed of Jake, the first time in several years. And then she did again on the following night. They were both very peculiar dreams, in fact they were quite upsetting. In one, she and he were arguing – pointlessly, irreconcilably – and then the scene somehow jumped to one in which Jake, heavily made up with lipstick and eye-shadow, was brandishing red-hot needles in front of her face. The following night, even more chillingly, the two of them were together in a ramshackle boat on a swollen river. The vessel struck something, capsized and then they were drowning. On both subsequent mornings she woke up thoroughly shaken. She realised then that she was still haunted. The dilemma of whether or not to join the expedition reared in front of her, demanding an answer, but now she found herself paralysed with indecision. Eventually, after much tangled debating with herself, she wrote back to Miranda and, with a recklessness prompted by mental exhaustion, agreed to join the family in India.

Naturally, she was filled with a thousand misgivings, not least the expense of time and money, despite the trust subsidising the accommodation and air fares, but in the end long reflection convinced her that it could well be for the best. It could be a closure, after all – a final farewell to this scarred and dysfunctional tribe.

They're not all bad, of course. The siblings are fairly easygoing: Miranda has always struck Esme as capable and focused, if a bit opaque, while Simon might be slightly less direct, perhaps more layered, but otherwise fairly safe. In fact, compared to their live-wire step-brother, they both come across as worthy but slightly dull, and in this not unlike their father. But then she remembers Jake's rather savage dismissal of Laurie: banal, but slippery too.

He seemed to think there was something shifty and untrustworthy about him.

Yet Laurie seems harmless enough after all, as is Stef's mother, once you get used to her idiosyncrasies – though what she is doing with the smug and self-aggrandising accountant is a mystery. In truth, none of them are the sort of people she would be drawn to were there no other connection, but above all else it is their very membership of the Daniel-Johnson axis that has discouraged Esme from developing any meaningful relationship with them. They might have no blood ties to Jake, but they are all revolving in his orbit.

Stef, however, is completely toxic. Deep, inconsolable misery oozes out of her like pus from a wound, and everyone seems terrified of her – Esme included. She feels flustered, unsettled, in her presence, and keeps being reminded of what made Jake himself such a difficult person to be with. Just as he did, Stef permeates the air around her, setting the microclimate. And, similar to Jake, she seems to be somehow controlling them all, dictating the agenda. Or is Esme being paranoid?

She wonders how they all got on growing up together, living under the same roof with Stef at the helm. Esme would bet on a bumpy ride, livened up by plenty of fireworks – all launched and thrown into the mix by Jake himself.

On the bare shoreline, the only feature to be seen is a double column of spindly shafts sticking out of the water in the distance. She wonders if it's some kind of art installation and makes her way towards it, but as she draws nearer she sees that the shafts are in fact the rusty remains of a pier, no doubt a relic of empire long since dismantled by the sea. There are other people there, probably attracted to it by virtue of it being the only manmade object to be seen, a solitary landmark in the grand emptiness. Some are couples, sauntering hand in hand under gaudy umbrellas or posing gaily for selfies. As ever, it is the women, in peach-coloured churidars or scarlet leggings, who contribute the colour and panache, while the men are mostly drab in their western-style collared shirts and tight trousers.

There are a few multi-generational families present, too, animated by the kind of voluble excitement that always comes with proximity to the sea. More distantly, she sees a gang of boys cavorting uninhibitedly in the surf, some in baggy swimming trunks, some fully clothed. Most venture no deeper than knee-high in the water, she notices, and those brave enough to go further aren't exactly swimming anyway, they look more like they are wrestling with the sea, pummelled and tossed by the giant waves.

Admittedly, Esme's negative attitude to Stef is conditioned by the lies she has told her and her consequent burden of guilt. Guilt piled onto the guilt she already felt for having broken with her darling boy, for not saving him. And then there is the burden of being, as Stef told her this afternoon, the surviving link with her dead son. She never asked for that role, and it is a heavy one. However, she ought to be feeling pity for the bereaved mother, not horror. Where is the charitable feeling she should have, the allowances she should be making, the generosity of spirit?

The truth is that, for all Stef's other faults, none of the reasons for resenting her are actually Stef's fault. They are nothing to do with her. The reasons lie in Esme's mind alone. Yes, it is her attitude towards Stef that she primarily needs to work on.

The sweat has dried on Esme's skin but the heat still hangs heavily on her, and she feels a strong impulse to throw off her outer clothes and dive into the heaving sea. She could swim for hours. Impossible, of course. Even without Thomas's advice, she is not tough enough to endure the leering stares of the boys and the families that would doubtless ensue. She pictures all the males congregating like flies from miles around to ogle her. Why does it have to be like this? It's not even the fact of being female, for there is a group of local women further along the beach, all fully-clothed and squealing with girlish laughter as they prance in the shallows. But then, even if she were not the only female in the sea, she would still be objectified as the only European female.

And so Esme suppresses her urges and contents herself with hunkering down on the sand, knees pulled up, straw hat tugged down. Apart from occasional sips from her water bottle, she is so still that after a while no one pays her any notice. She finds a degree of solace in the joyful abandon of the thrashing boys and the squealing girls, chasing each other through the waves and displaying the kind of innocent rapture that she hasn't witnessed since her arrival in this land. Such vicarious pleasure, though, cannot compensate for her sense of being cut off, stranded on the shore, watching their joy from the outside.

Trudging back across the sand to her bike, leaving behind their careless merriment, she feels a keen sense of exclusion growing in her like a slow ache. To be a traveller here is to be always on the outside. She should be used to it now.

She is not yet ready to head back to the hostel and decides to cycle north along the beach road in search of refreshment. Half a mile or so along she comes across a hippy-ish bar on the sand and stops. It has om murals on the walls and Bollywood tunes booming from giant speakers inside. She orders a pineapple lassi, finds a table on the terrace and listens to the restless energy of the music as she sips from her glass, frustrated that she cannot comprehend the words or enter into its vibrant spirit. In front of her, boldly painted fishing boats festooned with flags are pulled up on the beach, next to which small groups of off-duty fishermen are playing cards cross-legged in the sand. Again, she is outside the circle.

The light, she realises, is dwindling and thickening, and she glances at her phone. Much as she would love to watch the sun melt into the sea-horizon and savour her melancholy mood, she knows that she should start back before it gets dark. She must be present at the dinner tonight at the hostel, apparently a welcome and a thank you to all the attendees. She does not view the prospect with any kind of relish, but it is part of the package and she has no option. She drains her glass, pays and returns to her bike, still feeling a residue of sadness but fortified, too, by the time spent in the company of the sea and her own thoughts. It has given her a bit of brain space. The dinner might even turn out to be the unifying, together-time that they all need. An authentic common purpose – not just a sham. And she's up for it. For a week or so. Then she can say goodbye.

Chapter 21 | The Keralan feast

'Good evening madam, good evening Mr Maitland, sir.'

With clasped hands and a polished smile, Thomas is being particularly unctuous tonight. He ushers Cynthia and Oliver inside the dining room and waits proudly for the couple to pause and take in the long table covered with a linen table-cloth, the silver candle-holder at its centre and the napkins rolled inside silver rings. There are ten places laid out, each adorned with a little heap of maroon and saffron petals. Three stout candles are in the candle-holder, their flames flickering precariously as they are pulled in all directions by the overhead fans, and there are more candles along the sides of the room and on a cabinet where covered dishes are waiting.

'Where is everyone?' asks Cynthia.

'You are the first, madam. Please...' and he guides them to their allocated seats at one end of the table. He pulls out a chair for Cynthia, who is wearing a high-necked cream blouse, pale cotton slacks and a pearl necklace. Oliver, dapperly dressed in a navy-blue blazer and a striped club tie, settles down beside her.

'Ah, welcome, welcome!' They look up to see Flowery enter the room. 'How are you enjoying your stay? Comfortable? Are your rooms to your satisfaction? Is there anything lacking?'

Every time Cynthia is about to answer a question another one springs forth, until she is reduced to smiling and nodding in silence. Then Flowery whisks herself out of the door that she has just entered from.

'My wife is in charge of the kitchen,' Thomas explains.

'Your wife is a chef?' Oliver asks.

'She is the kitchen administrator,' Thomas tells him. 'There is a separate employee who performs the chef's duties.' He pours them both a full glass of water. 'Filtered, madam,' he says, before Cynthia can get her question out. 'And boiled.'

'Filtered *and* boiled?' Oliver repeats, sounding impressed.

Thomas is nodding and smiling. 'Nothing is too much a problem for our guests. We have no bugs here. No stomach troubles. Hygiene is the king!'

At this point, Stef and Laurie appear in the doorway and Thomas fussily performs the new seat allocations. Francis enters wordlessly from the opposite door and deposits on the sideboard an ornate silver vessel with a robust silver spoon poking out before stationing himself by the cabinet, hands folded in front of him and lips pursed below his neat grey moustache.

Miranda enters the room, then Simon, and lastly Esme. She is looking pleased.

'I've had a word with Shetty,' she tells Miranda as she takes her seat beside her.

'Who's that?'

'The chef. He's going to make special dishes for me. Vegan.'

'Why haven't we seen him?' Miranda asks. 'What's he like?'

'Obese. And jolly. He only works here at mealtimes, and then he's stuck in the kitchen. He's cool. A lot of the dishes will be the same for everyone, but if there are animal products he says he'll prepare a special version for me.'

'That's cool.'

Laurie is on his feet and tapping his glass with a knife. Stef, seated beside him, stares across the table with an impatient expression.

'Er, welcome, everyone, welcome. Although our gathering is not yet complete, in the sense that two members of the group have not yet arrived, we decided not to delay and to hold this special welcome dinner tonight, as planned. There was a chance that they would be here but as yet there's no sign of them, and we don't know for sure when exactly they will appear. Their loss, ha ha! Anyway, Stef and I thought it would be appropriate to host this informal get-together to welcome you all and to thank you for travelling five thousand miles to be present here with us. We're both deeply touched, of course, by your agreeing to come. For some of us, this is the first time we have been able to meet for several years, so tonight will be an opportunity to renew old acquaintances, to exchange notes and maybe, too, share a few memories before the official inauguration of the Jake Daniel Recreation Centre. The inauguration of the Centre is why we're here, in India, in Kerala, at this time, and is due to take place in the next few days – we haven't got a precise date for it yet. But we're not just here to witness the opening of the Recreation Centre, the main reason we've come all this way is to remember Jake. You may have noticed a third empty place at the table – that's his. He's the presiding spirit, as it were, the *raison d'être* of the whole enterprise and the person who unites us all. So let's remember him, let's celebrate him, let's honour him, and tonight, above all, let's also have a jolly good time!

'The food is always excellent in the hostel, but Shetty – the wizard in the kitchen – has made a special effort tonight and promised us a veritable banquet of Keralan dishes. We're all very grateful to him, and to Thomas of course, for being a brilliant host, and let's not forget the ever-fragrant Flowery.'

All eyes turn to Thomas and Flowery standing at the door, smiling and nodding. They have been joined by the rotund figure of Shetty himself, identifiable by his chef's toque and apron and also beaming and nodding proudly.

'Many of you have made significant contributions of money and time, which we sincerely appreciate, as will the children who will benefit most from what has come to be known as "The Project".

But I don't want to dwell on that now, let's save that for another occasion, for the inauguration itself. Tonight, Stef and I want to acknowledge the greatest gift, which is your presence here with us. So thank you all for coming, for being here on this occasion to say goodbye to Jake. And it *is* a sort of farewell, I guess, a difficult and emotional farewell, even if I'm certain that he will never actually leave us or be truly absent. I have no doubt that he will be with us in spirit and in our thoughts until our own time comes around.'

Averting their eyes from each other and from the other people at the table, Esme, Miranda and Simon all experience a sinking of their hearts at these words, while still managing to maintain a stoic expression.

'I know what a sacrifice it's been for all of you to be here,' Laurie continues. 'And not just you. Apart from our previously mentioned missing friends – one of them Jake's best friend at university – there are many other people who couldn't be with us tonight but whose thoughts and good wishes are with us. So I'd like to propose a toast to all of you – to those present and to absent friends. It's a toast in mango juice, in this case, in respect to our hosts and to this incredible country, but a heartfelt toast nonetheless. So thank you everyone, and cheers.'

As Laurie holds aloft his glass and takes a swallow, all the others follow suit. Then, as he lowers himself into his seat, everyone jumps as Oliver, sitting next to him, loudly clears his throat before himself rising to his feet with a serious, intentful manner. Laurie looks bemused – clearly this was not on the agenda.

'If you'll permit me, Laurence, I'd like to add a few words of my own,' Oliver announces, slowly surveying each face at the table. 'First of all I want to express our collective gratitude to you for bringing us all together in this marvellous place, and for organising this event so efficiently. Apart from anything else, it's a triumph of logistics. And let's not forget your lieutenants, too,

Miranda and Simon, who have played a crucial role, from what I understand, thereby making their own invaluable contribution to this noble cause and poignant adieu. And, not least, humble acknowledgement is due to Stephanie, a mother, a wife, a pedagogue, and a tireless campaigner, who is a shining beacon to us all. Lastly, I wish to salute the extraordinary woman here by my side, Cynthia, Stephanie's mother, who I trust will not be offended to be called the matriarch of this formidable family.'

Stef, arms folded, her eyes fixed on the opposite wall, is scowling, while Cynthia blinks up at Oliver, perplexed. She too has not been forewarned of this intervention.

'So I raise my glass to you, Laurence,' he continues, 'and also to dear Jake, whom I never had the fortune to know but who by all accounts gave himself so selflessly to the poor and deprived children of this corner of the subcontinent without any expectation of reward or hope of recognition, whose unique contribution made such a difference to so many lives, and whose example we should do well to follow. From everything I've heard Jake was quite a character; he was also an inspiration, and to my mind a hero, worthy of the utmost respect. And so, though this may only be a toast in mango, it's no less sincere and meaningful for all that. Thank you, Jake. And cheers, old son!'

Oliver throws back his glass and the others hesitantly follow suit. A solitary but spirited clapping sounds from the corner of the room, and all eyes swivel round to see Thomas enthusiastically applauding, nodding vigorously and smiling broadly. Flowery joins in, and, from the other side of the room, so does Francis, and soon those seated around the table are adding their own half-hearted applause.

Oliver nods and beams to everyone at the table as he sits down. Abruptly, Thomas stops clapping and issues a command to Francis, who is roused into action. He begins conveying a

177

succession of plates heaped with rice, chapatis, bhajis, dal, idli, roast chicken and spiced vegetables from the sideboard to the table. As everyone begins to serve themselves, Stef overhears above the clatter of crockery and muttered niceties the mocking tones of Simon at the far end of the table: 'Buttered parsnips anyone? No? God, that was embarrassing!' Stef pins a cold, medusa-like stare on him, but he seems oblivious as he helps himself to rice, and Laurie manages to deflect his wife's icy glare by passing her the dish of bhajis.

'You know,' murmurs Esme to Miranda, 'sometimes I wonder if we're all singing from the same hymn sheet.'

Stef is glaring pugnaciously at everyone now.

'That was very touching, wasn't it?' Cynthia murmurs to her daughter. 'He didn't tell me he had his own speech planned.'

'Sounded a bit scripted to me,' Stef hisses back.

'He's doing his best, dear!'

'And what did he mean "Quite a character"? What have you been telling him?'

'Nothing, nothing!' Cynthia hastily responds.

Stef looks sceptical but, when all is said and done, they can all go to hell as far as she is concerned. Right now she has other things on her mind. First and foremost: why haven't they heard anything from the Institute? She and Laurie have waited anxiously for the summons for the last three days, fearing the worst, aware that the time is passing. When there was no call yesterday she was on the point of going back to shake them all up, but Laurie dissuaded her. He keeps saying you can't hurry things here. It's Indian time. Better to wait. But what possible reason could there be for making them wait? There is something wrong, Stef knows it, and she has resolved to go there first thing tomorrow and find out.

Not only this – what has happened to Dougie and his friend? Some mishap or disaster? Why are they not here? Is it possible they are not coming after all? They and their precious cargo. It is all she can do to keep panic at bay.

Fretfully, she looks across at the three empty places at the far end of the table. Two for Dougie and his friend, one for Jake – that was her doing. Stef has insisted on this: 'Let's not forget Jake, in the midst of everything else going on,' she told Laurie. 'Let's not forget why we're here.' Sometimes India seems to her one big distraction. The point of the exercise is getting lost in the detail. Everyone is chatting away, not thinking of him. Well, she will carry the flame. She will always do that.

She turns to Laurie next to her.

'Do you think he would have appreciated this?' she asks him. 'All his closest friends and family...'

'He would have thought it was a huge joke, love. You know what he was like. He would have found it hilarious.' Under his breath he adds: 'Not least the old duffer's contribution.'

Stef almost laughs. Maybe one day she will laugh at all this. For now, it's a task to keep her temper.

'Stef...' Laurie says, turning to look significantly at her.

'What?'

'I think you're doing really well.'

'What are you talking about?'

'I just want you to know that you're doing a great job. Respect, and everything!'

'I really haven't a clue what you're talking about!'

She turns away, hugely irritated, and surveys the company with her unforgiving, hawk-like eyes. Miranda is chatting with Esme. 'It's not as if people don't recognise dirt when they see it,' she is saying. 'You only have to look at all the SUVs and lease cars and Mercs on the road. Have you ever seen metalwork so obscenely spotless? It's that old cliché, one rule for the rich, one rule for everybody else. And for ninety-nine point nine per cent of the population, the rule is squalor and neglect. That's what I can't accept...'

Stef thinks Esme has probably had enough of Miranda's preaching, and raises her voice to interrupt.

'Esme, did I hear you say that you've been all the way to the sea and didn't even have a swim?'

Startled, Esme is unsure how to respond, and her voice when she finds it is apologetic: 'It was actually rather rough. Really quite scary. Thomas advised me not to.'

'Oh, Thomas!' Stef says, loud enough for the hostel manager, then in the act of a whispered consultation with Francis, to turn his attention towards her. 'Ignore him! He's exaggerating! That's his job. Probably afraid of being sued if you get a mouthful of seawater. You should have gone for it, darling. Taken the plunge. Jake would have!'

'Yes, you're probably right,' Esme says. 'He would have.'

'Well I wouldn't,' Miranda says. 'And Jake was never exactly a great model when it came to safe conduct.'

Stef stares at her in disbelief. 'That's an extremely tasteless thing to say.'

'Hey,' Laurie intervenes. 'She didn't mean it the way you're hearing it. Simmer down, love.'

Stef sniffs haughtily, and loudly tells Laurie, 'At least he knew how to have fun.'

A few minutes later, Miranda leans across the table to say to Stef: 'I'm sorry if I said anything tactless – I wasn't thinking.'

'Yes, it was tactless,' Stef replies. 'But tact was never your strong point. And for God's sake will you stop bringing your ideas of social justice to the table! It's completely inappropriate!'

'We were just exchanging observations, Stef. It's no big deal.' Stef is about to make a retort when Miranda quickly adds: 'But I'll keep my opinions to myself, if that's what you want.'

'Now you're making me out to be some kind of censor.'

Miranda raises both hands, backing off. 'Okay! Sorry...'

Stef sees her mutter something to Esme, but refrains from commenting. Best to be magnanimous, she decides. Everyone's on edge, and she can't blame them. But she won't allow them to blame her, either.

Turning to her other side, she hears Oliver discussing single malt whiskies, of all things, with Laurie.

'It's become something of a hobby of mine, in my retirement,' he is telling him.

'I really don't know anything about them.'

'Truth be told, I didn't intend to get interested, and I'm not much of a drinker, either. But the more I dipped my beak in, so to speak, the more interested I became.'

'I wouldn't know where to start...' Laurie says.

'I have a very decent bottle in my room, as it happens. Glenmorangie. Ten years. Exquisite! We'll have a taster one of these evenings if you like.'

Laurie suddenly meets Stef's eye and coughs. Oliver also notices Stef following their conversation and issues another throat-clearing.

'Tell me, what do you know about Indian train gauges...?' Oliver blithely continues to Laurie.

'Next to nothing, I'm afraid,' Laurie admits.

'Dear God!' Stef murmurs to herself, rolling her eyes. Sometimes it feels that irritation is her natural state, because only she seems able to see that the world itself is irreparably flawed and fundamentally irritating. She tunes out of any further conversation around her, picks up her phone and swipes at it. A few minutes later she puts it down and stares at the plate in front of her. She's not even hungry. Getting to her feet, she looks about her and announces that she is going to her room. 'Goodnight, everybody. I'm sorry that I don't seem able to do conversation these days. It's a trick I can't get the hang of any more.'

Everyone at the table, as well as Flowery who is carrying dishes and Francis in the act of pouring from a jug of water, stops what they are doing to watch her go. With one hand raised, fingers fluttering in the air, Stef crosses the room and the door clicks shut behind her. There is an immediate, palpable sense of relief at the table. Laurie finds himself looking round at the company with an embarrassed smile.

It is Simon who breaks the silence. 'Right! So who's been hiding the beer? I could murder a lager right now. Hey!'

'Behave yourself, Simon' says Miranda, having just kicked him. 'Let's all try and be nice and grown up, shall we?'

Oliver turns to Laurie, as if oblivious to what has passed. 'Have you come across Glengoyne, perhaps?'

Cynthia leans her head back with eyes closed and slowly exhales. She wonders if they are all going to get through the next week in one piece. So far the omens are not good.

Chapter 22 | A dark horse

Seeing Oliver engaged in conversation with Laurie, Miranda leans over to Cynthia, sitting beside her picking at her food.

'I'm glad I've met Oliver, at last,' she says in a lowered tone.

Cynthia looks up. 'Of course! You hadn't met him before, had you?'

'Only via email, after he made that generous donation that has made all this possible.'

Cynthia turns to glance at Oliver and decides he is too engrossed in his conversation to overhear them. 'And do you approve of him?' she murmurs, a look of amusement on her face.

Miranda laughs. 'He's quite handsome...' she says, mouthing the words behind her palm. Then, still in a quiet voice: 'No – I don't approve or disapprove! I'm just very grateful. We all are. Do you?'

Now it is Cynthia's turn to laugh. 'Approve of him? Not always,' she concedes. He's a bit of a dark horse, you know.'

'Really?'

'Yes. One of the other guests here actually recognised him.'

'*Really?*'

Cynthia nods, still looking amused, as at a private joke.

'Is he famous, then?' Miranda asks.

'I don't truly know. When I asked Oliver afterwards, he was extremely evasive. He can be very modest, you know.'

Miranda raises her eyebrows. That would not be the first word she might use in relation to Oliver. 'What exactly did the guest say?'

'Well, nothing very explicit.' Cynthia is almost whispering now, and turns again to make sure Oliver is not eavesdropping. 'Actually I don't think he's staying here, but he's often in the garden with a newspaper. Jowly sort of fellow, you've probably seen him. I was sitting at another table and he leaned over and said, "He ought to write a book." I said, "I beg your pardon?" and he said, "Your husband" – of course he's not my husband, but I didn't correct him – he said: "Your husband should write a book about his life." I said, "Really? Why ever should he do that?" And he said: "Such an interesting life! People would want to know the ins and outs." Ins and outs? I really had no idea what he meant.'

'Didn't you ask him?' Miranda asks, intrigued.

'I didn't get a chance, because Oliver appeared just then and the Indian gentleman went back to his newspaper.'

'What did Oliver say about it?'

'Well, I didn't want to mention it then, with the Indian man sitting there, but I asked him later on, when we were back in our room, and he said he had no idea what he was talking about.'

'How odd!'

'Extremely odd,' Cynthia agrees.

'Aren't you curious? Don't you want to find out?'

'Well, yes, I suppose so. I expect I'll find out sooner or later. But it's sort of nice not to know, too, if you see what I mean. I thought he'd had a completely boring life, so it's good to know that there's a bit more to him than that.'

Miranda, who wants to know everything and abhors uncertainty, cannot agree.

'So he doesn't give much away?' she asks Cynthia.

'No,' Cynthia tells her. 'A bit of a closed book. But things do dribble out eventually.'

'So long as you're okay with that.' Miranda smiles self-deprecatingly. 'Not that I'm anything like an expert or anything, but they say that the only important question in a relationship is: Does he make you happy?'

Cynthia has her amused look again as she ponders this. 'Yes...

Well... We're very content. For the time being.'

'That's alright then!' Miranda says. 'And I bet he's got loads of useful tips when you do your tax return. There must be all kinds of benefits to be going out with an accountant?'

Cynthia giggles, suddenly sounding girlish, then resumes her serene, grandmotherly look. 'Well, we don't go out much, actually. We stay in most of the time.'

'It was a very touching speech he made just now.'

Cynthia thoughtfully cocks her head. 'Hmm...'

'I expect it's a bit overwhelming for him to be here, plunged into this family situation...' Miranda suggests.

'Oh, he takes it all in his stride. He's very accommodating, on the whole. In fact I think he probably finds it all quite fascinating. He's very *interested*, you know. He's interested in everything.'

'Hark, my ears are burning! Are you referring to me, by any chance?' Oliver interjects, having caught the last few words.

Cynthia turns to face him. 'Yes – speaking of the devil. With the big burning, flapping ears!'

He cups both ears and waggles them. 'It's amazing the things you hear sometimes, fascinating...' He looks at Cynthia significantly, to which she responds with a disapproving expression of reproach. Miranda notices this enigmatic, almost conspiratorial exchange.

As they start discussing the food, Miranda reflects on the closed book that is Oliver Maitland. She has not had more than a few polite words with him so far, put off by her first impressions, namely that he is a man of infinite leisure fond of broadcasting his opinions. Beware the man with too much time on his hands, is one of her maxims. Now, though, her interest is piqued. Unlike Cynthia, she is not enamoured of mysteries. She can't stand to leave a book closed for long, there is always a compulsion to peruse it, satisfy her curiosity and move on. Is he for real? She can't decide whether he is more interesting than he makes himself out to be or less so.

Later, following the dessert that Thomas introduced as a 'typical rice pudding', the six remaining diners decide to transfer to the veranda where they are served tea and jalebi sweets. Miranda sits alone at a table at the far end and gazes thoughtfully at the garden, only the first few feet of which are visible in the weak glow of the low-wattage bulbs above their heads. She is nibbling at the sticky orange sweet when her ruminations are interrupted by Oliver himself.

'Do you mind?' he says, laying down his plate of jalebi and pulling out a chair.

'Of course not.'

He grunts as he lowers himself, then expels a single, peremptory cough. Miranda throws him a glance, expecting him to initiate a conversation, but he is absorbed in examining his plate with overt suspicion. She is about to make a comment when he pre-empts her: 'A successful evening, all in all.'

'Yes, very.'

'A delightful supper. Apart from that so-called rice-pudding. My God, what was that chef thinking?'

'Yes...'

'What's his name – Shetty. I had a few words with him at breakfast this morning. Curious chap. Says he learned his trade in the army. Well, that's one place I *wouldn't* recommend for learning how to cook. As for this... I really don't know what to make of it.'

'Yes.' Then, after a pause, she adds: 'Have you served in the army, Oliver?'

'Me? Good lord, no.' He issues another of his habitual short barks. 'Been an accountant all my life,' he declares. 'Over forty years. It's been my wife, my life, my world.'

'What's it like coming out of that? Retiring, I mean.'

'Retirement? A tiny bit unnerving, perhaps, to begin with. But I've learned to take things slowly,' he answers.

'Where was your office?'

'Oh, I've had offices all over the place. London, Honk Kong, Singapore, New York.'

'Oh. I didn't realise. I imagined you working some place like Croydon or darkest Purley.'

'Purley?' he snorts.

'I don't know much about accountancy, as you might have guessed. I imagine it must be a bit repetitive, though, all those numbers.'

'Yes, it's mostly number. But I can assure you that it's never, ever boring.'

'Really?'

'People have this idea that accountancy is supremely humdrum and dull. In fact it's nothing of the sort.'

'I'll have to take your word for that...'

'Sometimes it can be a bit dull, of course, like any job' he concedes, 'but mostly it's extremely lively.' He laughs drily as if at a private joke, and there is plenty more to say but he chooses not to. After a pause, he continues: 'Anyway, yes, it's good to have a break from the treadmill. And I'm improving my golf strokes.' He regards her reflectively, one eyebrow cocked. 'And what about Miranda? I understand that we mainly have you to thank for putting this operation together?'

'I did a bit, yes, but it was my dad who set it all in motion. It's his thing, really.'

'Sad business,' Oliver says. 'Desperately sad. I imagine there's nothing more painful than a loss of this kind in the family.'

Miranda nods, dreading the inevitable next question.

'Were you and Jake very close?'

'Er... Well, we didn't see much of each other after he left home. He was a bit estranged from the family.'

'Estranged? Oh! And...what was he like?' he presses her. His eyes are twinkling slightly, regarding her with what might be ironical detachment.

'He was ...' she starts, searching for the right words. But suddenly she is finding his probing irksome. She doesn't feel like discussing Jake, and what kind of question is it anyway? How can you answer that kind of question? She has to say something, though. And after all, Oliver's curiosity is fairly understandable – how else is he to get a handle on all this? He only has Cynthia to tell him, and Cynthia was not exactly Jake's greatest fan. She decides to give him the positive version of Jake, and starts again: 'Well, that's actually an extremely hard question to answer. Jake was impossible to summarise in a few words, because he didn't fit in any particular category. He lived in his own world, went his own way and made his own rules. He was original, and unpredictable, and quite undisciplined, I guess. He had theories about everything, grand ideas.' She laughs now, remembering. 'Like the cosmos, how it affected his life. He read a book called *The Dark Gods* when he was about fourteen, which was about how malignant forces in the universe are thwarting and undermining everything, sabotaging the greater good, and how they've done that throughout history. Jake decided that they were specifically out to get him, and complained of being under "psychic attack". He was a bit paranoid, too. And a vagabond. He kept running away from school. He went all over the country, phoning Stef from wherever he ended up. Or worse, he wouldn't telephone at all. Once, after she had had no news of him for a week, he called from France to tell her he had decided to live there. But he came back three days later, hungry and penniless, of course. He ran her ragged.'

Oliver listens attentively. His face shows amused interest, but she knows that he is carefully weighing and analysing every word. When she pauses, he whistles in wonder.

'Crikey,' he says. 'Quite a handful, then.'

'A true wild child,' she agrees. 'He wouldn't be tied down.'

He nods. 'Clearly. Rather like his father, then...'

She does a double take at his words. 'I don't know anything about his father.'

'A bit of a shady character, I gather.'

'Was he?'

'An unknown quantity. So I've heard. And a nomad.'

Miranda is about to ask what he means when they are both surprised by a low rumble.

'Ah! Sounds like another storm on the way,' Oliver says.

More long groans follow, sounding closer now.

'So what is it that you've heard about Michael?' Miranda asks.

'What? Oh, nothing really. A few rumours, that's all.'

'Such as?'

'Well, I don't like to spread gossip, you know. Ask your step-grandmother. Cynthia will tell you. The fount of all knowledge...'

'Oh, go on. In what way was he a nomad? We never heard anything about Jake's real dad.'

Oliver turns to look at her briefly, and she thinks she detects something like annoyance in his shadowed face, annoyance with himself or with her or possibly both.

He seems about to say something when his words are cut off by a louder growl of thunder, much closer, and at exactly the same instant the lights on the veranda are extinguished.

'Whoops...' The two of them are cast in total darkness now, and all conversation on the veranda stops. There is a banging from inside, then a scrape of shoes behind them, a flickering glow of light, and the unruffled voice of Francis in their midst.

'Yes, please, one moment.' He is carrying two lanterns with guttering candles. 'Please sit down. Yes, no problem.'

Then a firmer light shines from Oliver's direction. He is on his feet and is using a torch to manoeuvre round the table where he and Miranda have been sitting. 'Cynthia? Are you there?'

'Yes, Oliver,' comes Cynthia's voice.

'We ought to get upstairs.'

'Oh. Wouldn't it be better to stay here until the lights come back on?' she asks.

'No, no, it's much safer in our room. Don't worry, I'll guide you.' He reaches Cynthia's table, helps her to her feet and, grasping her arm, steers her inside the building. 'Off we go then. Good night everybody. Good night! Good night!'

'Good night, Oliver. Good night, Cynthia.'

They shuffle indoors, and Laurie, Simon, Esme and Miranda are left on the veranda, with Francis fussing around them, setting lanterns on the tables and tidying the chairs before he too disappears inside. There is another low roar of thunder and the four of them huddle together around one table, discussing the events of the day and listening to the dry booming in the night, a grumbling, dissatisfied sound, rainless and unresolved.

Chapter 23 | The guided tour

The rapid hammering at the door feels as if it is on the side of Stef's skull.

'Professor Daniel?'

She gets to her feet, a little shakily. She woke late after a disturbed night, and now something has happened to her right ear – it feels blocked, as if she has been swimming underwater, and all sound is echoey and unbalanced. She puts it down to the heat.

There is the hammering again. She hesitates, then turns to fetch her dark glasses from the dressing table and puts them on. It makes things worse, for now it is difficult to gauge directions and distances, but she leaves them on anyway as she unlocks the door and opens it a few inches. Thomas is there.

'I have a message for you from Sister Margaret at the Institute,' he says.

'Yes?'

'She kindly says, Professor, that if you are available this morning she will be very glad to meet with you in her office at ten o'clock.'

'At ten o'clock...'

'Yes, Professor.'

'That's in half an hour.'

'Yes, Professor.'

Stef nods, absorbing the information. The news is good, nevertheless she feels the wings of panic in her breast. She dismisses Thomas, rinses her face and makes her way downstairs. She finds her mother, Oliver and Miranda seated at a table outside. Oliver is describing some of the most common birds to be seen in Kerala, but stops in mid-sentence on Stef's approach.

'Where's Laurie?' Stef asks her mother.

'I think he went to buy some fruit,' Cynthia tells her.

'Here he is!' Miranda announces. Laurie has just appeared on the drive; he is chewing and has a bag of lychees in his hand.

'The nun called,' Stef says as soon as he has reached them. 'She wants us there at ten.'

'Ten?' Laurie queries, consulting his watch. 'That's rather short notice.'

She nods, pulling up a chair at the table and slumping into it. She is still feeling disorientated.

'Well, that's good news, dear,' Cynthia says.

Stef nods again and stares past her mother at a large yellow-winged butterfly perched on a plant in the flowerbed. It seems to be throbbing.

'She said she'd show us around the school,' Laurie says.

'Now that's exactly what I was wanting to do,' Cynthia says. 'Do you mind if we tag along?'

'Er, sure, why not?' Laurie says, glancing at Stef.

'I'd like to come too,' Miranda says.

'Mmm,' Laurie hesitates. 'We don't want to overwhelm them.' He looks again at Stef, but she won't give any signal either way, her eyes hidden behind her sunglasses.

'I'm sure it will be fine,' Cynthia says. 'They must be used to showing people around! You must come, dear, after all your hard work. Are you joining us, Oliver?'

Stef winces inwardly, but says nothing.

'You go,' Oliver tells Cynthia, in a rare display of sensitivity. 'I'll stay here. There are emails that need my attention. I can go some other time.'

'We need to go now, then,' Laurie says.

'Right,' Stef hesitates. 'Wait a moment.' She rises unsteadily to her feet and re-enters the hostel, hurrying upstairs back to her room before anyone has time to ask her if she's 'alright'.

She locks the bedroom door and sits on the bed, her eyes restless, her nerves jittery at the prospect of going back to the Institute. She can't think of the place without thinking of Jake, and now her head is full of Jake and there is a searing pain in her stomach. She throws off her sunglasses and screws her eyes shut, breathing deeply and evenly for several seconds, then snaps them open once more and rises to consult the mirror above the dressing table. God, what a wreck she is. What would Jake say? Most likely he'd snigger with scorn.

A few minutes later, Stef, Laurie, Cynthia and Miranda are emerging in single file from the hostel grounds. They make the short journey to the orphanage in silence. In the office, there is no sign of Sister Grace, the nun who was there on their previous visit, instead they find a very young-looking novice with a swarthy complexion and a shy demeanour. She nods as if they have been expected and ushers them back along the passageway and into a musty, cluttered room where a dozen plastic chairs are ranged around beige walls. There are box files and dog-eared ledgers on a shelf, framed and faded colour photographs of children and nuns on another, and a cluster of silver trophies in a cabinet. Apart from these, the only decoration is a picture on the wall showing a pale-skinned Jesus preaching. Below are the words: 'Welcome to the Holy Fellowship of Christ.' The novice, who says her name is Charity, brings a tray with a jug of lemonade which she pours into glasses and distributes before withdrawing with a nervous smile.

Seated on the uncomfortable chairs, the four of them clutch their glasses of lemonade without drinking, all wary of picking up a bug. Stef removes her sunglasses and approaches the shelf to search for Jake among the solemn faces in the photographs, but he is not there. She is examining the faces when the door swings open and Sister Margaret strides in. She seems to be still burdened with the armful of files she carried the last time they saw her, though this time she deposits them as soon as she enters, stretching out her hand to greet the visitors.

'Mr and Mrs Daniels, thank you for coming at such late notice.' She looks around at the others, smiling politely. 'And these are your friends?'

'These are members of Jake's family,' Laurie says, and introduces Miranda and Cynthia to Sister Margaret, who scrutinizes each one on being told their name and relationship to Jake.

'Now,' she begins in a business-like tone, 'it is important that we finalise details of the ceremony that we have organised to accompany the inauguration of the Recreation Centre, which we are building with your own generous aid and in memory of your own dear son.' Stef and Laurie resist the urge to exchange a glance, each marvelling thinking at how much more rehearsed Sister Margaret seems to be compared with their previous encounter.

'But first,' the nun announces, 'we are going to look at some of the good work we are doing here in this school. Please follow me and we will visit some classrooms.'

And with that Sister Margaret sweeps up her armful of files, wheels round and exits from the room, marching briskly along the passageway. The others hasten after her, taken unawares by the sudden shift in momentum. She swings round the corner without looking back and enters the large outdoor area enclosed by the three storeys of the Institute's central structure, nodding to the few nuns and children she encounters there. Finally she pauses at a door at the far end of the yard, satisfies herself that her retinue is behind her and disappears inside.

The visitors follow in the nun's wake and ascend a flight of stairs, straining to hear her high-pitched voice which is now providing a mechanical-sounding commentary that mostly seems to consist of timetables, numbers of pupils and the success rates of their job placements after leaving the Institute.

'The sisters have been here for more than thirty-five years, doing good works every day, you know, very hard work no doubt,' she tells them. 'And with only very limited funding available. It is a great tribute to them. We will see some of the hard work they are doing.'

When the nun turns off the first landing and marches along the corridor, Miranda pauses to wait for Cynthia, panting as she struggles to keep up. Sister Margaret has come to a halt at an open doorway halfway along from which a steady murmur of young voices emanates.

'Here you will see the children working.' They crowd around the doorway, peering into a small crowded room where a dozen or so children are seated at desks, cutting strips of coloured material with long scissors. Bright paintings and collages are tacked onto the walls and there are piles of magazines on tables. Three nuns are stooped over individuals, directing them, talking in soft tones in Malayalam. The children, aged between around seven and twelve years old, are neatly dressed and groomed, intent on their snipping and sorting. None pays any notice to the visitors.

Sister Margaret looks expectantly at the party. 'You see how they are working hard.'

'Did Jake work here?' Stef asks.

'Jack? It is quite possible, no doubt.'

They proceed down the corridor, halting at two more doors to observe similar groups of well-dressed children engaged in tasks. Then they return back along the corridor to the staircase, where they troop up to the next floor and enter another corridor. Again they stop at open doors to regard the students. The age range seems wider here, from about five to sixteen or seventeen years old, and most of the children appear to have a disability. In one room, a large, fleshy boy gapes up at them with a broad smile on his face. A much thinner boy beside him has eyes that point in different directions and, again, a toothy smile.

'You see how happy they are?' Sister Margaret declares. 'They are very happy. Because of the hard work they are doing.'

'What is it that the children are doing?' Laurie asks.

'Can you not see? They are doing work,' Sister Margaret replies. 'Making things. Sewing. Sums. It is training for when they leave.'

'And are they all orphans?' Cynthia enquires.

'Not at all, madam. Many are orphans, but many also have mothers and fathers who are not able to look after them no doubt.'

'And are they all Christians?' Miranda asks.

'No,' the nun answers shortly.

They proceed to the next room where a boy with callipers is seated at a sewing-machine next to another who is engrossed in a drawing. To one side sits a girl staring blankly at a picture book. On the open page of the book Stef can see a tractor with a line of geese behind and sheep on a green hillside. The girl doesn't seem to be taking in the scene. Something about her draws Stef's attention. She is ten or eleven years old and has paler skin than the other children. When the girl eventually turns to look at the visitors, her eyes meet Stef's and are revealed to be an almost luminescent green. Something about her fixated stare is familiar to Stef, and she struggles to place it. Then she remembers: the woman they encountered on their previous visit to the Institute. She has the same intense expression. Perhaps this is her sister, or her daughter. Stef attempts an encouraging smile, which the girl registers but does not return.

'Did Jake work with handicapped children?' she asks Sister Margaret.

'I do not know. I was not here all those years ago, you see. I was working hard in Africa. In Somalia. I was there for eight years in the refugee camps. But no doubt he was here. Now we will see the

196

toilets.' And she is walking swiftly back along the corridor towards the stairs, files still cradled in her arms. Stef lingers at the threshold of the classroom, reluctant to leave, but the girl has turned back to the farmyard scene in front of her, seemingly still oblivious to it, and Stef has to hurry to catch up with the others.

The toilet block is eventually reached through a door at the back of the building. It is a neat, single-storey, pale green structure, more modern-looking than the other buildings they have seen. It is raised a couple of feet above the ground and accessed by a ramp as well as steps. Rows of wash-basins stretch on either side, where a few pristinely unformed children are rinsing their hands. Others are running up and down the ramp in ones and twos. 'This is our most important new development,' Sister Margaret is saying, 'funded last year by a Swedish charity organisation. It is monsoon-resistant. The girls and the boys have their own separate sections, you see.'

'It all looks very clean,' Cynthia ventures.

'Of course!' Sister Margaret confirms. 'It is all very clean, madam. Cleanliness is next to godliness. The girls need have no fear, you see. It is all good. And now I will show the vegetable garden.' And she briskly leads the way around the side of the toilet block to an area of allotments, each tidily demarcated by short wooden stakes, where she points out rows of beans, tomatoes, peppers and aubergines.

Next she shows them a small exercise area where a dozen or more children are lining up to throw balls to each other, supervised by two young nuns, both African. Other children ranged around the edge are patiently watching.

'You see how we need more space!' Sister Margaret tells them.

Laurie takes the opportunity to say: 'That's why the Recreation Centre will be so welcome.'

'Indeed, yes!'

'Are we going to see the Recreation Centre?' Miranda asks.

'Would you like to see it?' Sister Margaret asks.

'Well, yes,' Stef says. 'Wasn't that the plan?

'We don't want to put you out,' Laurie adds, 'knowing how busy you are, but it would be useful, sure.'

Sister Margaret nods in grave acknowledgement. 'Come!' she says, and leads the procession back around the buildings to a partially concealed space behind a row of bushes to one side of the new toilet block. Here they are faced with a concrete, single-storey structure swathed in bamboo scaffolding. A heap of cement is piled in front, and there are ribbons barring the entrance, but there are no signs of workmen or activity of any kind. They stare in puzzlement.

'Is this it?' Miranda asks uncertainly.

'Indeed yes, madam,' Sister Margaret replies.

'It's not finished,' Laurie says.

'Yes, but it will be ready very soon.'

'In time for the inauguration?'

'Unfortunately it is true that the Recreation Centre will not be technically finished for the inauguration,' the nun tells him. 'But we must bear in mind that your time with us is so limited, you know, and we do not want to delay the ceremony, so we will proceed anyway.'

'I don't understand,' Laurie says. 'Why is the building work not finished?'

Sister Margaret smiles at him and spreads her hands. 'Why, why,' she says. 'Many reasons why. But it is nearly finished.'

'Well, when will our ceremony actually take place?' Stef asks.

'We are thinking, in six days time.'

'Six days? So it won't take place on the day of Jake's birthday, as promised?'

'What day is his birthday?'

'The day that had been arranged for the ceremony, months ago,' Stef answers. 'The tenth of May. Friday.'

'That is impossible.'

'What do you mean, "impossible"?' Stef says, a note of belligerence in her voice now. 'Look, this was all planned! Months ago! Tell her, Miranda.'

'I am afraid that Friday the tenth of May is absolutely impossible, due to the circumstances,' the nun tells them.

'What circumstances?' Stef demands.

'We have a very important meeting with the members of the state government.'

'Can't you rearrange the meeting?'

'No.'

'Oh, really!' fumes Stef. 'Well what about the eleventh of May?'

'No, that is a Saturday. It is a day when many staff are absent, you know.'

'Sunday?'

'Sunday? Unfortunately that will not be possible.'

'Why not?'

'Sunday is impossible. Absolutely. The children will be having services on that day. We will be in church. I am afraid the first day that is possible is Monday the thirteenth of May.'

'The thirteenth...' Stef repeats despondently.

'But why won't the building be ready?' Miranda asks. 'We weren't informed of any construction delays. We were told that the Centre would be ready by now.'

'I did not tell you, Miss Daniels. You had communications with Sister Mercy. She is not here now. She is in Bangla Desh.'

'Miss Johnson, actually,' Miranda corrects her. 'I am Jake's step-sister. So what is the problem, specifically?'

'There is no problem, Miss Johnson. Just details, you know. Regulations. The paperwork is not yet in order. And the wiring system. The building work is not yet complete.'

'Well, this is terribly disappointing,' Laurie says, eyeing Stef, trying to gauge her mood behind her sunglasses. 'After all, the construction work has been underway for a very long time.'

'Yes, that is undoubtedly true, and I must apologise, but Professor Daniels, you must understand, this is India, you see, and not everything happens the way it does in your Western countries.'

Her gaze is directed so severely at him that Laurie feels that to argue would be to deny responsibility for global inequality and his country's colonial record. He glances again at Stef, but is unable to meet her eye.

'Well, it is a disappointment,' he says. 'A major disappointment.'

'When do you expect the work to be complete?' Miranda asks.

'That we cannot say.'

'Soon?'

'Yes, very soon.'

There is another awkward silence, and Laurie, to fill it, says, almost apologetically: 'Well, I'll have to speak with the building contractors, find out what's going on.'

'We just have to be patient,' Cynthia says. 'After all, it must be done properly. No good doing a botched job if it's going to be in use for years to come. For generations, probably!'

Sister Margaret looks uncomfortable now.

'The ceremony will take place as planned,' she assures them.' It will be very good, very beautiful. And the Recreation Centre will be useful, also. A great gift. Sometimes we cannot hurry God's gifts, but, as you say, madam, we must be patient.'

'The ceremony is not taking place as planned,' Stef says. 'It is taking place three days later than planned. And it will a pointless ceremony because the building won't even be ready! It's completely unacceptable.'

'Sorry, madam, but we have fixed that the formal inauguration ceremony will take place on Monday the thirteenth of May. That will be the day when our fine new Recreation Centre will officially open, that will honour the memory of Jack.'

'Who?' Stef growls, feeling her gorge rise.

'Your son. The ceremony will be next Monday at ten o'clock in the morning. There will be a grand opening. The welfare officer of Allapoorha's town council will be present, and I very much hope that you all can be present also. Come.'

The four westerners stare dumbly at her as she moves swiftly away. She halts and turns to them.

'Let us go!' she prompts, and this time they obediently follow, back the way they have come as far as the school gates.

Here Sister Margaret shakes hands with each of them, still holding her files, and leaves them with a nod and a slightly stiff smile. The four of them continue to stand uncertainly inside the Institute's gates, as if reluctant to leave. Stef, behind her sunglasses, appears aloof, unreachable, while Miranda and Cynthia look on awkwardly, unwilling to offer comfort, knowing from past experience how sympathy or any kind of physical contact will be shunned. Laurie feels impotently angry and obscurely guilty – after all, he is the one who has been responsible for The Project and it now seems that it is not even to be brought to any kind of conclusion, at least not the one that they have been expecting. But he must contain himself. After all, what can he do? The decision, it seems, has been made.

'That woman's a bloody clown,' Stef finally declares. 'I'd sack her if I was the local bishop, or whoever it is that employs her.'

'She's doing what she can, dear,' Cynthia tells her. 'It's probably outside her control.'

'Nonsense. She's clueless. She should be doing something useful, back in the refugee camps or wherever she was before coming here. You can see she's out of her depth.'

'I'll get on to the contractor as soon as we get back,' Laurie assures her, though he knows that it will be futile. When he has spoken with the construction firm previously there has been an unbridgeable gulf of communication between them. Any contact with them can only lead to more frustration. Nothing is in their control here. After all, they're on Indian time. That's the reality. You go with the flow, or you don't go at all.

'Come on,' Miranda says, and they shuffle back across the road, past the sun-blasted church, across the second road, back to their shady lodgings.

In the lobby they wordlessly disperse, avoiding each other's eyes, each wrapped in a fog of disappointment. Stef repairs to the veranda where she lights a cigarette. As she smokes, her eyes sweep the garden, her eyes stern, then sunk into themselves as her thoughts range darkly.

'How was it?' Esme's voice. Stef turns to see her on the veranda behind her.

'What?'

'Did you sort everything out at the Institute?'

'No darling, we certainly didn't. It's a madhouse. Have you had any news?'

Esme looks perplexed. 'News?'

'Of those two. Dougie and his friend. Why aren't they here yet?'

'I think they're on their way.'

'Why do you say that? Have you heard anything?'

'Dougie didn't answer my last text. The last I heard from him was that they're on their way and should be here tomorrow or the day after.'

'Do you trust him?'

'Er, well I don't see why he should say that if it's not true,' Esme says, looking confused.

'People say all sorts of things,' Stef says. She throws her cigarette butt onto the decking and grinds it out. 'Why don't you text them again? Or call them.'

'Okay. I will.'

'Good. Thank you. Now, excuse me, Esme.' Stef marches inside and upstairs. *Did you sort everything out? No, darling, we didn't. Too much in this place is bloody unsorted.* Nothing is going according to plan, and she feels deeply uneasy. And she wants a drink. She won't, but the thought is there, the ache is there, persistent, festering, infecting everything.

Chapter 24 | On the train

Jules stares out of the carriage door, his eyes swivelling compulsively from side to side as they fix momentarily on objects flying past – the needle-thin minaret of a mosque, a herd of shaggy goats, a cricket match, a group of defecating men, a row of schoolgirls in a school yard. All vanish out of sight after a couple of seconds. It is a moving picture, a silent film, a postcard parade of frozen tableaux, transfixing, hypnotising, dizzying. It's early morning, following a disturbed night. He doesn't know how long he has been crouched here at the open carriage door, absorbing the show. His brain is a kaleidoscope, a restless, heaving mash-up of such images. And yet totally serene. It is befuddled and bewitched. It is stoned. Yesterday, he and Dougie swallowed lumps of hash for this thirty-hour journey south, and it is still has him in its spell, floating high, aloft, sublime.

For the umpteenth time a vendor behind him in the carriage calls out to him to buy a cup of sweet coffee, or a plastic comb, or a tinfoil tray of something smelling spicy and hot. The vendors might be women or men, many are old, often they are blind or one-armed or afflicted by some kind of horrible skin disease, and all are clearly desperate, teetering on the borders of subsistence. The extent of the poverty and misery here is shocking. He has no idea how to respond. He shakes his head and turns back to the travelling circus outside.

Back in Britain, Jules doesn't do drugs. He used to – pills mainly, usually at weekends – but these days they interfere with everything else. Work especially. Jules is a self-confessed wage slave: he works for an advertising firm, dons a suit every morning and boards a train, putting in the hours. It isn't the most inspiring work, but it's regular, it's got 'prospects', and he can switch off at 5.30. Aged twenty-four, he is on the lower rungs of the ladder, and he is fairly content with his lot. He still parties, of course, but less often. In fact, since hooking up with Dougie he has gone all domestic. That's okay. Despite their ups and downs, the two of them have grown to be a good fit, they function well together. No more flings, no more dramas, no more searching for a soul-mate. Dougie, he is sure, is as close as he will get to the perfect partner. He doesn't question how long it will last, but he is happy the way things are right now. And so, it seems, is Dougie. Currently his partner in crime. Who is now asleep, has been for hours. Jules couldn't sleep. He spent most of the night here, by the carriage door, watching India fly by, entrancing even in the dark, and he is still high as a kite, and loving it.

Funny, that Dougie is literally out of it. He was once the druggier of the two, but he reacts completely differently. He falls unconscious. Maybe it's his age, older than Jules, going on thirty-one. Back home, Dougie works in a magazine office as a subeditor. One day, he says, he will move across to the content side of journalism, be a proper writer, but for now he is happy enough proving himself as a proficient subeditor. He has done most drugs, he says, was most loyal to MDMA, but apart from the odd binge his druggy days are behind him. He says. He is getting serious. But look at him now. Look at both of them.

The two have lived together for nine months. They have been a couple for just under a year. Jules moved into Dougie's larger, more comfortable flat in Dalston, where everything is elegantly white. Jules has had to learn minimalist ways. Yes, they have had their barnies, of course, but these have dwindled over time, and in the last couple of months they have not rowed once. And now, embarked together on this 'holiday' – this wacky shared trip, a helter-skelter caper through India – they have grown ever closer

205

as they dip back into their younger, wilder selves, awaken their dormant roisterers, and revel in their recklessness. It's as if haring around this crazy place has sealed their bond. Like they are in a capsule, hurtling through space, safe in their love pod from the flying debris, the radiation, the solar flares and asteroids.

He has never mentioned it to Doug, but in the last few months Jules's niggling worry about their relationship has been that it had become a little *too* domesticated. Too tame too soon. That way boredom lies. Not for him, necessarily – Jules has sincerely appreciated this period of stability and steadiness as they have moulded their lives around each other. But in the future, if nothing were to change, if they continued being cosy without allowing their inner anarchists the occasional excursion – well, who knows how it could go? If nothing else, this trip has shown them that they are capable of having fun, of throwing caution through the window, of letting their hair fly and chasing the party flame. No doubt they will return to their relatively safe lives in London, but now they know that they can go a bit wild too and still get on.

Dougie, of course, had wild times a-plenty in the past. Every so often, his time at university comes up, his crazy days with Jake. In truth, Jules is sick of hearing about them. Enough already. Now, let this be their wild time to eclipse all wild times. This is what they should remember in the days and years to come.

Jules doesn't know what he was expecting by coming to India, but he never expected this. Everything so far has been a shock, a rush, a sensory onslaught. But the best of it has been learning how tight he and his lover have become. Which is just as well, in the circumstances, because everything to do with this expedition has been stressing Dougie out and putting a strain on both of them over the last three months. Ever since that email from Miranda, bringing everything back, reawakening old anxieties. It was the Great Cunt, putting his oar in, stirring things up, just as he always did.

There was to be a ceremony, Miranda wrote. In, of all places, India. Where the shite had made such a contribution. My arse he did, said Dougie. Jake had never contributed anything in his selfish life – apart from bullshit. It was just possible that the Cunt had done some good in India, but he doubted it. Jake was just not the altruistic type, Dougie said. He had gone out there to have a good time, and because he had nothing better to do.

Nonetheless, this was the place they had settled on to memorialise him. His mother no doubt. Who by all accounts is living in la-la land. They couldn't think of anywhere else where he might have done some good, so they settled on the orphanage in India where he had spent eight months on a gap year. As if the orphans hadn't suffered enough.

That email from Miranda burst open the whole can of worms. Dougie was excited, suddenly, he couldn't stop talking about Jake. They had met at uni, in a gay club of all places. It was weird from the outset, since Jake was patently not gay. He had girls buzzing around him like flies around dung, yet suddenly he was into queer culture. Better music, he said. Soon he was joining Dougie and his set on a regular basis, spending evenings together in gay pubs and clubs. Dougie and Jake got close. They exchanged witty banter, shared daring jokes, sized up hunky males and speculated on their potential. It was all a big laugh for Jake, and everyone played along. Jules suspected he was slumming it, condescending, but Dougie dismissed this, saying they were just having a laugh and why did they have to live in a gay ghetto, why be so binary? Jake, he said, was pan-sexual.

At the time Dougie was in a brittle relationship with another guy who hated Jake, but in the end it was Dougie and the other guy who split. Jules strongly suspected that Jake had something to do with that, but Dougie denied it. Why did he always defend him? It was infuriating. There seemed to be something about Jake that Dougie was both drawn to and repelled by. What the fuck was it? Couldn't he and his mates see through the charm, the irony, the role-playing? Evidently not. Even if they could see it, there was something else too. What? And so, to his chagrin, hearing Dougie go on about Jake, Jules reluctantly found himself longing to have met him, just to be able to judge for himself. But that wasn't going to happen.

Eventually Dougie and Jules fell out over it. Over who or what Jake was, what he represented, where he was really at in his soul. Jules came out and accused his lover of having sucked up to the Great Cunt, of flirting with him. He fancied him of course. Must have. Dougie reacted badly to that, in fact he was royally pissed off.

Everything blew up. There was a scene in the Gloucester Arms a few months back, with Jules dramatically storming out. The end of the affair.

But they got back together. They had it out, talked it through.

The trip to India was discussed, and eventually, after much humming and ha-ing, tears and hugs, they decided they would go together. That was the deal. Well, it was a tall order, far-fetched, not to mention expensive, but they could combine it with an overdue holiday, their annual leave. A first week on the road having fun, a week in Kerala for the big event, and a week to recover on a beach somewhere. They planned it carefully. And all the time Jake was hardly mentioned.

Of course none of their meticulous planning came to much. The roller-coaster took over, rolling on under its own momentum, and they didn't mind at all. In fact it was a total blast. They didn't have to think, just tag along.

And now here they are, ten days in, hurtling towards their rendez-vous with the family – out of their boxes and loving every minute. They are dreading their arrival, of course, not least because it will mean returning to that fatal ground, the thorny past, the one that Dougie can't stop reliving and that Jules wants to deny – the source of their only strife.

For Jules, the big question remains unanswered. It is taboo, *verboten,* and so far they have successfully steered away from it – but it's one that torments Jules. Namely, whether Dougie and Jake ever actually ended up together, even for a night. It shouldn't matter, but for Jules it really does. It has always been there in his mind, but he has forbidden himself from asking it. Discord would surely follow, the pact would be broken, the dream ruptured.

He consults his phone. Arrival in three hours time, plus however many hours late the train is. If he weren't stoned, Jules reflects, he would still be loving it. But he is, bent out of shape as he is, all over the place as he is, scattered and bedazzled and begrimed, and he doesn't give a shit. Let the future in. He doesn't care at all.

He gets out his phone again, this time for a selfie by the carriage door, with India whizzing past behind. He hardly recognises the image on the screen. His face is flushed and his scarf is tied around his forehead, hair sprouting out on top. Dougie's last words to him before he crashed out were: 'Dude, I have to tell you: you're a pineapple.'

Carefully, painfully, Jules raises himself from his crouching position, steadies himself, and totters along the corridor to check on Dougie and their bags. Faces look up and stare as he passes. If they're not looking amazed they look amused. Why does everyone seem so amused by them here?

There he is, slouched against his jacket in the corner of the compartment, his face innocent and gorgeous, mouth slightly open, almost snoring. Jules gathers up the scarf and spreadeagled book he left to preserve his precious space opposite Dougie's seat and settles in. He contemplates his partner for a few seconds, then his gaze shifts down to their bags stuffed under the seat. He looks harder, then frowns. He gets up and, kneeling now, scours the space under Dougie's seat.

'Hey,' he is shaking him awake. 'Doug! Hey!'

Dougie opens his eyes all confusion and innocence.

'What have you done with your bag?'

'What?'

'Your bag. What have you done with your bag?'

'What bag?'

'Your backpack, dude. I can't see it!'

Finally Dougie rouses himself and looks under his seat. Then he looks under Jules's seat, then under the seats all around. The other passengers in the compartment, the ones who are awake, watch in mute curiosity.

'Where the fuck...?'

The two exchange a terrified look.

'Not again! Please God...'

Dougie starts questioning the other passengers: 'Excuse me, have you seen my backpack? My bag? Where is it? Did you see anyone take it? Hallo? Excuse me...'

They all shake their heads vacantly. Some of them look concerned. Dougie says, 'Stay here!' to Jules and charges along the carriage, searching on every rack and under every seat. Then he starts searching the next carriage, then the next, and then he gives up. There are dozens of carriages on this train, all packed to the rafters with suitcases, bags, carpets, rolled up blankets, even cages holding chickens. His backpack could be stuffed out of sight behind any of them, anywhere.

He returns to their compartment to find Jules with the same stricken face that he had on their first night in Mumbai. He looks up desperately as Dougie reappears, but seeing Dougie's own defeated expression slaps his head repeatedly.

'No, no, no...!'

'It's fucking gone, man,' Dougie tells him grimly. 'Someone's stolen it. I don't know where or when. Could have been any time in the last eight hours. But it's gone. Definitively gone. And we're fucked.'

Chapter 25 | The family merger

It is early evening, Tuesday or Wednesday, he's not sure which. Time seems to have stopped since they arrived at the hostel. The amber sky is sliced by distant strips of serrated orange cloud. Simon is seated in the arched and vaulted terrace that sits at the top of the stairs, over the entrance to the hostel building. He is drawing, while regularly swatting away those mosquitoes that haven't been deterred by the burning coil positioned a couple of feet away. Simon prefers this covered terrace to the balcony in his own room – not just because it has its own overhead fan but for its quirky feel: it's the only part of the hostel that for him has any character, with three arched openings to look out through. The left-hand arch reveals a trio of broad-winged birds wheeling somewhere far away, beyond the tree-line. Through the opening in front, nearer at hand, he can see Shibu training a hose on the scrappy flowerbeds and lawn, framed by the wall of trees behind. Simon is focused on the scene visible to the right, however, his pen moving deftly over the page as he attempts to reproduce the small temple on the far side of the garden wall. He is in a hurry to complete the sketch before darkness falls.

But while his eye and hand are occupied, his mind is somewhere else. Having reflected on the strange run of circumstances that have brought them all to this remote spot, his thoughts have turned to a more distant time, an era he has not dwelt on for many years.

There was never a good reason to mull over his early childhood. After all, his nebulous memories of his life with his mother melded long ago with his dream world, not to be trusted, while his first years growing up motherless are largely, for some reason, a complete blank. His real memories don't really start until his new family was forged, when he was all of seven years old, and even there the recollections are pretty patchy. Perhaps because that whole period was muddled and messy. In retrospect, the way things turned out, it could have been handled so much better.

It was never going to be an easy fit, the Daniels and the Johnsons. Simon has a clear recollection of the day when his dad came home with the news: two families were to be one. Miranda had warned him this might happen. He remembers not understanding what she meant. Another mummy? No, she explained, not a mummy. Well, sort of. But not a real mummy. And there would be a sort of new brother, too. But not a real brother.

To Simon it sounded marvellous. He didn't understand his sister's nuanced circumlocutions. A mummy and a brother! New! He hadn't met his new brother, but he had met the new mummy. Daddy had brought her home once or twice. They all had tea together. She seemed okay. He can't remember any impression more precise than that. And he was fairly content. It was only later that doubts started to creep in. Stef's visits became more frequent, and she was often accompanied by his brother-to-be, Jake. They all went on picnics or had lunches in pub gardens together. Even then Stef was distant and unpredictable. Wisely, she never attempted to mother him and Miranda, never tried to be what their real mummy had been, at least according to his imagination. Sometimes she looked at Simon and seemed to be looking through him, like he wasn't there. He could live with that. No, the problem was Jake. Baby Jesus. He was a couple of years younger than Miranda, and a couple of years older than Simon, but somehow he seemed both many years older and many years younger than either of them. He was certainly bolder, smarter, scarier even.

Like his mother he was aloof, almost threateningly so. Then, gradually, after a year or two, when the initial *froideur* on all sides following Stef and Jake moving in had thawed, Jake assumed a new function in the family. Imperceptibly at first, Jake – plump, freckly, ginger-haired – took Simon – thin, shy, rather miserable – under his wing, He adopted the unasked-for role of Simon's protector. And from having kept him at a distance Simon began to look up to his precocious step-brother as his model and mentor. More than that, to everyone's amusement, he began to *worship* him. That's what it amounted to. Jake became his guide, his leader even. And he did not just lead him, he was his *confidant*. Jake shared everything with Simon, his secrets and hankerings and, of course, all the playground gossip. He regaled him with accounts of his escapades and scrapes, and seemed to take particular pleasure in relating the mischief he had got up to at school, which Simon would absorb with awe and admiration. How he tormented the physics teacher, Dr Gawker, a bewildered-looking old dodderer who met every violation of his tattered authority with an expression of sheer panic, such as when Jake brought into the class stink bombs or a gadget from which cruel, mocking laughter issued at the press of a switch. Although a lot of it sounded like exaggeration, the stories were often confirmed by reports that seeped through the school, though the tales became more far-fetched with every telling. Jake was creating for himself a distinctly bad rep.

Naturally, Simon attempted to imitate his icon, at least in the lesser crimes, though he soon gave this up following one particularly embarrassing episode. It occurred quite early in his school career, and for years afterwards caused him to cringe with embarrassment whenever it was recalled – even when there was no one else around the memory would induce in him deep blushes. It happened after Jake had described to him inking his tongue during art class, transforming it into a startling shade of dark blue, which allowed him to scare the living daylights out of the other kids when he poked it out. This had struck Simon as an amazingly clever thing to do, and one morning, a few days or weeks later, during a more-then-usually dull art lesson, he had furtively daubed his own tongue a bright blue, so that when he licked his hand it also turned blue. He licked the other hand, and that became blue too. It was while he was admiring the blue stripes on his two hands that Miss Julie, the art teacher, came up behind and demanded to know what he was doing. Feeling suddenly hot and guilty, Simon opened his mouth wide and stuck out his blue tongue. For some reason, Miss Julie became absolutely furious, crosser than he had ever seen her (she was normally sweet and friendly and kind), causing Simon to burst into babyish tears. Everyone in the class turned and looked at him, some with worried expressions, others sniggering, which made him even more upset. Then the art teacher became flustered and frightened. She eventually became her kind self again in her efforts to quieten him down, but Simon could not stop bawling, and eventually she bustled him out of the room to the dispensary. The school nurse made him wash his mouth out several times, then put him on her knee and cuddled him until he was merely snivelling. At last Stef appeared to pick him up and bring him home. 'What on earth made you do that, you silly child?' she said, but though it was said without malice or anger Simon could never bring himself to tell her who had been the instigator. He had to put up with laughter and head-shaking from the rest of the family that evening and many times after as they recounted his foolishness among themselves and to visitors. For some reason he was never able to say that it was Jake – he was the one who had done it first, he was the real culprit. But Jake hadn't been found out, that was the point. He hadn't got into trouble; he was, as ever, immune.

What hurt most was that Jake joined in the general fun at Simon's expense, without ever owning up. Even when they were alone together he never referred to his part in it, never admitting that it was he, Jake, who had first been responsible for this particular mischief.

Meanwhile, he continued to egg Simon on, daring him to participate in further boundary-breaching feats and misdemeanours. He even taught him to masturbate ('This is absolutely brilliant, you'll thank me for this'). Then things got a little out of hand. Jake began to share with Simon his dark sexual fantasies: fucking women, fucking nuns and teachers, fucking little girls and pregnant women and mothers and old ladies. When he reflected on this years later, Simon was pretty sure that Jake was once more simply pushing the limits, seeing how far he could go. That was what he did all his life. And back then, at the very start of his iconoclastic career, it had clearly become Jake's mission to corrupt his naive *protégé*.

By now, however, Simon had wised up a little. He had learned his lesson after the incident with the inky tongue and its horrible aftermath, which had struck him as not just unfair but shameful too. It had dawned on him that Jake could not be completely trusted, and Simon was never again able to listen to him without a degree of scepticism. More than that, more than the intense embarrassment and stinging hurt, the episode planted in him a vague sense of betrayal.

As it turned out, the sense of betrayal was soon to be his default mode in his feelings towards his ex-mentor, for the time came when Jake, seemingly overnight, disappeared from his world. Simon looked around and suddenly Jake wasn't there. It happened during that crucial transition when Simon began to leave childhood behind and sample and adopt the first traits and mannerisms of manhood, the various ingredients that might one day define his character. Now there was no longer an older brother/protector/mentor/model by his side, nor was there ever again. From being privy to everything he was now permanently excluded. At school, Jake seemed to avoid Simon, and at home he was either ensconced in his room at the top of the house or out somewhere, usually some place he never felt it necessary to divulge. And when Jake reached the age of sixteen or so, he was no longer present on family outings and holidays either. As for Miranda, she had abandoned Simon a long time before, when Simon and Jake had created their own exclusive gang and she had found her own coterie of friends – so now she wasn't there for him either.

To Simon, aged thirteen and fourteen, this all came as a shock. It felt like Jake had ruthlessly shut him out of his world, and it undermined him. Looking back, his rational mind told him that Jake was alienated from all members of the family equally, it was not necessarily personal, but at the time it felt acutely personal. It was like a sharp wound, and though the pain dulled with the passing of time, it remained with him like a bereavement – something unwillingly accepted and rarely mentioned.

Which was why, years later, when Jake really did vanish from their lives, when he disappeared forever, Simon couldn't grieve. He had done his grieving years before. He had already cauterised the wound, and there was no feeling left.

Seated in his cushioned alcove, Simon is suddenly aware that the sky has turned from pale orange to deep pink, and that his hand has not made any mark on the paper for some time. Here, night drops like a thick blanket thrown over everything, total and absolute. It is already too dark to continue drawing. Pulling out and lighting a beedi, he stares unseeingly into the grove of black trees as he smokes, distantly aware of the bats darting and diving over the garden.

Much later, when Simon embarked on a psychology course at uni, he came across things that struck a chord – conditions and syndromes that he thought he recognised. There was one set of syndromes that were simply referred to as 'callous emotional traits'. Was Jake suffering from this little known phenomenon? Simon sent Miranda a link to an academic website that discussed the condition. In the email he wrote: 'According to psychologists, as many as one per cent of all children are thought to suffer from this...' But she wasn't convinced. 'More likely he had some kind of attention deficit disorder,' she replied, 'maybe combined with dyslexia? Or autism?' Simon didn't pursue it with Miranda, but he couldn't stop returning to the subject. Could Jake have been on the autistic spectrum? Or was it just that he was supremely selfish? If so, that might explain why his time in India is still so important to Stef: it nurtured a part of him that wasn't entirely ego-driven, something that might even approximate to empathy.

Miranda, of course, never understood Jake. They were poles apart – philosophically opposed at a very deep level. Miranda was a truth-seeker, while Jake pursued happiness. No, not happiness – happiness isn't a word that could be used in relation to Jake. Hedonism more like. From everything Simon heard, when Jake entered university he was consumed by a kind of competitive hedonism. Having returned from his stint in India – about which he rarely spoke – he now immersed himself in the frenetic social whirl that life at uni offered, relishing the abundant new opportunities to indulge himself, finding stimulation and self-gratification in every encounter. At the beginning at least, it was as if university liberated Jake, galvanised him. He seemed to exude a mad enthusiasm for his new life; on his infrequent visits home he was practically vibrating with it. It was obvious from his manner, from his complete indifference to his former life. He was emotionally absent, his attention was somewhere else – back at uni, where he finally found the kind of freedom that suited him best.

Stef obviously sensed this too, and though he seemed more than ever distant from her and antagonistic towards her, she inevitably found ways to justify it. It showed his total engagement, she said, his embrace of the other, or some such nonsense. Not only did she submit to his hurtful barbs, she actually cheered him on.

Simon wonders now what it could be like to have a mother that loves you so intensely that she loses all connection with reality, and how it would feel to be the object of so much passion. Staring into the night, he puffs pensively, then hurls away the butt with impatience. Maybe heaven, maybe hell – he'll never know. He stares at the pencilled page, now barely visible. An insect whines near his face and he jumps at an owl's sudden screech. He thinks of Jessica back in London, and feels an acute, unexpected loneliness. He remembers her arms, her touch, her tolerant look, and he misses her. Incredibly, his eyes are watering. He never cries – what's going on? Impatiently, he wipes his palms against his face, jumps to his feet and, sweeping his materials into his shoulder bag, rushes downstairs, the owl's siren-like howl ringing in his ears.

On the veranda, he finds Esme alone, reading, loosely wrapped in a shawl next to her own burning coil of mosquito repellent.

'Hey,' she says, looking up at his entrance.

'Hey.' She looks composed, self-sufficient, a welcome corrective to his own inner turmoil.

'What's up?'

'Nothing. Been thinking about your boyfriend.'

Esme looks puzzled, then annoyed. Her eyes drop back to her book, her face full of disdain. *Jake? Boyfriend? He doesn't exist for me any more. Isn't that obvious?* She scowls down at the page.

Simon hesitates, then moves off, towards the lounge. He longs for a beer but will settle for a lime soda.

'See ya.'

Esme doesn't answer.

Chapter 26 | The scapegoat

It is night and the veiled sky is emitting a series of long, meandering notes. Through the ragged curtain of clouds the moon flares sporadically like a bright, roving eye. Esme sits in candlelight, cross-legged on her mat, facing the open balcony door. She has her travel journal open in front of her, though she had to abandon any attempt to write in it since the lights failed and the candles supplied by Thomas proved to be richly atmospheric but completely inadequate. If she screws up her eyes and holds the page close she can write, but it's all too laborious. Instead, like the maddened moths careering around the candle flames, Esme's thoughts are tirelessly and uselessly revolving in her head. Despite all her attempts to steer them away, they keep returning to yesterday's exchange with Stef in the lounge, when she revealed that she would soon be in possession of Jake's book. She made it sound like a lifeline. Esme is cursing herself for having once, long ago, lied to her, and now it's too late to put the record straight. At the time it seemed unimportant, a trivial stretching of the truth, but now it has all got horribly out of hand. Somehow, her lie has infected other people.

She longs for the arrival of Dougie, if only to clear up the mess. Dougie, surely, can disabuse Stef. Can't he? If Esme's lie has turned into a weird reality, to the extent that Dougie has convinced Stef – perhaps even convinced himself – that the alibi once concocted on the spur of the moment by Esme is in fact real, then where can any possible solution come from?

A memory of waking up in Ajmer suddenly comes back to her. It was over a week ago, when she was travelling in Rajasthan, groggy after a long bus ride the day before. Her hotel room was cheap and bare, with white walls and wooden shutters, but clean enough, and the best available that she could find. She was roused awake earlier than she would have wished by a hubbub of voices close by. They were calling, laughing, in chattering conversation. When she opened her eyes, the room was crowded with people. They were milling around her, in bright red turbans and scarves, saris and lungis, some carrying bags bulging with vegetables. Strangely, they were all ignoring her. Occasionally a louder voice would call out as if selling wares. She blinked in confusion and half-rose in her bed, feeling a surge of panic. The figures were all over the walls. For a few seconds she felt delirious, then, with merciful relief, she understood what was happening. The narrow crack between the closed shutters had let in the world outside, the thronged street market, and projected it onto the walls of her room. She was in the chamber of a giant pinhole camera. The figures were illusions, and yet they were real. They were real, but they were illusions. Which was it? It didn't matter. The real and illusory had swapped places for a brief moment. A few minutes later, as the angle of the sun changed, the figures faded and vanished, leaving behind only the clamour of the market outside.

What now is real? Dougie would surely know. She just has to wait for him to throw open the shutters, dispel the hallucinations. Sometimes, at this distance, and so far removed from her present-day life, Esme feels that her whole life with Jake was little more than a dream or hallucination. Perhaps the golden eras of the past always seem that way?

Against her will, her thoughts fly back, right back to the beginning, to the very start of their fractious relationship and their first, innocent encounter. She was with Terry on a train heading back to Brighton. It was her first year at uni, and they had only been together a couple of weeks. She thought they were in love, or at least had a strong connection. It was the May bank holiday, and they had travelled a few stops along the line to an area of woodland somewhere on the South Downs where, Terry said, they was great potential for spotting birds – his great passion. She remembers she was wearing deep pink dungarees and monkey boots. They did see a few birds, but nothing that really stoked Terry up. There was plenty of opportunity for holding hands and kissing, though – probably the real point of the exercise. She was fine with that. On the return ride, Terry had to leave the train at the stop before hers, she can't remember why. They bid each other farewell with a lengthy snog at the carriage door, only to be interrupted by a raucous shout from the platform.

'Terry! Oi! Stop that right now! Desist! Leave that girl alone, for fuck's sake.'

The couple unclasped to see a dozen concerned pairs of eyes turned towards them. Terry, she saw, was tomato-red – he hated being the centre of attention.

'Hallo, Jake,' he said between gritted teeth.

On the platform was a grinning, scruffy-looking boy, slightly overweight, with gingery curly hair flowing over his ears and a scatter of freckles on his face. He wore a torn green tee-shirt, faded jeans and trainers, and he was holding a bike. He must have just disembarked from the same train.

'And who is your victim on this occasion?' he demanded.

'Jake, Esme; Esme, Jake. He's in my tutor group,' Terry explained to Esme, a note of resignation in his introduction.

'Has he been pestering you?' Jake asked Esme. 'I'm really sorry, he's totally out of order. He needs a leash.'

The whistle blew, and Terry had to jump off the train, blowing a kiss to Esme with a hurried 'Call you later!'

But Jake was still holding the door open, his eyes brazenly giving Esme the once-over.

'Are you staying on?' he asked.

'Mine's the next stop.' Why did she say that?

The guard was yelling at Jake, who now slammed the door, his eyes still on her, before suddenly shooting away down the platform. Esme would have waved to Terry as the train pulled away, but Terry wasn't looking at her, he was staring after Jake as he disappeared down the steps in front of him, bike held aloft.

The next stop was only another five minutes' ride. Esme had just left the station and was walking back to her shared house on the outskirts of Brighton when she heard a rattling commotion behind her. There he was: Jake, on his bike, panting hard, drenched with sweat, looking shattered from his marathon race from the previous station. She was completely taken aback.

'How on earth did you do that?' she asked.

He couldn't say anything for several seconds, and when he did it was to gasp something about a short-cut and demand that she buy him a drink.

Awed by his feat, and feeling somehow obliged to acknowledge it, she agreed to buy him a drink, and they walked to The Plough at the end of the street, had a drink (Jake had two), and she found herself giving him her telephone number when he requested it. And he had called her the next day. And the day after that. And so he drew her in, like a whirlpool pulling in a foolish swimmer who has dared to venture too close. And she was willing.

She didn't give in immediately to Jake's ridiculous seduction techniques. In fact she remained loyal to Terry for another three or four days at least, by which time her birdwatching boyfriend had lost his initial allure when compared to Jake's madcap charm and dogged persistence. She was seduced as well as appalled by Jake's sheer audacity and willingness to betray his so-called pal. And that was all it took to hook Esme: a cocktail of effrontery, arrogance, flair, immorality and charm. It embarrasses her now to think of it. She isn't proud of her youthful self. She surrendered like a child to Jake's roguish appeal.

The things she found out about Jake as she got to know him better were darker aspects of his original attraction. There was a constant series of revelations. For example, after being lured away from Terry's side, she soon became aware that this was part of a pattern. It emerged that Jake had a habit of lusting after his friends' partners – in fact most of Jake's enemies at college (who were numerous) seemed to have been victims of either backstabbings or unhonoured debts at the hands of Jake. Terry, of course, neither of them could face again – he would be spotted from afar and evaded with delicious, conspiratorial glee. But he was just one among many. There was a whole collection of ex-friends whom it was necessary to avoid. It became a regular occurrence when the two of them were walking in town or on the campus that she would find Jake no longer beside her, having abruptly dived into a shop or doorway. Sometimes, in a pub or across a room, she'd notice a stranger staring hard at Jake with an unsettling mixture of curiosity and loathing, then the stranger's eyes would turn to her, appraising or judging her, or, worse, regarding her with something like pity. Jake would brush off her questions with an airy reference to 'someone I once rubbed up the wrong way' or 'a bloke I fell out with a long time ago'. She didn't probe. His self-mystification was boyish, droll, and better left unexamined.

It was the same with his 'book'. She still has no idea if it ever even existed. When he had first mentioned it, late one night across a table in a gay club, she immediately latched onto it. Jake, of all people, was not a person she would associate with writing anything. He did not seem the reflective type, nor to possess the necessary discipline or ability to see it through.

'So what's it about?'

'Can't say.'

'Go on. Is it about us?'

'Can't say, I'm afraid.'

He looked evasive, but that was not unusual for him. Whether he sincerely found it difficult to talk about an ongoing work – as artists often do – or whether he was bullshitting – as he often did – she could not tell.

'At least tell me what genre it is!' she insisted. 'Is it fiction? Commentary? A critique?'

'I really can't say. Sorry.'

She left it at that. He wouldn't even reveal whether he had already started it or it was still incubating. Not long after, they broke up and she never got to the bottom of it. But it still intrigued her. It was a possible new clue that might have offered some insight into his interior life, which even after spending months in his company she was no nearer to piercing. He was a chameleon, all surface, everything else ungraspable. But this admission of his, or even this declaration of intent, afforded a glimpse into a more self-sufficient soul that she suspected lay beneath his flighty social front. Even the aspiration to create a work of art generated respect on her part, for it indicated a capacity – or possibly a yearning – for a more nuanced inner life than he pretended to possess. Esme herself would never be capable of writing a book, would never have the nerve, which perhaps accounts for her being in awe of those who do. She is a translator of other people's art, that's as close as she ever gets to true creativity.

Looking back, what she can't reconcile herself to, what she can never forgive herself for, is her acquiescence in his degeneracy, starting with her acceptance of the fact that he shafted his friends, stole their women and neglected his debts. His behaviour was shameful, but somehow it didn't turn her off. In fact, all the time she knew him those contradictory impulses of repulsion and attraction were sustained in a precarious balance. It was the story of their relationship. What did that say about her? And where did love come into all of this? Looking back now, Esme thinks she always knew that she did not love Jake – she thinks she knew it from the start – and, probably, he did not love her, probably never had. In fact she has the impression, though her memory is hazy on this point, that she even grew to dislike him while they were together. Whatever it was she felt for him had to come from someplace else, but not her heart. Curiosity, perhaps, fascination certainly, for who would not be intrigued by this eldritch outcast, this mercurial waif who resisted all attempts to pin him down or constrain him? But there must have been something else, something murkier, that drew her more than mere morbid curiosity or dark fascination. Even the sex – which had been brilliant at first, if sometimes a bit weird– became erratic after the first few weeks, and not at all central or essential. Much of the time he couldn't even do it, or lacked any desire. And he seemed to have an unhealthy interest in her own previous lovers, needling her, wanting to know the details of her past relationships.

Whatever it was, Jake left a stain that she can never truly wash away, like a residue of sin. It has lurked there, ever present, resisting all her attempts to cover it up. It is present even here in India. As present as Jake himself, for Jake's absence is the strongest presence at this misconceived gathering. How can one who is dead exert so much influence over the living? And the lies... Instead of being buried with him, they are still there, ready to surface.

Jake has become a dark reminder of their heedless younger selves. While he was with them, they allowed him to run wild, to entertain them for a while, and then, when he spun out of control, they let him go. After all, he was responsible for himself, who else was? And who else was there to blame for his own downfall? How could they have prevented it? He was their mascot of mischief, their licence for bad behaviour, and their scapegoat.

When it was all over, the deed done and the lies told, it was convenient for all of them to leave mother and son to their own tail-chasing fate. Let them consume each other. Eight years ago Esme had already had enough and was ready to move on to the next chapter of her life. As time went on, her dearest wish was to put the experience behind her; then, when this charade was concocted, she still nursed the hope that it could all be over and the various actors need never see or think about each other again. Even now she still believes that this can happen and that the past can be put away definitively, truth be damned. But the truth, it seems, is rushing to meet them. Jake's 'book' – the one she once suspected was a mere excuse of his, conjured up to cover his all-too-evident lack of productivity, and then became the fiction that Esme herself fed to his mother to get her off her back – has taken on a life of its own. It turns out to be either a collective illusion or an unexpected, resurrected reality come to ambush them. Either way it is at the centre of that same old whirlpool. Esme feels once again the pull of it, helplessly caught in the current.

Out of the night, cutting through the rolling thunder, comes a harsh cackling that makes her jump. Some crazy bird. Her nerves are all over the place. She should turn in. It won't be long now until it's all ended.

Chapter 27 | Mother's ruin

The hypnotic, machine-like buzz of crickets are the dominant soundtrack to this late hour of the morning. Stef sits immobile, poised like a bird on the edge of her bed. She is listening, while her eyes keep returning to the red suitcase that lies on the low table by the wall. Now is her time to view her baby. Just a glimpse. She couldn't while Laurie was there, in fact she hasn't allowed herself to since their arrival in this place. But after yesterday's debacle at the Institute and in the grip of the sheer inertia of this place that feels increasingly like a prison camp, she feels she has the right to indulge herself a little. Nonetheless, several more minutes pass before she slowly rises to her feet and steps towards the closed suitcase. She stands over it, still listening. Then, without more ado, she flips open the lid of the case. Laurie has transferred the contents of his case to the chest of drawers and wardrobe in their bedroom. He has left her space in each, and she has begun placing some of her clothes in the drawers, hung up the blouse and trousers that she will be wearing for the ceremony, but her case is still half full with shirts and underwear. She stares at them for a moment, then carefully sweeps them aside to uncover a litre bottle of colourless liquid. There it is, her little one. Mother's ruin. Her eyes are more animated now as they linger on the bottle. It is a necessity, this comforting presence and the freedom it offers. By bringing it, she has given herself the option, saving herself from the sense of being constricted, from the desperation that could propel her into disaster. Her fingers stroke the glass. There is a kind of distant comfort in doing so, though there is no pleasure or pain as such. Delicately, she picks up her little one and unscrews the lid, putting her nose to the neck and taking in the aroma. Then, just as carefully, she screws the lid back on, replaces the bottle in the suitcase and rearranges its covering of clothes. It is her darling, her consolation and hope. Or the substitute thereof.

She idly wonders what Laurie makes of her little companion. He has been so good in the past, so tolerant, so understanding. She has always depended on his indulgence, for, like others who have lost something precious, she has an imperative need for someone to grant her the benefit of the doubt, to always say yes, to say she's right, to forgive and not to criticise. Laurie has been good that way. He is kind, reliable, sympathetic. 'You're very good to me,' she once told him, in the early days of her loss, 'but I don't know whether you're good *for* me.'

'Of course I am,' Laurie answered. 'I'll get you through this.'

'What makes you so sure?' she asked.

'Because I love you.'

'Why should you think love is enough?'

'Love conquers everything. And anyway, no one is better equipped, because I know you.'

'Do you really?' she asked.

'Sure, trust me. I'll stick by you, you'll see.'

But, though he stuck by her, she didn't become the person he wanted her to be. And now he has assumed a harder stance that doesn't suit him at all. Again, is that what Stef really needs now?

Ultimately, Stef believes that only she can help herself. No one else will do. She is a fighter, and eventually she will win. All she requires is self-belief. It has always pulled her through in the past. When she was twelve years old, her father – her adored father – allowed her to accompany him and her two older brothers on a particularly arduous climb to the top of Helvellyn, in the Lake District. Her mother had protested that it was too long, too far, too challenging, and her brothers had agreed. She would slow them all down, they said. It was a treat they had been looking forward to for weeks and they were determined that their sister would not spoil it. Or perhaps they were afraid that she would upstage them. Anyway, she was equally determined that she would do it, she would show them, and, in particular, she would show her father that she was up to it. He would be proud of her. In the end, as a result of her stubborn insistence, her father relented, and she was allowed to join the party. It turned out to be as bad as they warned it would be – hot, gruelling, thirsty work. They all struggled during the climb, but in the end it had been one of her brothers who threw in the towel – winded, exhausted, with a sore ankle and blisters, he complained childishly, then, utterly vanquished, refused to go any further. With immense satisfaction, she watched him writhe and weep. She was glad they had to give up, turn around and descend the slope back down to the car, as her own body was nearly at the end of its endurance, but she was even gladder to see her brother in his state of abject defeat. Her self-belief had pulled her through. And her father didn't have to see her fail.

At home, Laurie says she spends too much time in her room. Well, that's her choice. So much safer. And it is the same here. Now, though, having spent most of the morning watching the rotations of the ceiling fan, perhaps it is time to venture outside. She unlocks the bedroom door and steps into the corridor. Descending the stairs, she passes through the empty reception, enters the heat of the garden and walks purposefully along the path towards the entrance gate.

Outside, the diseased dog she has previously noticed lurking about here lies motionless by the wall, seemingly annihilated by the heat. She has no idea where she is going. She could just keep on walking. She crosses the road and finds herself in front of St Antony's church, struck anew by its grand, flamboyant façade. It rears tall and defiant, almost a challenge. The doors are open, but there is no one entering or exiting – in fact there is nobody in sight anywhere. On an impulse she walks towards it and slips inside. Her mother attended a Sunday service here and declared her disappointment in finding nothing new or inspiring. But she is interested in faith – Stef is merely seeking refuge.

The cavernous, white interior is bare and empty, and she walks to a row of wooden chairs and lowers herself onto one, settling into the silence. She does not want to think. She will sit, eyes wide open, and try to empty her mind. That sounds like a plan. At least, it will suffice until something else comes along. That is how she lives her life now.

She becomes aware of a pigeon crooning somewhere high above, then, after a few minutes, of a woman at the far end of the church who has started sweeping. Nothing, however, disturbs the stillness. She stares at the simple cross above the altar and wishes she believed in something else, something outside herself – redemption, perhaps, or even love – but it is too late for all that. Stef once had strong beliefs, though not in gods. Primarily she believed in herself, of course, in her ability to overcome and ultimately prevail. Then, later, came her belief in literature, and from that came her belief in the power to change – change minds, modify prejudices, alter society, disrupt the status quo. Then, when she was still quite young, her belief stumbled. Not just that – the very notion of belief cracked and splintered.

Stef attributes the erosion of her capacity for faith to three significant setbacks in her life, three disappearances. The first was when she was a gawky fourteen-year-old and her father disappeared. He was an academic and a writer: erudite, wise, sharp-witted, funny – and a heavy drinker. Alcohol finished him in the end. She internalised it of course, though she mourned his passing fiercely. She was only really able to put it behind her when she left home. Next, there was Michael. Her brow creases as her thoughts fly back to those times, that pre-Jake era when her soul was welded to his. Michael was her true companion, her comrade-in-arms, her soul-brother. She thrived within the iron solidarity of his embrace. And then he disappeared – suddenly, inexplicably, when she was already pregnant with their son.

The third , final blow to her faltering faith came with Jake's disappearance, of course. With that her last remnants of belief perished forever.

Laurie is not a believer, not a true believer, unless you can count his touching belief in her, Stef. Jake, of course, believed in nothing, or nothing that she could discern. Perhaps he took after his father. Michael actually transcended belief systems, though he had made a damn good impression of having one, of living by it and through it. And though she might later have doubted whether his beliefs existed at all, whether they had ever existed, at the time they seemed to burn bright and strong.

Well, now I do believe in something, she thinks. I believe in a resurrection, if not *the* resurrection.

There is a movement behind her. One of the church wardens or helpers is closing the main doors. She sees him look curiously at her, and leave a side door open for her to exit. Clearly he thinks she is praying.

When Stef is disheartened, when she sees only grey walls or infinite, empty horizons, she reverts to time past. She thinks of her previous life, that gold-hued era when Jake was a growing boy. His precious, all-too-brief youth. What wouldn't she give to spend a day there now? The two of them didn't have a perfect relationship, far from it, but it was real. Real in the sense that death is real.

Her mother wants her to 'move on'. She doesn't say it any more – she knows better – but that's what she is thinking. And Stef has no wish to 'move on'. She has simply 'gone on', because there is no alternative. Why should she want to move on from her son? He is a part of her and always will be, with her every day, alive or dead.

She always wants him in her life. She knows too that she needs to go on, for the sake of her dead son, for her husband and for herself. But the raw grieving still hits her at unexpected moments, out of nowhere, like a punch to the throat. Yes, it's happening less frequently now. Most days the rawness has been replaced by numbness. And she knows that this numbness will eventually take over, will be her constant companion forever.

She recalls, for the umpteenth time, hearing the news, the uniformed messengers, the careful but unadorned words, the death sentence. All the details of that distant day are hazy and unreal, yet the fact that emerged was inescapably real. And she remembers falling, her heart caved in, her mind in seizure, her body melting.

The pain came later. The mental pain, the searing emotional pain, that was to be expected – what she could not have anticipated was the physical pain, which lasted for months afterwards. Burning waves of it radiated down her face, down her neck and across her ribcage. Friends were shocked when she'd double over in mid-sentence. Painkillers did nothing. There was no relief.

One of her shrinks told her that it was essential for her to give herself permission to walk away. But no, impossible. She would keep expecting a text from him, an email with an off-colour joke or a sarcastic reference to some lines from one of her old marching songs. How many times has Stef caught herself on her way to her computer or about to pick up her phone in order to dial his number or fire off a message or email demanding to know why he hasn't called? No, she won't 'move on'. She would sooner die.

Like love, like loss, grief is non-negotiable and irreparable. It is like a madness, something she carries around with her, inside her, wherever she goes. And it is delusional. Just a few days ago, in England, in the street, she noticed a tall youth from behind, and there was something about his shambling gait and the gingery shade of his tangled hair that drew her. Aware of her foolishness, she followed him through the streets for ten minutes or more, only desisting when he turned back for an instant and she was forced to see his face – so lacking, so void of her boy's animating spirit. He was a mere dull simulacrum, empty and false. As the pain swept through her anew, concentrated in her solar plexus now, she turned dizzily away and pretended to stare into a shop window, her mind intent on suppressing the burning ache.

A year ago she quit her job. Now she has nothing to occupy her, and it is a blessed relief. She no longer has to pretend to be interested in anything. She can give herself entirely to her pain. In some stupid way, it focuses her, gives her energy. It gives a geometry to her thoughts, even as her body fails. Last year she lost two teeth, this year one more. Gum disease, apparently. She is a spectator to her own disintegration.

Stef swims twice a week, if only to give some structure to her time. It's also a distant reminder of the hold that the sea had over her during her childhood. Back in Cornwall she swam nearly every day when the weather allowed, and she knew all the beaches. She had friends with whom she attended beach parties, with liberal doses of alcohol around blazing driftwood fires, and music and sex. Who was she then? Unrecognisable, that's for sure. The local pool in Winnersh has few echoes of those times, lacks the brisk rub of the ocean through which she once sliced like a sailfish. There is no thrill, no exhilaration to be had there. It's a pretence. So why does she do it? At least joined-up thought is impossible when you're performing the crawl. She avoids the more meditative breast stroke, and even running allows for a degree of contemplation, but these dull, repetitive lengths obliterate all but the most fragmented of thoughts. Mindlessly she counts the lengths, and with every one, as she dips her head in and out of the water, she glimpses more and more clearly the marker on the tiles swimming towards her, the black cross that indicates the end of another length – the inevitable, looming black cross.

Out of boredom, and to keep track of her progress, she began some time ago to enumerate the lengths as years in her boy's life. Length one: his first year, that virgin time, learning how to be a mother. You taught me so much. ... Length two: more confident, talking, talking. ... Length seven: bursting with energy, your freckled face, top marks at school. ... Length nine, moving in with the Johnsons. Crazy time. But you coped triumphantly, even to the point of adopting little Simon as your mascot. ... Length fourteen: issues, arguments, finding your selfhood. ... Length seventeen: more vicious rows, misunderstandings, sexual misadventures, absences.... Length eighteen: gap year in India, my darling, to discover how to give. ... Length twenty: at university, we didn't see so much of you. ... Length twenty-two: that black year, when you left us forever. ... Length twenty-eight: you might have been working: a gifted writer or a cartoonist, perhaps? An artist anyway. ... Length thirty: married, I think, to a wonderful girl, radically intelligent, a true match. Length thirty-three: the age of Christ at the cross – a new vocation? ... Length thirty-six: the first child, my own grandchild. ...

Etc., etc.

But at the end of every length: the black cross. Always there, waiting.

Her eyes return to the plain wooden cross suspended from the church roof. It is blissfully calm and cool in this building. Why is there no one else taking advantage of it? It's almost enough to turn one into a Catholic. She rests her eyes on the rapturous statuette of the Madonna attached to the column in front. Our Lady of the Shipwrecked, perhaps?

Tearing her eyes away from the idol, Stef rouses herself, shudders. She pulls herself to her feet and wavers unsteadily. This self-immersion is no good. It is a symptom of sobriety. This is what she can expect from the sober life. No good. Tentatively, bracing herself, she slips out of the side door and abandons the relatively fresh air of the church. After the first shock, she feels eerily soothed by the brutality of the afternoon heat, anchored by it, even as her muscles ache with fatigue and the blood pumps painfully in her head.

Twenty minutes later, re-entering the hostel, her fragile equanimity blows apart as she feels the eyes of Laurie, Cynthia and Oliver turn towards her inquisitively. They are grouped around a table in the shade of the veranda, and she knows they have been discussing her.

'Where have you been, dear?' her mother enquires.

'In church.'

'Goodness! Don't tell me you attended a service? Or were you admiring the architecture? It's so magnificent. Such a statement of faith!'

'Of colonial arrogance, you mean?' Stef says.

'Oh, please!' Cynthia protests. 'Not everything is political. It's a monument to the simple faith of the people!'

'"Simple faith"? That's terribly patronising, mother. So it's a monument to their credulity?'

Cynthia rolls her eyes, and Oliver turns a beady, twinkling eye on Stef. 'Have you not kept the faith, then, Stephanie?'

She looks up wearily. 'Faith in what?'

'Say no more,' Oliver declares gnomically, and he grunts loudly before thrusting back his head to stare at the sky through narrowed eyes.

Stef directs a brief, penetrating look at him. *What does he know? And why does he need to advertise the fact that he knows it?*

'I'm going to take a bath,' Stef tells the group, and as she heads up to her room the question occurs to her, not for the first time: *Is he shrewd or is he vacuous?* Either way, she decides, there is something false about that man, something dangerous perhaps.

Chapter 28 | The Rabbit Pie Summit

At two o'clock in the afternoon, peak heat and humidity, Laurie climbs the stairs in the hostel feeling his neck clammy, his back and forehead prickly. Slowly does it, lightly does it. Padding along the corridor he eases open the bedroom door, just in time to startle Stef with a tumbler of colourless liquid in her hand. They stare at each other for a couple of seconds, frozen. Then Stef turns away, takes a long swallow and sharply informs him: 'It's water!'

Laurie laughs dismissively. 'Hey! Easy! I wasn't spying!'

'Yes you were,' she says, and ostentatiously drains the glass.

Laurie tries to defuse the awkwardness by striding purposefully across the room and pretending to rummage though one of his drawers. But the unease lingers. It is comprised of equal parts embarrassment, shared guilt and shame. Since their arrival, there has been no mention of the subject of Stef's drinking, nor of the conversations on the subject that preceded their departure from England. The first of these took place five or six weeks earlier, really nothing more than an apparently off-the-cuff remark that Stef made to Laurie. They were discussing plans after dinner, she was pouring them both a third glass of wine, and she said: 'Of course, we won't be doing this in India.'

'Oh?' Laurie raised his eyebrows, trying to sound casual.

She shrugged.

'No wine in India?' he pursued.

'Shouldn't think so,' she replied airily. 'It's probably forbidden, isn't it?' He said nothing. 'Isn't it?' she repeated, briefly meeting his eyes.

'It's...frowned upon,' he said. 'I've never seen alcohol at the hostel or the Institute, of course.'

'That doesn't mean anything,' she said, taking a deep draught from her glass as if making up for the abstinence to come. 'Nuns are notorious boozers.' She contemplated her wine and after a pause said, 'Anyway, it wouldn't do.'

Laurie was initially mystified by this statement, but then decided that she probably meant that drinking during a gathering in Jake's name would be disrespectful to him. He made no response, his eyes focused on the raindrops splashing on the window pane as he processed the information, trying to calculate what impact it would make on his scheme.

No further reference to the exchange was made in the following few days, however. Stef continued drinking normally – the usual daily routine of wine, gin, more wine, vermouth or sherry, more gin, or perhaps a few shots of vodka or whiskey as the evening progressed, etc., etc. But Laurie was girding himself for a speech he had been preparing for months. It was an essential component – *the* essential component – of his scheme. The first step had been last year's proposal to Stef that they should wind up the Jake Daniel Trust, and should do so with one final, culminating gift, a permanent reminder of the contribution that Jake had made to St Antony's Institute. Stef's response was sceptical and dismissive at first, but when she came to see that Laurie was being decisive in a way she hadn't seen for many years, she started to take his idea more seriously. She started to listen, and even to contribute. Their vision started to take form. There would be a whole new building, something that, according to Laurie, the school desperately needed: a supervised, well-equipped space where the kids could play safely. It would be Jake's lasting gift to the place where he himself had learned how to give, and it would be a final farewell. There might be a ceremony, perhaps attended by his family and friends. It could coincide with Jake's thirtieth birthday (this was Stef's idea).

And so they had assembled the pieces, enlisting the help of Miranda and Simon, communicating with Sister Mercy at the Institute, and receiving (many months later) her joyous blessing. Miranda christened it The Project. Funds were raised, contractors found, and an architect and designer recommended. Finally, Oliver stepped in and made the final contribution that would ensure the scheme went ahead.

Stef, at first resistant, became almost enthusiastic. Inevitably, there was a large residue of scepticism still in her, but Laurie began to allow himself to believe that she was finally waking from her long slumber. She continued to drink, of course, and continued to dwell in her cocooned, cotton-wool world – that was to be expected – but there was a hint of optimism in her, too; when they discussed the progress of their plans, he thought he detected a spark of interest in her eyes that he had not seen for a long, long time.

The only part of The Project that Laurie didn't share with the others, the part that was his and his alone, was his own add-on scheme: The Ultimatum. And now Stef had prepared the way with her casual aside.

He picked his time. He prepared dinner, as usual. It was rabbit pie, one of his specialities; afterwards, in his mind, he referred to the evening as the Rabbit Pie Summit.

'So you don't think you'll be drinking in India,' he said, as they finished their plates.

She didn't look at him, but instinctively reached for her glass.

'Probably not.'

'It wouldn't be right, would it?' he pressed.

She did not reply.

'Wouldn't be right for Jake.'

She twiddled the glass, her eyes darkening dangerously.

'But what about when it's over?'

Silence.

'What about then? And what about us?'

She looked up at the ceiling before finally uttering: 'What *about* us?'

'What will happen to *us*?'

'Why should anything happen to us? What are you talking about?'

'What will we do?

'We'll just carry on, I suppose.'

'No,' Laurie said quietly. 'No, we won't.'

Hearing the new, unfamiliar note of resolution in his voice, she finally met his gaze.

'That's not good enough,' he went on. 'Nor is it what Jake would have wanted.' He hated himself for saying this, which probably a complete fabrication, hated his uncharacteristic preachy tone, but he had to pull out all the stops now, it was all or nothing. 'We can't just "carry on". It's not going to work. We have to change.' She was looking at the ceiling again, seemed slightly unnerved. '*You* have to change. You can't continue like this, Stef. You. Have. To stop. Drinking.'

'I have to stop drinking,' she repeated in a monotone. He could almost hear her thoughts whirring, calculating, could tell that she was put out that her drinking habit was being verbalised, dragged into the open. That was not how they did things.

'Everybody thinks so,' he pressed on in a more reasonable tone. 'It's not doing us any good. It's certainly not doing you any good. I mean, look at you. Do you remember when you were fighting? When you were engaged? Committed? It seems another life now, but it wasn't so long ago. I'll never forget the fire you had. That's what I loved you for, Stef. You were a fighter, a warrior. Remember? Don't you think you might have despised the person you've become? The self-destructive you? The marginalised you? The fellow-traveller? Just waiting for – for what? A squalid end-

241

game. Mere oblivion. And it's agonising to see.'

She was stung now, with eyes burning.

'A *fellow-traveller*? How dare you? Do you think I want this?' she demanded. 'This. Was not. Part. Of the plan!'

'At last! She admits it!' Laurie exclaimed. 'That's a start, Stef!'

She looked away, back to the wall, visibly seething.

'You're so ... yeurgh!' she scowled. 'You don't understand, you've never understood...'

'Oh, don't give me that! Don't say I don't understand. I understand very well that you – and me – are going nowhere. And that you seem to content with that. You're happy to give in. To screw up our marriage after all we've been through together. After all the bloody struggle. Look – something terrible happened eight years ago, something dreadful and ghastly and I'm desperately sorry, but you're not just punishing the world for it, you're punishing yourself, you're punishing me, and you're sabotaging our marriage!'

She rose, glaring down at him. Then her expression changed. She suddenly looked exhausted. 'Oh, just ... leave me alone!' she said wearily.

'Yes, I will!' Laurie said. 'If that's what you really want, Stef. I will. Because if you don't stop, if you don't get your life back on the rails, then for us it's over!' She stared incredulously at him now, clearly aghast. Perhaps she had never heard him like this. 'You said you'll stop drinking in India. Good! Do it! But make that the time to stop forever. It's your call. If you want to just "carry on", then I'm out. Full stop. The end. You're on your own.'

Stef's expression was unreadable, but he thought – later, when he was running over the altercation in his mind – that it might just have shown a glimmer of a new respect for him. As if she was remembering that he too had been a fighter, not just a hanger-on. He could mean business. He was not going to be taken for granted any longer.

With leaden steps she walked towards the door to leave the room – abandoning, he noticed, her wine glass on the table. She turned to face him.

'You're ... absurd!' she said. She opened the door, then stopped again and turned, her face now twisted, distraught. 'Oh God... I didn't mean that,' she whispered. 'I really really ... *hate* myself sometimes!' Then she went, the door closing softly behind her.

'But I love you, Stef,' he shouted after her. 'Love you!' And then, more quietly: 'Why do you think I'm still here?'

The next morning Stef made no mention of their talk, and life seemed to continue as before. She continued to drink her usual amount, no more or less. But Laurie was pleased. He thought the ultimatum had gone quite well, all things considered. At least, it could have gone far worse. Whether or not he believed that she would stop, he couldn't say. And whether or not either of them believed he would stick to his guns and leave her if she continued to drink, he couldn't say either.

On the morning of their departure, when they were packing their suitcases in their separate rooms, Stef had gone downstairs for something and Laurie entered her room. He saw her closed suitcase and, on an impulse, lifted the lid and groped around inside. As he heard her climbing back upstairs, he pulled out from among her bras and books the bottle of gin. Entering the room, she saw him with the bottle and froze. There was a long pause as they both assessed the situation, then she simply took the bottle from him and replaced it among her clothes.

Rising to face him, she said in a level voice: 'Trust me. Just trust me, okay?'

He didn't say anything. There was no point. He had to assume that this was her way of dealing with the situation, her technique. He wasn't going to question it now. And anyway – that wasn't their style; it wasn't the way either had dealt with Stef's slide into stupefaction over the years. Their way was: no words; nothing any more explicit than was strictly necessary.

Now, Laurie is sitting in the dingy dark of the chai shop in Allapoorha's centre. He is reflecting on the events that have led them to this point, and to this state of their marriage. No further reference has been made to his final warning since they arrived in India, and he has not seen her drink. The bottle in her suitcase has remained unopened. There has been no acknowledgement and no objection. Everything implied, nothing articulated. *Story of our marriage*, Laurie thinks to himself. *Perhaps the story of every marriage. But ours especially. And especially since Jake left.*

Laurie's feelings towards Jake are, as they always have been, ambivalent. Of course, while he was alive, he felt a genuine, if qualified, fondness for him – how could he not, having assumed the paternal role for some twelve years? He watched him evolve from a complex, needy boy to a complex and somewhat contradictory adult and was there for all the phases in between. He was there for him. But no one could ever claim the relationship was an easy one. From the start, Jake was a clingy, petulant mummy's boy, and completely indifferent to his new father-figure. He just wanted his mother all the time: the lap, the soothing voice, the constant caress. Laurie was aware it was incumbent on him to bond – Stef kept telling him so – and he tried. But in the end he couldn't and didn't bond very successfully with him. He remembers the constant reminders of the distance between them, seeing Stef and Jake together at the kitchen table or on the sofa or out on a walk, whispering, chatting, communing together as if enclosed in a conspiracy that excluded all others. It was at these moments that Laurie felt the restless, painful jabs that told him he wasn't just a stranger to Jake, but outside Stef's world too.

Eventually, Laurie stopped trying. Or perhaps he stopped

caring. Anyway, he had his own children to look to. He always had a fierce attachment to Miranda and Simon that he never could feel towards Jake. Christ, he even felt a stronger attachment to the dog! Despite the protective sympathy he felt for this strange little boy who had lost his father before he was even born, he always had to remind himself to take this absence into account when coping with the boy's waywardness. And Laurie had it easy, comparatively; it was Stef who later bore the full brunt of Jake's erratic behaviour, notwithstanding the intense closeness of their relationship. Long before adolescence, Jake showed signs of distancing himself from his mother, asserting his independence, sometimes in the cruellest ways. Later he became a full-on rebel: cocky, jeering, even rancorous. No one was safe from his jibes, least of all Stef, who seemed to accept the sulky sarcasm and his implicit or explicit criticism of her values with a toleration that she never manifested for anyone or anything else. She rarely allowed herself to get angry but instead lived in a state of constant forbearance. Yes, she was occasionally despairing, but never bitter. Typically, she was able to rationalise it, even approved of it: he had an artistic temperament, she said, or (on another occasion) he was creating the space he needed to find himself.

There were physical changes, too: Jake's hair graduated from light orange to a gingery chestnut, and came more and more to resemble the photograph of his father, Michael, that Laurie had once unearthed in Stef's drawer on one of his occasional trawls. Perhaps the genes were taking over. He was growing into his father's image. Laurie found himself getting to know Michael through his stepson's morphing into him.

How ironic that the thing that ultimately bonded father and son was the manner of their deaths. Michael first, then Jake – both victims of violent crashes. In each case, they were the drivers, of course, but it was kind of spooky, son following the father he never met even unto the grave, even unto specific mode of expiry.

Inevitably, the wilder Jake became, the more the hybrid family split into its component parts. After periods of harmony with Miranda and Simon, there suddenly seemed a gulf between him and them, as he went through his pyromaniac phase, his drinking phase, his druggie phase, his vanishing phase. Miranda and Simon's own adolescence was comparatively uncomplicated, and relatively pain-free. Unsurprising, really, in the face of Jake's own extreme teenage years. But the gap widened vastly from that time. In appearance, of course, Laurie was visibly linked to Simon and Miranda just as Stef and Jake shared physical traits, but more significant were the distinctive character traits that divided the two factions: Laurie and his two were cautious and considered where Stef and Jake were impulsive and theatrical; the Johnsons were emotionally contained while the Daniels threw themselves into everything.

Jake was a handful, alright. Sometimes, though it was never spelled out, Laurie was convinced that Stef blamed him for her son's waywardness. It was surely his failure to establish a fulfilled relationship with Jake (she seemed to hint) that accounted for his impossible ways. And it's true that he always counted this as another personal failure on his part. As if he had any choice in the matter.

Then, something miraculous happened. Just when Laurie could see his relationship with Stef unravelling in the face of Jake's provocations and constant demands on their attention, they were drawn together again. As Jake became his own man, as he turned against his own mother, Stef and Laurie found themselves united again, this time on the outside of his charmed circle that now only seemed to contain himself alone. Jake's sojourn with the Daniel-Johnson clan – because, in retrospect, that's what it seemed, a temporary lodging with a make-do family – was suddenly over. He went his own way – to sixth-form college, eventually to India and university – and was, it seemed, set up in life. To his delight, Laurie felt readmitted into Stef's confidence, their partnership re-established, and they were once more a team.

But it was a brief interlude, as it transpired. For everything changed again when the boy disappeared forever from their lives. Laurie and Stef were once more prised apart, and more divided than ever.

Now that they are finally putting the boy to rest, forgiveness and reconciliation must surely follow. Stef will put away her own wayward self, pack it away out of sight, and they will find themselves again. That's the theory, anyway. Even if Laurie can't allow himself fully to believe it. From what he knows of Jake, the boy is likely to throw something up, some last surprise that will sabotage everything. It would be entirely in character.

Chapter 29 | The great shame

It is early evening at St Antony's Hostel, and on the veranda Cynthia and Oliver are absorbed in a silent game of cards, occasionally looking up from their hands to ponder the squawks and screeches issuing from the trees at the end of the garden. At home, Cynthia plays patience most evenings between six and seven and once a week she joins friends to play canasta or bridge. Oliver is not normally a cards man. At his house, he drinks whiskey in the evening, often while listening to Vivaldi or Bach or almost anything else that's Baroque. Sometimes, depending on his mood, he will read – biographies usually, or the poetry of Milton or Pope. When he is with Cynthia he won't have more than two tumblers of Scotch and soda in an evening – any more for some reason sets off a sneezing fit which she finds irritating. He has a small glass of whisky in front of him now from a supply he has brought in his suitcase; Cynthia has a tall glass of lime soda. An anti-mosquito coil burns steadily next to them, filling the air with its acrid but not unpleasant fumes.

She is about to issue a sharp prompt to Oliver, who thinks too long before playing a card, when they both hear footsteps and look up to see Miranda crossing the garden towards them.

'Hallo, dear. Where have you come from?' Cynthia enquires.

Miranda displays the bag of mangoes. 'The market. I just felt like getting out. Would you like one?'

'May I take one for later?' Cynthia asks.

'Of course.'

Cynthia plucks a mango from the bag and Miranda offers one to Oliver. He shakes his head. 'Too messy for me,' he declares. 'The stickiest of fruits. Though they call it the king of fruits. It's the national fruit of India, you know, and a valuable source of vitamins A, C and D. But there's no way to eat a mango if you want to preserve your dignity.'

'You don't need to worry about your dignity,' Cynthia tells him.

'Thank you!'

Miranda is unsure whether they are joshing or quarrelling. 'Any news of anything?' she asks.

'No, nothing new to report,' Cynthia answers.

Miranda sighs, eyebrows knotted.

'Is something the matter, dear?' Cynthia asks.

Miranda shrugs. 'Just impatient, I guess. Too much waiting around. And Stef is getting antsy that the boys haven't arrived.'

'What boys?'

'Men, I should say. Dougie and Jules.'

'Why is she worried about them?'

Miranda shrugs. 'I think she wants them to be there for the inauguration. I don't see why it makes much difference, myself. She keeps saying that Dougie must be here. But we're all getting a bit tetchy, aren't we, being here? We're all stuck in limbo. Nothing's happening.'

'I know what you mean,' Cynthia confides. 'It is a bit unsettling. But let's be positive. After all, it won't be long. And in the meantime we're having a pleasant holiday. Isn't it splendid just being here?'

'Is it?'

'Yes. India *is* rather splendid, despite everything.'

'But this isn't India, is it? I just wish it weren't so boiling hot all the time. I'm afraid it's getting to me. I can't think straight. It was crazy to come at the hottest time of year, pre-monsoon and everything. I just wish we'd thought it through when we were planning the whole thing.'

'What was it Forster said?' Cynthia says, leafing through the book in front of her. 'Here we are: "There is nothing in India but the weather – the alpha and omega of the whole affair."'

'E.M. Forster?' Miranda asks.

Cynthia holds up the cover of the book: *A Passage to India*. 'I'm re-reading it. He's always been one of my favourite writers.'

'I don't know,' Miranda says. 'I've been thinking more and more that the alpha and omega of India is poverty, inequality and social injustice.'

'Ah, yes. India's great shame,' Oliver declares, joining the conversation.

Miranda is surprised to hear him utter these words. She has assumed that he is on the side of the haves against the have-nots.

'I can't bear it,' she says. 'I suppose it's a dilemma that every rich traveller in a poor country must face. It's always the same question: How to be good? How do you reconcile your own wealth – and however poor you are in Europe, you're rich in comparison to most of the people here – how do you reconcile that with the everyday misery here?'

'Yes,' Cynthia agrees. 'Especially when you compare the paucity of everything here with all the things we have at home. All that *stuff*! You only need to look inside the houses here, well, looking through the windows anyway – they're usually bare, empty of everything.'

'And they're the lucky ones – lucky to have houses,' Miranda says. 'Some people haven't even got a home, like those orphans. They're desperate. Everyone's struggling. You can see it in all those rickshaw drivers fighting for every fare. It's maddening, but heartbreaking too.'

'Socialism might be a start,' Cynthia suggests.

'And yet isn't that what they've got here, in Kerala?' Miranda says. 'In name, anyway. Haven't you seen all the red flags, and the hammers and sickles?' Cynthia shakes her head in surprise. 'The state government is supposed to be socialist, though it's hard to see much evidence of it on the surface.'

'Well, the surface doesn't reveal much here anyway, does it, dear?' Cynthia says. 'Everything is so opaque. Who knows what's really going on?'

'Socialism would be an utter disaster,' Oliver observes. 'India is the entrepreneurial country *par excellence*. It's the paradise of small businesses.'

'Hmm,' Cynthia wrinkles her nose. 'Anyway, I do think that sexual equality would be a significant step forward.'

'For sure,' Miranda says. 'But what is definitely not needed is more religion.'

'Oh, I don't know. Do you remember that statue of Mother Teresa we saw in ... where was it?' Cynthia asks Oliver. 'Outside that big cathedral? It was in a glass case at the side of the street,' she tells Miranda, 'and she had an infant in her arms, thin as a spider, with blue skin. I thought it was very moving. Don't you think that the Mother Teresas of India and all the other do-gooders are actually doing good?'

'You're ignoring all the propaganda that invariably accompanies their good works,' Oliver interposes. 'It would be instructive to do an audit, see what long-term benefits Mother Teresa actually accomplished in Kolkata. A museum, perhaps?'

'Oh, you're such a cynic,' Cynthia tells him. 'Individuals *can* make a difference.'

He unleashes a throat-clearing. 'Well, I agree that life is hard for some people here, but things may not be quite as bad as they seem to us westerners.'

'You can't ignore the misery and deprivation,' Miranda says. 'That's pretty plain to see.'

'On the contrary,' says Oliver. 'I'm constantly surprised by how *un*-miserable people are here. Even when they appear to have so little, most people seem to be fairly content.'

'*Content?*'

'Yes. Haven't you noticed? You only have to look at the orphans at the school, or even the beggars on the streets. They put on a sad face when they see us, but when no one's looking they're having a whale of a time.'

'Oliver, you're exaggerating,' Cynthia chides.

'You can't really believe that,' Miranda says.

'Certainly I do. Look at him.' He points to the mange-infected dog that usually loiters outside the hostel entrance and has now wandered into the garden, contemplating them mournfully from a safe distance. Large patches of its coat are missing, exposing livid red sores on pink skin. 'He's got a rotten life,' Oliver continues. 'He's the lowest of the low. Yet you see him or dogs like him cavorting about without a care in the world. Once they're distracted from their scratching, of course.'

'Oliver: please stop,' Cynthia remonstrates. 'Are you really comparing that dog with impoverished Indians?'

'Well, I suppose I'm comparing a certain attitude to life. Or the resilience of the spirit. Or...'

'You do talk rubbish,' Cynthia interrupts. 'You remind me of that absurd Urdu proverb that Forster quotes: "What does unhappiness matter when we are all unhappy together?"'

'We must agree to disagree on that topic,' Oliver says. 'Right now I believe it's time for my afternoon constitutional.'

'What about our game of cards?' Cynthia asks.

'We'll have to resume later,' he tells her, consulting his watch. 'I must do my walk. Won't be long.'

Cynthia looks at her own watch. 'You're *so* punctual,' she says. Oliver beams, and she turns to Miranda. 'I'm afraid he takes that as a compliment.'

After Oliver has donned his hat and marched out of the gates,

Cynthia sighs, 'I apologise on his behalf, Miranda. Sometimes I wonder what planet he's living on. Actually, a lot of what he says is intended to provoke.'

'I kind of gathered that,' Miranda says.

'He does love a good argument. And I'm afraid I don't usually rise to the bait. He's probably missing the kind of weighty man-to-man discussions he has with his friends in the Lodge.'

'Lodge?'

'Whoops. Yes, he's a mason. I probably shouldn't have mentioned that. It's just a boys' thing really. They meet up once a month, decide where to allocate their charitable funding and drink a lot. He looks after their accounts.'

'Ah – he's their accountant.' Miranda hesitates, then continues: 'You know, he gave me the impression that he was rather a top-flight accountant in the City before he retired. In fact he told me that he's worked all over the place – New York and Hong Kong.'

'Really, dear?' Cynthia doesn't look particularly impressed. 'I find the world of money completely inaccessible to me, to be honest. It's just not my culture.'

'Nor mine. That Indian gentleman seemed to know about him, though, didn't he? Have you found out any more?'

Cynthia shakes her head. 'I'll find out eventually. I'll let you know, I promise. As long as it's legal!'

'He said something else to me the other night – the night of the big dinner. He seemed to know something about Michael.'

Cynthia looks up sharply, suddenly interested. 'Michael? Stephanie's friend?'

'Partner. Jake's dad.'

Cynthia tuts. 'Whatever he was. That man.'

'He said he didn't want to spread rumours, but I should ask you about him.'

'He said that? I can't think what he meant,' Cynthia says. 'I didn't know the man. Well – I met him once or twice, but I can't say I actually got to know him.'

Miranda's brow furrows, then she shrugs. She suddenly feels exhausted. She can feel the sweat flowing in rivulets down her neck and under her shirt and wonders for a moment whether it's possible that, for westerners, this subcontinental climate is absolutely antithetical to rational thought. 'I need to have a shower,' she tells Cynthia, rising to her feet. 'The third today. I'd have one every half-an-hour if I wasn't worried about water shortages!'

'You *are* a good girl,' Cynthia says. 'You're the only person I can really talk to here – the only person apart from Oliver, anyway. And the only person I can talk to *about* him. I can't talk to my daughter, of course. That's completely out of the question...'

Miranda smiles, picks up her bag of mangoes and leaves her step-grandmother to her cards and her Forster. Stef with her Woolf, Cynthia with her Forster – the two of them are closer to each other than they like to think, Miranda muses. Both living in an imagined past, the one where they feel most comfortable, and which provides the lenses that best suit their vision of life. Miranda doesn't exclude herself from this syndrome, but doesn't completely buy into it either. Life, for her, is in the here and now. She has given up on Hesse's *Siddhartha* – she has always found more relevance in the ambiguous and complicated world of *sansara*, the material world, than in listening to the over-simplified, stripped-down wisdom of the river. That's just romance.

Chapter 30 | Art in the afternoon

After taking her third cold shower of the day, Miranda picks up her Hesse and joins Simon and Esme in the alcove on the top terrace. It is five o'clock in the afternoon, the cicadas are buzzing loudly, and conversation is sparse. Esme is reading, sitting in profile on the terrace wall in her wide-brimmed straw hat and wearing a lacy, burgundy-coloured blouse above a wide, white cotton skirt. Simon is drawing her against a background of ragged creepers and trees.

Simon's busy hand movements are in direct contrast to Esme's stillness. Miranda takes a seat to one side of her brother in order to observe his rapid act of creation. It is something she has only rarely witnessed in the last few years. She used to love watching him draw, seeing his thick black graphite pencil flying over the paper as if possessed. His strokes are decisive, he rubs and smudges, brushes the page every few seconds, and transforms the white space into recognisable shapes and images. And it transforms *him* too. Usually quietly spoken, unwilling to put himself forward, when he draws he becomes a master: in command of the page, wielding his skills, able to create or – with a finger or eraser – destroy at will. Miranda would feel a part of her fulfilled if she were able to enter into that esoteric rite. Why would you need anything else, she thinks, when you can magic up your own world? It makes her feel barren.

Although Miranda is generally satisfied with her life, with the choices she has made and the point she has reached, she is not without regrets. Not being artistic is one of them. She might have had culinary skills, or a musical bent, a talent for garden design or carpentry, but she feels earthbound and dull in the presence of creation.

Regarding Esme too – so self-possessed, simultaneously calm and dynamic – Miranda feels other, more mundane pangs of inadequacy. Esme is graceful in a way that Miranda, in her own perception, can never be. She appears to be comfortable in her own skin. And there is something else – Miranda can't quite put a finger on it. Is it a kind of physicality? Miranda has never thought of herself as a sensual being. Yes, she has had lovers, she has even reached the heights of ecstasy, but her sexual side is locked away, only brought out when required. Esme, on the other hand, seems to wear it on the outside, a cool everyday sensuality like a soft flowing dress. It's as if she has an instinctive connection with the physical world that Miranda seems to lack. Maybe it is missing in most people, she has never really noticed. Its presence in front of her now makes her wonder what her own life might have been like, how different it might have been, if she were easily able to attract the looks, admiration, friends and lovers that she imagines Esme can. Sometimes she feels a richer life is there, just out of reach.

Miranda herself had a late start to her sexual life. She was in no hurry, and she certainly had no wish to give up her innocence casually, the way some of her friends did. It has been satisfactory, she reckons, if not exactly scintillating. But is that good enough? She is sure that Esme has regular, sizzling, scintillating sex.

She has had three significant romantic relationships, each one cautiously embarked upon, each relatively long-lasting, and each eventually terminated by her on the grounds of future incompatibility. She wants to bear children, but she must be absolutely sure of having the right partner before committing herself. And if the right partner has not made himself known by the time she hits thirty-five, she has decided, then she will be a single mother.

She wonders about Simon, still energetically sketching. He has never discussed his girlfriends with her. They have never had that sort of relationship. That would be another regret. She would have liked a confidant in the family, someone to share more, and she would have liked a greater insight into Simon's world. He is very much his own person with his own precise agenda. Some might view him as introverted, buttoned up even, but she sees him as a kindred spirit alive to the world. The fact that contact between the two of them has only been sporadic in recent years is irrelevant; she's not sure how that happened, but now she feels secure again in his comradeship. Their journey to India, if nothing else, has cemented their sibling solidarity.

There is something about him that is needling her, however. Yesterday, when he briefly went up to his room leaving his sketchbook on the table, she unthinkingly picked it up and leafed through it, and was astonished to find numerous drawings of Jake. They showed him in different attitudes, lounging or reclining, looking out of the page at the viewer or away into the distance, his fleshy face turned to one side, his wavy hair straggling over his neck or encased in a motorcycle helmet. His expression is smirking in some, more winsomely questioning in others. They seem to be recent sketches, as they are interspersed with others showing Indian birds, trees and buildings. She has wanted to ask Simon about them but has not found the right moment, and now she thinks she probably won't. As soon as she saw the imaginary portraits she felt guilty, as if she was intruding on his diary. Are sketchbooks private? He never minded her leafing through them in the past.

She recalls the period when Simon, as a little boy, was spending all his time in Jake's company. He seemed to have fallen completely under his step-brother's spell. She remembers feeling excluded and drifting away from both of them. But though she was hurt by Simon's new attachment, one that seemed deliberately to shut her out, she soon adapted, hooking up with a clique of girls at her school. And then things changed again. Jake, who had never confided in her or even paid her much notice, started to take an interest in her. First of all (she must have been about fourteen) she became aware of him staring at her while they were watching TV or over the dinner table. 'What's the matter?' she would ask, but he shook his head innocently as if he didn't know what she was referring to. A couple of times she noticed him staring at her chest. It was shortly after Miranda began wearing a bra, and the way he looked suggested he had only just become aware of her breasts.

He was suddenly paying more attention to her. One afternoon, while Simon was at some school event, Jake entered her bedroom and sat with her for a while. She was writing in her diary, which she quickly put away, but he noticed and asked her about it. 'It's just something I like doing,' she responded.

'What do you write?'

'What I've done, what I've been watching and listening to, stuff like that.'

'Every day?'

'Yes.'

'That's a bit weird,' he said

'Why?'

'Can I read it?'

'Of course not.'

'Why not?'

'It's private.'

He didn't persist, but something about his questions made her even more careful to keep the diary well hidden when she wasn't in her room. She placed a scrap of paper on it so that she would know if someone had found her hiding place and opened it. The paper was always exactly where she had placed it, but she still had her suspicions.

Jake started coming into Miranda's room more often, usually

when Simon was out. 'He's so babyish,' he told her. 'He just wants to play stupid kids' games.'

He began to discuss books with her, which was odd because she never saw him reading. He seemed to know a lot about the books that she pored over, and asked her opinion of the authors. He seemed to know everything. Miranda felt flattered, and obscurely proud of this new intimacy. They shared jokes, exchanged opinions. They played games, too. At first, they would play card games, then, when these got boring, Jake would make up dice games, in which they would have to do dares according to the throw of the dice – silly things like stealing a biscuit from the kitchen, drinking water from the wrong side of the glass, moving bookmarks in Stef's books or rearranging Laurie's shelves. It was during one of these dice games that Jake suggested a variation. He said, 'Let's play that if I throw a one, I have to kiss you for one second, if it's a two, for two seconds, three for three seconds, four for four seconds, five for five seconds, six for six seconds. And when you throw, you have to kiss me the same.'

'What do you mean, "kiss"?' she wanted to know.

'Like this' he said, kissing the back of his hand.

'On our hands?'

'No – a proper kiss. On our mouths. You know how to kiss, don't you?'

'Of course I do.' She had never actually kissed anyone on the mouth, but she had seen it done on TV and was curious, so she agreed to try. She had her doubts at first, but she thought it was okay because Jake wasn't her real brother. They played it a few times. She didn't mind. They didn't use their tongues or anything – that would have been gross – but she found it interesting.

Then Jake got bored of that and proposed something else: a tying-up game. She would tie him up and he would try to escape, then he would tie her up and she would try to escape. They did that a few times; he always managed to wriggle out of her knots, but she rarely succeeded in freeing herself from his. Once, after he had secured her hands behind her back in one of his tightest knots, she became aware of him looking at her strangely. Then he began unbuttoning her shirt. She told him to stop, but he didn't, he carried on until her shirt was around her shoulders and her pink-spotted bra exposed. She struggled hard, but couldn't release herself. He stared transfixed at her breasts. Then he touched them. His touch was soft and tentative. She protested, she was blushing bright red, she threatened to scream, call for Laurie who was in his study in the basement, but they both knew she wouldn't, it would just be too shameful.

Eventually, after what seemed like a long time during which he continued to stare and prod at her breasts, all the time making humming noises while she screwed her eyes tight shut, he rebuttoned her shirt and released her. She could hardly raise her eyes to look at him, but whispered fiercely: 'Go now! Get out of my room.'

'Why?' he asked, all innocence.

'Just go!' she hissed, her face still red, but now as much with fury as embarrassment. And with that he shrugged and left without another word, and that was the last time he came into her room.

She was never able to erase that event from her memory. It was strange, shameful, and poisoned her relationship with Jake from that point on. Now, years later, she thinks she has forgiven him his abuse of her, though can't work out why. Why was Jake always forgiven? Why is he still?

Simon was never aware of any of these goings on, though Miranda often longed to share them with him, to confess this aberration in which she was as guilty as Jake. But the right time never came, and now she knows she probably never will tell him. Would he ever want to hear it?

As for Jake, he was moving on, anyway, spending less time with his step-siblings, more time by himself. It was shortly afterwards that his interest in lighting fires began – little conflagrations that he would make in the garden or the park or an alley near their home. One day smoke began seeping out from under his bedroom door and Stef rushed in to discover a fire that he had lit in a wastepaper basket and was now getting out of control. She went ballistic, started yelling and swearing, and doused the fire with a tub of water from the bathroom. She later exonerated her Baby Jesus, of course; later, Miranda even heard her describing the incident to someone on the telephone and laughing about it. She sounded almost proud. She didn't find his next trick so amusing, though, when he took to roaming, travelling all over the place, sometimes hitching across the country and camping wild.

Miranda rises from her seat, pulling her shirt and cotton trousers off her sticky skin. She feels tired and headachy. It's as if they are locked down in this place, prisoners of the heat. 'I'm going to lie down,' she says. The others nod and she leaves.

Pulling shut the door of her room, Miranda curls up on her bed and feels vulnerable, the way she did all those years ago. She wonders how Esme would have reacted to Jake's nasty games. Probably a lot more forthrightly. Surely Esme, of all people, was a match for him. When she'd had enough she simply gave him the boot. At least, Miranda assumes that's the way it happened.

Esme... emanating strength. Everyone loves Esme. Even Simon isn't immune. Miranda has noted the approving glances and, even stranger, the sneaky, sideways leers that her normally reserved and reticent brother has allowed himself. And then there is Stef, fawning and flattering. Miranda can't imagine Stef ever singing her – Miranda's – praises or fawning over her the way she does over Esme. But Stef has fixed ideas on everyone. Once she decides she likes someone, that's it: they're in her team and can do no wrong. Of course, Miranda is well aware of Stef's opinion of *her*. Not for the first time, she wonders whether Stef always disliked her, or whether the antipathy developed over time.

Well, it won't matter much soon. Once all this is over, and Miranda has prised her father out of Stef's grasp, Stef won't matter very much at all...

She gets up and walks to the window. In the garden, the Indian man in the baggy white suit is there, the one Cynthia mentioned. He is absorbed in his newspaper, unfurled on the table in front of him next to a teapot on a tray. A few feet away, in the shade of a bush, she sees the mangy dog that Oliver took as an illustration of a poor man's carefree state of living-in-the-moment. It is prostrate, apparently asleep, but twitching nervously, and panting fast as it contends with the afternoon's relentless heat. Man and dog are ignoring each other.

On an impulse, Miranda crosses the room and, locking the door behind her, rushes downstairs. She hesitates for an instant before entering the garden, then, stepping onto the lawn, casually walks to the table a few feet from the one unoccupied by the Indian man. He looks up at her approach and she offers him a cordial smile. He nods back politely then returns to his newspaper. She sits down, and a minute or two later Francis appears and she orders an apple juice. She glances at the Indian man, wondering how best to engage with him. The direct approach is probably best, she decides, so she waits for a couple of minutes after her apple juice arrives, then leans towards him.

'Excuse me, sorry to bother you...' He turns an obliging face to her, showing his greying moustache and grey, carefully combed hair around his ears. He has quick eyes behind clinical steel-rimmed spectacles, and she guesses him to be in his early sixties. 'I understand you know Oliver. What an amazing coincidence!'

His face lights up, suddenly animated.

'Mr Moorland? Yes, I am a great admirer! It was such a pleasure for me to discover he is staying here.' His voice is thin and surprisingly high-pitched.

'Moorland? Do you mean Oliver Maitland?'

'Oh... yes. That's it! Maitland. Oliver Maitland, yes. Such a clever man.'

'I didn't know he's so famous!'

'Famous! Well, in his field, yes. You could say he is famous.'

'His field of accountancy?'

'Accountancy, yes. He is a bit of a wizard, you know,' the man laughs, looking uncomfortable now. 'But I suppose not that famous, no. If you are in my profession he is quite well known. He made quite a name for himself when he worked in Hong Kong a few years ago.'

'Are you an accountant?' Miranda asks.

'Me? No, no. I am retired.'

'What from?'

'Well, my work was in banking. Finance, you know. And various business affairs. In Mumbai. It is the business capital of India, you know. Do you like India?'

'Yes,' Miranda answers. 'I've never been to Mumbai, though.'

'Oh, it is very big. Very rich, you see? Full of millionaires. And billionaires!' He laughs uneasily, and Miranda realises that he is acutely embarrassed. He suddenly pushes his chair back and, folding up his newspaper, gets to his feet. 'Well, it is a great honour to meet you, madam. Please give my regards to Mr Maitland. Thank you.' And he is away, walking fast across the grass to the hostel gate.

Miranda sips her lemonade, mystified. What a strange man! What could he have been feeling embarrassed about? And how, if he's such a fan, could he have forgotten Oliver's surname?

She reaches for her mobile phone and starts tapping.

Chapter 31 | A true likeness

In the alcove, Simon and Esme are remotely aware of Miranda's steps receding down the corridor and the sound of her bedroom door closing. Simon's attention is on the white pad supported on his knees and the image taking shape on it, while Esme is focused on the page of her book. Simon's fluttering hand and the circling flies are once more the only movements. After a few minutes Simon holds up his sketch and regards it appraisingly. He looks across at Esme who remains immobile, absorbed in reading.

'Not there yet,' he mutters to himself. Esme looks up and straightens her back, pulling her shoulders back.

'Where are you trying to get to?'

'Somewhere that … to a point where it chimes. Something that's really recognizable. Unmistakably you.'

'Does it matter?' Esme asks. 'As long as it's an okay drawing? Does it have to resemble the subject?'

Simon rises his eyebrows. 'That's like saying does it matter if you have a true or a false image of someone, or true or faulty vision. Of course it matters. That's the point of the exercise.'

'So you don't believe in art for art's sake?'

'Well, yes, sometimes. But if you're interested in reality, accurate representation is the whole *raison d'être*! For me, anyway. And I don't call it art, it's just me trying to nail something, I guess. Nail it down and get it right.' After a pause, he continues, still contemplating the image: 'I suppose if I were a proper artist, I might indulge myself more, isn't that what art for art's sake is? I'm not ruling it out. But I'm trying to do something specific, achieve a true likeness. It's a matter of technique more than anything.'

'I suppose it would only be a true likeness in your eyes, anyway,'

Esme remarks. 'Somebody else might draw me completely differently.'

'Fair enough,' Simon says. 'Everyone will have a different version of you.'

'Do you draw a lot at home?'

'No,' he replies. 'Haven't done it for a while.'

'So why have you got the urge now?'

He shrugs. 'It's something to do. Nothing much else to do, stranded here, stuck in the doldrums. And it's better than thinking all the time. Remembering. Better to focus on what's in front of you, what you can see. And it's relaxing.'

'Like yoga, then,' Esme says.

'That's right,' Simon agrees. 'It's cathartic.'

There is a sound of voices and Esme looks down onto the garden 'I thought Miranda was going to lie down,' she comments. Ian leans over the parapet and sees his sister talking to Mr Pereira. He watches them for a moment then returns to his pad.

'Have you drawn your sister?' Esme asks.

He shakes his head. 'Not for years.'

'Why not?'

He shrugs again. 'Maybe she's too familiar to me. 'You're more interesting.'

'Am I?'

'Yes. You're a bit of a mystery – in my eyes, anyway. Plus you're a good sitter.'

'Mystery is in the eye of the beholder,' Esme says, smiling. 'Anyway, it's not exactly difficult. Though normally I hate being stared at. I have to erase you from my consciousness and forget you're there.'

'So you're erasing me...'

She laughs. 'It's a sort of yoga technique.'

Simon wonders whether she really hates being stared at, or

whether a part of her enjoys it. 'Can you erase me for a bit longer?' he asks. 'I want to try another.'

'Sure. My diary's pretty free right now.'

She resumes reading, and he stares at her for a long time before putting pencil to a fresh sheet on his pad. As he draws, the question occurs to him how it would come out if he drew her not so much as he sees her as how he views her, how he responds to her, as if he were looking inside her. He has no idea, because, yes, she is a mystery. Once again the old question boomerangs back: how did she and Jake fit together? How did they function? And how did that happen? Easy to see why he should fall for her, she's a catch all right. He didn't deserve her. But what did she see in him?

He puts down some tentative preliminary lines, then pauses. He is pleased that he and Esme seem to be easier with each other now. He's on the point of asking her aloud about her relationship with Jake but stops himself in time – he really doesn't want to bring Jake into this private space of theirs right now. There is no place for him in this charmed circle. Though he can imagine him hovering somewhere on the outside, watching with ironic amusement.

Instead of bringing up the subject of Jake, he asks: 'Have you ever been sketched before?'

She looks up from her page, screwing up her face as she casts back into her memories.

'A girlfriend at school used to draw me sometimes. She drew everybody.'

'You're such a great subject.' She turns down her lips and frowns, as if to say that she can't understand why she is a great subject. Then a mischievous imp gatecrashes Simon's mind, plants words in his mouth. 'Have you ever been drawn nude?'

She laughs. 'Definitely not.'

He is staring directly at her.

'Would you like to be?'

She laughs again. 'Er...'

'I'd love to have a go. At a nude portrait of you, I mean.'

She looks unsure what to make of this. 'You're joking, right?'

'Serious! Would you like me to?'

'Er...'

'We could do it in my room. Or yours.'

'I don't think so, Simon.'.

'Oh. Why not?'

'I ... just don't think it would be a very good idea.'

Their eyes lock for a moment; eventually he smiles and says: 'Okay.'

She continues to regard him with an amused but doubtful frown, then shakes her head and returns to her book. After another minute, though, she snaps it shut, swings her legs onto the terrace. 'I think that's enough sitting for me, anyway. I'm going downstairs.'

Simon puts down his pad and says: 'Esme – I hope you haven't misconstrued anything.'

'No!' she says, too quickly. Then: 'I don't know; have I?'

'I just thought we could be friends.'

'Friends? Well, that's what we are.'

'And it might add a bit of interest to our time here.'

Now she has a definite grasp of his drift and looks impatient, irate even. 'No. I don't think so. Don't be stupid.' And with that, she is gone.

Simon contemplates the scant lines of his newly started sketch and frowns. *Blown it. Dumb or what? Anyway, it's crap. What is any of this for, this attempt at art? What am I trying to prove? That I'm better than Jake, who Stef said was an artist but never created anything?* His eyes return to where Esme was sitting. *It was a really bad idea. And it wouldn't have worked.* Then he smiles faintly to himself. *It was worth asking, though, if only to see her reaction.*

Chapter 32 | The wedding venue

Stef's quiet vigil in the soft, grey, early morning air is disturbed by a footfall, and she turns to see Esme emerge onto the veranda behind her. She is wearing a skimpy vest and leggings, her face scrubbed, her hair pulled tight back. She halts to contemplate the cool serenity of the garden, her posture strong and erect. She hasn't noticed Stef, but seeing her eyes sweep slowly towards her as they survey the scene, Stef decides she ought to signal her presence before Esme discovers her unbidden. She doesn't want to take her by surprise, or make her think she's being spied on.

So Stef clears her throat and Esme's eyes immediately find her, though without the least display of surprise or shock, almost as if she has been expecting to find Stef here at this early hour.

'Good morning, Stef.' Her voice is hushed, as if reluctant to ripple the morning's fragility.

'Hallo, darling! Have you come to keep me company?'

Esme walks over and leans her weight on the veranda post.

'I had no idea you were here. It's early.'

'I couldn't sleep, so I decided to make a virtue of insomnia and enjoy the early-morning coolness. Do you have the same problem?'

Esme shakes her head. 'I normally sleep okay, but I like to rise early for yoga. And then I looked out and thought I'd come down to sniff the air in the garden. And to refill my water jug.'

Stef sniffs, then inhales deeply. 'Certainly feels good to me. Actually this is the only time of day when you can breathe properly!'

Esme offers a tight smile. 'How are you feeling?' she asks.

Stef hesitates. That question again.

'Same, same. Waiting, waiting. That's all one does here. It's like being stuck in the middle of the sea without any wind in your sails. Have you contacted Dougie?'

'I tried, but it just rang. I sent him a text and an email,'

'Belt and braces, eh?'

Esme nods.

Stef looks sulky, then changes subject: 'Did you hear Simon at the welcome dinner? The sod. After Oliver's little encomium – he made a snide comment. So insensitive and rude. I know Oliver is a little OTT but it was good of him, don't you think? He didn't have to say anything.'

'Simon can be very... thoughtless.'

'The speech was complete cobblers, of course, but at least he tried. Most people have rallied round. Anyway, none of it matters. I don't give a toss about any of them. Because, in the end, I'll come out on top!'

Esme looks quizzical.

'I'll have the book, darling! That's what matters!'

'Ah.' Esme pushes herself away from the veranda post. 'Right. Well, I must get on with my sun salutation.'

The older woman looks up at her, her expression miffed, then resigned. Her facial expressions change by the second, Esme notices. Sometimes she has the face of a lost girl. Now she sighs and smiles wistfully. 'Your yoga. Of course. You're very dedicated.'

'I try! Anyway, see you later. Take care.' And she is gone.

Stef continues to sit for a while, then, rummaging in her top pocket, produces a packet of cigarettes. She lights one, breathes in, and breathes out a long jet of smoke. A sudden metallic explosion cracks the air, making her jump, but it's just the first clang of the temple bell. The muezzin has already done his thing. More clangs follow, each one making her flinch. After a while the tolling stops and is replaced by a snaking thread of song issuing from the same direction. Everything is so busy here, she thinks: nothing is still for long. When it's not voices and engines it's drumming and clanging. Where is there peace in this unquiet land? Jake must have heard the same constant clamour, but he probably enjoyed it.

A few minutes later Stef pushes open her bedroom door. The room is semi-dark, the only movement the soporific, cyclical motion of the ceiling fan. Laurie is lying on his side on the edge of the bed, an expression of innocent satisfaction on his face. He snuffles, grimaces, twitches. Is he dreaming? No, it's a fly settled on his cheek. She doesn't bother to wave it away, it will only come back. She half-opens the blind, enough to allow her to look out, and settles into the wicker chair by the window. With the light leaking in and the temple music vying with the birdsong, Laurie slowly emerges into consciousness. He groans, blinks his eyes open, and stares at Stef with surprise.

'Hallo, there!' he says.

'Hallo.'

'Been up long?'

'A while.'

Reaching for his glasses, he puts them on and clasps his hands behind his head on the pillow, gazing across the room at her. Her face is turned towards the window.

'So what's the plan for today?' he asks.

'I thought I might go to the school.'

'Oh? Have you heard from them?' She shakes her head. 'Do they know you're going?'

'Not unless their god has informed them of the fact. I've only just decided. And they can't bloody object. I just want to spend a bit of time with the kids.'

'Shall I come?'

'No.'

His doubtful look seems to be saying, *You'll just get in the way, they won't welcome you hanging around*, but he refrains from comment, instead pushing back his sheet and hoisting himself to his feet.

He dresses quickly and goes down for breakfast, allowing Stef to shower and change without rush. Half an hour later she is descending the stairs. From the lobby she hears Oliver's booming voice and Laurie's quieter tones in unequal conversation in the restaurant. She strides past without looking in and heads outside, out of the hostel grounds, past the two beggars in the lane outside the gates. They hardly acknowledge the Europeans any more, only half-heartedly extending a palm as they hurry by.

In the lane she sees saffron-beaked mynahs and black-breasted bulbuls hopping nervously about in the dust. She crosses the square in front of the church, eyeing the trickle of people converging on its open doors, and enters the school gates. Sister Grace, the stern young nun who was there on their first visit, is in the office. She's talking on a mobile phone and looks vaguely embarrassed when Stef enters and stands in front of the desk, patiently waiting. Casting suspicious looks at her, the nun ends her call and listens to Stef's request to assist in one of the classes. Somewhat unexpectedly, she gives a curt nod and gestures wordlessly for her to carry on up to the classrooms.

Feeling almost deflated at being denied a confrontation, Stef makes her way to the teaching block and looks into the classrooms on the second floor. There is no sign of the girl with the green eyes. Selecting one of them at random, she enters and asks the short, elderly nun presiding if she can join in and help out in some way. Stef is not sure if the nun understands her but at least she makes no objection, waggling her head vaguely before turning back to the little girl next to her, concentrating on slicing through a length of material with long sewing scissors. Stef finds a thin-faced boy on his own, pulls up one of the miniature chairs scattered around the tables and squeezes herself into it next to him. The boy, who looks ten or eleven years old and has a withered leg, looks briefly alarmed, then reverts to what he was doing as if she isn't there. At first she simply watches him, then, slowly, without a word exchanged, she begins to hand him a spool of thread or a thimble or a tape-measure, until eventually he allows her to help him cut and sew. The room is hot and dimly lit, with only small, high windows admitting the air and light, but Stef feels surprisingly at ease, moving from child to child. The quiet satisfaction it affords her is a revelation. Apart from some initial lingering stares, the children seem relaxed in her presence, devoid of any preconceptions or prejudices and not treating her any differently from the nuns. They cannot communicate verbally but this does not seem to be a hindrance. One little boy of four or five climbs unasked into her lap, producing in her an unexpected swirl of emotion. She wonders if Jake worked here, in this room, and how he interacted with these tethered scraps of humanity. If only she could know.

After an hour or so, Stef looks up to see, through the open door of an adjacent classroom, the strange woman she and Laurie encountered on their first visit. She is crouched down, brandishing a bundle of twigs that she is using to sweep the floor, creating billows of dust in the sunlight. As their eyes meet, the woman's face lights up once more and she assumes the same radiant smile as before. Stef wonders if she might be half-witted and smiles uncertainly back. She is about to go over to speak to her when she feels a tap on the shoulder. Sister Margaret is standing beside her, looming tall. 'Mrs Daniels! You are here!'

Feeling awkward in the child's chair, Stef struggles to her feet.

'I thought I would come to lend some assistance. Is that alright?'

'Certainly. It is fine. But please do not interfere or get in the way of the teaching. The hard work of the sisters is very important!'

'No, of course not. I don't want to be in anybody's way.'

'No doubt. You are very generous with your time.'

'I have nothing better to do.'

'God will bless you.'

'I'm a teacher too, you know,' Stef volunteers.

Sister Margaret looks only marginally impressed. 'Yes?'

'Yes. Older children. Or rather, students. University students.'

'Oh,' the nun smiles with a hint of condescension, 'that is very different.'

She is about to hurry on her way when Stef says: 'Sister Margaret! Who is that woman over there?' She turns to point to the smiling woman in the next room, but the woman is no longer there.

'Which woman are you referring to?'

'Oh, no one. She's gone. Actually there was something else I wanted to ask you.'

'Yes?' The nun is looking a bit impatient now.

'I was wondering if there's anyone who was in the school when Jake was here.'

'Yes.'

Stef is agreeably surprised by the answer. 'Can I speak to them?'

'Certainly. There is just one sister who was here at that time. Sister Solace. She has been here for thirty-one years.'

'Does she speak English?'

'Yes. But she is deaf.'

'Oh.'

'It is alright. She will understand you. Sometimes we think that she is only as deaf as she wants to be!' She laughs gaily at her own joke.

'Where can I find her, please?'

The nun consults her watch. 'At this time she will be in Room 3C, on the third floor. She is attending the handicapped children in year five.'

Sister Margaret turns and leaves. Stef pats the young boy beside her, who continues with his task without a look or a word to her. She hurries to the staircase at the end of the corridor, ascends a level, and passes three doors until she finds one with 3C scrawled in black paint over the lintel.

Inside are half a dozen severely handicapped children, all wearing bibs, with two nuns helping them to eat a porridge-like substance from plastic bowls. One of them is Sister Charity, who has been previously introduced to Stef, the other is old and hump-backed, with sunken cheeks, milky eyes and thin white hair pulled back behind her habit. She seems to have no teeth.

Stef stoops next to her and says in a raised voice: 'Sister Solace?' The nun turns quickly and squints up at her with an old woman's scowl. Her face wrinkles up in an unspoken enquiry.

'Are you Sister Solace?' Stef repeats.

The nun cocks a gnarled hand to her ear. 'Yes?'

'I am Stephanie Daniel.'

The nun grimaces.

'I am Stephanie Daniel,' Stef repeats, louder.

In a strangled, heavily accented voice that is difficult to understand, the nun says, 'I know who you are.'

'Oh!' Stef is taken aback. 'Did you know my son?'

'What?'

'My son. Did you know him? Jake Daniel.'

The nun looks disgusted. 'I know your son.'

'Do you remember him?' Stef asks, delighted.

'I know him.'

'Can you tell me about him please? Anything.'

'What?'

'What do you remember about him? About Jake? What did he do here? What was his job?'

The nun continues to look disgusted. 'No good,' she says.

'Sorry?'

'No good.' She turns back to the child she is feeding and brusquely pushes a spoonful of the porridge-like meal into his mouth, which she immediately wipes with the cloth held in her other hand.

'Who is no good?' Stef asks. 'Sister Solace?'

'Your son. He is not a good man,' the nun announces, without looking up.

'What are you saying? Why was he no good?' She sees Sister Charity look over at them and realises her voice sounds shrill and desperate.

Sister Solace doesn't answer or look up.

'Sister Solace?'

Without turning, the nun waves her arm as if shooing her away.

Stef stares at her, blinking in disbelief. She is confused. She wants to persist, but Sister Charity's concerned expression dissuades her, and reluctantly she straightens and walks out of the room. There is a stone in her stomach, and she feels dejected and perplexed. She is anxious to leave the building now, but walking back down the stairs she once more encounters Sister Margaret.

'Did you find her?'

'Yes. But I couldn't understand her. Or she couldn't understand me.'

Sister Margaret chortles briefly. 'She is very old.'

'I think she remembers Jake, but she wouldn't tell me about him.'

The nun laughs again. She sounds infuriatingly cheerful today.

'She is sometimes angry. She is so old. You must ask her another time.' Then, noticing Stef's crestfallen expression, she adopts a more serious tone: 'She does not want the Recreation Centre, you see.'

Stef is roused out of her misery.

'She doesn't want it? Why ever not?'

'She is so old-fashioned. But I think it will be very good for the children to have something like that. They will certainly want it.'

'Yes, and not just the children now but the generations to come – long after Sister Solace has gone to a better place.'

If Sister Margaret detects a note of sarcasm she does not show it. In fact, she seems to be struggling with something else.

'Not for generations, actually.'

'Why shouldn't it?'

'Well, you see, although it is a great fortune and a blessing no doubt for the children to be able to use this new facility, generously donated by Jack's Trust, however we must also accept that it will only have a limited life.'

'I don't understand.'

Sister Margaret cradles her hands as she gazes at the wall behind Stef, her head waving from side to side as she picks her words.

'Well, as you have no doubt been notified, Mrs Daniels, this Institute will not exist next year.'

In response to Stef's bewildered stare, she continues: 'Have you not been informed? The Institute is due to be closed.'

'What are you saying?'

'Our state government has decided that it will be better for the Institute to close and for the children to be dispersed.'

'You're joking.'

'No I am not joking, Mrs Daniels,' Sister Margaret responds gravely, all humour now gone. 'Indeed this is a very serious matter. Not one for joking.'

'But what will happen to the children?' Stef asks. 'Where will they go?'

'They will be dispersed. That is to say, some will be adopted among local families, and where there are no local families available they will go to other families in different parts of the country. And some will go to special needs institutions that are better equipped than our little school.'

Stef lets out a lungful of breath, extracts a tissue from her pocket and wipes her sweat-soaked brow. Her head is thumping, and she feels that annoying echoey sensation in one ear.

'But this is disastrous!' she declares. 'Outrageous! What about all your work?'

'Thank you so much, Mrs Daniels, for your so kind endorsement, but it is the modern way, you know. After all, it is the same in Europe too, is it not? Is it not correct that there are no longer orphanages in your own country?'

'I don't really know,' she confesses, annoyed by her own admission.

Sister Margaret answers for her. 'Very few, I believe. It is now community care, is it not? That is the way things are. And Kerala is proud to be a pioneering state in the dismantling of these institutions. It is the modern method.'

'So what will become of this place, the school?' Stef asks.

'After rebuilding work, it will be a hotel and wedding venue.'

Stef stares, dumbstruck. 'A *wedding venue*?' she finally manages.

'Yes, actually it will be rebuilt from scratch. It is going to be a valuable addition to the tourist infrastructure.'

When Stef does not comment, Sister Margaret smiles sympathetically. 'This is what they call *progress*, Mrs Daniels.' She pronounces the word as if it were a technical term.

But all Stef can think about is the little boy she sat next to in the classroom. And what about the girl, the one with the luminous, empty eyes? And she thinks about the smiling woman too, the one who was sweeping. What will become of *her*?

'And you?' she asks the nun. 'Where will you go? And the other

277

nuns?'

'Ah, there is always someplace for us, no doubt,' Sister Margaret tells her, her smile now sad. 'There is a great deal of hard work to be done everywhere, you see. All over the world.'

'So – the Recreation Centre, Jake's Recreation Centre, is useless,' says Stef. 'Bloody pointless. A complete waste of time and money. How long have you known about this?'

The nun looks sorrowful, head to one side, as she adopts the tone one might use to a child. 'Some time now. But you know, here, we don't really know anything. Things happen. And sometimes they don't. I am sorry that you were not informed. Emails were sent, you know. Perhaps in your junk folder?'

Stef keeps silent.

'And the Recreation Centre will be used,' Sister Margaret continues. 'Have no concern. For a little while. When it is completed, no doubt.' There is another silence. 'All we can do is follow God's will. There is always so much hard work to be done in His name.'

Silence.

'Now I will leave you,' says the nun, joining her hands and bowing her head. 'Goodbye, Mrs Daniels.'

As Sister Margaret continues on her march upstairs, Stef is left feeling crushed, her head thrumming. How long has she had this headache? Making her way to the school entrance, she passes through the gate and makes her way to the church. For once the great doors are closed. She has nowhere to go. So she slowly makes her way up the road towards town, head bent down, ignoring the stares of the local people. A child's voice sweetly calls to her, 'Hallo! Where from?' but she doesn't look up. There are no words, she has nothing to say. She cannot be diverted from her task, which is to place one foot in front of the other, until hopefully she will arrive somewhere.

Chapter 33 | Lake Punnamada

Esme steps out of the shower, methodically dries herself and slips into her clothes. Going downstairs to the restaurant, she contemplates the day ahead and her steps slow down as she feels the weight descend, the pressure tightening around her neck and shoulders, as if the restorative effects of her morning yoga are being negated or reversed by the prospect of meeting her fellow guests at breakfast.

Thankfully, however, the room is still empty at this hour. Helping herself from the bowls of fruit salad and curd, she is interrupted by Francis entering the room with his usual taciturn face.

'Good morning, madam.'

She smiles back. 'Morning!'

He waits impassively by the door, then, when she is seated, crosses the room to her table. 'I will take your breakfast order, madam.'

She orders bhaji puri and tea, which she wolfs down as soon as they arrive, keen to vacate the room before anyone else appears. By the time she climbs back upstairs she has formulated a plan for the day. It boils down to one word: escape. The hostel, whose enclosed grounds and air of seclusion had once offered her a shelter and refuge, now feels like a prison. And following this morning's encounter with Stef and yesterday's clumsy and equally excruciating approach by Simon, she has an urgent need to put as much distance as possible between her and them, and can think of no remoter or more appropriate place than the middle of Lake Punnamada. Until now Esme has been put off exploring Allapoorha's fabled waterways by the sight of dozens of the *kettu vallam* houseboats moored off the lake shores. The former rice barges, with oiled jackwood hulls, teak decks and canopies of plaited palm thatch and coir, have been adapted for the tourist trade and now dominate the lake. According to her guidebook, it is *de rigueur* to do a boat tour here, it's the first thing to do if you're a tourist, so it would be perverse to come all this way and not do it. But she has no wish to join one of the organised tours, far preferable to do it her own way while supporting the local economy; she will find something smaller-scale.

This does not prove to be any kind of problem. Half an hour later, as she is walking towards the lake on a back-street that runs alongside one of Allapoorha's canals, she hears a voice coming from below her.

'Boat tour, madam?'

The tone and timbre trigger an impulse, following her training in India's tourist spots, to keep walking, but then she remembers why she is here and looks round to see a short man crouching by the side of the canal below the street. He has pockmarked cheeks and wears a dhoti, a torn white vest and a scarf wrapped around his head.

'Boat tour?' he repeats. 'On lake. Very nice.'

The man springs off his haunches and points to a gondola-like vessel tied up a few feet away and furnished with rugs and a basic divan. After a brief negotiation she climbs in, and they're off.

The boatman, whose name sounds something like 'Dosh', squats behind her at the stern of the boat as she settles back on the divan with her hat and sunglasses in place, content that the craft's lack of an engine is making minimal impact on the environment, with no troubling noise or pollution. However, her sense of conducting herself ethically is soon undermined by the laboured grunts of Dosh behind her, each one stabbing her with a pang of guilt. From ethically sound she has become, in the eyes of him and of anyone else observing them, just another spoilt and privileged westerner who can afford to pay lackeys to provide a day's entertainment – probably at the expense of the lackey's health. Passers-by on the canal banks look down on her reclining on the divan with what she interprets as knowing sneers. How easy it is to fall into predetermined roles! Then, making her feel even worse, the slow rhythmic slapping of the single paddle is also accompanied at regular intervals by the sound of the boatman's hawking and spitting into the water.

After a few minutes, they enter the placid expanse of lake and she starts to feel better without the accusing eyes looking down on her. But that's when the inquisition begins. 'Which country, madam?' 'What is your profession?' 'Married?' 'Boyfriend?' 'How old?' 'Where stay?' 'How long in India?' 'India is good place?' She replies in monosyllables, eventually not even turning round to answer, just throwing the information he requires over her shoulder and making it very clear she is answering on sufferance.

Dosh gives up and resumes his hawking and spitting, but now with a sulky resentment, or so it seems to Esme. His eyes are doubtlessly scrutinising her from behind, measuring her up and assessing her wealth. But even without this sensation of being watched by the disgruntled oarsman, it would be hard to unwind and admire the flat lake, glistening silkily in the morning light, for there are large houseboats loaded with Indian tourists trundling past every few minutes, each one creating a mighty wake that sets their own vessel rocking madly.

'Perfect?' comes the voice from behind.

She turns, uncomprehending.

'Perfect?' Dosh says again, almost pleading with her to agree.

'Not really,' she answers him. 'Can we get away from the main route? Away from the big boats?' When he finally understands he steers a diagonal path across the lake, and as the water becomes calmer, their path now crossed only by small shikaras bearing heaps of vegetables or odd fragments of machinery, she begins to relax. Over the dense silvery grey of the water there are dragon-flies and egrets and cormorants, and she even spots brilliantly coloured kingfishers skimming over the surface – one, perched on an island of driftwood and weeds, even has a silver fish in its beak, though it flees before she can raise her phone to photograph it. There is none of the breeze she was hoping for, however – if anything the heat hangs more heavily here than in the hostel garden, causing her scalp to itch and perspiration to pool on her neck. The sky, pure blue when she emerged from the hostel, is now a soupy grey, and the air is thick and sultry. Every so often the boat passes through swirling clouds of tiny flies, but thankfully the insects ignore her.

Although she feels soothed by the lake's tranquillity, there is a niggling unease at the pit of Esme's stomach that she can't shake off. Disappointingly. far from leaving her preoccupations behind at the hostel, she finds that she is carrying them with her, even here on this boat. Her thoughts keep returning to her fellow guests – or inmates, as she can't help regarding them: Stef with her peremptory, egoistical neediness, Simon with his sneaky designs, and most of all there is the invisible but overarching figure of Jake and his mythical book – she still can't bring herself to believe fully in it. Notwithstanding, until she sees it, or at least until Stef has it in her possession, Esme feels in thrall to that book.

Behind her, Dosh shoots more of his sputum into the lake. She sighs, then whips out her phone, checks her messages, and fires off yet another plea to Dougie to let her know of his whereabouts and ETA. She is pinning her hopes on him to set the record straight, even though, by now, she does not expect any reply from him and is beginning to wonder whether he will arrive at all. He might not even be in the country, might have bailed out at the last minute.

It is fitting that Dougie holds the key, for it was the lure of his exotically queer world that prompted Jake's later explorations of his own identity. He was already strongly drawn to it before he and Esme split up, though that certainly wasn't the reason for the split, that would have happened anyway. As far as she can recall, there was never a moment or a decisive factor, she just accepted their separation as inevitable, part of the natural cycle of their relationship. Maybe, too, she simply ceased to tolerate him, or ceased to tolerate her own allegiance to him. Esme, above all, is a person who needs to like and approve of herself, and eventually the self-reproach and guilt got the upper hand. After one particularly messy row with Jake, she casually informed him she didn't want to be with him any more, almost in passing. She can still picture the momentary shock and disbelief on his face; it was probably the first time he had ever been rejected. To his credit, he didn't argue, didn't even assume his usual look of wounded self-pity, he simply nodded, smiled and walked out of her room for the last time.

Perhaps naively she thought that that would be the end of it; he drifted away and, for a while, was out of her life. Exams were approaching and she had other things on her mind. From what she heard, his immersion in the gay scene became more intense, though, typically, he went too far, adopting the role, wearing it like it was his. A few weeks after their split she ran into him and he told her that he was now gay. He even said something about being born in the wrong gender. She wasn't particularly surprised or saddened, in fact she didn't take much notice of his words at all, buried as they were within his usual meandering, solipsistic, stream-of-consciousness spiel that she had stopped paying attention to some time before. She was only surprised that she didn't much care.

A day or two later, Stef called, unable to reach her son. She didn't seem to know and Esme didn't feel inclined to tell her that she was no longer with Jake. Why not? She couldn't exactly say. That was the first lie of omission. Was it the note of fear she heard in Stef's voice? Her need of reassurance? Was it pity, after Stef mentioned that Jake hadn't called home for two weeks and she was worried. Jake of course refused to use mobile phones, didn't use Facebook or Insta, rarely looked at his emails. He was the only person Esme knew who still resorted to public telephones, and only then as a last resort. She suspected that this was so his mother couldn't reach him. Esme had no problem with that, if anything Jake's rejection of modern media added to his charm. 'I'm not introverted enough for social media,' he said once. Now, though, Stef was cut off from her son and clearly stressed about it. Esme assured her that she would remind Jake to ring her, though afterwards she didn't seek him out to tell him, in fact Stef's call and her promise dropped completely out of her mind.

There was another call from Stef a few days later. She was still anxious, still in the dark. Esme knew then how crucial their relationship – hers and Jake's – was to his mother, it must have represented some kind of stability in her son's chaotic life. So, again, Esme bottled it, unable to bring herself to confess that she was no longer responsible for Jake because they were no longer together. She heard herself reassure Stef that everything was fine, that they were both wrapped up in their studies but everything was great. She would tell Stef, obviously, if anything was wrong.

As it happened, Esme had an encounter with Jake on the following day. She was waiting for a friend in the Prince Albert when a strange woman approached her. 'Well, hallo,' she greeted her in an unusually deep voice, and Esme found herself looking into Jake's eyes. 'Meet the new me!'

Agog, Esme looked him up and down, taking in the exaggerated make-up, the hoop ear-rings, the blond-dyed hair, now combed and straightened, the frumpy violet blouse and the knee-length skirt above black boots that rose halfway up his calves.

'You're blonde!' was the first thing that came into her head.

'Like it?'

'And I've never seen you clean shaven!'

He nodded, pleased at his effect on her.

'Are you cross-dressing now?'

'Only on special occasions,' he said, his voice camp and ridiculous.

'What's the occasion?'

'Well, I *was* hoping to get a card from you this morning,' he said, eyelids fluttering.

She put her hand to her mouth. 'Oh my god! Sorry! Happy birthday!' And she made herself lean forward and plant a kiss on his cheek.

'Forgiven. Anyway, must dash. I've got a hunky new date.'

'Have you called your mother?'

'Who?'

'She wants you to call.'

'Okay, message received. I'll call. Bye bye, sweetie! Wish me luck! Byeee...' And she watched him mincing out of the pub, marvelling at the lengths he would go to.

Esme assumed he must have spoken to Stef because she stopped calling her. He must have told his mother to stop bothering her. Nor did Esme hear from Jake for several weeks, though she heard *about* him, his new persona was the subject on everyone's lips. She felt obscurely embarrassed. This was her ex people were discussing! At least they weren't laughing at him – rather, they spoke in a kind of awed admiration. Esme tried to stay out of their gossipy chit-chat, though she couldn't help being intrigued.

Once, in The Lanes, she spotted him in a plastic, electric blue skirt, the same calf-high boots as before, and a scarlet jacket that matched his lipstick. His hair was still dyed blond and he was arm in arm with Charlie, his gay Burmese friend. He had a contented, slightly dazed look on his face. She felt an odd mix of emotions – jealousy, a little, and curiosity too, but in a strange way it also restored her faith in him.

Esme is aware of Dosh addressing her again: 'You paddling?'

She turns round, not sure if she has heard correctly.

'Pardon?'

'You paddling?'

'You want me to paddle?'

'Front paddle,' he clarifies. 'Very nice exercise.'

Well no, she doesn't want to paddle and she doesn't need the exercise. She has agreed to pay one thousand rupees for this service and isn't prepared to part with that small fortune in order to work up even greater torrents of sweat. But instead of saying this, she makes the usual fudge of pretending to laugh as if he is joking (maybe he is) and mumbling something like 'Later, perhaps'. She takes a drink from her bottle and glowers, thankful that he cannot see her brooding anger.

And then the guilt – temporarily banished by her irritation at his interrogating and spitting – seeps into her again. Perhaps she ought to help him out. He's not a strong-looking type, and it might even correct his clear assumption that she, a mere western woman, won't or can't row, might show him that she is no memsahib being transported on a cut-price stately barge. More importantly, it might assuage her gnawing conscience.

Without warning, an eerie, high-pitched wail cuts through the dense air of the lake. Startled, Esme turns to see Dosh, mouth open but still smiling at her, apparently singing. Perhaps he is serenading her, though he appears to be simply repeating one phrase over and over to no particular melody. For all she knows he is singing: 'Whore, whore', or 'Spoilt, stuck-up memsahib'. She decides to ignore him, and, extracting her phone once more, starts swiping crossly at her social media pages. She gives up after a minute or two – she's not in the mood for pointless gossip. What is she in the mood for? She doesn't know, all she knows is that she was seeking some respite from the tentacles of the Johnson-Daniel octopus and has not found it.

A week or so after seeing Jake in The Lanes, Esme was racing across the campus with a friend, late for a lecture, when she glimpsed him across the lawn, also moving fast, his hasty gait so different from his usual lazy stride that she had to stop for a second or two to look more closely. It *was* him, this time in man-dress. He looked as if he was on a mission, fixated even, and a bit troubled. He was still clean-shaven, and his blond hair was now cropped short. Thinking back on it later, she thought he also looked a bit shifty.

The next time she saw him, he was alone in a pub holding a tall, thin glass of something fizzy with exaggerated care, as if he might snap it. This time his hair was dyed a radiant gold, but he looked vague, distant, and skinnier, she thought. She detached herself from the couple of friends she was with and approached him. He didn't seem to recognise her at first.

'Hey!' she said. He narrowed his eyes, then she saw recognition dawn. 'Long time. What are you up to?'

'Nothing!' He looked guilty, a state she would never have associated with him. And yes, he had lost his plumpness. Close up, how strange he was with his short, gold hair, almost ethereal. His fingers were grimy, she couldn't help noticing, and his nails were chewed back.

'You on the wagon?' she asked incredulously.

He stared at her hard, as if trying to comprehend her words. 'What?'

She laughed, gesturing to the glass of lemon-coloured liquid in his hand. 'On the wagon. I never thought I'd see you with an unalcoholic beverage.'

He looked down at his glass, then looked up at her, dumb, absent. It was as if he wasn't really there. That was when she realised. She had thought he might be already drunk, even at this hour of the day (it was around noon), but when she saw his glassy eyes, his pupils tiny dots, she realised the truth. No, he was not drunk. He was completely out of his tree. And, apparently, in the gutter.

She said something silly and trite, couldn't afterwards remember exactly what, and turned away, walking quickly back to her group. But instead of joining them, she swerved past and went outside where she took great gasps of air and wiped away the tears that were stinging her eyes. So that's what it was. Now he really was lost. More than anything she felt a profound disappointment. What a waste.

That was the last time she ever saw him. A day or two later, Stef called. Her voice was leaden.

'I've just heard.'

'Heard what?'

'About Jake. He's chucked it in. And you didn't even tell me!'

Esme had no idea what she was talking about.

'It's a tragedy and a complete waste! Not to mention the money. He'll still have to pay it back.'

'I'm sure he will,' Esme said, still flailing.

'But how? How will he ever get a job even?'

The penny suddenly dropped. Jake had quit his course.

'It doesn't have to be a disaster,' she told Stef.

'How long have you known? Why didn't you tell me?'

'Honestly Stef, I've only just found out,' Stef answered, relieved that finally she could speak truthfully.

'Oh. Well I'm in bits, Esme. It's not too late. Can't you persuade him to carry on? Please!'

'Not if he's really made his mind up. You know how stubborn he is.'

'But try! Tell me you'll try. Please! He might listen to you.'

'Right. I'll try.'

'I said I'd come down but he said he won't see me. Refuses!'

'He's in a strange place right now, Stef.'

'Is he? Is he alright? Is he happy?'

'To be honest, I'm not seeing so much of him these days. It's all a bit mad right now, with exams and everything.' Second lie, again of omission.

'Of course it is. I apologise, Esme, I don't want to land this on you. Just tell me that he's alright. I don't know who else to call.'

'Yuh. Well. He seems very...preoccupied.'

'Preoccupied? What do you mean?'

And that was when Esme dropped her third major lie, just two words. She didn't know why she uttered them, probably because it seemed to be what she sensed Stef wanted to hear.

'He's writing.'

There was a short silence. Then Stef's words tumbled out rapidly, almost beseeching: 'Really? *Writing?* Oh my god. He's writing. That explains a lot. But writing what?'

'I – I don't know, Stef. It's a book. I think.'

'My *god*! ... He's writing a book. How exciting! So *that's* why he dropped out. What kind of a book?' Esme could hear the desperate pleasure in her voice. She was almost purring and weeping at the same time.

'He doesn't say. He's very secretive, you know. Something he's been thinking about for a while – maybe a novel or something. He's staying with a friend, actually, somewhere outside town, so I don't see him that much. He said he doesn't want distractions.'

And this was the routine for the next few weeks. Jake seemed to

289

have stopped contacting Stef altogether, with the result that she was calling Esme at regular intervals and Esme had to repeat the lies: Jake was hard at work; he was writing all the time, or in the library researching; he was looking fine.

In reality, Jake seemed to have disappeared from the scene. There were reports, though, that he and Charlie were cooped up together, living in some kind of suburban smack den, that Jake was dealing, that Jake looked awful. Why didn't Esme hear the alarm bells? Surely that was the time to intervene? And why didn't she tell his mother? She might have saved him.

That is the burden that she has carried all these years. If she'd cared enough, or dared enough, she might have saved him. Once, Esme believed that Jake was indestructible. He was so unknowable, so unbelievable, that he had become almost fictional, and how can an artifice ever come to harm? And even if he did, why would it matter? Jake himself was a mere construct, and wasn't this junky thing just another role, a twist in the plot, a new stage of the game? And for his next trick...

But the next report she had of Jake was that the character had become so unreal, so outrageous, that it was no longer sustainable. It had been dropped from his own production, and he had come a cropper. Game over.

After that final gesture of his, there was no going back, no further edits or revisions of the story were possible. Nor was there ever a good time to disenchant his mother. And anyway, it was in keeping with all the other illusions surrounding her golden boy. That's all there was to it. The lies were preserved in aspic, along with all the other false memories.

Back then, she was able to persuade herself that she was saving Stef further distress, but now, eight years later, there is no such excuse. Why didn't she come clean this morning? That this mythical book was Esme's invention and had nothing to do with

Dougie? She was responsible, she was the one who first planted it in Stef's mind for no good reason.

But then again, how could she have told Stef that she – Stef – was the gullible fool, that she had swallowed this fantasy hook, line and sinker?

Dosh's weird singing has thankfully stopped, replaced once more by his hawking and spitting. They are in another busy thoroughfare with the water churned up by gargantuan houseboats filled with parties of tourists, most of them thrusting out their mobiles to take selfies when they are not pointing them down at her. She turns once more to scowl at the boatman, gesturing at the thundering vessels and the rocky wake they create.

'Yes, madam,' he says, and soon after he turns off the main waterway and into a tiny, well-hidden backwater. Here it is a different world, quiet and secluded, where there are tumbledown shacks and women beating clothes against rocks, rinsing buckets of snails, and hacking at unseen objects with menacing-looking machetes. The water is a viscous dark brown filled with a detritus of rotting mangoes, coconut shells and plastic bottles.

When their boat can advance no further, Dosh jumps onto a bank and fastens it to a post. Esme looks at him perplexed.

'You walk? See paddies?' he asks, gesturing to the expanse of flat green rice fields stretching into the haze in front of them and crossed by a row of spindly pylons. She looks doubtful, thinking *This wasn't part of the deal.* On the other hand, she's curious. Never one to turn down a new experience, she decides that at least it will be a change from the humid sweatbath of the lake. She climbs out of the canoe and feels the reassuring solidity of the ground underfoot. Dosh points up a dirt trail and urges her on. She hesitates, then follows the trail, her guide following a few paces behind. She grows increasingly suspicious. Images of assault flash into her mind, but these are quickly banished by her complete confidence in being able to deal with any situation – and anyway, there are people about. Every few minutes they pass flimsy shacks or dwellings from which very old or very young faces peer out inquisitively. She is beginning to relax, enjoying the long vistas to either side, free of the closeness of the lake air, when Dosh calls to her to halt. They are in front of a hut where an old crone in a faded red sari is crouched over a pot, briskly stirring. Odours of coriander, ginger and onion bubble out. Dosh says something to the old woman, who grins toothlessly up at Esme and points to a rug on the ground.

'You eat,' Dosh tells her from behind.

So that was the plan, he wants her to buy a meal, for which he'll get a healthy baksheesh. Better than a physical assault, she reasons, but still a crafty ruse, and one that confirms her in her role as a naive consumer.

'You eat,' Dosh repeats, coaxing her inside the squalid hut. Esme waves her hands and shakes her head, but Dosh perseveres. 'Amma, amma,' he repeats. Then he finally manages to say, 'Mother', gesturing to the woman. Esme is mortified. It's not a sales pitch, there is no trickery. He is introducing her to his mother, who wants her to join them for a meal.

Chastened and disarmed, Esme can only submit, and, planting a grateful smile on her face, she clasps her hands and bows her head. At the old woman's instigation, she lowers herself onto the rug, accepts a banana leaf and lets the woman dole out the contents of the pot onto it. Dosh receives his own portion and sits crosslegged opposite her on the rug. His mother squats a few feet away, watching them eat with a pleased expression.

Later, as they return to the boat, with the air and light ripening to the heavy texture of late afternoon, Esme feels a new affection for Dosh. Yes, he is irritating, but his heart is sound, and he's generous – he wouldn't accept any money for the meal. She sits back in the canoe as he takes up his oar and starts the soft, slow row back to their starting point in Allapoorha. This time, she offers to help out, and despite the sweat streaming from her forehead and trickling down her back she feels happy to share the task. She even begins to appreciate his tuneless accompanying serenade.

An hour later, back on the quay, she counts out one thousand rupees. Dosh holds the wad of notes briefly to his forehead, bows, and clasps his hand to his heart.

'Perfect?' he asks.

'Absolutely perfect,' she tells him.

Chapter 34 | A chillum in the garden

Under the parasol in the garden, Cynthia lifts her eyes from her novel, nose twitching. Opposite her, Oliver is jabbing aggressively at his tablet.

'What are you doing?'

Oliver looks up in surprise.

'I'm writing a letter.'

'An email?'

'Yes. I'm writing an email. Why?'

'Can't you do it any quieter?'

'Quieter?'

'Yes.'

'I wasn't aware that I was making any noise.'

'Well you are. And you're panting.'

'Panting?'

'Yes.'

Oliver stares at her in bafflement as he leans back in his seat, creasing his brow and stroking his moustache.

'I wasn't aware that I was panting.'

'Well you are. You do. It's like that thing you do with your throat. Unconscious.'

'I'm sorry,' Oliver says. 'I suppose we all do things we're unconscious of all the time. Especially when we're getting old.'

'*You* do.'

Oliver looks wryly amused now as he squares up to her, still caressing his moustache. He can see that she is in a mood, no doubt brought on by the afternoon's oppressive air this afternoon. The grey sky above them is a dull, featureless expanse weighing down on them all, and she has a headache.

'You do, too,' he tells her.

'What do I do?'

'You make involuntary noises.'

'I don't!'

'You do, I'm afraid.'

'What noises do I make?'

'Well, you snore sometimes.'

'Snore?'

'Sometimes.'

'Well I'm sorry if I snore.'

'You twitch your nose, too.'

'Do I?' Cynthia is looking worried now.

'Sometimes.'

Cynthia's nose twitches in annoyance. 'Well that's hardly an involuntary noise. And at least I don't puff and pant while I'm typing.' After a pause during which the two regard each other with dry amusement, she says: 'You're always on that thing.'

'What thing?'

'That tablet thing.'

'Yes...'

'Is that another sign of growing old?'

He guffaws. 'Absolutely not!'

'Well, I suppose it's a good sign that you're on top of the latest technology.' She pauses, then adds: 'And I suppose I should be grateful you're still *compos mentis*. Half of my friends seem to be either in the process of dying or going gaga.'

'I promise I'll always be *compos mentis* for you.'

'How would you know?'

'Even when I'm not *compos mentis* I'll be there for you.'

'But will I still want you to be? And will I want you to be around when I'm incapacitated? Do I want to depend on you?'

'We can always depend on each other.'

'You're certainly dependable.'

'Thank you.'

'And when we go out it's always you who gets the drinks. Old-fashioned, but gratifying too, I suppose.'

'It's my prerogative. Anyway, that's a detail. More important, I'm always there for you to talk to. We always have stimulating conversations.'

'You can certainly talk! Sometimes you don't shut up!'

'It's true that I am a good communicator.'

'You are, dear. Since you got that new smartphone you text as much as a teenager. But you can't spell. The grammar is especially terrible. Often your texts are meaningless.'

'It's my fingers. I can't type properly on a phone.'

'A text from you is usually followed by a second one explaining the meaning of the first, but it's equally atrociously spelt.'

'I've always been hopeless at spelling.'

'And they're sometimes quite insulting.'

'They're not intended to be insulting. You know I'm only joking.'

'If anyone else were to read your messages, they'd be shocked. The ones to me, anyway.'

'Sorry.' He is about to add something, then stops at the sound of a blaring horn somewhere nearby. Suddenly there is an explosive tumult, as an auto-rickshaw lurches into the hostel's driveway, pulling up noisily outside the entrance. The engine is killed, and there are knocks and voices from inside before two dishevelled figures spill out, blinking at their surroundings. One wears a creased yellow gilet, the other a red bandana; both are unshaven. The couple watch in amazement as the two passengers are immediately involved in a complicated financial transaction with the driver involving raised voices and baleful looks. Roused by this invasion of the hostel precincts, Thomas emerges from the lobby with Flowery close behind, while Francis materializes on the veranda from the restaurant, spectating from a respectful distance. Thomas barks at the rickshaw driver, the driver responds in defensive tones, resentment and accusation boiling over. Eventually, one of the passengers thrusts a banknote at the driver, who mutters and scowls but pockets it anyway, then climbs back into the rickshaw and roars off.

'Yes, kind sirs?' Thomas says with a somewhat strained equanimity, anxious as he is to restore the customary calm of his establishment. 'May I be of assistance?'

'Hi, yes. I think we're meant to be booked in here,' says the one in the gilet.

At this point Cynthia calls over: 'Is one of you Douglas?'

'I'm Douglas!' answers the gilet-wearer, who walks over to where Cynthia and Oliver are seated, followed by his companion, their bags abandoned in a heap on the ground. Oliver sees Thomas give instructions to Shibu, who has also arrived on the scene, then the manager and Flowery withdraw into the building, leaving Shibu to heave the dusty bags inside. Francis lingers on the veranda, watching serenely from the shade of the porch.

Dougie wipes his palms on his jeans before exchanging handshakes with Cynthia and Oliver. 'How do you do?' he says, his Scottish-accented voice surprisingly soft and well-spoken. 'Although to be honest I've got no idea who you are.'

'Oliver Maitland,' Oliver says, 'and this is Cynthia, Jake's grandmother. Welcome to Allapoorha. Where have you come from? The moon, perhaps?'

The new arrivals exchange a look and a slightly mad grin. 'It's a long story,' Dougie says. 'We've been travelling non-stop for the last thirty hours. This is my partner, Jules.'

Oliver gestures at a couple of chairs for them to pull up and join them at the table, and calls to Francis, ordering four lime sodas.

'You are friends of my grandson, I understand,' Cynthia says.

'Yes,' Dougie replies. 'Well, I am. Or, er, was. Jules didn't know him at all.'

'But I've heard a lot about him,' Jules says, 'so I feel like I do.'

'So – is everything on schedule for the big opening ceremony?' Dougie asks.

'No, actually,' Cynthia answers. 'It was supposed to be tomorrow, but now it's going to be on Monday. At least we think it is. That was what they've told us, anyway. The day keeps changing. Time is rather elastic here.'

'Ah… Indian time…' Dougie says. He starts explaining some of the unforeseen delays that have kept them away when the lime sodas arrive. The newcomers dispatch theirs in a few deep swallows.

'Stephanie will be glad to see you,' Cynthia says. 'I don't know where she is now. You'll probably see her at supper. The others are around somewhere.'

'Is Esme here?' Dougie asks.

'Esme's gone on a boat tour of the lake, apparently,' Cynthia tells him. 'You missed a lovely Keralan feast on Monday, a sort of general welcome to everybody. Oliver made a speech.'

'Shame…' Dougie glances at Oliver and decides he hasn't missed anything. Following a lull in the conversation, he looks over to Jules, who is gazing fixedly into the garden. 'Well… Perhaps we'd better check out our rooms.'

'Yes, I expect you'll want to shower off the dust after all that travelling,' Cynthia says. 'It's very clean and comfortable here.'

'Just what the doctor ordered,' Dougie says. He stands and looks at his companion. 'Shall we?'

Dougie and Jules head inside, but before they can be admitted to their rooms they must submit to the admission procedure, which involves Thomas laboriously completing all the forms necessary for the register. Jules provides his details with unconcealed impatience, annoyed that they have been allocated separate rooms. He was aware of the arrangement, for they have already discussed it at length, and he had acquiesced as a special favour to Dougie after the latter received a very sensitive and apologetic email from Laurie asking them to make this concession to local sensibilities to avoid the possibility of any awkwardness in this traditional Christian establishment. Nonetheless, Jules continues to nurse a resentment about it – but then he is generally resentful about everything to do with their sojourn at the hostel.

Fifteen minutes later he is letting himself into Dougie's room and they are exchanging impressions of the place and the comedy duo who greeted them on their arrival. Looking about him, Jules notices how his lover's few remaining possessions are scattered proprietorially about, as if to claim this as his own personal territory, and thinks he detects a note of contentment on Dougie's part to have his own space.

When Dougie shuts himself into the bathroom for what he warns will be a 'long session' of cleansing and purging, Jules tries to impose his own stamp on the room, first lying on the bed then wandering around, opening drawers and touching random objects. He makes a critical appraisal of the silver sacred heart on the wall, studies the view from the window and feels more strongly than ever an unease about this place and their presence in it. He has made no secret of the fact that he does not want to be here and wants to get away as soon as possible, once this toe-curling 'ceremony' is done and Jake is definitively consigned to history. The news that the event has been delayed is particularly irksome – he was counting on being able to leave on Saturday, the day after it was originally scheduled.

He bangs on the bathroom door. 'I'm going out,' he announces. 'Just a walk, check this place out.'

Dougie yells something in reply, and Jules exits the room,

descends the stairs and quickly crosses the reception area, aware of Thomas at his desk casting a long look in his direction as he does so.

Offering a matey thumbs-up to Cynthia and Oliver, still ensconced under their parasol, he heads past them towards the trees at the far end of the garden. But what appeared from Dougie's window to be a thick grove of trees turns out to be a largely impenetrable tangle of vegetation ending in a rusty iron barrier. However, it'll do. Installing himself behind a matted trunk, he slips one hand into his pocket and pulls out a chillum and a box of matches. The chillum is half-smoked, left over from the last train ride. Checking that he is out of sight of the hostel, he forms a cup with one hand so that the chillum is poking out between his fingers, applies a lit match to the bowl, and draws deeply. But it is too dry, too hot, and he is immediately convulsed in a coughing fit, his throat rebelling against the fiery inhalation. Spluttering billows of smoke from his mouth and with eyes watering, he clutches the trunk of the tree.

'Fuck!' he shouts a moment later as a searing pain spreads over his hand, from which he frenziedly shakes off a swarming multitude of large black ants.

Once he has slightly recovered, he wipes his eyes and tries again, holding a match to the bowl, but again he is wracked with explosive spasms of coughing. He bows over with his hands on his knees, not wishing to put them anywhere else that might harbour biting or stinging creatures. But then, when he straightens up, still reeling, eyes still streaming, and panting hard to catch his breath, he receives another violent shock to see, a few feet away, a figure observing him. Immobile, face half concealed behind large, wrap-around dark glasses, she is all in white, in a loose cotton shirt, baggy trousers and a western scarf wound around her hair. He stares dumbly and for a moment is tempted to run away. The figure draws closer, a little unsteadily, and stops in front of him.

'Are you alright?' Her voice is raspy and sharp.

Jules nods wordlessly but warily, his eyes still tearful. She gestures towards the chillum still in his hand. 'I wouldn't let the manager catch you doing that. This is a respectable establishment.' He nods again, coughs again. 'Who are you, anyway?'

'I'm Jules,' he says eventually, his voice a hoarse whisper, and he has to repeat it louder when she frowns in puzzlement.

Then she pulls out a pack of cigarettes 'Think I'll join you. Thomas doesn't much approve of smoking on the premises, but we all do it anyway.'

'I...I don't know who Thomas is,' Jules gasps.

'The *manager*,' she says, as if speaking to a simpleton. 'Light?'

'What?'

'*Have you got a light?*'

He quickly produces his box of matches, tries to strike one, fails, and fails a second time.

'Indian matches,' she tuts, taking the box and managing to light her cigarette on the first attempt. 'Are you sure you're alright?'

He nods.

She inhales deeply, still watching him. 'So, Jules, have you been having a good time? Has India treated you well?'

'Sure, it's, er, terrific.'

'Good! And are you glad to be here? Here, I mean, in this spot? What do you make of it?'

'I don't know,' his voice is still a whisper. He realises that even the two inhalations of the chillum have got to him, for his head is spinning and his tongue is dry. He clears his throat. 'We've just arrived,' he explains in a firmer tone.

'Yes, we've established that. You woke up the entire neighbourhood.'

'Oh. Sorry...'

'Don't worry about it darling, we're all dying of boredom anyway.' He blinks at her and she continues to contemplate him impassively as she smokes, as if he is a mildly interesting specimen dropped from a bird's beak. She seems to be enjoying his discomfort. 'I'm guessing that you're Dougie's friend.'

He nods. 'And you're...?'

'Jake's mother. You know who Jake is?' He nods. 'Well, I'm mum.'

He doesn't know what to say.

'You can call me Stef,' she says. 'None of that Professor Daniel rubbish, please.' She studies him, noting his suspicious expression. 'You're very young, aren't you? Are you *stoned*?'

'No, no...' he tries to laugh casually but his voice comes out cracked, setting off another coughing fit.

'Don't worry. It'll all be over soon. And then you can go back to whatever it is you do. Be normal again.'

Trying to appear normal now, Jules nods and wheezes.

'What *do* you do, anyway?' Stef continues. 'What's your job? Do you have a job?'

'Advertising.'

'Oh my god, that's sounds terminally dull.'

'Not always,' he says. He straightens his back and manages to meet her eye with an equal directness. 'But it's just a job. And you? A professor, right? That sounds like it could be dull, too, sometimes.'

'It is,' she admits, a note of regret in her voice.

'And are you enjoying your stay here?' he asks, trying to join in her game and if possible commandeer it.

She snorts derisively. 'Are you mad? Oh, I'm having a *whale* of a time. Brilliant.'

He frowns at her, unsure of where she is drawing the line between being serious and satirical.

302

'Why ever should you think that I'm having a good time?' she asks, undoubtedly serious now.

'I didn't mean ...'

'We're not here to *have a good time!*'

'No, right. Sorry. Okay. I didn't mean that. So where do you teach, Mrs ... er .. Professor, er, Stef?'

'No, no, no, that's all wrong. Just Stef, darling. I work in a *university*. Or used to. I teach *Women's Studies*. Know what that is?'

Jules nods but she tells him anyway, emitting jets of cigarette smoke as she does so.

'Women's literature. Politics. Philosophy. All that stuff. You know: a woman's function, role and subjection in a patriarchal society. Hierarchies. Complicity and revolt. The second wave, the third wave. That sort of thing.' She pauses. 'Are you keeping up? Do you know what I'm talking about?' He nods, and she continues in a less declamatory tone: 'But literature more than anything else. Do you read?'

Jules nods.

'What do you read?'

He looks panicked, unable to think of any books he has read ever.

'Do you read Virginia Woolf?' Stef asks.

'Yes...'

'Good!' she says approvingly. 'Well if you know anything about her you'll know she had a very unfortunate life. Combating male hierarchies and beset by illness and madness. And death of course. "Death is the enemy. It is death against whom I ride with my spear couched and my hair flying..." Her words, not mine. What's your favourite Woolf novel?'

'*Orlando?*' he suggests.

She nods. 'Good. I think we're going to get on.' She throws her

303

smoked cigarette into the undergrowth, then, with a 'Oh, Christ!' goes in search of the butt and stamps on it twice before grinding it savagely into the earth. 'Don't want to burn the place down,' she tells him. 'Not yet, anyway. By the way, darling, have you brought the book?'

'Sorry?'

'Jake's book.'

Jules feels panicked again. 'Oh, er ... dunno. You'd better ask Dougie. He knows about it.'

'Really?' she says. She's looking more searchingly at him now. 'And where is Dougie?'

'In his room. Or was. Washing.'

'Hmm. Alright then. We'll ask him when he comes down.' She sighs, lips pursed disconsolately, then she perks up suddenly. 'Come on, Jules, let's join the party.' And she takes his arm and guides him out of the trees, back across the lawn to the hostel, leaning rather too heavily on him, he can't help thinking. He feels rudderless, confused and outmanoeuvred, and wonders if it's the dope or her performance that is making him feel like this. Whichever it is, it's a rum introduction to the family.

Chapter 35 | At Sri Vidna

Esme hears her phone ping as she is disembarking from the boat. Once she has paid Dosh and traded expressions of good will and mutual respect, she consults it while walking alongside the canal. It's a message from Dougie: *at sri vidna la la lassis cu there?*

Her heart leaps. At last!

She makes a quick search on the phone and quickly finds it: Sri Vidna is just a few streets away. She texts back: *Be there in 10*.

The thought of lassi makes her salivate. All she can think about here is her next drink. Water is the only real solution, but anything liquid will do, and the prospect of a sweet lassi is enticing. She is also mightily looking forward to seeing Dougie. Apart from the answers he might have, the end he might bring to all the desperate ambiguities, he will provide a tenuous solidarity and a refuge from the cloying embrace of the clan. She and he have not always kept up since hanging out together at uni, but they got on well enough at the time, often going out as a group with others in the local gay crowd, and they were able to bond in the face of Jake's eccentricities. Since the funeral, they have only maintained cursory contact via Facebook, and have never alluded to the past. It was as if they were both glad to shovel that period of their lives out of sight. She has heard mention of Dougie's partner Jules, and feels a mild curiosity towards him.

Esme turns left onto a main road. As if in defiance of her sleepy late afternoon mood, Allapoorha is as frenetic as ever, with the constant bustle of buying and selling at street stalls, the honking rickshaws, the overloaded local buses clearing a path before them and leaving clouds of thick black exhaust in their wake. As ever, the stench of urine permeates the air. Weaving through the crowds, she looks steadfastly ahead as she has trained herself to do, ignoring the stares and forcing herself to maintain her composure as snarling motorbikes pass daringly close, almost touching her. She crosses the road and climbs an iron pedestrian bridge that bestrides another canal, descends onto a much quieter street and walks two or three hundred metres west to the Sri Vidna Hotel.

There are no rooms at this 'hotel', instead she finds a tiled dining space at the top of a short flight of broad marble steps. It is fan-cooled and, with its luridly bright plastic tables and chairs, looks almost clinically clean. At the far end, seated at one of the formica-topped tables, Dougie is absorbed in conversation with a fair-haired, soft-eyed man who can only be Jules. Both are adorned with beads around their necks, scarves with Vedic writing and colourful baggy trousers, and both have stubbly chin-growths. If it weren't for the straws poking out of their lassis and the orange plastic chairs on which they are sitting, they could pass for lads out on a jaunt, the kind of adventure-seeking backpackers on the India trail that she has seen everywhere on her travels. But the straws and the modern, primary-coloured surroundings make them appear out of place, a bit like overgrown children.

Dougie spots her and waves across the room.

'So...' she sighs, joining them, 'where's my lassi, then?' She already feels hot and short-tempered from her short walk from the lake.

'Darling Esme – you look absolutely delightful,' Dougie says as he gets up to embrace her. 'It's been so long! Hey, I've really missed you. You're looking fabulous.' She smiles, pleased at the fuss he is making. The warm pleasure it gives her makes her think that perhaps she has been lonely in the last few days without realising it.

'Actually, I'm knackered,' she tells him, 'despite having spent the afternoon reclining on a divan being rowed around a lake.'

'That sounds divinely decadent. Meet Jules, my, er, accomplice...'

Esme and Jules briefly embrace, and they all sit down. After she has ordered a drink ('No straw!' she instructs the waiter), she has a chance to examine Dougie at closer quarters while listening to his rushed account of their last ten days, taking in the slightly broader face and pudgier features that he has developed since the last time they met. He also appears more relaxed than she remembers – looser, perhaps, and smoother, less edgy. He has a sort of glow of travel on him and a sparkling excitement in his eyes.

As for Jules, he strikes her as more serious and thoughtful than first impressions suggested. He is clearly younger than Dougie, probably in his mid-twenties, with a narrow, unshaven face, a pointy nose and small, regular teeth. He looks confident, alert, witty and watchful, probably a good complement to Dougie's slower, more deliberative style.

Her plain lassi arrives and she swallows it thirstily while attempting to answer questions about where she has been in the last three weeks, her time at the hostel, impressions of the family and future plans.

'So what's life at the hostel like?' Dougie asks.

'It's a bit unreal,' Esme tells them. 'You'll find it very weird after travelling. It's like nothing ever happens there. Like a sort of stagnant pool. Everyone's festering, waiting for something to happen – and trying to avoid Stef. She's the one who lays down the rules. She reigns over us like a big spider at the centre of a sticky web, Yet she's the one who looks most uncomfortable to be there.'

'She seems to be on another planet,' Jules says. 'She took me aside and started grilling me about Virginia Woolf.'

'That's her favourite subject,' Esme says. 'Apart from Jake of course. She's a specialist on women's writing: Woolf, Sylvia Plath,

Simone de Beauvoir, all those early feminists. But especially Virginia Woolf.'

'Not a very cheerful lot,' Jules says.

'Not cheerful at all,' Dougie comments. 'Sylvia Plath wrote poems about concentration camps and put her head in an oven. Virginia had manic episodes and drowned herself in a river. De Beauvoir was charged with debauching a minor. None of them were exactly a barrel of fun. But then Stef never struck me as a party animal.'

'Oh, I suspect she knows how to have a good time,' Jules says. 'There's a party in her head, isn't there? It's great. Endless booze. Everyone's invited.'

Esme feels a surge of irritation. *What does he know?* 'I don't think anyone's invited. In fact I think she's not having a such a great time.' It strikes her as bizarre to be defending Stef – but she's too easy a victim. And what right has Jules to be attacking her? 'Miranda says Stef might be turning a corner,' she adds. 'I think that's what this whole thing is about. She's going to start over, turn a new leaf.'

'So that's what we're doing here,' Dougie says. 'It's all beginning to make sense.'

'But she's living in cloud-cuckoo land, isn't she?' Jules asks. 'You know, lost the plot? Constantly pissed?'

'It sounds like word has got around…' Esme says.

'Don't look at me,' Dougie says. 'But it's not exactly a secret, is it?'

'You told me she's been that way since the Old Cunt's funeral,' Jules says to Dougie.

'I beg your pardon?' Esme exclaims.

'Whoops,' Jules covers his mouth. 'Sorry. Tactless.'

But Esme is giggling. She isn't in the least offended, in fact it's a relief to hear Jake's name taken in vain. Perhaps these two rebels have the right idea after all. Who needs solemnity? Jake never did, anyway.

'We know who you mean, Julian,' Dougie says.

'Of course we do,' she says. 'He got called a lot of things in his time. You know what they used to call him at home? Baby Jesus. I don't think Jake would have minded being called a cunt.'

'Badge of honour,' Dougie agrees. 'He was a wanker and he knew it. Love him or loathe him.'

'And you've done both in your time,' Jules says.

'You know, I've never told you,' Dougie tells Esme, 'but I was really disgusted when he walked out on you.'

'What do you mean?' Esme asks.

'When he dumped you. It was a bit sudden. You must have been gutted.'

'When *he* dumped *me*? Er, who told you that? He didn't dump me. *I* dumped *him*!'

'Oh. That's not what he told us.'

'That doesn't surprise me at all,' Esme tells him, finishing off her glass. 'Actually, I think he was a bit traumatised. No one had ever done that to him before.'

'Well, that puts a different light on things!'

'If that's what Jake told you, he probably said the same thing to Stef,' Esme remarks, drumming her fingers on the table as her mind assesses the implications. Maybe she shouldn't be feeling guilt towards Stef after all. Then she remembers the other reasons to feel guilty.

'He probably did!'

'By the way – a word of warning,' Esme tells them. They both look up with worried faces. 'It's Jake's thirtieth birthday tomorrow. That's why the ceremony was scheduled for then. So Stef's going to be pretty extreme... I was thinking of a day out somewhere. Somewhere far away.'

'In case of crossfire?' Dougie says. 'Sounds reasonable. Maybe we'll tag along.'

'And something else that might persuade you to put a bit of distance between yourselves and the hostel – she's planning to have a serious chat with you.'

'Really?' Dougie asks, face dropping. 'What about?'

'The book, of course.'

Dougie winces. 'Ah...'

'Apparently, you've got it...'

'Well...'

'She's got the highest expectations' Esme says. 'She thinks it's a potential masterpiece, and she's counting on you to produce the rabbit out of your hat. It's what she's living for.'

'Oh hell,' Dougie says with a groan.

'And to be honest,' Esme says, 'it came as a bit of a surprise to me. I didn't even know of the existence of this book.'

'Er – yes you did,' Dougie responds. 'Stef said you were the one who told her about it in the first place. She was interrogating me about it at the funeral.'

'Well, yeah...'

'I didn't have a clue what she was on about,' Dougie says. 'You could have knocked me down with a feather. I mean – Jake? Writing a *book*? Come on!'

'He *might* have been writing a book,' Esme says. 'He did mention it once.'

'He mentioned it? Esme, that's not quite the same thing. He mentioned a lot of things. He might have mentioned that he was the king of Peru, but no one actually believed him.'

'But if you don't believe he wrote a book, why ever did you tell her you're bringing it?' Esme asks. 'And exactly what is it that you're bringing her?'

Dougie and Jules exchange a nervous glance. 'Well, that's the thing. You see, I found these notebooks of his. Just recently. I was clearing out a cupboard, and there they were, and I remembered he had left them in my room once. Before he went awol. I've never actually looked at them. But they might just have been the beginnings of a book. Possibly. A skeleton of a book. So I wrote to Stef, because I thought she might be interested.'

'Interested? She's obsessed! She's asked me about it at least a dozen times. I told her I didn't know anything about it. But whatever you've got will set her mind at rest. Doesn't matter what it is, even if it's a shopping list: she can die happy.'

Dougie pinches his cheeks together and turns a solemn look on Esme. 'Trouble is – I don't have them any more.'

Esme stares at him. 'So you don't have it...'

'No.'

'We woz robbed!' Jules says theatrically, having followed the exchange with mute interest. 'On the train. Some wanker took the bag they were in.'

'Oh Jesus...' Esme says, exhaling. 'Holy fuck.'

'Quite,' agrees Dougie. 'And I haven't got a clue what to do. I mean... where do we go from here?'

A silence hangs between them.

'Well, short of writing a book in the next few hours and passing it off as Jake's, you'll just have to come clean,' Jules says. When no one responds, he says to Esme: 'What I don't get is, if you weren't aware that he wrote a book, why did you tell Stef he wrote a book?'

Esme shrugs. 'It's what she wanted to hear.'

Jules looks confused. 'Oh. Right. So you thought that's what she wanted to hear, and so you lied to her... Sounds a bit ethically dubious to me.'

'I didn't really think it through.'

'Evidently,' Jules says.

Esme frowns. She doesn't feel Jules knows her well enough to start criticising her. After a pause, she sits up straighter and says to Dougie: 'And, by the same reasoning, it's probably unwise to mention his habits. His habit.'

Dougie suddenly looks more serious, screwing up his features. 'She doesn't know about his habit?'

'I have no idea. It's not like we're on intimate terms. She hasn't mentioned it, so she probably doesn't.'

'Er, what are you two talking about?' Jules asks.

They look at him, suddenly uncomfortable.

'Jake had a habit,' Dougie tells him.

'You never mentioned that.'

Dougie shrugs. 'It was just another vice. He collected vices. Like his gambling.'

'Gambling...?' Jules echoes.

'He was an idiot, I told you that. He would try everything. He was a compulsive gambler. Stayed up all night playing online poker.'

'Did he win?'

'Occasionally. But never as much as he lost. And he lost big time. That's how he picked up a habit.'

'How does that work?'

'Duh. He started dealing to clear his debts. Him and Charlie. And then the inevitable happened: he began enjoying the merchandise a bit too much.'

'Who's Charlie?'

'A friend. It was Charlie's bike he came off.'

Jules is looking very disgruntled now. 'So what else haven't you told me?'

'Hey, what is this cross-examination?' Dougie says. 'Do I have to tell you everything?'

'Yes. Full disclosure, dude.'

The two are staring at each other belligerently, making Esme wonder whether she should leave them to sort things out.

'It's just a bit weird you haven't mentioned these little details,' Jules continues in a petulant tone. 'You've told me a lot of other stuff about him. It's like you've given me the sanitised version.'

Dougie shrugs again. 'I thought I'd mentioned it.' Jules looks sceptical, his eyes dark and troubled. 'It wasn't a secret,' Dougie continues, more defensively. 'It just didn't come up. Didn't seem important.'

'Well, obviously it *is*,' Jules tells him. 'And it would be rather important to Stef.'

'Why?' Esme asks. She can see he's getting angrier by the second, and he's beginning to get on her nerves.

Jules turns his flashing eyes on her. 'You've already said she's obsessed about a book he wasn't writing. And she doesn't know he was a junkie, and a problem gambler, and a dealer? Does she have a clue? And doesn't she have a right to know – I mean, she's his mother!'

'I don't see what difference it would make,' Esme says. 'Why add to her misery?'

'It just doesn't seem ... right,' Jules responds sulkily, rubbing his bristly chin. 'Or very honest. Somebody ought to tell her.'

'Don't be crazy,' Dougie says. 'If she doesn't know now, now is not the time for her to know.'

'It might actually do her some good,' Jules says, his voice rising again. 'You know, bring her down to reality.'

'What, by toppling her golden boy from his pedestal?'

'*Golden boy*,' Jules scoffs. 'If only she knew! This drugged-up, dissolute, phoney queer who dealt heroin, gambled recklessly and shafted all his so-called mates. She doesn't know half the story. Golden boy? More like *golden void*. Golden illusion! Golden fantasy! I mean who was he really? You all talk about him so much, but who was he really? I don't think either of you have any idea.

He was anything you chose him to be. Actually, I think he was a fraud. In fact, he was a total fiction! Like this so-called book he was supposed to be writing. Doesn't exist! Never did!'

Esme and Dougie stare at him, surprised by his vehemence.

'Steady on, old fruit!' Dougie says, in a comic approximation of Sean Connery's brogue.

'Maybe it's him up on his shitty golden throne that makes her drink like a fucking fish,' Jules is almost shouting now, seriously aggrieved.

'Hey,' Dougie says. 'Simmer down, man. Too hot for this. I don't know why you're getting in such a stew.'

'Because you've been lying. To her and to me.'

'Don't be an arse. I haven't been lying to her *or* to you.'

'You haven't been giving me the whole picture. Which makes me think there's a lot more to tell.'

'That's bullshit,' Dougie tells him, his tone appeasing.

'Is it?' Jules says, huffily.

There is a silence, and all three turn their gazes to the window, avoiding each other's eyes. As they do so, they become aware that it is now dark outside, and simultaneously of the fizzing whine of insects zapping angrily into the blue insectocutor on the wall above them.

'Anyway,' Dougie says eventually. 'It's not up to us. Even if now was a good time. It's not our gig.'

'I really think a few things need to be straightened out,' Jules says, looking pointedly at Dougie. 'Some home truths need to be aired. Too much bullshit, y'know, bad for the soul. Too many secrets. Can't do any good.'

'Yeah, man. Let's all start living the truth. Don't be a dweeb,' Dougie said.

'If anything,' Esme ventures, 'tell Laurie. He could handle it.'

'Maybe I will,' Jules says grudgingly.

'No! Don't even do that,' Dougie exclaims. 'For fuck's sake, it's going to be stressful enough just being here. Let's not make it any worse by stirring up a hornet's nest. And the past is a hornet's nest. That's why we don't do the past, remember?'

'Let's just tell the truth,' said Jules. 'Truth is the great healer. And it sounds to me like Stef needs healing. She deserves the truth. If no one else does, I'll tell her.'

'I think I'm going to be sick!' Dougie says, clearly exasperated. 'Why are you being such a numpty?' Esme can't tell how angry he is, or how genuine his anger is. 'And anyway,' he adds more calmly, reverting to his more usual ironic tone, 'there is no single truth. Hasn't India taught you anything? Get real, baba.'

'Yes, baba,' Jules agrees, joining his hands in prayer and turning his gaze heavenwards. 'There are as many truths as there are leaves in the forest." And that's one of them. Let's dwell on that.'

'Hey – you guys haven't gone all spiritual, have you?" Esme asks, clutching at the chance of turning this private row into something humorous.

'No,' Dougie says. 'We haven't. But...' He suddenly assumes a crafty smirk. 'We have got some superlative *charas* stashed away, if you're looking for enlightenment.'

Esme shakes her head. 'I don't even smoke tobacco any more,' she tells him. 'And anyway, it's far too bloody hot.'

'Fucking hot...' echoes Jules.

'So I shouldn't be expecting any great wisdom from you two,' she says, mocking. 'India hasn't exactly touched your souls. *Hey, I'm not enlightened,*' she mocks them. '*I'm just stoned.*'

'That's just about right,' Dougie agrees. 'We don't do the past. We don't do gods. We don't do enlightenment. But we do get high. Spread the word!'

'Yo, spread the word,' Jules says. 'Just don't tell the cat's mother...'

315

Chapter 36 | The Tamil temple

It is still dark when Esme wakes to a soft knocking at her door. At the same instant, her phone alarm rattles. She swipes the alarm, jumps out of bed and hurries to the door. Pulling it ajar, she finds Shibu's sleepy face on the other side. They exchange a wordless nod and smile, both content that the pre-arranged call has been successfully accomplished. Shibu walks along the corridor to knock on the next door on his list while Esme steps quickly into the shower. By the time she gets downstairs, Dougie is already waiting by the rickshaw they have booked for the ride to the railway station. It is not yet six o'clock.

Light filters into the sky as they bounce towards the station. There are just the two of them on the excursion now, after Miranda, Ian and Jules all opted out – for which Esme is privately glad. She isn't in a convivial frame of mind, though she appreciates the opportunity to spend some time alone with Dougie, even if she is fairly sure that he would not have agreed to come but for his terror of the inevitable encounter with Stef, and the admission he will have to make to her.

At the station they join a milling crowd on the concourse – lively, even at this hour. They don't board their train until seven-thirty, however, an hour after the scheduled departure time. As soon as the train sets off, Esme feels her mood lift. She addresses a few comments to Dougie, sitting opposite her, but he appears to be self-absorbed or just sleepy and she doesn't attempt to draw him out. Then, an hour or so later, during an extended wait on the line with the train immersed in a profound, sleepy silence, Dougie turns his attention away from the fields and removes his ear-buds.

'Just remind me why you chose this place?'

'The temple? It's an important Hindu monument, apparently,' Esme tells him. 'Tamil-style, so a rare thing in Kerala. It's supposed to be architecturally significant. The guidebook calls it unique and unmissable.'

Dougie nods, not showing much enthusiasm. In fact, he seems to Esme to be peevishly discontented, which she ascribes to the distinctly frosty mood of last night, when Jules made known his general disapproval of everything.

'Plus I thought we should get out of the Christian zone,' Esme adds.

'Why?'

'Just for the change. We're surrounded by it in Allapoorha, it's suffocating. Most of India isn't Christian, yet we're stuck in that bubble.'

Dougie grunts and reinserts his earbuds, cutting off further discussion. Esme returns her attention to her book. Until this enforced stop, her eyes have been flickering between her book and the rural landscape crawling by outside, but she was taking in little of either. Instead, her mind has been seething with unresolved questions, mostly to do with how much Stef is entitled to know. Is Jules right, that it's unethical to keep her swaddled in her blanket of illusion? Who decides? And who bears responsibility for the collateral damage if the blanket is snatched away? If Esme had her way, she would overrule any suggestion of enlightening Stef regarding the full extent of her son's multiple failures – there can be no risk of harm if she is none the wiser. But if truth must be served, it should probably come from her, no one else, in which case she should do it before Jules or anyone else blurts it out thoughtlessly. She is pretty sure that subtlety is not Jules's strongest point. As for Dougie, she would normally be confident that he would never willingly fess up – at uni he always shunned confrontations – however, if he is put on the spot and admits that

Jake's precious book is irretrievably gone, who knows what else might tumble out?

She was hoping to chew it over with Dougie in the course of this day-trip – maybe later, when he is more receptive. His eyes are clouded now, and won't meet hers. In fact, Dougie is hardly aware of Esme at all, for he too is preoccupied by the prospect of Stef's confrontation with the truth, and depressed by it, and even more preoccupied by the wall that has sprung up between him and Jules. There has been some kind of communication breakdown since their arrival in Allapoorha, an inexplicable distancing – the first time they have felt anything like it since leaving England.

Last night, after meeting Esme at Sri Vidna, the three of them went to find something to eat and ended up in a nondescript dhaba on the main road, where they exchanged stilted small talk over a very mediocre meal. At one point Jules announced that he would not after all accompany them on today's excursion to the temple, he needed some down time, he said, whereupon, on an impulse, Dougie nodded as if in approval. 'Good, we could both do with some time out.' He saw the sting in Jules's face but said nothing. Dougie doesn't know why he said what he did. Something to do with Jules's somewhat stony manner. Not even a shared chillum under the trees afterwards succeeded in healing the rupture. Later, they went to their separate rooms with hardly a word, just a brief, evasive caress. The truth was that they had nothing to say to each other. Maybe they have simply been too much in each other's pocket over the last couple of weeks and are now emptied of conversation. Whatever the cause, something has definitely shifted. It's as if, now that they're no longer travelling, now they have stopped moving, they are living in two different places, as if they have disembarked at different stations. But at the bottom of it, Dougie is convinced, it all comes back to Jake.

Esme was the original link between Dougie and Jake at uni. She had known Dougie, Charlie and other members of the local gay scene, had had a few drinks with them, been to a few clubs, had a few laughs. She introduced them to Jake. Dougie can clearly recall his first impressions of Jake – of his sloping, shambling walk, his feet splayed, of his slow smile and clear gaze that was both ironic and innocent, and of his complete dedication to self-indulgence. Later, when they became more relaxed with each other, he remembers asking him if he ever had gay inclinations, Jake looked up, his green eyes sparkling mischievously but otherwise straight-faced. 'Hey, Doug: we're all gay now!'

For a while, Jake was up there with the angels, at one with the cosmic flow. Then one day his shining chariot crashed and burned and he disappeared from view.

He remembers when, several years later, he was telling Jules about the local scene, including Jake, and being taken aback by Jules's rather prim reaction to Jake's honorary membership of the town's queer culture. He evidently found his 'conversion' distasteful. He was an interloper, he said, an entryist, and it was insulting. He sounded almost resentful. Dougie countered his primness with humour and hooted with laughter. 'Don't be such a fucking prude,' he told him. 'What does it matter if he was gay or straight or bi anyway? You didn't know him. He was a joker. He could be whoever he wanted to be.'

'So he was just having a laugh at your expense,' Jules said.

'Look: he was off the map,' Dougie insisted, 'a wee bit eccentric, an original,' and he whipped Jules's arse with the drying-up towel before turning back to his sinkful of dirty dishes. 'Okay, maybe he was just messing around. What does it matter?'

'I just don't like tourists. And I feel sorry for his girlfriend,' Jules loftily declared before stalking out of the kitchen. After that, Dougie felt he was treading on eggshells whenever he mentioned Jake in front of his lover. Jules was implacable – apparently infuriated that Dougie could be so tolerant of what he saw as Jake's imposture and infiltration. He seemed to suspect that Dougie wasn't being honest with him. And he was obviously jealous. But the man's dead. How could he still be nursing that animosity?

With screeching brakes and repeated triumphant blasts of its bovine-like klaxon, the train finally trails into their station. The three-hour ride turned out to be four and a half hours, so that Dougie and Esme eventually arrive at their stop two and a half hours later than planned. They quickly find a rickshaw for the last leg of the journey to the temple, whose soaring multi-coloured gopura towers dominate the town. Before entering, they pause to take in the towers' dense and gaudy population of plaster gods, heroes and beasts, some grinning or gurning, some blue-skinned, some with multiple arms and protruding tongues or elaborate feathered headwear or all of these.

After worming their way through the mêlée of devotees and beggars around the temple's entrance, they are made to discard their sandals, forcing them, once inside, to sprint barefooted across the furnace-hot ground from one patch of shade to the next. Contrary to their expectations of being scrutinised and hassled, they are treated by the worshippers with complete indifference. Stick-thin sadhus sitting cross-legged in the dust gaze nonchalantly at them, ancient women with matted hair and leathery faces look straight through them, and even the beggars ignore them. There is the usual scattering of semi-comatose dogs flung randomly about the temple grounds, but these show only the mildest curiosity, raising their heads to offer a listless glance before returning to their twitchy slumbers. At this midday hour, with the temperature pushing forty degrees, it is simply too hot to give much attention to the pale-skinned sightseers.

They are able to enter all but the most inner of sanctums, including dim, incense-swathed chambers filled with people ostentatiously prostrating themselves on the ground while others perform private pujas in silent concentration. At one end of the complex, at the top of petal-strewn steps, they pass a huge stone bull, Nandi, swathed in a brilliant white shawl, in front of which a fleshy man stripped to the waist and with his forehead daubed with ash is stoking a small ceremonial fire on a raised brazier while his equally fleshy companion receives monetary donations from a line of worshippers. Elsewhere in the temple, they gaze upon blackened, impish-looking stone figures and a forest of stumpy lingams striped with white bands.

Finally, after roaming around the scattered structures in search of the best vantage points and photo angles, they find a thin strip of shade on the peripheral wall of a tank of greenish-brown water where they can crouch out of the sun's glare. In the middle of the tank, black cormorants are drifting like flotsam around a platform a small image of Ganesh, over which a tattered flag droops lifelessly. In front of them another of the tall gopuras rears up. Dougie squints in wonder at the carnival of garishly-coloured figures crowding it: sinuous *yakshini* flaunting their spherical breasts, thrusting hips and voluptuous lips, jostling for space with fearsome, teeth-baring and lavishly moustached warriors and a menagerie of coiled snakes, regal elephants and prancing monkeys. Sporadically, showers of pigeons scatter from the tower and reassemble on it a few moments later, careless of the holiness of their perches.

The busyness of the towers is in marked contrast to the sluggish activity on the ground. A lethargic procession of local people files past, some lanky and thin, balancing unwieldy bundles on their heads, others bent and bandy-legged, leaning on crudely fashioned staffs. There are more purposeful types, too, whom Dougie assumes to be part of the temple hierarchy. The younger ones look like trainee priests – wrapped in fresh white dhotis, with neat top-knots, beads strung around their necks and caste strings across their bare chests. They seem possessed of a swaggering self-assurance, not deigning to rest their eyes on anyone. Then there are plumper, older and more solemn figures with shaven heads, whose slow, imperious gaze sweeps haughtily over the foreigners as they pass.

'How is it that they can just stroll along without being scorched?' Dougie wonders aloud.

'Indian feet,' Esme tells him. 'They're hardier.'

Dougie feels bewildered by everything he has seen. It is the first Indian temple he has entered, his first close-up encounter with the Hindu faith, and he feels more confused than before he entered. Religion here seems to him like a closed circuit, without any reference to the world outside. The temple is impressive enough, and he's in awe of the locals' stoic disregard of the aggressive heat, but he can't relate to their dogged devotions. To him, it is all unfathomable.

He wonders what Jules is doing right now, but resists the temptation to text him. Knowing him, he's smoking ganja on Allapoorha's lake, or lounging on the beach – not stranded here in this god-infested hothouse. This sightseeing expedition has turned out to be harder work than he bargained for, and, wearily wiping his neck with his scarf, he ponders on when it might be reasonable to suggest embarking on their return journey. It seems that an immense measure of time has elapsed since they boarded the train this morning. Esme, absorbed in her guidebook, seems in no hurry to leave.

'Any word from Jules?' Esme asks, seeing him consult his phone and sensing his restlessness. Dougie shakes his head, putting the phone away.

Esme returns to her book, and silence descends once more.

'So what does it say?' asks Dougie, gesturing to the guidebook.

'About where we are. This place,' she answers. Abruptly she shuts the book and sighs. 'Actually, it feels completely inappropriate.'

'What does?'

'This... sightseeing. In a temple. It feels voyeuristic to be gawping at people in prayer. It makes me uncomfortable.'

'I'm with you on that, Esme,' Dougie tells her, feeling a wave of relief. 'In fact I share your sentiments completely.' Until now they have been circulating around the complex in silence, taking it all in, but neither of them, it transpires, able to appreciate what they are seeing.

'Plus it's all a bit irrelevant,' Esme adds. 'Because ... you know, it's not why we're here. In India.'

'You mean we should be giving all our attention to Jake?'

She frowns. 'No. Yes. I don't know.'

For the umpteenth time Dougie consults his phone and sees the time. 'Well, whatever, we're going to have to shift soon anyway if we're going to catch the Link Express back to Allapoorha.'

Esme nods. 'Let's go now.'

They gather their things and hasten back over the hot ground to the entrance where they collect their shoes and hail a rickshaw for the ride to the station.

The train is only fifty minutes late, and once they have settled in a compartment, back in the train's soothing, clanking motion with maize fields on either side, they are more talkative than on the outward journey and begin to exchange travellers' tales on their Indian experiences.

'It sounds like you've had a lot of fun,' Esme tells Dougie.

'Don't get me wrong,' he replies, 'it's been a ball. At least, it was until yesterday. In fact it was wild! I haven't had so much fun since I was a student.'

'Since you were hanging out with Jake?'

'Well, yes, that was fun, definitely. But not all my uni memories are to do with that delinquent. He only turned up in my last year.'

'Did you ever have a physical relationship with him?'

Dougie jerks up and stares at Esme. 'Whoa! Where did that come from? Are you serious?'

'Oh God, sorry, sorry. I don't know why I said that! It just came into my mind.'

'Christ, give me a break! What kind of question is that? I might expect that from Jules. I get it from him all the time, implied if not in so many words...'

'Forgive me, Dougie, I'm so stupid. I didn't realise he felt like that. And it's none of my business anyway.'

'Sadly he does. He's actually jealous of what may or may not have happened eight years ago.'

'Maybe that's not so strange...'

'Yes, it is. It is!'

Subdued now, Esme lets her eye wander to a low elevation of hills on the eastern horizon, above which she is just able to make out a group of large, floating birds lazily circling on outstretched wings.

Dougie follows her gaze, screwing up his yes. 'What do you think they are?' he asks.

'They look like buzzards. Or vultures, perhaps. They've probably found carrion, or some half-cremated corpse.'

'Ugh!' he grimaces.

'It's good. Life being recycled.'

When the birds are no longer visible, Esme says: 'You've been together with Jules for quite a while now, haven't you? Sorry – I'm being nosy again...'

'No, it's alright. Yes, quite a while. And we have a brilliant relationship. Well, it was brilliant until we got here.'

'The curse of the Daniels...'

'Maybe revisiting the world of Jake has exposed some fault-lines, shall we say? The age difference, for example.'

'Between you two? Does that matter?'

'Probably not,' he concedes. 'But something's amiss. I'm just beginning to wonder whether this whole thing is a gigantic folly.'

'Coming to India?' Esme asks.

'No, I mean agreeing to come to Allapoorha. To the hostel and the ceremony and everything.'

'Yes, maybe it was,' she replies, 'but maybe it was necessary, too.'

The train suddenly grinds to to yet another halt in the middle of fields, and they both retreat into their own thoughts. Esme notices the sky's blue modulating, changing tone, bringing to mind memories of previous train rides in India at this time of day – the hour when the waning sun has cast a buttery hue over the land. Dougie for his part is reflecting on Esme's inquisitiveness regarding his relationship with Jake and why it should matter to her. He supposes that what she actually wants to know is whether her boyfriend really was authentically gay, whether he went all the way. It is natural enough for her to be curious, nonetheless he finds her curiosity intrusive. He himself has never dared to question her on own sexual relations with Jake. Not that he isn't curious, too. Would it be offensive or tasteless to ask?

'So,' Dougie says to Esme, breaking the heavy silence, 'how did you deal with the split?'

'What are you talking about?'

'When your relationship with Jake ended. Him "coming out". Were you okay with that?'

'Oh. Sure. But it wasn't my business any more. Actually it was a huge relief. It allowed me to take a step back. Then I had a brief but torrid affair with a tutor.'

At this they both burst out laughing, attracting the looks of fellow passengers. 'Who?' Dougie demands.

'No names,' she says. 'Well, alright, he was called Dominic. And he was amazing.'

He cackles uproariously. 'I'm glad to hear it!'

The thought that there is, indeed, life after Jake, contrary to what the last few days and weeks have told them, is cheering, and as the train shudders back into motion Dougie seems restored to his previous good humour. 'I tell you what, though,' he tells Esme with a nudge. 'I don't half fancy some of the guys with tashes in these parts.'

'You're joking!'

'They're rather gorgeous! They put Freddie Mercury to shame.'

'I can't say I'd noticed,' Esme says.

'Liar. And talking of gorgeous hunks, what about Shibu?'

'Shibu at the hostel?'

'He's the one we saw last night, right? He's rather lickable.'

'As I said, I hadn't really noticed.'

'Then you're walking around with your eyes closed, sister.'

'Listen, you'd better behave yourself,' Esme says. 'You're almost a married man!'

But the thought teases her. Shibu? It wasn't completely mad. She'd give him a closer look when they got back, maybe.

Chapter 37 | The misdemeanour

'Good morning, Cynthia!'

'Good morning, dear! How are you this morning?'

'Good,' Miranda answers. 'Do you mind if I join you?'

'Not at all. Isn't it wonderful?'

'What is?'

'The morning. Being here. India!'

Miranda takes a seat opposite Cynthia on the veranda. It is eight o'clock, and the air is vibrant, knife-sharp and filled with chattering song. A few yards away, Shibu is hosing the green-brown lawn and the flowerbeds, oblivious to the restive flies and seemingly lost in his thoughts.

Miranda looks around her anxiously. 'Has Stef been down?'

'I haven't seen her. She's normally down a bit later.'

'It's a tough day for her, isn't it?'

'You mean Jake's birthday?' Cynthia asks. 'Yes, it always is, every year. She normally hides herself away and doesn't reappear until the next day. And today will be especially hard. The ceremony was supposed to take place this morning.'

'I know...'

'But we must get on with things, as normal. That's the best policy. Act as if everything will be alright and perhaps it will be. That's my philosophy.'

'Yes...' Miranda agrees without much conviction.

'I understand Esme has gone on some sightseeing expedition with Dougie and Jules. That's a good idea. You should have gone with them.'

'Jules didn't go in the end, and I thought I'd better stay here. Dad might need me...'

'That's very thoughtful, dear' Cynthia tells her. 'He's very lucky to have you. You're a rock.'

'Well... actually, I feel a bit, you know, apprehensive.' Her eyes drift over to Shibu, now fiddling with the valve on his hose.

'Oh, dear!'

'It's like a kind of dread. Something I can't put a finger on. and then there's something else that keeps nagging at me.'

'What's that, dear?'

'Well, it's something I found out. About Oliver.'

Cynthia's expression hardens almost imperceptibly, her face now subtly veiled. 'What have you found out?' she asks in a neutral tone.

Miranda watches Shibu as he resumes his hosing, then turns to look straight into Cynthia's eyes, 'Did you know that he changed his name?'

'No, I didn't know he changed his name.' She looks bemused now.

'He never mentioned it, then?'

'No.' Cynthia gazes meditatively across the garden. She sighs, then adds, a little irritably: 'Well, there must be a good reason for it, I suppose. It's not against the law to change your name.'

'No, of course not,' Miranda hastens to reassure her. But, with her jaw set and arms folded, Cynthia is wearing an expression that Miranda recognises – the sort she adopts when she has reached a decision that she will not budge from, overriding any advice, counter information or second thoughts that might sway her. She is notoriously obstinate in that way.

There is an uncomfortable hiatus in the conversation, and Miranda is about to expand on what she has discovered when the silence is broken by the characteristic guttural bark that heralds the approach of Oliver himself. He is crossing the grass towards them, looking trim and dapper in a fawn-coloured cotton jacket, fawn short trousers and his Panama hat, with a newspaper folded under his arm.

'How was your walk, dear?' Cynthia enquires, her light-hearted tone astonishing to Miranda, as though nothing remotely concerning him had just passed between the two women.

'Capital. It's the best part of the day. Good morning, Miranda,' he adds, seating himself at the table.

'Where have you come from?' Miranda asks him.

'Down the road. Just a stroll. Half a mile, nothing more. I can't have breakfast without my constitutional.'

'I've had my tea, dear,' Cynthia tells him. 'And I think I'll just leave you both now, if you don't mind.' She rises and hastens indoors, and they hear her dashing upstairs.

'Dodgy stomach,' explains Oliver curtly. He unravels his newspaper and produces a pen. 'How are you with crosswords?'

'Cryptic?'

'Of course.'

'Then, no, sorry. Can't help you there.'

'Fair enough.' He frowns at the newspaper. 'I'm stuck on twenty-three across.'

Just as she is about to say something, they both sense a movement from inside the hostel. Simon emerges from the restaurant, yawning. 'Morning,' he says on seeing them.

'Good morning!' Oliver responds, suddenly jovial.

Simon looks around the garden and up at the sky. 'Sunny again. How monotonous.'

'Ah, but you never can tell what's lurking,' Oliver says. 'There was rain in the night – not a whiff of it now.'

Simon eyes him sleepily, then turns to his sister. 'Have you had breakfast?'

She shakes her head.

'Are you going to have breakfast?' he asks.

'Okay, let's go. Good luck with your crossword,' she tells Oliver, who nods smartly and reverts to his puzzle.

In the restaurant, waiting for their eggs, Simon murmurs to her: 'Something oily about that man. And deeply boring!'

'Oliver? No, I don't think so,' she tells him. 'He's actually rather mysterious.'

'You can be mysterious and boring.'

'Actually, he's turning out to be a bit more interesting than we thought.'

Simon scoffs. 'How interesting can an accountant be? Anyway, he's a phony.'

'Why do you say that?'

'He's all front. This act of his, efficient, suave, man of the world, all that crap – it doesn't ring true. He's a phony alright.'

Flowery, smiling effusively, arrives with a tray laden with tea, cups and saucers, milk and sugar, just as Laurie enters the room.

'Good morning, Professor,' she greets him in her high, fluting voice.

'Good morning, Flowery.'

'Your usual breakfast. Professor?'

'Marvellous. Thank you, Flowery,' he beams. Flowery bustles out and he joins Miranda and Simon at their table, snapping open his tablet as he does so.

'How's Stef?' Miranda asks. 'Is she okay?'

'Sound asleep, I think,' Laurie answers abstractedly. 'She had a rotten night, seemed to be awake most of it, then she finally drifted off around dawn.'

'Oh dear.'

Laurie is peering into the screen of his tablet, apparently unconcerned, making clear that he wishes to change the subject. 'Anyway ... what's been happening in the world?' he asks, addressing no one in particular.

'Oh, you know. It's still spinning,' Miranda says. 'Oliver is stuck on twenty-three across and Cynthia has the runs.'

Laurie winces at her. 'I think you might be over-sharing, love,' he says. 'Too much information.'

Simon sighs. 'She's a sad product of the times, your daughter,' he tells him. 'She doesn't get it that most information is unwanted.'

'How do you know?' Miranda asks.

'And superfluous,' Simon adds.

'But you must have the information first, in order to decide what is superfluous,' Miranda tells him. 'Anyway, I like information. It's what makes the world go round.'

'I thought it was love,' Laurie says.

'Or money,' adds Simon. 'Information's an add-on, like an uninvited guest. And it's dangerous because you can never unknow it. Anyway, it's all subjective, and fakeable. Miranda's got something on Oliver,' he explains to Laurie. 'She thinks he's more interesting than he appears.'

Laurie briefly chuckles, but he is reading, not listening.

'What do *you* think?' Miranda asks her father.

He looks up. 'What?'

'Do you think Oliver is more than he appears?'

'Probably,' Laurie says, returning to his screen. 'You can't take anyone at face value these days.'

Flowery arrives with two plates of well-cooked fried eggs which she places in front of Miranda and Simon. Laurie contemplates the eggs doubtfully, takes a slice of toast for himself and starts to butter it, grimacing at the butter's greasy texture.

'Cynthia says he's a dark horse,' Miranda tells him.

'Oh, yes?' He chuckles, smearing a thin pink layer of jam over the butter. 'Well Cynthia's a bit of a romantic, as we all know. She loves anyone with a dash of mystery, preferably with a few spicey stories thrown in. They seem to get on, anyway, that's the main thing.'

'Can't really associate the word "romantic" with Oliver the accountant, myself,' Simon says, setting about his eggs.

'You shouldn't underestimate him,' Miranda tells him. 'That's why you need good information.'

'Hey, you're in classroom mode again,' Simon admonishes her. 'Stop lecturing, sis.'

'Imagination can take the place of information, sometimes,' Laurie says. 'Dreaming's allowed too, you know...'

'Oh, but isn't imagination self-deceiving?' Miranda asks, 'I always thought that dreaming's for reality-rejecters.'

Simon stops eating and contemplates his sister with a worried expression. 'So, not only have you got no sense of humour, you're paranoid, and you want a world where everything is known about everybody and dreamers are persecuted.'

'Not persecuted, just...kept in their place.'

Simon regards her with pity. 'Join the human race, sis. We're not all information-processors.'

For the next few minutes, as they progress through their breakfasts in companionable silence, the three of them feel more united than they have for years. It is as if the present crisis has solidified their bond, and it gives Miranda a frisson of hope. *United* – she thinks – *still a team after all these years, in the face of all adversities.* She can count on the team. With their support she can confront and overcome the tasks ahead.

She decides then that she can consult her father in the first of these, the thorny issue regarding Oliver. Before that, though, she will have to tackle Oliver separately, lay her cards on the table – notwithstanding Cynthia's sentimental wish to sweep them away out of sight. Once she has got Oliver's version she can provide Laurie with the full picture and they can proceed from there.

Having reached her decision, she is keen to see it through before she can be deflected. With an apology and an excuse to Laurie and Simon, she abandons her eggs and returns to the veranda, where she finds Oliver still wrestling with his puzzle.

'Hallo, again!' she says as she takes her seat opposite him. He looks up, surprised to see her.

'Well, hallo! Breakfasted? Really can't get on with the breakfasts here, myself. It's the one failing of this place. But otherwise I think everything's superb, don't you? And the staff are outstanding!'

'They're all very friendly,' she says.

'It's more like a proper hotel than a hostel. Must say, I was worried when your father told us we'd be staying in a hostel. I was expecting to see rows of dormitory beds and clogged-up shower-trays. But the rooms are very satisfactory. And I'm sleeping quite well, too, now that I've got used to the dawn chorus, not to mention the muezzin and the prayer songs. Ear-plugs help.'

'I never go anywhere without ear-plugs.'

'Ah, a light sleeper, like me. Well I'm an early riser anyway. Force of habit. I wake early. If it's too early I'll listen to the World Service back home, but here it's the perfect time to be up and about. I do my early-morning constitutional – that's the one I've just done – then I do my late-morning constitutional before lunch and my afternoon constitutional after my siesta.' He looks up at her amiably. 'You'd be most welcome to join me, if the whim takes you. Relaxes the muscles, soothes the bones, clears the mind. The best antidote to all this waiting around, I find.' He clears his throat and beams at her. There is an unappealing smugness in his face and Miranda decides to dive in.

'You know, I had a funny conversation with that Indian gentleman who's often here. Mr Pereira, I think he's called. Though I haven't seen him since then. He was here nearly every day last week. He said he knew you.'

'Oh?'

'Yes. Well, heard of you, anyway. Apparently he's a great fan! But he called you Oliver Moorland, not Maitland.'

'Perhaps he mistook me for someone else.'

'I don't think so. He was very sure. He's a businessman and said he knew all about your career.'

'Good lord.'

'Yes – small world! He said you had quite a reputation in your day. And that you worked in the City. High finance.' Oliver continues to regard her with a poker face, waiting. 'So that tweaked my interest, obviously, and I looked you up. Or looked up Oliver Moorland, anyway. I'm not sure which is your correct surname.'

'You looked me up...' He casts a casual glance over his shoulder.

'Yes, just a quick Google search, nothing very in-depth.'

'And what did you find?' His voice is low and steady now, with not a hint of smugness, and his eyes are fixed on her.

'Well... I suppose you can guess...' Lowering her own voice a fraction, she asks: 'Does Cynthia *know* you've been in prison?'

Oliver does not flinch or display the slightest sign of surprise.

'It sounds like you're confusing me with someone else, Miranda.'

'I don't think so. There was a photograph in a newspaper, and it was you!'

'I see.'

'So does she?'

'No.'

'I didn't think so.'

'And actually she doesn't need to know.' His voice has descended to a soft murmur.

'Really?'

'Believe me, it would be far better if she weren't to know. She might get completely the wrong end of the stick.'

'It was fraud, wasn't it, that you were convicted for? '

'There's no advantage that I can see in mentioning it,' he quietly insists. 'Not to anyone.'

'The article said it was a six-month sentence, but you only served three months.'

'Thirteen weeks, to be exact. And no, it wasn't fraud.'

'What was it?'

'It's completely irrelevant now, Miranda, it's past. I've done my time, and it's behind me now. It's behind us all.'

'Was it cooking the books?'

Oliver sighs deeply, lowers his head, then meets her eyes again, his face devoid of any pretence or charm.

'It's a complicated business, Miranda, and I couldn't possibly summarise it in a few words even if I wanted to. But it's important that you know that in my eyes, and in the eyes of many of my colleagues, I did nothing wrong. Whatsoever.'

'The judges must have thought so!'

Oliver sighs again, exasperated but patient. 'Let me begin to explain. I offered consultancy. I performed audits. Accountants are not just bean-counters, you know, telling you how many beans make five.'

'I expect any number of beans can make five in your world, from zero to a million.'

He frowns now, losing patience. 'You're determined to paint me in a bad light, Miranda. It's understandable, I suppose. You're shocked, I see that. But bear in mind that many people benefitted from my work, not just rich people, and I repeat, in the eyes of most people – people like Mr Pereira – I did no wrong. At most it was a professional misdemeanour. In terms of moral culpability, I would put it in the same category as shoplifting.'

'Shoplifting!'

'It's all relative, of course. It's a question of degree. And I didn't actually steal anything from anybody. I advised a few firms where to invest, how to maximise efficiency, how to get the best value from investments, that sort of thing.'

'Oh, is that what they call "creative accounting"?'

'If you like. But a lot of my work was simply auditing.'

'Well, I don't understand much about finance or big business,' she admits. 'I'm totally ignorant, really. Like how does it happen that auditors are employed by the same companies whose books are being inspected? No one has ever been able to explain that to me.'

'No, you're right, Miranda. You don't understand much about finance or how companies operate or how audits work. Suffice to say that it was all above board, and I can assure you that there are much bigger fish than me, much more powerful and much, much richer, who got away scot-free for doing exactly the same work...'

'That's not surprising...'

'...and that it's largely a matter of bad luck who, in the parlance, gets nicked. And I happened to be the one who got nicked, although most people recognised that I did nothing fundamentally wrong. Nonetheless, I was given a sentence. And consequently I thought it expedient to change my surname to avoid the kind of misguided probing that you are now subjecting me to. And I reiterate, Miranda, that if word of my past "misadventures", shall we call them, is generally circulated, it will benefit absolutely no one, it will simply cause distress and unnecessary hurt. Why would you want to do that? As I have said to you, I have served my time, that part of my life is behind me, and if it makes you feel any better I have never profited from anyone else's misfortune, in fact I have never made a great deal of money at anyone's expense, nor am I particularly well off now. What little I previously earned is mostly gone, and now I have a relatively modest lifestyle. I have enough to get by, enough to pay my golf club dues and to enjoy the occasional holiday, and enough to make periodic contributions to charitable causes, including, as you well know, your own trust, which is what enables us all to be here today.'

The two exchange a long, mute look, and at last Miranda says: 'I don't know what the best thing to do is, Oliver, to be honest. I'll feel remiss if I don't tell Cynthia what I know, but I'll probably feel bad if I tell her, too. I'm usually quite good at taking decisions, but I'm a bit flummoxed. I just assumed that you would prefer to be open and honest with Cynthia.'

'My relationship with Cynthia is none of your concern, Miranda, but I might as well mention that Cynthia and I have a very good relationship, a healthy one that is mutually supportive, and that is largely due to an unspoken pact we have according to which neither of us delves too deeply into the other's private affairs. Least of all those that are in the past, which is where they should remain.'

'Got it.' Miranda nods and rises. 'Thank you, Oliver, for your candour.'

'And I appreciate yours, Miranda,' Oliver says. 'I have complete faith in your good sense and I am sure that you will do the right thing.'

She nods again, and turns to leave. 'One moment,' Oliver stops her. 'I haven't finished yet.' He emits a throat-clearing, more subdued this time, then continues in the same low, steady tone: 'I just wanted to advise you that it really wouldn't do to spread false rumours when there are one or two skeletons in your own family vault...'

Miranda looks at him curiously. 'Meaning...?'

Oliver leans forward, and looks directly into her eyes. 'Meaning there are a few things I'm sure you wouldn't wish to be divulged. Not with Stephanie in her extremely fragile state right now.'

'What are you talking about?'

He leans back again, the look of smugness back on his face.

'I wouldn't want to give too much away.'

'Are you saying you know something about my family?'

'I'm just saying, sometimes discretion is an undervalued quality, and can save all kinds of complications.'

'What do you know?'

'Surely you don't believe that you're the only one who can do a bit of digging?'

'Is this about Michael?'

'Ooh, possibly. Jake's father. Your father. Various skeletons... I'm afraid I can't be more specific right now.'

They exchange a long, silent look as Miranda processes his words, wondering if she has understood him correctly. Then, still without saying anything, she turns and goes inside and up to her room.

Locking her door, she sits on her bed feeling numb. Her heart is beating fast, her hands are trembling, and her mind is enveloped in a fug of panic. All her previous confidence has melted away as she relives the conversation that has just taken place. It already feels like a fantasy, pure fiction, but the hard truth is inescapable. There is an interloper in their midst. Suddenly, there are question marks everywhere, her family's precious solidarity looks very fragile, and she no longer feels up to confronting the cover-ups and dilemmas that beset her. Everything is false, everything a facade, and there is no help at hand, no one she can now confide in. She frowns cagily at the floor beneath her as if at a minefield. Nothing is what it seems, everything is hollow. *So far everyone has been terribly polite, but actually no one is saying what they're really thinking. And the heat is rising and the monsoon is about to break. In the end it might just drown us all.*

Chapter 38 | The hidden treasures

Despite the general anticipation of a difficult twenty-four hours, Jake's birthday begins on a lighter, happier note than the hostel guests have been accustomed to. No one dares to spell it out, but the lighter mood is not unrelated to the non-appearance of Stef. In the breakfast room, the mood is quiet and unhurried, and Laurie and Simon, following Miranda's sudden departure, are content to linger over their tea, discussing nothing in particular.

As they are about to leave, Cynthia and Oliver enter the room. Laurie understands immediately Cynthia's tacit enquiry – raised eyebrows, concerned eyes. 'She was sleeping when I left her. Had a bad night.' Cynthia nods and follows Oliver to their usual table near the garden door.

Laurie takes his tablet into the lounge while Simon fetches his sketchpad from his room and goes into the garden. To his surprise, he finds Jules at a table tapping on his phone.

'Didn't you go with the others to the temple?' he asks.

'No. I was feeling a bit travel-weary,' Jules says. He has a solemn air about him and does not appear disposed to conversation. That suits Simon well, for he is content to settle on the veranda with his sketchpad, drawing in silence. He considers for a moment making another attempt to reproduce Esme on the page, but quickly jettisons the idea. She did not even invite him on her temple expedition – hardly surprising, given the embarrassment that has wrapped itself around their dealings over the last couple of days.

Then, everything changes. There is a banging, raised voices, and out of the dining room door Stef appears, a severe, somewhat stricken expression on her face. Ignoring Simon, she strides across the grass to Jules.

'Morning!' she says, a little too heartily. 'Where's Dougie?'

'He's on some kind of sightseeing trip with Esme,' Jules answers. 'They left early this morning.'

'Sightseeing?' Stef almost spits out the word. 'Where? When will they be back?'

'They went somewhere... I don't know. Somewhere inland, I think,' he tells her. 'I've got no idea when they'll be back.'

Stef is twisting her mouth, chewing her lip. 'Are they avoiding me?' she demands, but doesn't wait for a reply, heading back inside.

For the next hour they are aware of her prowling around the building, moving fretfully from room to room and once even shouting at Thomas, who looks utterly distraught and uncomprehending. Nobody can discover the reason for her outburst, and the other hostel guests exchange nervous glances from their positions in the garden and lounge.

Cynthia and Oliver are the first to desert the scene, announcing that they will make an outing to the lake, for which Thomas has booked places on a tour aboard a rice barge. Jules, who abandoned the garden after his brief encounter with Stef in favour of his balcony, then lay disconsolately on his bed, finally decides that he too needs an outing. He finds Simon still drawing in the garden and proposes an undemanding jaunt somewhere, anywhere. Simon readily agrees and goes in search of Miranda, finding her in her room looking tense and a bit rattled. She readily agrees to join them, and they decide to explore the dusty rural track heading south from St Antony's church, away from the town.

As soon as they are outside the hostel grounds they experience an immediate release of the pent-up tension. Allapoorha's traffic is left behind surprisingly quickly, and they find themselves walking between maize fields and irrigation ditches in which water buffalo are contentedly wallowing, snouts poking out of the reedy water. Every so often they pass farmers on high wagons laden with produce or small boys on outsized bikes, all eyes agog. Their faces betray neither friendliness nor hostility until Simon hails them with 'Namaste', whereupon they reply with 'namaste' or 'namaskar' and warm smiles. Women with tottering bundles on their heads also eye them guardedly, but they too respond with shy smiles when greeted.

After a period of strolling along in silence, Simon voices what they are all thinking: 'It's weird, how enmeshed we are in the waiting and the fretting and all the complications at the hostel, and yet, just a few minutes away, there's this other incredible world. It's like being in a cinema or something that's absorbing all our attention – a complete distraction from this other reality.'

'It's a relief to get out into the real world,' Miranda agrees, though she is still unable to shake off the anxiety that has seeped through her since the morning's uncomfortable exchange with Oliver.

'But which is the realer world?' Simon asks. 'This, or *that*? I'm starting to lose the ability to tell.'

'What's real is that we came here to remember Jake,' Miranda reminds him, 'and we keep losing sight of him amid all the hysteria.' No one responds to this, and she muses aloud: 'He probably came down this way too.'

'Quite likely,' Simon agrees. 'He was here for eight months. He can't have been with the kids all the time.'

'We don't really know what he got up to. I can't imagine him here. But let's pretend we're following in his footsteps,' she says.

'Oh Jesus, let's not. Why spoil a good walk?' Simon says.

Jules looks up, surprised and encouraged by Simon's heretical tone. 'Jake certainly does cast a long shadow,' he says. 'I mean, don't listen to me, I've only just got here and I'm nothing to do with any of this. I'm on the outside. Don't even know why I'm here, to be honest. But then, so far as I can see, nobody even wants to be here anyway. Except his mum.' Miranda and Simon say nothing, both slightly uneasy at this trespass on their family territory. Unfazed by their lack of response, Jules continues: 'So tell me. What's the deal? Why here?'

'Because Stef says so,' Simon answers.

'Well, actually, it's more dad's thing,' Miranda corrects him. 'He set it all up to begin with. Because this is where Jake worked, where he chose to come and help out with the local kids.'

'That's the official version...' Simon comments.

'That's what's so confusing,' Jules says. 'There are so many versions. I didn't know the guy so I'm trying to get a handle on him, but I really can't. It's like he was a composite, or rather he was a different person according to who you speak to. I mean, it's none of my business, but what was he doing on a motorbike, anyway?'

Miranda raises her eyebrows, surprised that this is what is bugging Jules. 'He had a thing about bikes,' she tells him.

'It just sounds completely out of character,' Jules says. 'From what I've heard, he was a bit of a party animal. Not the type to go around in leathers or tinker with engines.'

'No, no – he wasn't a "biker",' Miranda tells him. 'He just loved speed.'

'I can believe that...'

'It was probably something to do with his dad, too,' Simon adds.

'What about his dad?'

'His dad died on a motorbike.'

'Holy shit!' Jules is agog. 'I didn't know that.'

'He was in a road accident,' Simon explains. 'In Germany, I think. That's what was so ironic, or tragic, or whatever, about Jake going the same way.'

'Well ... wouldn't that have put him *off* bikes? That sounds like a more logical reaction.'

'Not for Jake,' Miranda says. 'If you knew him you'd get it. He was always ... perverse. He liked to defy expectations.'

'I'm gobsmacked,' Jules says, then mutters, more to himself: 'Doug never mentioned that.'

'There are all kinds of things that aren't mentioned about Jake,' Simon says.

'Yeah, so I gather,' Jules says. 'Like his drug habit.'

Both Miranda and Simon swivel round at this statement.

'Eh?' Miranda frowns.

'His life in drugs. Another hobby of his, apparently...'

'He was taking drugs when he was fifteen,' Miranda patiently explains. 'That's hardly surprising. And hardly a life in drugs.'

'Smack? Was that normal?'

'Heroin? Who told you that?' Miranda asks, bristling.

'Doug. And Esme.'

Miranda raises her eyebrows and feels dizzy. She feels herself falling into the pit again, the kind of trap in which Jake specialised. 'That's news to us,' is all she says.

'As you said, there are all kinds of things that are unspoken,' Jules says.

'Knowing Jake, he was just messing about,' Miranda reasons, scrabbling to find a footing.

'Well, it wasn't like messing around with motorbikes. I think it was a bit more serious than that. He was dosing himself every day, apparently. And you know whose bike it was he crashed on?'

'We just heard it belonged to one of his friends,' Simon says.

'Yeah, Charlie's.'

'Charlie?'

'His dealer. His drug buddy. Just about the only friend Jake had at that point in his life, according to Doug.'

'We don't know anything about Charlie,' Simon tells him.

'A Burmese guy. He'd been doing a degree course, got busted, and was thrown off the course. Started dealing to support himself. Got close to Jake. He was the one who persuaded him to dye his hair. Apparently everyone in Burma, or Myanmar, whatever it is, all the dudes there dye their hair weird colours. So he dyed his gold.'

'I don't remember him at the funeral,' Miranda remarks.

'And then there was this book he was supposed to be writing.'

'What book?'

'He was supposed to be writing a masterpiece when he died.'

'Is that what Dougie told you?' Simon asks. 'It doesn't sound like the Jake we know.'

'Exactly! Which Jake? There are so many Jakes.'

'It's true – I did hear Stef mention it once or twice,' Miranda says. 'She did say something about a book. She'd heard it from Esme.'

'I think that was bullshit,' Jules says. 'Though why she should make it up is a mystery. I just don't get it. And what about his gambling addiction?'

Miranda and Simon exchange a worried look. 'What gambling addiction?' Simon asks.

'Didn't you know? He lost a fortune online. That's why he had to start dealing drugs – to pay his debts. That's what I heard.'

'Look,' Miranda says, her head swimming again. 'How do you know all this? It all sounds like rumour and gossip.'

Jules shrugs. 'Maybe. I'm just telling you what I've picked up from other people.'

'So you're not sure?' Miranda says.

'Nope. But then nobody is sure about anything where Jake is concerned.'

'Well, if you're not sure, maybe you shouldn't be spreading it around. It's probably nonsense. Just dangerous gossip. You should know better.'

The other two look at her and exchange a glance, surprised by her accusatory tone.

'Sorry,' Jules says. 'I should've kept my gob shut. It's really nothing to do with me.'

'You're right, it's not,' Miranda says. 'In fact, you're just muddying the waters – which are already very muddy indeed. It sounds like fake news to me. And you're trolling someone who's dead.'

'Hey, easy! What's fake anyway? And what's real? The only way of knowing is when everything's out in the open. Don't you get pissed off with all this pussyfooting, padding around the truth? It's like no one wants to question the myth.'

'Myth?' Miranda says.

'This mythical figure that Jake has become for all of you,' Jules says. 'It's not exactly healthy, is it? He's like one of those sacred cows.'

'He was no saint, that's for sure,' Simon agrees. 'Even if he was in Stef's eyes.'

'Yeah – the immaculate one,' Jules says. '*Baby Jesus.*'

Again, Miranda bridles at this intrusion into their family's inner life, at Jules's knowledge of the names they once used. She stops, and the other two also stop.

'Jules – can you just give it a rest? Or at least change the subject? I thought we were trying to get away from all of that. Plus it's his birthday!'

'Hey, Mirrie, he's only telling us what he's heard,' Simon says. 'It is allowed, isn't it? To discuss this thing, to discuss Jake? Who's the reason why we're here?'

'No, she's right, I'm blabbing,' Jules says. 'My bad. I'll shut up. In fact, I'm going to turn back. I think I'm a disruptive influence. And it's nothing to do with me. But one last thing...'

'What?' Miranda says, jaw clenched.

'Is he really dead?'

'*What?*'

'Are you sure he's dead? I mean, has anyone actually seen the body?'

'You're crazy,' Miranda says.

'Or we all are. It just occurred to me. I mean, since no one seems to know anything about him for sure. I just wondered whether he ever really died...'

'He's dead!' Miranda shouts. 'Believe me. He's well and truly dead!'

Jules sighs. 'Okay, okay! Or maybe he's sitting somewhere now, in a castle or on a mountain or something, or maybe in a nuthouse, just watching us all squawking all these stories about him to each other. He's probably splitting his sides.'

With that he turns round and starts walking back the way they have come. 'Laters!' he calls behind him. The other two stand for a few seconds, watching him go.

'How come he seems to know much more about our brother than we do?' Simon asks.

'It sounds like he's got some kind of axe to grind,' Miranda says. 'Come on – forget about him. He's angry.'

'Why should *he* be angry?'

'No idea. Come on.'

And they continue their walk, faster now, staring moodily at the dusty road in front of them, each wrapped up in their thoughts.

After a few minutes, something catches Simon's eye, an incongruous shape lying on the far side of a field where women are crouched with sickles.

'Hey – what's that?'

Miranda looks to where her brother is pointing. A cluster of ancient-looking towers are visible above a thick row of bushes and trees.

'That's interesting! Temples? Or mausoleums?' Miranda wonders. 'I didn't see anything in the guidebook about anything here.'

'There's a path. Let's take a closer look.'

The footpath leads between fields towards the glade of trees where the towers are nestled. The sickle-wielding women look up in amazement as they pass. Approaching, they can make out the rough stonework of dilapidated Hindu monuments, their pointed sikhara towers girdled by an array of crumbling vestibules, porches and chhatris. The nearest of them is enclosed within a low wall. Leaning over the wall they are surprised to see half a dozen sleek-skinned buffaloes, tethered and chewing on a heap of dried grass with hens scratching on the ground around them.

'Wow! How about that?' Simon says. 'It's an old shrine or something, serving as a farmyard barn.' They are suddenly aware of a tall, turbaned and bespectacled figure a few feet away, staring statuesquely.

'Namaste!' Simon utters, a bit nervously.

Without returning his greeting the man disappears behind a wall, only to reappear a few seconds later next to them. He is wearing a long white shirt above striped boxer shorts, with a pure white, curlicued moustache on his face. His turban is a simple yellowed rag wound like a bandage round his bony head. Bowing stiffly with palms joined, he beckons to them to follow, and leads them back the way he has come, into the yard where the cattle are. He points to the temple and stands to one side, sentry-like. They tentatively enter but can make nothing out in the dim light. Simon pulls out his phone to train torchlight onto the walls, and an extensive faded frieze is revealed that takes their breath away. Men and women are depicted, some with multiple faces, some with the heads of elephants or dogs. There are shaven-headed, dhoti-wearing priests, too, as well as giant fish, prancing horses and lissom snakes, all painted in muted shades of pink and blue and violet. The more they look, the more there is to see: fiery stars, looping rivers and trees on whose intricate branches extravagantly plumed birds are perched. The frieze's state of neglect only enhances its precious beauty.

'It's so beautiful,' breathes Miranda. 'Pure magic!'

Simon is equally entranced. 'It looks like it might be hundreds of years old,' he surmises, 'and yet it's completely abandoned.'

When they have had their fill, the tall farmer gestures to another ruin a few metres away. This one seems to be used to store farming equipment, but above the piles of empty sacks and coils of rope there are more murals – painted warriors and wrestlers, men with drooping moustaches and serpents twined around their arms. Others figures wield scimitars or hold aloft ceremonial umbrellas or are mounted on huge peacocks.

The mute farmer waits for them to take it all in, then points to two more derelict buildings among trees on the far side of a field. He beckons again, and they follow in the wake of his long measured strides. Both of these other temples have elaborately carved figures outside and more murals within, but here the stale air is pungent with the acrid odour of bat droppings and they don't spend long inside.

'We're not in any hurry are we?' Simon asks his sister.

Miranda shakes her head, and he extracts his drawing pad from his shoulder bag and perches down on a root beneath the shade of a tree. Miranda hands the tight-lipped farmer a couple of notes and returns his solemn bow, watching his bone-thin legs as he walks away, poking like spikes out of his shorts. She settles down beside Simon, now busily sketching the ruined temples. Half-closing her eyes, feeling the perspiration dry on her skin, she soaks in the tranquillity of the scene and feels that at last she has found something of real value in this land – the first encounter here that has truly humbled her, and revealed a deep power that until now she has only suspected.

The friction of her exchange with Jules slowly ebbs away, and even Jake and Oliver's dark secrets and Cynthia's overt denials recede into insignificance. The tangled politics and stifling confinement of the hostel's pressure-cooker become distant and small, like tiny details on a miniature painting.

When the two of them eventually make their way back across the fields they are in a state of quiet rapture.

'That was an utterly wonderful find,' Simon says as they turn back along the Allapoorha road. 'Almost miraculous.'

'It makes me think how much more there must be, other hidden treasures waiting for us to unearth them,' Miranda observes. 'They don't even merit a mention in the guidebook.'

An hour later, re-entering the hostel grounds, Miranda feels newly fortified. Instead of the revelations and threats that previously preoccupied her, her head is full of the delicate and other-worldly murals that she and Simon have stumbled upon. There is no sign of Jules or any of the other guests. Simon disappears upstairs and she settles down on one of the chairs on the lawn to cool down after their hot walk and reflect on India's labyrinthine inner life. It has the meticulous depths of a Mughal miniature, and the intricacy of a termite's nest.

A movement to her right draws her attention: it is the black, distempered dog that can usually be found asleep outside the hostel gates. It clearly thinks it belongs here. It pauses in the middle of the drive, a few feet away from Miranda, and they regard each other. She gazes in horror and pity at its tortured flesh, and then wonders if it has a name. With its tongue lolling and a look of defeat in its misty eyes, the dog looks utterly miserable, and Miranda wonders if it might be dying. It must be thirsty, anyway, and the thought occurs to her that she should find some water for it. She is just about to get up and fetch a dish into which she can pour some water when Thomas bursts out from the lobby in a rare display of frenzied excitement.

'Get away, get away!' he shouts, and stoops to pick up a stone to throw. Miranda sees the dog's limp tail rise and even briefly wag at its first sight of the hostel manager, perhaps anticipating a game, but as soon as it sees him stoop down for a missile to hurl, it turns and flees back through the gates, tail firmly wedged between its legs, in as unlikely a show of energy as that of his persecutor.

Once the animal has vanished out of sight, Thomas turns to his guest, panting slightly. 'I'm so sorry, madam. That brute, it is always coming in here!'

'It doesn't bother me at all,' Miranda says. 'No problem, honestly!'

'But it is a problem, madam. It comes in here at all hours, disturbing the guests. Someone should shoot it! Or I will put some poison out for it.'

'Really...' she starts, but Thomas is already on his way back to his office, straightening his jacket and patting down his hair as he walks.

Disconcerted by the incident, with her previous equanimity set off balance, Miranda marvels once more at the complexity of responses India ignites in her. It is a succession of conflicting emotions. Or perhaps it is the hostel that does, or perhaps it is their peculiar circumstances – she cannot decide. Undoubtedly, however, she has until now been too focused on the country's negative aspects. She must look further and deeper for the real India, and she must engage with it more if she wants to go beneath the multiple, irreconcilable surfaces, warts and all.

Chapter 39 | Meeting in the market

Stef wakes late feeling jagged. She is alone. With a great effort, she dresses, then pockets her cigarettes and goes down to the restaurant. Before entering she surveys the room from the doorway. It is empty but for her mother and Oliver sitting in silence, vacantly chewing. There is no sign of Esme or the new arrivals, Dougie and Jules. Dougie was not around last night either. She feels an impulse to go back upstairs and hammer on his bedroom door, but of course they might be sleeping late and would not take her intrusion kindly.

Nibbling at her overcooked eggs, her mother appears withdrawn, and neither is Oliver his normal ebullient self – no doubt Cynthia has issued him with instructions to be tactful and reticent on this of all mornings. Cynthia looks up and sees Stef at the door and offers a reassuring smile, which Stef recognises as an attempt at empathy. She is in no mood for commiseration or empathy, however, she is in no mood for anything except to find the book on this particular day. That would be the best birthday gift.

'Stephanie?' her mother calls as she marches past her table.

She halts at the doorway onto the veranda, not turning. 'What?'

'Where are you going?'

'Outside.'

'What about breakfast?'

'Please don't tell me to have breakfast. I'm not thirteen any more.'

Simon is on the veranda and Jules is in the garden with his phone, but there is no sign of Esme or Dougie.

In answer to her questions Jules tells her they have departed on a sightseeing trip, probably for the whole day. She feels a queasy swirl of doubt and fear in her stomach. Could it be possible that the book is beyond her grasp after all?

Back in her room, on the balcony, she feels her whole body trembling as she lights her cigarette. Of course, in his absence, Jake's birthday has always been a troublesome day for her, one that at home she has habitually spent in isolation, socially distanced, insulated from any possibility of meeting other people. Not that she found any solace in her own company, more that she has never had the slightest wish to subject herself to anyone's misguided hushed sympathy or tactful evasions. It is a day on which, more than any other, her son's ghost preys on her and his memory consumes her. It is a day when she thinks back to the twenty birthdays that he had on this earth and dwells on all the birthdays that he has not had. Today, however, she is afraid. Now more than ever, she is conscious that such thoughts will drive her mad.

Stubbing out her cigarette in the plant pot, she returns inside the room and sits stiffly on the bed. There is no comfort here, it is a prison. Her eyes flit compulsively to the red suitcase in the corner, but she can't permit herself to go there. Although she longs above all else for that sweet oblivion – the numbing of the numbness that has been available to her on each of the previous seven birthdays – it is a relief that she cannot allow herself today.

She has both longed for and dreaded this birthday. If everything had gone according to plan, it would have been marked by the ceremony that she has mentally prepared for over many months. It was to be a catharsis. Instead it is a null, a void, merely another useless expanse of empty time – a day like any other.

She picks up a book, and a few seconds later flings it down again. She closes the shutters, then re-opens them. She goes to the mirror, then lies on the bed. When she hears Laurie's footsteps in the corridor, the thought of his presence in the room fills her with panic, and she jumps to her feet and rushes out, passing him without a word, feeling his worried eyes on her. She goes down to the lounge, then out on the veranda. Nowhere is safe from her anger. She even has a tetchy altercation with Thomas when he is unable to tell her in less than multiple compound sentences with numerous subclauses why there is no television and what she can do to procure one. She sees her mother and Oliver cowering from behind their books and newspapers, and finally decides that she can no longer inflict herself on the company.

'I'm going to take a walk,' she tells Laurie, back in their room.

'You're going to take a walk,' Laurie repeats, parrot-fashion.

'Correct.'

'Where?'

'No idea.'

'Do you want company?'

'No. Bye.'

So, with sunglasses and a sun-hat, she walks briskly into town. She is followed most of the way by the revoltingly mangy dog with lolling tongue and defeated eyes that seems to frequent this neighbourhood, its scarred, mottled skin simultaneously disgusting her and tearing at her heart. Fortunately, halfway along the busy main road, the wretched animal stops, and when she glances behind her a few moments later it is gone.

Still feeling queasy and trembly, she finds the noise and fumes even more oppressive than usual and decides to lose herself in Allapoorha's pulsating market. She walks purposefully into the press of alleys, channelled between mountains of polished aubergines, mounds of chillis and fields of onions. Glassy-eyed goats stand quizzically in doorways and pigs snuffle in the dust. There is a comfortable anonymity here. No one looks, no one follows, no one is interested. For once, even the beggars leave her alone.

Soon, however, she is assailed again by that familiar itch, her unquenchable restlessness. Her head is a mass of conflicting emotions, and her eyes are burning, darting feverishly to left and right as if in search of something. Jake is everywhere, inescapable, an invisible companion that she both cherishes and rebels against. Today of all days, she needs a break from him.

Then, without warning, as if illuminated by a sudden flash, she is there – the girl from the school. She is walking and skipping along the narrow lane in front of her. Stef quickens her pace, and when she is a few steps away she calls and the little girl turns and sees her. Her eyes look panicky at first and she appears to be on the point of running away, but instead she hesitates, eyeing Stef uncertainly, and allows her to come up close. Removing her sunglasses, Stef crouches down to the girl's level, smiling up into her searing green eyes.

'Hallo, darling! Do you remember me?' She looks her up and down, takes in her clear, cinnamon-toned skin, her soft dark hair parted in the middle with tendrils curling down on her shoulders, her thin arms cluttered with bracelets. She appears embarrassed, but not frightened. Stef continues to smile, feeling protective and brimming with love for this shy scrap of a girl. She has to keep her here, prevent her from disappearing into the crowd. Looking around, she spots across the lane a sweet-seller frying gulab jamun, the sweet syrup balls that Laurie made her sample on one of their rare forays into town together. Next to the blackened, oil-filled pan is a piled-up pyramid of them already cooked. Stef points to the stall and gestures an eating motion, and the girl lets her steer her across the lane. Stef manages to communicate to the squatting sweet-seller that they want two of the newly-cooked sweets. He plucks a couple of them from the pile, places them on a leaf-dish and wordlessly presents them to Stef, who in turn hands them to the little girl. She accepts the leaf, examines the balls, picks up one of them and nibbles a tiny piece from the side. Crouching down again, Stef asks her: 'What is your name?'

The girl ignores her, then, when Stef repeats the question, looks suspicious.

Stef points to herself. 'My name is Stef!' She points to the girl. 'You?' She repeats this twice more without any sign of comprehension on the girl's part. Finally the stallholder barks at her in Malayalam. The girl mutters a word that Stef can't understand.

'She name Juditz,' the sweet-seller tells her.

'Juditz?'

'Juditz,' the man repeats, as the girl puts the remainder of the first sweet into her mouth.

A light suddenly dawns. 'Judith!' Stef exclaims. The girl looks up, as if acknowledging her name. 'Your name is Judith!' The girl lets a shy grin escape, lighting up her whole face. She steps back into the street, and suddenly there is an angry roar. With a yelp Stef pulls the girl back, out of the path of a motorbike that seemed to be heading straight towards her. The bandana-ed driver thunders past without acknowledging them or slowing his pace, but the girl seems unperturbed, as does the stallholder. It's so natural, so normal here to be an inch away from disaster or death. As the girl concentrates on her second gulab jamun, Stef's protective arm around her shoulders, the shopkeeper says something to her and the girl responds monosyllabically in her language. Then, wrapping the half-eaten sweet in the leaf, she twirls on her heels, shrugs off Stef's arm and, without warning, darts away down the street.

'Wait!' Stef calls after her, and begins to follow, but the sweet-seller tells her, 'She late! Go school.'

Something in his tone warns Stef from pursuing little Judith, so she nods curtly at the stallholder, pays him ten rupees for the sweets and walks off in the same direction, though at a slow enough pace to suggest to anyone watching that she is not attempting to catch up with the girl.

Weaving through the scrimmage of stalls, shoppers and animals, Stef feels strangely lighter, and her vision seems clearer, as if a light has been switched on and she can view the way ahead. With a renewed sense of purpose, she makes her way back to the hostel, though once there she feels overwhelms by a mighty exhaustion. Her room, to her relief, is empty. She closes the shutter, adjusts the ceiling fan and undresses before throwing herself down onto the cool white sheet, and is asleep in seconds.

Her sleep is deep but dreamless. She lies like a stone in the bed, the fan tugging gently at her hair. Through the shutters, the light changes but the volume of birdsong is constant, even while the tune and the individual components are in endless change and tireless motion. She is deaf to all of it, and in the end it is a soft shuffling noise in the room that wakes her. Opening her eyes she sees Laurie creeping across.

'What are you doing?' she croaks.

He stops and turns, apologetic.

'Didn't want to wake you, love. Just getting some gel. Thought I might read on the balcony before dinner.'

'Dinner? What time is it?'

'Seven o'clock, about.'

She sits up with a start. 'My God! I've been asleep for hours!'

'And that's brilliant! You obviously needed it.'

She notices the subdued light through the shutters. She can't remember the last time she slept so well. Then the memory returns to her of her encounter in the market and she feels a warm caress of contentment.

'I saw her!' she announces to Laurie. 'I saw the little girl this afternoon.'

'Which little girl?' Laurie asks.

'You know! The little girl we saw at the school. She was in the classroom. Do you remember? Green eyes. Her name is Judith.'

She can see Laurie look blank, then pretend to look interested though failing to wipe away his puzzlement so she doesn't pursue it, simply remarking, 'She's a lovely little thing. So fragile.'

'They all looked like great kids,' Laurie says. 'And so happy. I think the school is doing a really impressive job. It's just a tragedy that they're going to close it down.'

Stef grunts, shaking off the unwelcome thought.

'So whatever's going to happen to her?' he asks.

'She'll be – what was the word – *dispersed*."

'It sounds totalitarian!' Laurie says.

'She and her mother,' Stef says

'Isn't she an orphan?' Laurie asks. 'Isn't that why she's there?'

'I think she has a mother,' Stef says, remembering the woman at the gate, the one sweeping in the classroom, the one with the same piercing eyes. 'Some kids are there because their mothers can't look after them. They're illegitimate, or there are problems in the family, or maybe the mother just can't cope.'

Laurie nods, opens the door to the balcony and is about to step out when Stef speaks again.

'By the way – you haven't mentioned the closure to anyone have you?'

He blinks innocently. 'Of course not! You told me not to...'

'I *asked* you.'

'...though I'm still not sure why.'

'It doesn't make a lot of difference, does it?' Stef says.

'Exactly. It doesn't, so why...'

'So it doesn't matter, does it? So forget it, please.'

Laurie sweeps his hand across his forehead as if to erase the thought. 'It's already forgotten, love. Don't worry. Don't worry about anything.'

He smiles reassuringly, and steps onto the balcony, closing the door behind him.

Stef hears him settle down with his book and sighs impatiently. Then, pushing back her pillow, she lies back on the mattress, eyes closed, hands splayed on either side of her head. She thinks of Judith, a faint smile on her lips. Then another thought intrudes, the thought that she woke up with this morning – the necessity to find Dougie and collect the book. He might have returned.

Rising, she slips on her clothes, rinses her face and goes downstairs. Bingo! There, through the open door in the lobby, she sees Dougie and Jules in one corner of the lounge, enveloped in the room's funereal gloom. At last! An adrenalin shot of elation shoots through her. The moment of catharsis might just have come.

They seem to be locked in an earnest dialogue, and only when she is almost upon them do they stop and look up at her. Both show alarmed expressions.

'Good evening, gentlemen! I hope you've had a productive day.'

'Stef!' says Dougie, rising to greet her. 'Hallo!'

She stops an arms-length away, careful not to fall within embracing distance.

'Well, what a long time it's been! Jules and I have already made our acquaintance, haven't we Jules? But you've been avoiding me. Do you mind if I join you?'

'By all means,' Dougie says, and waits for Stef to lower herself onto one of the overstuffed chairs before he does the same.

'Have you recovered from your journey?' she enquires. 'I didn't see you at dinner last night, or at breakfast this morning.'

'No, we met up with Esme last night and had a curry. And this morning I was away early with her on a trip.'

'A trip! *Sightseeing* I hear?'

'Yes.'

'And there's me thinking you'd be tired out after your long travels! Oh, well. It doesn't matter. I'm just very pleased to see you at all. Because, you know, we really appreciate your participation in our little gathering. A bit late, admittedly, but you got here in the end.'

'We couldn't make it any sooner, Stef,' Dougie explains. 'Really sorry.'

'Where have you been, out of interest?'

'Just.... travelling. We had a couple of incidents. Got sidetracked.'

With a brittle smile, Stef gives them a lingering look that is both sceptical and disapproving, then snaps it shut. 'Well, as I say, you're here now. Though, I must confess, Dougie, lovely as it is to see you, I'm actually much more interested in my son's book. You've probably guessed it's been very much on my mind.'

'Yes, I imagine it has been,' Dougie says.

'I know you were close to Jake in those final months. And you probably knew how he cut me off.'

'No, I didn't.'

'He did. Didn't want anything to do with me. Then he announced he was leaving his course, leaving his studies, and leaving university. Of course, I was extremely pissed off.'

'Of course.'

'And then I found out that he'd been writing. Writing! Well, what a revelation! You can imagine how I felt. But then, afterwards, there was no trace of anything. In fact we thought that whatever it was that he was writing had been thrown away or stolen. It was a complete mystery. Until you told me you'd had it all this time.'

'I had no idea that I had it...' Dougie says.

'Really? *Really?* You've been hanging onto it for eight years without even knowing you had it? I find that extraordinary!'

'I honestly didn't know. It wasn't like it was a manuscript or anything,' Dougie explains. 'It was a half-dozen exercise books stuffed into a plastic bag. I hadn't given it a second thought.'

'Extraordinary. So what was it? What was he writing? Don't keep me in suspense!'

'Actually, I've got no idea, Stef.'

'He didn't tell you?' She leans forward, incredulous. Dougie shakes his head. 'And you never asked him?' Again he shakes his head. 'And you never even had a peek?'

'I told you, I didn't know I had it.'

'Well, as I say... extraordinary!'

'I suppose so.'

She sighs, shaking her head in disbelief.

'Anyway, I'd very much appreciate if I could have it now.' She looks at him expectantly, eyes like searchlights burning into him.

'Er... This is the thing, Stef. I don't have it right now.'

She looks once more disbelieving, again with her brittle smile. 'Why not?' He shakes his head, unable to find the right words. 'Please don't tell me you've left it in England.'

'Er, no, no, I did bring it. But actually I left it in a hotel.'

At this, Jules swivels round to gape at Dougie, but Dougie ploughs on. 'Totally careless, I know. Completely ridiculous, really. We got up early, you know, to catch the train, and it was dark, and I left it in a drawer.'

'In a *drawer*?'

'Yes, but it's alright. I called the boss. The manager. And he's got it and he's going to send it.'

'Send it where?'

'Here.'

'Here?' Stef repeats.' But it'll never get here in time. We're leaving in a few days.'

'It's alright. I told him to send it express. My expense.'

'Express...' Stef looks bemused, her face an amalgam of bewilderment, disappointment and suspicion.

'So nothing to worry about at all,' Dougie assures her. 'It'll definitely arrive tomorrow. Or possibly the day after.'

'Are you winding me up?' she says finally.

'No! No, not at all. I'm really sorry, Stef, I'm such a fool. Really I am. But don't worry, honestly, it'll be here in a day or two. No problem. Seriously.'

Not hiding her suspicion, Stef cocks her head, squinting at Dougie. Then she clicks back into motion, possessed of a sudden energy. 'Good!' And she's on her feet, spinning round and striding out of the room.

Jules, who has been staring at his friend in shocked awe, lets out a long, low whistle and turns his gaze to the floor, shaking his head.

'Are you off your fucking head?'

'Probably,' Dougie admits, looking miserable.

'What did you say that for?'

'I couldn't think what else to say?'

'Why didn't you just tell her it's gone? That there's no chance she'll ever set eyes on her precious book?'

'Did you see the state she's in?' Dougie asks him. 'Do you really think she's up to hearing that?'

'So when are you going to tell her?'

'After the ceremony.'

'What, you'll just tell her you forgot what really happened, which is that you lost the fucking bag with the fucking book on a fucking train? It just slipped your mind. *Really?*'

'No! It just won't arrive by the time we're all out of here! We'll blame the Indian postal service!'

Jules cackles. 'Brilliant! You've thought it through!'

'No, actually I just thought of it now.'

'Well, it's still brilliant! But you're gonna come a cropper, pal, with your tangled web of deceit.'

'I had no choice...'

'You should stop digging, mate. Put away that shovel. You're just making it worse!'

'Maybe.'

Jules puts his arm around Dougie's shoulder, and whispers in his ear: 'But I love you anyway, you fucking prat!' He looks around surreptitiously, assures himself that no one is watching, turns Dougie's mouth towards him and plants a long kiss on it. They both pull away guiltily, again glancing around. No point in creating a fuss in this respectable Christian establishment.

'Come on, dude,' Jules says. 'You're looking stressed. Let's go upstairs.'

Chapter 40 | A death denied

It is Saturday morning, a day like any other at the hostel. But as Miranda, leaning on her balcony, contemplates the day in front and wonders how to fill it, it occurs to her that Saturday in the hostel does have subtle differences after all. For there below her, Shibu, whom she has never seen when he is not working, is today doing something for himself. Perhaps it is his day off. He is dressed the same, but there he is, in a patch of shade on the drive, painstakingly polishing his Suzuki scooter.

Most of the time he is busy on errands and mundane tasks – sweeping, carrying, cleaning, hosing, flapping up and down the corridors in his rubber sandals, leaving his wide smile floating behind him like a Cheshire cat's. Occasionally she sees him on this very scooter, usually roaring out of the grounds and returning half an hour later with bags of vegetables or crates of drink and other goods wedged between his knees or strapped onto the saddle behind him. But now he is pouring what she can only describe as his love onto the machine, and it is the first time she has noticed him as a being independent of his dogsbody role at the hostel.

There is something compelling in watching him bent over the gleaming chrome and metal, his devotion to his task. It is clearly an object of great pride to him, something that engrosses him. Cleaning and polishing, he radiates a soothing calm. She finds herself wondering if he has a home to go to, if he has a wife and how old he is. He may be ten years older or ten years younger than her, she couldn't say. She resolves to ask him – that can't be too hard. She could even ask him now, grab this opportunity, on his day off, to engage with him, this scion of his country and its people; she could delve beneath the politeness, sidestep the manners and divisions that separate them. But how? She must first draw him into some form of conversation.

Suddenly gripped by the urgency of speaking with him, of catching him before he can finish his labour and perhaps roar away, she rushes downstairs and into the garden.

He looks up as she approaches and immediately stands straighter, expecting no doubt a request or an order. But when she makes it clear that she is stopping purely to admire his bike, the enormous smile instantly lights up his face. She points to the lustrous machine, makes appreciative gestures. 'Your scooter?'

He looks puzzled.

'Is this your scooter? It's beautiful.' She touches her heart, and he nods and his smile intensifies. He has, she thinks, a rare grace, with his soft eyelashes and long, slender fingers. She attempts a few more simple questions and gestures, and Shibu finally understands that she is interested in him too, not just his Suzuki. He nods and smiles and starts talking, and suddenly a barrier is breached and he is chattering, his words an unstoppable torrent. His scattershot knowledge of English is chaotic, probably derived from the random contacts he has made with hostel guests, many of them probably not English themselves.

'Yes I student but now stop. ... Finish study. ... Work now. Not live Allapoorha. ... Home not here, understand, my parents in little village, in Kochi district. Not far. Wait...' he looks up at the sky, strumming his fingers against his lips 'Hundred fifty kilometres! Father, he shop. Mother, she schoolteacher. Sister, sister, she sick, but she getting better. Er, her name Anjana. Ten years old. ... Where you from? Married? Children no? ... I go England, but very expensive. And cold. Rain, rain. Snow. I see on television. ... I go one day, just to see. And learn speak English. Necessary speak English. Very important, yes yes. ... I Hindu. But I have Christian friends. Most people here Christian. My friend Minosh, he say

Europe people bad. Europe girls, always short dress, little skirt, when they go swimming they show boobs. But Hindu women. They show only this,' he points to his midriff and laughs wildly, throwing back his head. 'But we have temples, you know? Khajuraho? Sex sex, all things they show. Too much sex! But Hindu good boys. Only, little bit crazy. Like Hanuman, you know Hanuman? He monkey god. Every Tuesday he fast. Eat nothing nothing, all day, only evening he eat.' He starts counting on his fingers, mouthing the days of the week. 'Tuesday Hanuman day. And he no eat meat. He no drink, drugs, nothing nothing. He good boy, but little crazy.' He grins again, showing his teeth, twirls his fingers around his head, eyes aslant, then suddenly he throws back his head and unleashes another mighty spate of laughter.

Miranda tries to follow, to respond and engage, but begins to feel engulfed. It's all too difficult and exhausting. Shibu, seeing her struggling and her confusion, stops laughing, then once more smiles brightly – his default mode. She knows now there can be no real communication.

She smiles back, nods, and gently withdraws, going inside, leaving him to polish his scooter. Well, she reflects as she climbs back up the stairs to her room, she has engaged – or attempted to. She has tried, but she is none the wiser. There is altogether too much here, too much to take in, too much to explain, and too many layers. She cannot cross over after all. There may always be men like Shibu who are eager to share but are still unreachable, other hidden murals to discover in some lost ruin, but they are all mere fragments of a much bigger picture that she will never see or understand. She may be permitted a glimpse, allowed in a few inches only, and the real India will always be a few inches further away, just out of sight. She must accept that now.

That evening, sitting by herself on the veranda, she is recalling this failed attempt and reflecting on the gulfs and barriers that exist between all of them – not just her and Shibu – when Cynthia approaches. It is dark, around half-past nine, and Miranda has emerged from a dinner at which all conversation between the guests was reduced to low mumbles interspersed with long silences. Stef wasn't present – no surprise there – and Laurie was seated at a table with Cynthia and Oliver. The elderly couple were hardly speaking to each other, she noticed. Dougie and Jules were at their own table, and again, conversation seemed to be sparse. Esme joined Simon and Miranda at their table, though there seemed to be an inexplicable chill between her brother and Esme; they could hardly look at each other let alone converse, so the talk was extremely fragmentary at their table, too.

Fortunately, no one felt inclined to prolong the agony, everyone dispersing in different directions as soon as they could reasonably do so once the food was consumed. Miranda opted to brave the mosquitoes and sit outside, periodically illuminated by breaks in the cloud cover that reveal the nearly-full moon. Tonight it is looking fat and squashy, almost mustard in colour. She is listening to the various night-time sounds – clicking cicadas, the laments of owls and canine howls – when Cynthia joins her at her table. They exchange a few pleasantries, but it is all a bit stiff and Miranda is aware of a tension, an expectancy hanging between them as if Cynthia is wrestling with some dilemma. She notices her hands fidgeting below the table. But finally she seems to come to a decision.

'Miranda, dear, I don't know what it is you found out about Oliver, but I think you should keep it to yourself.'

'So you *do* know?' Miranda asks.

'No, I don't know anything. And I prefer it that way. All I know is what you have told me, that he has changed his name. Now I have no idea why he might have done that, but I respect him enough to know that there must have been a very good reason. I trust him, on the whole, and I'd really rather you didn't take this any further.'

'Okay,' Miranda says. 'Did he ask you to speak to me?'

'Certainly not! Oliver would never do that. No, I came to ask you because something has not been right since you had your little chat with him – right with him I mean – and I want to be able to assure him that whatever secrets he may have, I will never require him to reveal them if he decides that they are best kept packed away.'

Miranda is unsure of how to respond, but Cynthia continues her speech without waiting.

'I think I told you that he's a bit secretive. And I have never asked what there might be that he needs to be secretive about. It almost seems like bad manners. Anyway, we never know all there is to know about other people, do we? Probably better that way.'

'He seems to have had quite an eventful life,' Miranda says finally.

'Stop right there,' Cynthia tells her firmly, holding up a palm. 'That's all I need to know. Though I can't really believe an accountant's life can have been that eventful. And if he's told you otherwise, don't underestimate men's tendencies to exaggerate. Not least accountants, I should imagine. I dare say Oliver's rather prone to glorify his past. Anyway, the long and the short of it is that I'd rather not know all the details. As long as he hasn't actually killed anyone, his past is his affair, and best left alone.'

'That's pretty much what he told me when I questioned him about it,' Miranda says.

'You "questioned" him? Oh dear. Well, that might explain his subdued mood in the last couple of days. He hasn't exactly been cheerful since you spoke to him. He's been very quiet. It seems that whatever passed between you has left rather a bad odour.'

'I'm sorry if I've blundered into something. I know I can be a bit of a bull in a china shop,' Miranda tells her. 'But I was intrigued after I spoke to that Pereira man. And – I'll be honest – I was even more intrigued when Oliver hinted that he knows some of our own family secrets.'

Cynthia looks up with a start. 'He said that?'

'In a roundabout way, yes.'

Cynthia is looking flustered now, her hands under the table fidgeting ever more compulsively.

'It was like he knows something, something that he didn't think we'd want revealed.'

Cynthia looks away without meeting Miranda's eyes.

'Does he?' Miranda persists.

'How should I know, dear?' Cynthia says, a little defensively, perhaps.

'Is it about Michael?'

'I really think we should drop the subject,' Cynthia says.

'Or could it be something to do with my father?'

Cynthia looks up, clearly puzzled.

'Laurence? I very much doubt it!'

There is a pause, and then Miranda continues.

'Well, anyway, whatever it is, it got me thinking. About Jake, mostly. How there always seemed to be a bit of mystery in his life. Like a void. And it occurred to me that I know nothing about his father. He was never discussed at home. Never. Jake certainly never mentioned him, nor did Stef. So I thought I'd do some digging on my laptop. About Michael. And it's very weird.'

'What's weird?'

'Well … You never really liked Michael, did you?'

'Who told you that, dear?'

'I can't remember. Dad, probably. And that was the impression I got from Stef.'

'Stephanie has a lot of silly ideas.'

'I found out his surname, anyway. Donohue. Michael Donohue.'

'You know his surname?' Cynthia exclaims, alarmed.

'Yes. That was easy. It's on Jake's birth certificate. But I couldn't find out much more about him. There was nothing there.'

'Nothing where?'

'Nothing anywhere. On the internet. Nothing about his accident, for instance.'

'His accident...'

'You know. The crash. How he died. I emailed a friend who works in a legal practice, and she couldn't find any trace of it either. No police or court reports. No inquest. No death certificate. Not even any National Health data.'

Cynthia does not respond, so Miranda continues: 'So I thought I'll ask Stef. She might know why there's nothing about him.'

Cynthia looks more than alarmed now, almost horrified, encouraging Miranda to press on.

'So what was it you didn't like about him?'

Cynthia has adopted a cowled expression, gazing steadily into the trees.

'Well, I didn't trust him,' she replies, finally. Then she adds, in a whisper: 'And I was right.' She turns to Miranda. 'But I wouldn't broach the subject with Stephanie if I were you, dear. Not now. In fact, not ever.'

Miranda looks mystified, then Cynthia rises to her feet. 'Come on,' she says, more decisively, 'let's take a stroll.' And she starts walking across the lawn, away from the hostel, guided by the moon's waxy, intermittent light. Miranda falls into step, and soon they are among the trees and plunged into near-total darkness. They halt, unwilling to risk the tangled undergrowth, and face each other a few feet apart. Unable to see each other's expressions, they feel themselves enveloped in a cocoon of both intimacy and vulnerability, and almost exhilarated by the possibilities of complete candour it offers.

When she speaks again, Cynthia's voice is calm, reduced to a soft murmur in the night. 'I'll tell you something about Michael. In truth I hardly knew him. Stephanie kept me at a distance where her personal life was concerned. She was rather bolshy in those days, always on demonstrations or meetings or sit-ins, or some such thing. She was very political, and I'm afraid she didn't really want me in her life.'

'That must have been very hard for you.'

'Actually, we hadn't been particularly close for some time. She was always rather remote. At least she was after Roger died – my husband. She was fourteen.'

'It must have been awful for you both.'

'It was. But life moves on. You just have to take it on the chin when someone close to you dies. You accept it.'

Miranda thinks she hears a judgmental note in Cynthia's voice, as if she's not just referring to her own loss.

'Anyway,' the older woman continues, 'we moved to Penzance, and it was around that time that Stephanie discovered politics. Then she went to university and I hardly saw her. That's when she got involved with Michael. When she was doing her postgrad.'

'Did you actually meet him?'

'Once or twice, when she brought him down to Cornwall. Usually when they were out of money.'

'What did you think of him?'

There is a pause, then: 'Frankly, I thought he was a bit of an odd fish.'

'Was there anything in particular about him?'

'No, dear. Nothing I could put my finger on. Well, he was rather evasive. Cagey. He didn't like me asking about his home or family. I could tell he was hiding something. Goodness, I really shouldn't be talking to you like this. Behind Stephanie's back. She wouldn't like it at all.'

'But you know something about him, don't you?'

Cynthia stays nothing. Now that Miranda's eyes have adjusted to the darkness, she is aware of dappled spots of moonlight around their feet. Cynthia's profile is clearer, but her expression is still masked.

'Is it something about the accident?'

After another pause, Cynthia corrects her: 'His disappearance, you mean.'

Miranda is puzzled. *'Disappearance'? Is that a euphemism?* 'Do you mean it wasn't an accident?' she asks.

'I mean that actually – between you and me, mind, no one else – there was no accident.'

'You've lost me.'

'There was no accident. There was no crash. It simply didn't happen.'

Miranda pauses to take this in. 'You mean he didn't die...?'

'Not then. Maybe he did later, I don't know. He just disappeared.'

'But Stef went to his funeral.'

'There was no funeral. That was another fabrication. There was no funeral and no burial or cremation.'

'So Michael could still be alive...' Miranda says, trying to take it in. 'Did Jake know?'

'Not as far as I know.'

'Does Dad know?'

'I don't believe so. Stephanie told everyone the same story about the accident and the funeral. It was her secret. And mine... She had to tell me, you see. But she swore me to secrecy. She'll never speak to me again if she ever finds out I've told you – so please, please, Miranda, keep this to yourself.'

'I just don't understand why Stef had to lie, why she said he'd died in an accident. And why was he so evasive?'

'I didn't understand either, at the time,' Cynthia says. 'I always assumed that she lied in order to save face. She couldn't allow it to be known that someone had walked out on her, someone that she had apparently been deeply in love with. But let me tell you something else. Stephanie's father died when she was young. And she took it badly. She didn't show it at the time, but she took it very badly. And I believe she just couldn't tolerate being abandoned a second time. You see, Michael walked out on her when she told him she was expecting their child. She couldn't admit it. So she concocted this mad story to justify why she was a single mother. I thought it was a bit extreme at the time, I really did. Perhaps it made it easier. In the end I think she came to believe it herself.'

'And then, twenty years later, it was like she was abandoned a third time...' Miranda muses. They start to walk again, weaving slowly between the trees. 'No wonder I couldn't find anything out about Michael,' Miranda says. 'He didn't die.'

'Now do you see?' Cynthia says with a weary sigh. 'It's all very complicated. And extremely delicate. Now – if you don't mind, I'm very tired. I really must turn in. But Miranda, I beg you, please keep this to yourself. There's absolutely nothing to be gained by telling anybody else. Believe me. A little discretion goes a long way.'

Miranda is struck by the similar form of words that Oliver used to her yesterday morning. 'So why are you telling me?' she asks Cynthia.

'Because I'd rather tell you the truth than have you barking up the wrong tree, and coming to all sorts of conclusions, and telling Stephanie all kinds of things. She's in a very highly-strung state right now. As you know. So you mustn't start talking to people. Please. Now, goodnight, dear. I'll see you tomorrow.'

And with these stern words she crosses the lawn, leaving Miranda alone at the edge of the trees. She stands stock still as if frozen, deaf to the soft scrape of the cicadas and the occasional solitary whoops and hoots from the trees. The thought that keeps hammering at her brain is that it was so unnecessary, Jake's death. There was no motorcycle accident, so no need for Jake to re-enact it. Jake had a father. Maybe he still has. He could have saved him.

She feels a great heaviness inside. Stef's terrible lie came to be a self-fulfilling truth. So futile, so unnecessary. A hollow life, leading to a hollow death, all an illusion. Walking back slowly across the lawn, she stops and turns her face to the scudding moon. It is distant and alien, refusing to judge or comfort. It makes her feel profoundly alone, stuck here on earth, gravity pulling her down. She knows she'll have little sleep tonight. With a final, rueful sigh, she tears her face away and heads indoors.

Chapter 41 | The necessary lie

From her balcony, deep in shadow, Stef views the figure of Miranda standing alone on the grass, isolated in the cheesy moonlight. Inside the room, Laurie is unconscious in bed, no doubt dreaming. He has always possessed the precious gift of being able to sleep anywhere, in any circumstances, usually eight hours of unbroken slumber. Stef has never enjoyed this facility. She herself slept a little in the afternoon. She has not left her room today, kept herself to herself, skipped dinner, and has been sitting smoking on the balcony ever since Laurie came upstairs after dinner. From her half-hidden vantage, she heard the soft voices of Miranda and Cynthia on the veranda below, apparently deep in conversation, then watched the women cross the grass and disappear into the trees. A little later she saw them return separately. Now Miranda's frozen stance, lost in thought, is an eloquent sign that something significant has taken place. It convinces her that a confidence has been broken.

She knew it would happen one day, knew that her mother would feel compelled to unburden herself of her lie – the guilty lie that Stef herself laid on her all those years ago. Possibly she had already shared the truth with her friends, though she doubts it, just as she doubts that she would have done so with her family; Stef would have known immediately if her siblings were privy. She suspects that Oliver knows, though. Something in his clumsily arch manner tells her. It was inevitable, after all. Her mother lives in a world of untruth, yet she herself is not a natural deceiver. She cannot handle outright lying, always preferring the implicit, unspoken deceit, the embarrassed obfuscation. How very English.

It was a lunatic lie, no question, one conceived in a moment of hysteria, and not calculated to survive even this long. But it was a lie born of pride, one born of love, and she was young. Stef blames herself for many things, but, perhaps strangely, not this particular lapse of reason. Love, after all, like lust, is a lapse, a madness, a weakness, a momentary failure, and should be forgiven. And Stef's devotion to Michael was mad because it was absolute and unquestioned – as was, she believes, his to her. They had something that was unique, authentic and true.

Or so it seemed.

Which made it all the more painful to be confronted by his reaction when, one cloud-flecked late-summer day, as they lay in bed, she announced that she was pregnant and had decided to see it through. She immediately saw the shock in his eyes, the panic, and though he quickly – somewhat magnificently – overcame it, he never managed to hide the fear. It was there in his voice, or rather just under his voice, a constant, shifty undertone. Suddenly there was a limit to his solidarity, and the end came soon after.

She often wonders how he would have reacted had he ever actually set eyes on his beautiful son. It is the unanswerable question that has haunted her for thirty years, though in her own mind the answer has always been obvious: his heart would have melted, as hers had. And he would have been a fine, strong daddy.

But Michael vanished from her life before he was ever able to see his beautiful boy. It was his denial of their bond that struck her spirit hardest. They had something real, and he walked away. Like a coward, a weakling, a base, treacherous turncoat, he abandoned mother and unborn child.

Comrade – I have left you because you have left me. My struggle goes on, and I cannot (will not) be tied to what we both know to be a bourgeois construct. Far better to go now than a few months or years down the road. Our time together is passed. Do not think you will see me again. I cherish our bond more than you will ever know, and I wish all the best things in life for you and our child. I have never loved and respected anyone the way I have loved and respected you. The struggle goes on. M.

Bloody bollocks! Stef tore up his note as soon as she found it. The hackneyed phrases were false and meaningless. But still, the pain went deep. The betrayal and the humiliation were so huge that she couldn't admit it to anyone. It was impossible to talk about it, for she resolutely refused to be a victim. It was her first denial, her first defeat, and there was absolutely no redress, zero comfort, nothing she could do about it. So when they asked about him, their comrades and fellow-squatters, she told them he was active in another part of the country, and she was going to join him. In fact she retreated to Cornwall to stay with her mother, allowing her to sever all links with the Caucus members before the pregnancy became apparent.

She didn't regret any of it. With Michael's defection there perished the core of her crusading zeal. She felt nothing for her old revolutionary values. She felt nothing about anything. It was the strangest time of her life. While in Penzance, she swallowed a bottle of barbiturates and was found unconscious in her bedroom by her mother. An ambulance sped her to hospital where she had her stomach pumped.

She and her foetus pulled through, but she had no choice now but full disclosure to her mother. During a soul-baring session that she can never delete from her memory, she poured it all out: her pregnancy, Michael's paternity, his desertion, her despair. Of course she swore her mother to secrecy, about this and about her foolish suicide attempt, everything. Her mother, who always hated Michael, accepted the news meekly and promised not to betray her. Thus was he expunged – never mentioned again by either of them in each other's company.

Omissions and prevarications, however, never survive long in a family. Six months later, beaten down by continual questions from her sister, Stef's second big lie was spewed forth. She was in a savage mood, caught off-guard, and it was the first thing that came into her head. She informed Rebecca that the father of her unborn child was Michael, and that Michael was dead. His motorbike had spun off the road in Germany. Death was instant. Yes, it was devastating, but now she would live for Jake.

She regretted the stupid, unforgiveable lie almost as soon as she heard herself utter it, but simultaneously she knew that it could not be unsaid. On the plus side it saved a thousand futile conversations. She told her brothers and whoever else was interested the same story, repeated it so often that she absorbed it into her skin, almost coming to believe it herself. There was even a certain poetic truth in it: it symbolised the violent decease of their relationship. And, after all, it didn't hurt anyone.

For a moment, in Penzance, she had given up. The mountain was too steep, her love for Michael too deep, the prospect of life without him too daunting. But she picked herself up. It was an aberration, the exception that proved her true mettle. Head high, she began to look to the future. After Jake was born, she moved on. She was offered a teaching post in Cardiff, where no one questioned her on Jake's paternity. Things got a bit awkward later, when her new colleague, Laurie Johnson, came into her life, but he was given the same authorised version as everyone else. It was a necessary lie. Her only regret was that it became the version that was eventually relayed to Jake. She had anguished long and hard over this, and eventually concluded that Jake would be happier knowing that his father had not walked out on him. Stef had buried her own grief, now Jake would never need to grieve, would never be able to – how could he grieve for someone he'd never known? Far better for him to believe that his orphaned state was a random, intentioned act.

Nonetheless, the fact that Jake grew up with a lie has never stopped being a source of torment to Stef. She always intended to tell him the truth, had even set his twenty-first birthday as the date for this truth-telling, but that birthday never came. So Jake lived his whole life under the illusion that his father had been the victim of a pointless accident. That's all he had to know, and he never asked to know more. Yet somehow, cruelly, like a vicious joke played by the gods, that fallacy had determined his ultimate fate.

Eight years after Michael's disappearance, Laurie took her on. Laurie, mild and naive, who found something noble and admirable in Stef, came to her aid like a gallant, guileless knight, and Stef admitted him into her life. He became a valued ally, taking on her family of one without doubting her, though there were still negotiations to be made, mostly unspoken ones. There was also the fact that Laurie had his own children: Miranda and Simon. Somehow the two families had to be forged into one. In theory it was feasible. United and newly armoured, the composite family could move forward. Everything might have fallen into place. There was cooperation, respect, loyalty and a sort of love between them. But what family was ever perfect? It was a flawed compromise, however well it worked on paper.

Stef never spoke about her loss to her new stepchildren. Her previous existence and the tale of how Jake had come into their lives was never discussed. Laurie knew of her campaigning past, of course – he lapped it up. In fact it was his sympathy and belief that cemented his devotion. Not straightaway, but pretty early in their relationship. The irony was that for Laurie Michael assumed the role of some kind of martyr, his 'death' became iconic, a Che Guevara-like immolation. Stef had told him plainly it was a stupid accident but she could see Laurie responded to the romance of the story. Fortunately he respected her wish not to return to that chapter of her life, and she was always able to suppress the subject.

378

Even if It was in some ways a convenience, this alliance with Laurie, Stef had always known that she would get by. She knew that as soon as Jake was born. From that point on, Stef could look forward and build a recognisable future. Jake might have been Michael's parting gift – he had supplied the seed – but Stef was the vessel and the nurturer. Now she had something solid, something that wouldn't let her down or be whisked away, something that she could focus on and believe in. Michael, so unapproachable on an emotional level, so intellectual, always withholding a part of himself, had bequeathed her something valuable, something real, that she could love unreservedly. Intellect did not enter into it.

Instead of her previous adherence to praxis, Stef's crusading zeal was now directed into her passion for literature. Having consistently believed in both the transformative power of the word and the revolutionary potential of women throughout her adult life, she was able to devote her career to both of these in the form of feminist literature. She lectured, she taught, she persuaded, she proselytised. Her greatest models and mentors were a distinguished lineage of revolt: Mary Wollstonecraft, Mary Shelley, Virginia Woolf, Simone Weil, Simone de Beauvoir, Sylvia Plath, Andrea Dworkin. She has studied them exhaustively and taught them assiduously to her receptive university students.

Nowadays, of course, she does neither. She has left all her icons behind. – abandoned them when she realised they could no longer fire her or lend her conviction. They became mere ghosts. At first she went through the motions – convincingly enough, she hoped – but they were hollow. She never mentioned to Laurie or anyone else the death of her faith, they still do not know that light has died, and for them her old beacons are still shining brightly. For her they simply guttered out. How fragile those old beliefs must have been, after all. Woolf and Plath were the last to go, though she harbours a residual loyalty to both.

Eventually, Stef sees Miranda abandon the lawn and, with hesitant, sluggish steps, enter the building. Cynthia has certainly given her something to think about. But now, must Stef see Miranda as an enemy too, part of the forces that, if not ranged against her, constitute obstacles to attaining the truth? The truth about Jake, that is, that work in progress. She will stand up for him, and discover the direction he was taking when he suffered his brutal end, and retrieve it, and make it live. Though he is gone, his future survives somewhere, in a parallel universe maybe, but still real. It haunts and taunts her, just beyond her grasp. But it is there, waiting for her, and she is resolved to rescue it.

Stef will always fight her battles to the end – even if the game is up, she will still be standing, still on her feet, armed with her last, unstaunchable belief. It is stronger than that which clings around the god in St Antony's church, the one that so spectacularly fails to deliver, and will outlast the Institute too, that repository of faith which will soon die and become a wedding venue, for it is belief in love itself; it is belief in the power of belief.

There is Little Stef – the one who climbed the mountain to prove to her daddy that she was a winner – and there is Big Stef, the one who surrendered to grief and found solace in the bottle. And she believes that it is Little Stef who will pull through.

Heaving herself to her feet, she goes to the edge of the balcony, into the moonlight, her eyes narrowed and unrelentingly sober. She craves a drink. But she lights another cigarette instead and scowls at the dumb moon. She will win in the end, and everyone will see.

Chapter 42 | The spy

On Sunday, the storms which in the last few days have confined themselves to the night intrude into daytime hours, beginning in the early morning when the dawn polyphony was drowned out by a violent rumbling followed by a ferocious assault of rain. The downpour ends suddenly, shortly before the hostel guests descend for breakfast, leaving the front lawn a muddied swamp with a haze of vapour rising from it. Throughout the day the sky continues to moan intermittently, with billows of black-rimmed clouds rearing in the west, and there is another burst of rain in the afternoon that lasts less than ten minutes.

In the hostel itself, however, all remains curiously muted and outwardly calm. Again, there is no sign of Stef during the whole day, nor of Dougie or Jules until the late afternoon, when Miranda, sitting on her balcony, sees Jules heading out of the hostel on his own, followed half an hour later by Dougie headed in the opposite direction. She wonders if something has come between them that might account for them going on their separate expeditions on Friday and for Jules's tetchy tirade against Jake.

There are other unexplained signs of discontent among them, too. A couple of hours earlier, Miranda watched Esme and Simon pointedly ignore each other when Simon briefly appeared in the garden while Esme was seated there absorbed in her book. Is it the kind of coolness that might follow some kind of emotional entanglement? That would be completely infuriating – the last thing she needs to cope with right now.

And then there is the fault-line she has detected in the outwardly congenial relationship between Cynthia and Oliver, and the unsettling knowledge that the latter is not only hiding something from the former but seems to have some kind of inside information on the whole family which would apparently blow them apart. There is discord all around her. Only her dad, Laurie, seems immune to the chaos. Yet she knows that he too is seething with anxiety and anticipation; as ever, he has taken on too much, carrying the burden of Stef's simmering turmoil and the responsibility of seeing The Project through to the end.

The feeling of imminent disaster, of everything being held together by the thinnest of threads, strikes her yet more forcibly at dinner, which is accompanied by repeated peals of rumbling thunder filtering in from outside – the sky once more recording its displeasure. As it's Sunday, Thomas has arranged for them all to be seated together at one large table, but there are now four empty places, belonging to Jake, Stef, Dougie and Jules. The absences seem to impinge on those present, for conversation is as moribund as it was on the previous evening. It is a toothsome meal of chicken, rice, dal, okra and white beans in a spicy coconut and chilli sauce, but no one seems to be particularly enjoying it. After Miranda has pushed her plate away, feeling her stomach over-stretched, Esme leans over to tell her that she has booked her train ticket for the day after tomorrow – the day following Monday's ceremony.

'So soon?' Miranda asks.

'My flight is on Friday, so I want to make the most of the last three days. I thought I'd spend them in Kanyakumari.'

'What's that?'

'It's the town on India's southern tip. Cape Comorin, it used to be called.'

'It sounds fun,' Miranda tells her, wondering if it's feasible that everything really will be wrapped up on Monday. It seems hard to believe.

'Hope so,' Esme responds. She gets to her feet and looks round at the table. 'Goodnight, everyone.'

Everyone returns her salutation, then, a few minutes later, Laurie too gets up and leaves the table, followed shortly after by Simon. Only Oliver, Cynthia and Miranda are left, and Miranda seizes the opportunity.

'Cynthia, do you feel like a little stroll around the garden with me?'

'A stroll?'

'Yes. Actually, there's something I wanted to ask you.'

She looks vaguely alarmed. 'Oh, yes! Yes, of course. Come on, then. We'll be back soon, Oliver.'

'Good, good. Off you go. I'll be in the lounge.'

'Delightful! Come on, then.' And Cynthia is quickly on her feet, shuffling rapidly towards the door with Miranda hurrying behind, surprised at the older woman's alacrity and conscious of Oliver's suspicious eyes on them.

Outside, Cynthia takes Miranda's arm and allows herself to be guided along the route towards the trees that they followed on the previous evening. Thunder rumbles overhead, with frequent sparks of lightning, but there is no suggestion of rain.

'I hope he doesn't mind,' Miranda says.

'Oliver? Good lord, no. He does whatever I tell him.'

After a minute or two, at a safe distance from the hostel building, Cynthia asks: 'So what is it you wanted to ask me?'

'Well – there are a couple of things that have been bothering me, after our chat yesterday.'

'I can guess what it's about.'

'Yes.' Miranda pauses, then: 'It's about Stef. And Michael.'

'Oh?'

'First of all, despite what you told me about Michael, it doesn't explain why I could find no records of him – of his very existence. And secondly: what was he hiding?'

'Pardon?'

'You said: "I could tell he was hiding something." And you said he was cagey and secretive. Did you find out why?'

Cynthia pauses on their stroll and Miranda senses her barrier going up again.

'I'm sorry, dear, that's all I'm prepared to say.'

'Why?'

'I've already broken my word to Stephanie. I really can't say anything else. It wouldn't be fair.'

'Oliver knows too, doesn't he? That's why he's being so enigmatic. "A shady character", he called Michael. "An unknown quantity".'

'He shouldn't have said that.'

'And why did you say you were right not to trust Michael?'

'*I* shouldn't have said that.'

'Well, it's a bit odd for Oliver to know something about Jake's dad that no one else in the family knows. What about Stef?'

'She doesn't know. And she mustn't!'

'It must be something terrible.'

'It would hurt her, that's all. And she's been hurt enough.'

'Okay,' Miranda concedes. 'So you can't object if I do a bit more digging around. It'll be a lot easier now, after what you've told me. Because if he didn't die then, when she said he did, it changes everything. I could find out if he's still alive, maybe…'

'No! No, you must never do that!'

'Why ever not?'

'Some things are best left alone,' Cynthia insists. 'It's better for everyone.'

'Hmm.' Miranda can sense the other woman looking severely at her.

'Miranda, please!'

'This is all so bizarre! Oliver has revealed something to me that he doesn't want you to know, and you know something about Stef that you don't want me to know. And you don't want Stef to know any of it. It's all very complicated.'

'It does sound complicated, when you put it like that,' Cynthia concedes.

'And you can't expect me to stop now. I'm really intrigued. Don't worry, I'll be completely discreet.'

She can hear Cynthia breathing hard though her nose, clearly wrestling with a decision.

In a low voice, Cynthia says: 'If I tell you what I know, you must promise never to divulge it to anyone. Not to Simon, not to your father, and certainly not to Stephanie.'

'Of course I won't, if you don't want me to. But you don't have to tell me either, if it upsets you.'

'It would cause such irreparable damage,' Cynthia continues, as if to herself. She resumes her slow stroll through the trees, Miranda keeping pace.

'I did discover something about Michael,' Cynthia says. 'Many years ago. Something rather disturbing, when he was staying with me in Penzance. The three of us had gone to Porthcurno beach, and they were having a swim while I watched the bags. When they were round the point, out of sight, I did something that I'm not very proud of. I looked in Michael's wallet. I was suspicious, I told you. There was something about him that wasn't authentic, something that didn't ring true. And I'm a good judge of character usually.'

'What did you find?'

'Tucked away in the back of his wallet, there was an ID card. With his photo on it but a different name. Don't ask me to tell you the name because I won't. I don't remember what else was on the card, lots of acronyms, but I do remember the badge on it: a crown with a circle thing underneath, and the words "Metropolitan

Police".'

'What?' Miranda's jaw has dropped.

'I put everything back, and I never mentioned it to either of them.'

'He was a policeman?'

'Yes. Unbelievable. Stephanie was going out with a policeman. Who later turned out to be the father of her child. And he was living under a different name.'

'A different name? That would explain the lack of any trace of him online.'

'I expect so.'

'It's insane. Did she know?'

'Almost definitely not.'

'And you didn't tell her?'

'Of course not. Well, I wanted to. I thought I would when the right moment came. But then, a few weeks later, she came to stay with me and told me that she was pregnant, and that Michael was no longer on the scene, so to speak. I thought I would say it then, but she was very upset. She had become extremely attached to Michael. She called him the love of her life. I thought it would unbalance her completely if I mentioned it. So I left it alone. *Then* she started telling everyone this absurd story about Michael dying in a motorcycle crash in Germany. I thought she was mad, but she insisted I go along with it. And I never told anyone. Until I told Oliver.'

'Ah...'

'I didn't mean to! But you see, I'd made a note of Michael's name, all those years ago – or the name on the card, at least. Maybe *that* was a false name for all I know. Anyway, Oliver knows a lot of people with special knowledge of these things, so I mentioned it to him. I didn't say whose name it was or what it was about. I made a little game of it. He has these contacts, you see, in his lodge. His freemason's lodge. One of the other members of the lodge, someone he plays golf with, is in the police. Or was. Something high up in Special Branch. So I asked Oliver to ask him if he could find anything out about this name. Make some discreet enquiries, you know.'

'So – let's get this straight. You had this knowledge all that time, that Michael wasn't who he said he was, and you waited years and years. And even after he was out of your lives completely, you still wanted to find out the truth.'

'Yes.'

'What did you hope to discover?'

'Anything that I could tell Stephanie. You see, she always claimed I hated Michael. She's held it over me, as if somehow I was responsible for him walking out. Which is absolutely absurd. Anyway, she's never mentioned Michael since she first told me all about him walking out. I think she still harbours a kind of loyalty to him. Completely irrational. And – well, I thought it might help to build some bridges between us if I told her something she didn't know. Something that might explain why he went away, something to make her feel a bit better. She was hardly talking to me at all. She hardly talks to me still. My own daughter doesn't speak to me...'

'But why would she blame you?' Miranda asks.

'Oh – I don't know. Families are strange things. Little capsules of ... lunacy, for want of a better word. They're always riddled with unspoken blame and guilt and abiding resentments. Things get twisted.'

'So you didn't hate Michael...?'

'You see?' Cynthia says. 'That's just what I mean. Everything gets distorted. No, I didn't hate him. Not really. I just didn't completely trust him. And I was right!'

'In what way?'

'Well, he was totally untrustworthy. He was a rat!'

'What did you discover?'

Cynthia's voice drops to a dramatic whisper. 'That Michael was spying on her.'

'What?'

'Spying! He was a police spy. A mole! He worked for something called the National Public Order Intelligence Unit. It is, or was, part of Scotland Yard, and his job was to go undercover and infiltrate protest groups. Quite hard-core ones, you know – ultra lefties and anarchists. Well, I had no idea that Stephanie was involved with those kinds of people, but she must have been, or else she mixed with people who were. As I told you, Stephanie was very radical in those days. I don't think she ever did anything seriously illegal or anything, but anyway... When Oliver found out about Michael being an undercover agent, I had to tell him the whole story. I couldn't *not* tell him. But I gave him strict instructions not to tell anyone else. He promised!'

'I knew that she was an activist when she was younger.'

'She lived in a commune or something with others in the same group. And Michael was one of them. And of course she got together with him, and they had a baby – Jake. But what she didn't know, and what she must never know, is that Michael was a spy. In fact he was a complete shit. He went way beyond the limits of what he was permitted to do, having relationships with people in the group he was supposed to be spying on. And then Stephanie became pregnant with Jake and I suppose he couldn't handle it – he got out fast.'

'Oh my God!'

'He just disappeared. And he has never been seen since. At least not under that alias. Oliver found all this out through his friend. But it's a huge secret. That's why you must never tell anyone. Stephanie would be destroyed. As far as she's concerned, Michael was almost a god. But in reality he was weak. He couldn't cope.'

'I suppose his superiors couldn't allow it. It would have blown his cover. So what happened to him?'

'Apparently he went to Australia. That's all that's known about him. But this happened thirty years ago. He might have come back to England by now.'

'Or he could be dead,' Miranda says.

'Yes. He could be,' Cynthia agrees. 'It doesn't matter. He is to us, anyway. As far as Stephanie's concerned, he just fled. Couldn't face being a father. This was a long time ago, you know. Men were much more callous then.'

'But doesn't she have a right to know?'

'Right? What is a "right to know", dear? I don't know if there's any such thing as a "right to know". And, as I said, I've only recently found it out myself, through Oliver. And we've discussed it, at great length, and decided to keep it to ourselves. Stephanie must never know the truth. Certainly not now, when she's putting her son to rest, and not any other time either. What good would it do? She believed in Michael. She believed that he loved her, just couldn't face being a father. She never mentions him, of course, but I think she's sort of forgiven him. It's much easier to do that than believe he's a rat, and that their time together was a charade, that he never loved her.'

'Maybe he did love her,' Miranda suggests.

'Oh, come on! How could he have truly loved her, and yet deceived her like that? Betrayed her! Possibly he did feel something for her. But the fact remains: she doesn't know that he was using her. That makes all the difference. He was a complete fraud. Rotten through and through. She has no idea he was a traitor. If she did, she would know that he probably never did love her.'

They walk on for a while without speaking, both wrapped in

thought. They have traced a wide circle through the garden and are now back in front of the veranda. At the end of the veranda, below a hanging bulb that has dozens of insects whirling frenetically around it, Oliver is sitting with his book, a cup of tea on the table in front of him.

'Now listen,' Cynthia says in an urgent whisper. 'Apart from Oliver, you're the first person I've mentioned this to. Only you and me and Oliver know the truth. And I suppose a few spooks in Scotland Yard. And I'm absolutely firm about this: I don't want it to go any further. Alright, dear? And I'm going to have a stern word in Oliver's ear. I thought he was the soul of discretion...'

'It's all so unbelievable,' Miranda says. 'It's hard to take in. I can't help feeling that it's better for Stef to know the truth.'

'Some things are better left alone, dear,' Cynthia tells her. 'I firmly believe that. Now I'm going to join Oliver. Think on what I've said. And I implore you, for the love of God, please don't breathe a word of this to anyone. You must promise me. Promise?'

Miranda hesitates. She hates giving promises. Hates being tied down, especially when it comes to the truth.

She grasps Cynthia's arms, squeezes. 'Don't worry, Cynthia. Trust me. I'm not going to give you away!'

'That's not what I meant! Miranda!' But Miranda is walking away. Cynthia can hear her sandalled feet rushing upstairs, and a feeling of deep dread settles on her.

'Tiresome girl!' she says aloud.

She's still fuming when she joins Oliver at his table.

'What was all that about?' he asks her.

'She thinks she knows it all!'

'Miranda?'

'She has no right, she really hasn't!'

'No right?'

'She's interfering, and she's forcing my hand!'

'How is she she's forcing your hand?'

'She and you together!'

'What?'

Cynthia turns to face him, her expression as severe as he's ever seen. 'Oliver, I don't know what you've been up to. I don't want to know. But you've been letting a few cats out of a few bags, and I'm very cross. I just want you to know that! You've been extremely foolish!'

Oliver looks guilty, the colour rising in his cheeks.

'My dear, I wish I knew what you're talking about!'

Her face softens. She pats his arm and sighs. 'You do, though. We both know that you do. But let's leave it at that, shall we? Suffice to say that you've placed me in a very awkward position.'

She rises and goes inside without another word.

He coughs, juts out his lower lip and narrows his eyes. Breathing heavily, shaking his head in exasperated fury, he stares sulkily into the night.

Chapter 43 | Death at the Institute

It is the big day. Laurie smiles reassuringly at his wife, who is seated rigidly upright on the stool in front of the mirror, almost unblinking.

'You look fine,' he says.

She doesn't meet his eyes in the mirror. 'Of course I don't. It's better that you say nothing than lie.'

'How's your headache?' Now she glares at him in the mirror. He shrugs and turns away. *She's right. Better to say nothing.*

He looks at his watch: 9.30. So early yet so hot. Even at this hour there is no relief, the heat vibrating in the air outside to the stridulating rhythm of the cicadas. He turns back to his wife. Her make-up only seems to accentuate her fragile, volatile mood. She has been looking rough in the last couple of days, with dark folds under her eyes, her skin sallow and dry, her calves pocked with insect bites. Sweat glistens on her brow and forms dark patches under her arms. At breakfast this morning, she was silent, morose, almost lifeless, refusing to engage with her mother or Oliver or anyone else. He thought she had never looked so old. Now, though, her eyes glitter as if possessed of a crackling, high-voltage energy, dangerously over-charged. Anger emanates from her like a radioactive glow, warning anyone in the vicinity to keep their distance. Sometimes when he looks at her, Laurie has to turn away, almost seared by the intensity, but then he looks again a few seconds later and she seems transformed into something much gentler and more vulnerable, a completely different person. It reminds him of those optical tricks that can represent two entirely different images, like the drawing of a wine glass that, seen from a different perspective, perhaps in a different frame of mind, appears instead to be two faces kissing.

He pulls out his phone, glances at it, puts it away. He wants to hear Mozart. He wants to hear laughter, or cricket scores, or any sort of normal, unfreighted conversation, but above all he wants to be somewhere else. Like tomorrow.

There is a soft knock on the door. Laurie strides across the room to open it and finds Shibu there, standing gawkily to attention in a check shirt and crisp white dhoti.

'Please, downstairs...'

'What is it?'

'Come, please.'

Laurie turns and exchanges a worried glance with Stef. The two of them briskly leave the room and follow Shibu down to the reception. Thomas is standing upright behind his desk, but it is the other figure in the lobby that draws their attention. Half-hidden in the shadow, tall and erect in her blue and white habit, Sister Margaret stands as still as a plaster saint, her fingers interlocked. It is the first time they have seen her outside the Institute's precincts and she looks alien.

'Sister Margaret!'

'Good morning Mrs Daniels, Mr Johnson. How are you this morning?'

'What's the matter?' Stef demands. 'Has something happened?'

'Yes, I am afraid so.' They stare at her in alarm. 'I'm afraid I have very bad news.'

'What?'

'It is very bad. Very sad. We are bereaved, madam.'

'I – I don't understand!' Stef stutters in a hoarse whisper, eyes wide.

'We have had a death in the night. Our Sister Solace. She has gone from us.'

'Sister Solace?' Stef repeats with incredulity.

'Yes. She was very old. Now she is in God's hands.'

There is a pause. Stef looks relieved now. 'I'm very sorry to hear it,' she tells the nun. 'Was she ill?'

'No. But it was her time,' Sister Margaret answers in a matter-of-fact tone. 'God has decided. It is the best thing for her, no doubt.'

'Oh, well...' Stef hesitates, as if unsure of how to respond to the news. Just then, Cynthia and Oliver appear from the lounge, newspapers in hand. They, too, are formally dressed. From the garden, Miranda also joins them.

Sister Margaret continues. 'As you may imagine, Mrs Daniels, we are in great shock. Our little community is in mourning.'

'My deepest condolences,' Stef mutters.

'Unfortunately it is impossible to continue with the inauguration ceremony.'

'What?'

'We cannot continue with the ceremony,' Sister Margaret declares. 'It has been cancelled.'

'No!'

'I'm afraid it was necessary. It would not be appropriate. So I have cancelled it.'

Stef looks stunned, frozen to the spot. 'You can't,' she says, her voice cracking.

'So when can the ceremony take place?' Cynthia asks.

'That I cannot tell you.'

'But we're leaving in three days! We must have the ceremony as soon as possible.'

'I am sorry madam. I will let you know the new schedule after I have spoken to the sisters and to the other members of our community.'

Stef approaches the nun, palms joined in a kind of prayer.

'Please. Please let us go ahead with the ceremony. We cannot leave here unless we do. It is vitally important!'

Laurie looks askance at his wife, shocked by her sudden, unfamiliar display of humility. Recovering himself, and conscious that he must show solidarity, he chips in: 'It's absolutely imperative, Sister Margaret. We are very sad about Sister Solace, but can it not go ahead tomorrow instead? We have flights booked on Wednesday and it's too late to change them now.'

'I am sorry, Mr Johnson. I will let you know as soon as a decision has been made. It is outside my control.' Her face expresses sincere sympathy but her voice is as clipped and business-like as ever. She clasps her hands again. 'Now...'

Moving towards the door, she is about to step out, but then turns to address the group of westerners in the lobby. 'She was the longest-serving member of our community, you know.' She bows her head stiffly, then is gone.

Stef lets out a sound that is both a growl and an anguished groan and hides her face in her hands. Laurie puts his arm around her shoulders and he too appears stunned.

'It'll be alright, love. Don't worry. We'll get the ceremony done.'

'It's the most awful...' Oliver begins, but he is interrupted by Cynthia.

'We'll make sure of it,' she says. 'They must go on and do it. We'll insist. I'm sure they'll make a concession.' Stef raises her head and glares at her mother. 'They will, dear,' Cynthia assures her. 'Don't get yourself in a state.'

Back in their room, Stef savagely smokes a cigarette and vents her fury to Laurie.

'That bitch! She always hated Jake.'

'Sister Margaret?' Laurie asks.

'Sister Solace. She was poisonous, vile.'

'I've never met her,' Laurie says. 'I don't even know who she is. Is it someone who knew Jake?'

'Yes, and she hated him.'

'Well, I don't suppose she's done it on purpose. Died, I mean.'

'I wouldn't put it past her, the vile old bitch!'

'Listen, love, let's not get too worked up,' Laurie says. 'It won't do any of us any good getting upset and angry.'

'I'm *not* upset! I'm *furious*! And can you blame me?'

'No, of course not. It's perfectly understandable. It *is* upsetting. I'm just saying let's not make it any worse than it is. Everything will be resolved. One way or another we'll get through this, and then it'll be over and we can go back home.'

'Oh, don't give me that Pollyanna bullshit! I'm not stupid! It's too late! You know what you are? You're a bloody appeaser! And you're not helping. In fact you're the usual fly in the bloody ointment.'

'I beg your pardon?'

'A bloody fly in the bloody ointment!'

Laurie gapes at her, aghast. He doesn't remember seeing her this incensed.

'Just leave me alone,' she sighs, her voice now low and weary.

'Alright. Alright, I'll do something. I'll go to the school and I'll talk to Sister Margaret, see if I can get some sense out of her. Fly in the ointment? That's very harsh, Stef. You should stop biting the hand that's trying to support you!'

'Shut up! I don't need supporting!' she bellows.

Laurie stares at her again, speechless now. Then he stomps out of the room, slamming the door behind him. She hears his angry steps on the stairs and clenches her fists, staring at the ceiling and muttering wordless curses. Then she shakes her head violently and sits heavily on the bed. 'Give me strength!' she snarls between clenched jaws as she screws her cigarette stub into a saucer.

A few minutes later there is a soft knock on the door. Stef jumps to her feet, hackles risen, braced for the next assault, apology or any other anodyne nonsense. But, thrusting open the door, she is taken aback to see a thin, elderly white woman, richly swathed in a yellow and turquoise sari. It is her mother.

'What the bloody hell are you doing?' she demands.

Cynthia flinches, then smiles brightly. 'Don't you like it, dear? I bought it in Trivandrum.'

Stef blinks, speechless.

'I heard you shouting. Can I come in?'

Once inside with the door closed, Cynthia turns a stern gaze on her daughter. 'Now, what's the matter?'

Still agape at her mother's attire, Stef finally shakes her head in disbelief and sits back down on the bed, drained. 'You know what the matter is.'

'No. I don't.'

'Everything's shit.'

'Only if you let it be. You need to calm down. Why were you shouting at Laurence?'

'Because he doesn't have a clue.'

'None of us has a clue. We just have to adapt.'

'This was all planned months ago. I didn't even want to do it. And now it's all shit. I can't trust anyone.'

'You can't expect to control every eventuality, dear! This is India! We're not in Winnersh now.'

'No, we're not in Kansas...'

'Kansas?'

'He should have seen this coming.'

'Seen what coming?'

'Everything. Nothing has gone right since we arrived.'

'My dear, Laurence has worked his socks off to pull this together. So has Miranda. And Simon, and all your donors and everyone else who has lent their support. Can you not see that?'

'Of course I see it! But it's not enough! Laurie is just not up to it!'

'Not up to India? Well, you may be right. But he's stood by you every step of the way. And sometimes I think you don't appreciate how much you owe him. He's given everything! But do you ever show him any gratitude? Or do you take him for granted? You criticise him, you lie to him...'

'What lie?'

'What lie? The lie you told him and everybody else too. You know very well what I'm referring to. About Michael!'

'Oh, that lie...'

'Yes – that one. The lie in which you made me complicit.'

'I had to, obviously.'

'No, it's not at all obvious, dear. You even told your son that his father was dead.'

'Keep your voice down!' Stef hisses. 'Of course I did! But I would have told him the truth. I was going to.'

'When?'

'When he was an adult!'

'Well that wasn't about to happen, was it?'

'What do you mean?'

'Jake! He was never going to grow up! You wouldn't let him. You kept him in a state of infantilism.'

'How dare you say that! Jake was a great credit to me *and* to his father!'

'But you lied to him! You never even gave him a photograph of his father! He wasn't even allowed to mourn!'

'I always had Jake's interests at heart. Nobody else did! I did everything for him. He was a strong, original, creative human being! How dare you accuse me of not being a good mother! How would you know anyway?'

'What is that supposed to mean?'

'You were never there for us! When Daddy died. Just like you were never there for me when Michael died!'

'But he *didn't* die!'

'Keep your voice down! He died for *me*! And you couldn't show me an atom of support when I needed it!'

'I lied for you! You made me!'

'You hated him!'

'I didn't hate him. But I didn't trust him! He was a bad, bad man.'

'I loved him!'

'Stephanie, it's time you took that man off his pedestal! There are a few things you don't know about Michael!'

'I know everything there is to know about Michael!'

'Do you? Do you really?' Cynthia sits down opposite her daughter. 'I didn't want to tell you this, but I have no choice. Because if I don't, someone else will! You didn't know that he was spying on you, did you?'

'What?'

'Michael was a police spy. An informant. It sounds absurd, but it's the truth!'

Stef raises a level gaze towards her mother. Her eyes are stony.

'How do you know that?' she asks in a leaden voice.

'Because Oliver found it out. A friend of his was in the police. Michael was spying on you all! On your group in that commune, or whatever it was. He took you all in.'

'No, he didn't.'

Cynthia furrows her brow.

'He didn't take *me* in,' Stef tells her.

'You *knew*?'

'I found out.'

'How did you find out?'

'After he disappeared. I did my own research. I even found the grave of the dead child whose identity he assumed.'

'That's abominable!'

Stef nods. 'Yes. But it's for me to feel abominated. Not you. Not

Oliver. It's my business.'

'Don't you care that he deceived you?'

'I care very much. But it's *my* business.'

'What about his son?'

'That was my responsibility. I would have told him about his father.'

'You could have told him that his father was alive!'

'Why?'

Cynthia opens her mouth but no words come out. She is unable to answer. But then she quietly says: 'Because he was his son.'

'He was my son too. And his father wasn't involved any more. It was my decision.'

'It might have helped him.'

'Mum, you don't know the first thing. You have all these theories about the world, all these high ideals, but the reality is more complicated. Actually, the world is a very messy place, not always amenable to high ideals.'

Cynthia's expression softens and she smiles. 'You sound like me talking to you when you were seventeen.'

'Don't be ridiculous. And stay out of my private life!'

'You dragged me into it, dear, when you made me agree to your lie.'

'There were good reasons for that!'

'What were they? That you couldn't face the world knowing that he abandoned you? Or knowing that you were taken in? That your lover was deceiving you for two years? That he didn't love you?'

'Of course he loved me.'

Cynthia stares at her, baffled, as if she is trying to decipher a map or understand a cryptic crossword clue.

'My dear, you're not making sense.'

'He loved me,' Stef insists. 'He lied to me, but we all lie. He loved me. I know it. End of story.'

'Then you're living in a fantasy world, dear.'

'There are worse places. I could say the same about you and your boyfriend.'

'Oliver?'

'He's a leech. And an idiot. If you can't see that then it's you who's living in a world of illusion.'

'Stephanie, I'll pretend you didn't say that. You're a very cruel and heartless person. I might say that Jake was also living in a world of illusion, as you put it. Except he had no choice!'

'You might say that, might you? Cruel and heartless? Perhaps you were a cruel and heartless wife!'

Cynthia freezes. 'Is that what you think? Is that what you've thought all these years? Is that why you hate me?'

Stef takes a deep breath and closes her eyes.

'Don't be ridiculous. Can you go now, please.'

After a weighty silence, Cynthia gets up and crosses to the door, then stops.

'Stephanie, one day you might understand that God has put us on this world to be pleasant to each another. Not nasty.'

'No, mother, you're wrong. Actually, life's a bloody bitch. And we're entitled to do or say or believe any damn thing we like in order to get through it!'

Cynthia sniffs, pulls open the door and turns towards her daughter.

'Then you're twisted. I always knew Jake didn't give a jot about anything or anyone either. Now I know where he got it from.' And with that she leaves the room.

Chapter 44 | The resolution

Esme's phone pings jarringly while she is engaged in the dhanarasana pose on her yoga mat, with her spine curved to its limit, her abdomen stretched tight. She tries to expel from her consciousness the electronic intrusion and her irritation with it, but after a further half-minute she surrenders to the distraction, uncurls herself, and breathing evenly lies still for several seconds before reaching for her phone. It is a text from Dougie: 'Going crazy. Feel like a walk?' She puts the phone aside, message unanswered.

Even after completing her second yoga session of the day, Esme still feels conflicted. Everything has been thrown into confusion since the cancellation of the ceremony, and all the attendees have been left with too much time on their hands. Half an hour after the unhinged bout of screaming upstairs that was heard by all the hostel's residents, Cynthia descended looking pale and pensive, and she and Oliver have now ventured out on some excursion. Simon and Jules also went out somewhere, Miranda disappeared into her room, and now there is no sign of Stef, either. Esme longs to leave behind this cauldron of strife and stress, longs to get back on the road, but the postponement has thrown her plans awry. The prospect of escape to Kanyakumari beckons tantalisingly, a vision of release from the madness on India's southernmost tip. In her heart she knows she ought to stick it out, attend the ceremony as planned, whenever it is rescheduled, but she doesn't know if she is strong enough to remain here any longer.

Mired in indecision, she sits by her open window, unable to respond to Dougie's message. Above all, she must have a clear head – the last thing she needs is to enter the muddy waters of the boys' skewered relationship, for Dougie is sure to want to unload onto her.

Her attention latches onto a long-legged spider in one corner of the window frame, whose delicate limbs are patiently working at the strands of a web. She marvels at the web's mathematical intricacy and the spider's total dedication to its task.

The boys? They aren't boys. Why does she think of them in that way? Perhaps because that is the way she has regarded them since her first sight of them at Sri Vidna, festooned with beads and scarves, like vagabonds with their chin-growths, yet like boys sucking on straws. Jules in particular didn't seem to her properly grown up yet – or at least he made *her* feel properly grown up in his company. Though that didn't feel right either. When do you ever really grow up, she wonders? Is it when you start looking back on your youthful transgressions?

Thinking back to that first encounter with Dougie and Jules, she broods over the unguarded candour that she recklessly allowed herself: was she too honest? Why did she share so much? She might not have said anything were it not for the possibility – no, probability – that Stef would mention the book to Dougie. That was definitely on the cards. But she needn't have revealed as much as she did. To Jules especially, who is, after all, a stranger. And he seemed so indignant. Was it just jealousy, as Dougie suggested? She can't make him out. She wonders whether Jules would have fallen under Jake's spell the way others did. Why were certain people drawn to Jake? It was always a mystery to her. They seemed to have nothing in common with him or with each other. Were they simply the privileged people on whom he himself bestowed his interest, members of an élite club or society whose totem was Jake himself? What would Jake would have made of Jules?

Suddenly, Esme hears an angry buzzing and sees what appears to be a wasp charge through the open window as if on a mission. It hovers for an instant over the spider web, then dives down at the spider itself. In fascinated horror she watches as the wasp systematically severs each of the spider's legs, making rapid work of its butchery, until only the bulbous torso is left twitching on the sill. Then the wasp makes a final assault on this remaining body part, scoops it up and flies back out of the window with the torso grappled tightly to its insect chest. All is quiet again, and only the perfect web and the spider's severed legs on the sill testify to its having been there. Esme feels obscurely traumatised by the swiftness of the execution, how the wasp barely hesitated before targeting and efficiently dispatching its hapless prey. How superfluous, how laboured, how pointlessly irrelevant all her human concerns suddenly seem, and how fragile. All her desires and frustrations, all her plans and programmes, all the petty problems currently dividing Dougie and Jules – all pure self-indulgence.

Still feeling faintly disturbed, she buckles on her sandals, gathers her hat and sunglasses and lets herself out of the room, padlocking the door behind her. She will ask Thomas if she can take a bike out, have a wander in the country lanes hereabouts. Hoping she doesn't run into Dougie before she can carry out her plan, she hears a door slam above her as she is descending the stairs, and Stef appears above her.

'Esme, darling!' she exclaims, catching her up.

'Hallo, Stef.' Esme is alarmed at how scarily intense the older woman's eyes appear. Unthinkingly, she offers Stef an embrace. It is quite unlike her, just as it is out of character for Stef to submit to Esme's comforting arms. The two women pull apart after a few seconds, both slightly unnerved by the close contact, and continue side by side to the bottom of the stairs.

'I'm so sorry about the delay,' Esme tells Stef.

'So am I, darling. It's maddening.'

'I wish I could help move things along.'

'Come with me!' Stef says. 'I'm going to the school. I've got to speak to that nun. It's the only way. She has to sort this out.' There is something feverish, almost manic, in her expression.

'Of course,' Esme hears herself saying, her heart sinking. She is anticipating an emotional scene, a confrontation, an embarrassment – but there is no possibility of backing out now. Returning Thomas's guarded greeting, the pair emerge from the hostel gates at as brisk a pace as the midday heat allows. The black dog outside the gates pauses its miserable scratching to contemplate them as they pass.

As they are crossing the open space in front of the church, feeling the crushing weight of the sun, Esme hears Stef murmuring.

'Sorry?' she says, uncertain whether she is being addressed.

'Nothing, darling. Poetry. "Hourly the eye of the sky enlarges its blank dominion."' Esme glances at her without understanding. 'Plath. You know, Esme, I feel so close to Jake here. Being here, being with you all, his friends, it brings him closer. I'm convinced he is here too, walking with us.'

'Maybe. But isn't the point of all this to say goodbye? To lay his ghost to rest?'

'My God, Esme! "Lay his ghost to rest"? That sounds so brutal. I don't see it that way at all.'

'Don't we have to do that, eventually? To really say goodbye?'

'You, maybe. But can you really? You know, Esme, I'll never forget everything you did for him. You were a true friend. Perhaps the only one.'

Esme is once again struck by how wrong Stef could be. So deluded. After all, it wasn't what she or Dougie or anyone else did for Jake, it's what they saved him from doing – up to a point. Then they got tired. If only she knew. But they wouldn't let her. So whose fault is that? Not Stef's. And then, the shocking thought hits her, almost like a physical blow: it wasn't Jake who was the scapegoat, it was Stef herself. And she still is their scapegoat. Deep down, Esme thinks she always knew that.

At the time, of course, Esme persuaded herself that her lies to Stef – the active lies as well as the lies of omission – had been manufactured purely in order to soften the blow for her. But now she sees the inescapable, unembellished truth: it was simply easier that way, easier to placate and humour Stef, easier, ultimately, to blame her. After all, she was the one who took on the role of the grasping and self-deluding mother, surely it was only fitting to deceive her, who deceived herself so completely? After the possessive mother routine, she took on new roles: grieving Stef, unstable Stef, drunk fantasist Stef. And in this way she became the archetype, the totem witch whose historical function has always been to carry the sins of the community, to shoulder the burden of blame. For don't they all believe deep down that she is the responsible one, the one who produced this egotistical monster in the first place? It's so much more convenient to believe that. She fits the role – why not let her be the scapegoat?

Esme hears Stef murmuring to herself, perhaps reciting more lines by Plath or Woolf. Suddenly she halts in mid-stride.

'Wait!'

Esme looks at her expectantly. Stef seems to be listening.

'What is it?'

'Hear that?'

'What?' Esme asks.

'The birds. What language *is* that?'

But as soon as Esme tries to concentrate on the birdsong, trying to separate it from the noise of traffic and human voices, Stef has set off again and Esme has to hurry to keep up with her.

'Stef…' she says, in her gentlest, most hesitant tone as they wait to cross the road. 'I've been thinking a lot about Jake recently.

Well, we all have. And remembering all kinds of things. And I remembered what a great mimic he was. Was he always so good?'

There is a short, shrill eruption of mirth from Stef. 'Jake? Yes, he absolutely was. A natural. He was bloody incorrigible! Superb! And hilarious! He used to take the piss out of poor Laurie constantly. I'm sure he took the piss out of me too. I wouldn't be at all surprised. He could imitate anybody within seconds of meeting them. He'd absorb their essence, whatever it was that made them who they were, and reproduce it to a T. And it could be bloody embarrassing. But he was so clever. He really should have been an actor.'

Esme nods without replying. Yes, that's what he was alright – not an artist but an actor. Of course he was, seeing as mimicry was his particular gift – perhaps his only gift. He made a lot more sense when seen in that perspective. All the time, he was acting the part of somebody else. Impersonating them, perhaps trying to be them. He stole people's girlfriends because he wanted to be them for a while. He was always trying out – trialling – different personas. Everything he did involved some form of mimicry, from mocking his tutors to coming out, cross-dressing and even morphing into a heroin addict, right up to the very end when his own last act was a copy of his father's – even his own death was a mimicry.

But recognising the actor in Jake brings Esme no closer to arriving at the key to him, the crux of the enigma: if everything he did and everything he was was an act, who was Jake really? The same old question.

The two women enter the Institute gates, Stef accelerating her pace as she leads the way to the reception office. Before reaching it they encounter Sister Margaret coming out.

'Sister Margaret, I need to speak to you urgently,' Stef begins, peremptory and unswerving.

The nun wears an impatient expression. 'I have already spoken to your husband, Mrs Daniels,' she says.

'This is completely unacceptable. It's just not good enough. We're here, we came all this way, to do the right thing for my son. This is all about him!'

The nun raises both palms to her. 'Mrs Daniels! This is unnecessary...'

'No! Listen to me! It is very necessary. It is absolutely crucial. This is the whole reason we're here! You can't just...'

'Please let me finish!' The nun's high-pitched voice rises a few degrees higher. 'I have already spoken to your husband, Mrs Daniels. I have arranged for the ceremony to take place tomorrow. We had planned to spend a day of remembrance for our dear sister, but that will now take place on the following day. We shall formally inaugurate the Recreation Centre tomorrow, as you wanted. At nine o'clock a.m. I hope you will be there, with your family and friends no doubt.'

Stef is wide-eyed, flummoxed, at the nun's announcement. 'I... I – of course. Thank you. Of course we will be there.'

'Good. Until tomorrow then, Mrs Daniels.'

The nun speeds along the corridor towards the classrooms.

'It's Daniel,' Stef shouts after her retreating form. 'Professor Daniel!' But the nun does not stop, disappearing fast round the corner. 'Why the hell can't she get my name right?' she says to Esme.

'She seems so frantically busy,' Esme says. 'It's like she hasn't got the bandwidth for details like that. But isn't that the greatest news! Laurie must have persuaded her.'

'Possibly,' Stef concedes, sounding doubtful.

'So...!' Esme turns to retrace their steps out of the Institute, but Stef doesn't follow.

'You go,' she tells her. 'There's something I need to do here.'

'Are you sure?'

Stef nods. 'Someone I need to speak to. Thanks for coming. Thank you for being here. You don't know what a pillar of strength you are.'

Esme smiles modestly, waves, and as she hurries away feels the pressure of expectation and obligation dissolve off her skin like fairy dust. Mingled with the relief is the awareness of the strange hold that Stef has over her now. She is somehow in thrall to her, she can't explain why or how, even though proximity to her is so lacerating and life-sapping.

Nonetheless, despite that invisible chain, she knows what she must do. Again, she can't explain, it is beyond reason, but she is resolved. She knows as surely as she has ever known anything that she will forgo her train ticket tomorrow and will stay for the ceremony. She doesn't know how she could have ever conceived of there being any other option.

Later, at the hostel, she meets Dougie for a lunch of curd and bananas, offering sympathy without committing herself to any kind of advice on his suddenly undermined relationship with Jules. Despite a brief reconciliation, they have apparently fallen further apart. Relationships are not subject to rules, she tells him, they must go their own way. She senses the disappointment in Dougie at her unhelpful and anodyne analysis. Then she retires to her room, emerging a couple of hours later to borrow the hostel's bike and cycle to Allapoorha's railway station to find out whether another ticket to Kanyakumari can be had. She cannot know whether she has made a wise decision, but she is certain it is a right one.

Chapter 45 | Terra incognita

Stef carries on along the corridor, then crosses the yard to the school building, where she ascends the staircase. On each floor she flies along the corridor, scouring the rooms through the open doors as she passes, but without seeing the face she is searching for. On the third-floor corridor she meets Sister Margaret again and curses inwardly.

'Mrs Daniels! Can I be of assistance?'

'It's Judith. I was looking for Judith.'

'Judith?'

'The little girl. Eleven or twelve years old, with bright green eyes.'

Sister Margaret frowns, eyeing Stef with suspicious eyes. 'Ah, yes! Judith. I know the girl. She is out.'

'Don't tell me. She's in Bangla Desh.'

'Sorry?'

'Where is she?'

'She has gone to the market.'

'By herself?'

'Yes, by herself. It is her turn on the rota to do shopping. She has not come back yet.'

'What time will she be back?'

Sister Margaret waggles her head. 'Possibly in a few minutes, no doubt.'

'Right, thanks.' Stef starts to turn back towards the stairs, then pauses. 'Tell me, is Judith an orphan?'

'Yes.'

'She has no family at all?'

'She has one sister.'

'A sister? Is it the woman I've seen here, at the school, sweeping?'

'Yes, Elizabeth does work for us here. She works cleaning and cooking. Sometimes in the garden. Why do you ask, Mrs Daniels?'

'Nothing at all. Just curious. She...looks at me.'

'Looks at you?'

'Yes. She's a little strange. She smiles at me.'

Again, the suspicious look. 'Smiles?'

'It's as if she knows me. I don't know. It's probably my imagination.'

'Some of the people here are "strange", Mrs Daniels. They are very poor. They have great problems. Some of them have been abused.'

'But the little girl, Judith, she's not strange. She's such a sweet girl.'

The nun now turns her sober, appraising expression on Stef. She herself is, as ever, unreadable.

'Well, I won't be keeping you, Sister,' Stef tells her. 'Thank you so much for rearranging the ceremony at short notice. I truly appreciate it.' With that, she spins round and heads back downstairs to the entrance. At the gates, though, instead of crossing the road in the direction of the hostel, she finds a patch of shade beneath a jacaranda tree a few paces from the Institute gates and waits. She sees several people enter and leave the school gates, and the gatekeeper throws her the occasional curious glance, but there is no sign of Judith. Finally she spots the little girl on the far side of the street, weighed down by two large, blue-chequered bags that are bulging with carrots, onions, parsley and much else. She is wearing a patched yellow dress and her usual motley collection of bracelets.

Stef steps forward. 'Judith! Hallo!'

The little girl stops and for the first time offers her a full, heartfelt smile. Stef can see now the similarity in this and Elizabeth's smile. Elizabeth has the same smile but with the volume turned up to maximum. Judith puts the bags down, and Stef notices with concern the deep creases that the bags' handles have left in her flesh.

'Oh, you poor thing!' she says, turning up the palms of the girl's hands and gently rubbing the red marks. 'Poor, poor thing. It's so lovely to see you,' she croons at her. 'And you're such a sweet girl! Have you been to the market?' There is no sign that the girl has understood her words. It is frustrating, but there is comfort enough in seeing the girl's happy, guileless face. Stef rummages in her bag and produces from her purse a grubby hundred-rupee note. 'Here...'

Judith contemplates the note uncertainly.

'Take it,' Stef says, pressing the note on her. The girl casts glances up and down the road and finally accepts it, pushing it into a fold in her dress. She smiles again, briefly, then picks up the bags and continues to the school gate.

'Goodbye!' Stef calls after her. Judith stops and looks around expressionlessly, then disappears inside. Stef stares for a few moments at the space where she was, then rouses herself and walks quickly away.

As she crosses the chequerboard square in front of the church, she wonders how much little Judith knows of her parentage. Sister indeed! And does she ever miss the father that she never knew?

It is true what Cynthia said: Stef never spoke to Jake about his own father. She never spoke to any of the children of how it had happened – how Jake had come into their lives. As far as they were concerned, Jake was the product of a previous relationship, that was all. It didn't require any elaboration. One day, she would explain more fully to Jake, in private. She would set the record straight. But there was never a right time to set the record straight.

Terra incognita

Now was never the right time. One day the right time would make itself plain, and then it never could. Consequently, Stef has kept her secret intact, her own private narrative: the tale of how Michael bestowed this amazing gift when he was no longer in her life, when he himself had already renounced it.

She walks slowly along the track towards the entrance to the hostel, alongside the stream/sewer that runs below it with its stagnant grey contents, and flinches instinctively when she spots a rat scurrying along the bank in front of her before disappearing into the open mouth of a cement pipe. She doesn't falter, doesn't hesitate or cross to the other side, for she is resigned now. In this at least Laurie has been right: acceptance works better here, just as this slow saunter is the only viable pace in these ridiculous temperatures.

She passes the pink and orange temple, now deserted, with no trace of the beggars in front. The only sign of life is the dusty, diseased black dog. Curled up by the wall, it raises its head to look at her with apprehensive eyes, then yawns and resumes its prone position, twitching its wrinkled, inflamed skin.

She recalls again how Michael looked at her with that new, unfamiliar mien when she first told him of his gift – sad and panicky, like an animal. She was shocked. In her naivety, she had expected Michael to embrace the news. He might first have taken a detached, intellectual interest in his creation before fully accepting it, but this reaction of near-horror was hideous. After all, for all his emotional absence, Michael was not heartless. But then, what did she know?

When Stef enters the bedroom, Laurie looks up from his seat at the table, a wary look in his face.

'Have you heard?' he asks her. 'That it's back on?'

She nods. 'Well done, Laurie. But if you're expecting an apology from me, don't bother. I don't feel apologetic.'

413

'I wasn't expecting anything,' Laurie says. 'Least of all an apology. An apology from you is rarer than hen's teeth.'

'Good,' Stef tells him, kicking off her shoes and stretching out on the bed. 'We're agreed about that, at least. It's not my style.'

She closes her eyes. After a few seconds she senses Laurie standing next to her, no doubt surveying the deep lines of her face, then she feels the touch of his lips on her forehead. 'What are you doing?' she demands, eyes switched open.

'Nothing, Stef,' he says with a sad, sympathetic smile.

'Well, don't,' she mutters impatiently. 'Let's just get on with things.'

'Alright. Anyway – I'm off.'

'Where are you going?'

'To the lake, with Simon. Thomas says you can rent canoes.'

'Male bonding in a canoe?' Stef responds. 'How quaint! Just watch out for the backwoods boys! On the other hand – maybe they have little sisters!'

Laurie pretends not to hear. 'Maybe you should spend a little time with your mother,' he says.

'Obviously you're not expecting me to apologise to *her*,' Stef says.

'Obviously not.'

'Good.'

'But she's not looking very happy,' Laurie tells her.

'Nothing I can do about that.'

'She's worried,' Laurie says as he heads for the door. 'We...' He checks himself, then carries on out of the room with a cheery 'Byee!'

...*We all are*, Stef finishes his sentence. Everyone is worried about Stef. If only they'd let Stef be. She can't stand their sympathy and tactful evasions, their manufactured small talk and studied insouciance. Patience. All this will soon be over.

414

She closes her eyes again, but after a few seconds they flick back open. She can't rest now. Too much going on. She casts a glance to the red suitcase by the wall. Soon they would all leave, leave it this behind. Leave Jake behind, leave his book behind. She cannot fill the void left by the lost book – that would have enabled her to let him go with a lighter heart, but at least he'll never be truly gone. There's Judith.

Tomorrow, with the ceremony done, it is just possible she can stop thinking about Jake and there will be some chance of repose. Now, though, he is very much here, her thoughts are on him like a tongue returning again and again to a cavity, and she cannot control it. She recalls his face when he was Judith's age. It was never still, because he was such a spitfire – truculent, bolshy, high-spirited. Stef could never dream of this placid child, Judith, being so naughty. Yet there was something in her eyes too, some burning spirit of defiance and independence that Stef could recognise. It was there for sure.

Ah, how she misses that distant period of Jake's life; despite the bolshiness, there was innocence too, and even a layer of unabashed affection that only she seemed able to see. Later, when those first intimations of revolt grew and took him over, part of her relished his rebellious instinct, while another part feared it. How sad that she never discovered what he was revolting against.

And yet, despite his mission to stir everything up – or perhaps because of it – he was always a charmer. God, he was a right wicked charmer. Nobody was completely immune.

She rises restlessly from her bed and crosses to the window. Peering between the shutter's slats she sees Esme below. She's pushing a bicycle, wheeling it out of the hostel grounds. Then, mounting it, she rides away. How mysterious. Where is she going? She doesn't know Esme any more, perhaps never did, but she so much wants to know her. She suspects that there are vast areas of

Esme's life that are rich and teeming, worlds that she longs to have some insight into. The thought occurs to her for the first time: does Esme actually like her? What if she had become her daughter-in-law, the mother of her grandchildren? Would they have loved one another? Would they have even got on?

When he was older, much later, seventeen or eighteen, Jake developed a fascination with motorbikes. Doubtless, this was perversely related to what he knew to be his mother's terrified aversion to them. In fact, Stef was completely relaxed about motorbikes *per se*, she was just averse to any situation in which Jake could put himself at risk, a fear the boy played on mercilessly. But especially when it came to bikes. He raced around country lanes as if he was fleeing demons. Maybe he was.

Like Esme, Jake had vast interior worlds to which Stef was denied access. After all, he must have inherited plenty from his father, whose hinterland was *terra incognita*, pure and simple. Michael was completely opaque, his door permanently locked. She remembers the incident that first allowed her to prise it open – just a crack. It all started when Marta, a fellow member of the Caucus, spilled her troubles to her and Michael, confiding to them her need to get away from her volatile partner, Richard. Apparently, on a previous occasion when she had tried to leave him, Richard, who was by all accounts a psychopathic bully, had attacked her. Michael's response was so understanding and supportive, and Stef was so proud of him. In the following days Marta came more often to their squat to consult with them, seeming to bond particularly with Michael. Richard, however, got completely the wrong end of the stick, misread the situation, and became convinced that Marta and Michael were having a physical relationship. Suspicion and paranoia grew in him, and one weekday morning, the worse for alcohol, he followed Marta as she made her way to the squat. Stef was out, and Richard went round the back of the house to see Michael and Marta sitting at a table, seemingly engaged in an intimate dialogue. He dashed to the nearby High Street and stole a knife from a kitchen shop, with which he returned to the squat. Knocking on the door, he pushed his way inside and confronted Marta. She screamed at him, he screamed at her, and Michael attempted to eject him. At that point Richard pulled out the knife, whereupon, according to Marta, Michael suddenly went into a different mode. With a few fast and efficient moves, he disarmed Richard, who was big and burly, forced him onto the floor and pinioned his elbow back, pressing on his wrist until the man was screaming for mercy. Neighbours arrived, the police were called and Richard was arrested. The incident had a banal conclusion: Marta, who did not press charges, decided to give him another chance, Richard spent a few days in custody and was eventually charged with shoplifting and possession of an offensive weapon, for which he received a fine.

Except that wasn't the end of the story. A few days after the dramatic struggle at the squat, while Richard was still in a police cell, Marta took Stef aside. She was so grateful for Michael's intervention, so impressed, but there was something worrying her too. Silly really, probably nothing, but it bothered her. Marta had been on scores of angry confrontations with the police and SPG, and she had only ever seen the kind of procedure that Michael used against Richard, that highly trained display of force, on demos – as deployed by the police.

That was when the first seeds of doubt were planted.

A few weeks later, after Stef had announced her pregnancy, Michael was gone and Stef was plunged into moody reflection. The more she thought about it, the more it all began to make sense. All the little clues, all the details that didn't seem to fit. As she probed deeper, more of the truth oozed out. It was unsavoury, it was unsettling, but it was undeniable. She had been a cog in a much greater plan, a more squalid scheme than she ever could have thought possible.

And yet he loved her. That much she knew.

If only he had known his child, the consequence of his outrageous deceit. She could have forgiven him, they could have been reconciled. Stef is certain of that, too.

After a protracted period lost in reflection, Stef finds herself still standing rigid behind the blinds. Rousing herself, she eases the shutters open and steps onto the balcony. Darkness is about to fall and she sees bats flitting in and out of the weak pools of light cast over the garden below. They are like darts fired from hidden, silent guns, charged with a mad, demonic energy. She lowers herself onto the seat and lights a cigarette. The evening is full of sound – the rasping of cicadas, the grunting of frogs or toads, and, closer, the infuriating whine of mosquitoes. Every so often she claps the air next to her, or slaps at her skin, though rarely quickly enough to make a kill. Despite the blood-seeking assaults, she is determined not to move from the balcony, not until it gets really unbearable. She gazes up into the flower moon, stealing surreptitiously behind thick bundles of rain-heavy cloud, and waits.

Chapter 46 | The ceremony

Laurie stands at the open window, hands clasped behind him, eyes fixed on the garden. The morning is monstrously hot and the trees roar with their customary chorus of song. Yesterday evening purple clouds were gathered in puffy battalions and during the night unleashed their load with unforgiving fury, but that deluge seems like a dream now that the skies have reverted to their familiar cobalt blue and the air is as sticky as ever.

Laurie is wearing a linen suit, a thin, dark red tie and brown leather shoes. His lips are tightly pursed, his brow furrowed. It is once again the morning of the ceremony. It has to happen today, there can be no further delays. His mind is still smarting from the verbal lashing that Stef gave him yesterday, an outburst unlike any he has previously experienced from her for its bluntness and sheer rudeness. While her anger seems to have abated, she has still not uttered a word of remorse, nor a sincere word of gratitude for his having bargained with Sister Margaret to ensure that the ceremony takes place today. What has happened to their camaraderie?

True, she has been acting in an unusually subdued manner since then, calm even, but she has rebuffed all his attempts to reach out. Her mind is elsewhere. He can only put it down to the impending event – the end of so much and, he hopes, the beginning of so much, too.

'I will be her rock and her foundation,' he keeps telling himself. He is determined to retain his composure, and not give in to the hysteria that constantly threatens to overwhelm the occasion.

Stef emerges from the bathroom dressed in the same outfit as yesterday: blue slacks and a white pleated blouse. A brooch with a turquoise stone hangs on her chest. She looks perfectly calm.

'The sun has got his hat back on, I see,' she says, joining him at the window. 'That rain was quite uncalled for.'

'Thomas thinks it will return tonight.'

'Thomas thinks that, does he? Well, Thomas ought to know.'

They continue to regard the lawn through the bleached morning light, then Stef flips her wrist to consult her watch. 'Right, dear husband. It's time to go. Let the ceremony commence.' Perfectly serenely, without a hint of a wobble, she puts on her sunglasses, glides across the room to the door and waits for Laurie to collect himself and follow her lead. Which he does, somewhat suspicious of her strange new equanimity.

They make their way downstairs, where Thomas is manning his desk. He seems stiffer than usual, practically at attention, so that Laurie almost expects him to salute them as they pass as if they are heading out to battle. Laurie half turns towards him with a nod and the hint of a smile, which are not returned.

It's not a funeral, it's a celebration, Laurie silently intones.

Stepping outside is like plunging into a cauldron. They stride purposefully across the lawn to the shelter of the trees on the far side, then follow the path in the shade. Ten minutes later, just inside the Institute's gates, they encounter Sister Charity standing with hands invisibly joined within the sleeves of her pale-blue habit. She releases a tight little smile and a bow.

'Good morning, Mrs Daniels. Good morning, Mr Johnson. I hope you are well today?'

Laurie nods and returns her tight smile.

'Follow me, please,' the nun tells them. She leads them across the yard to a passage at the far end, which brings them to the area outside the uncompleted Recreation Centre. The building is still cordoned off with orange rope, and seems to be in exactly the same state it was in when they saw it the previous week, except that now the sacks of cement have been draped with a vermilion cloth edged with gold banding. In front, beneath a white canvas canopy providing shade, are two rows of chairs. Cynthia and Oliver are seated in two of them. Stef's heart sinks to see Cynthia dressed in her yellow and turquoise sari, her fan flapping energetically in front of her. She will just have to ignore it. Oliver nods at the new arrivals and noisily clears his throat; he has a camera strapped around his neck. Cynthia attempts a half-smile, which Stef pretends not to see.

Sister Charity points to two seats in the front row into which Stef and Laurie settle themselves. A few minutes later Esme, Simon and Miranda appear, trailing behind another nun who steers them into the second row of seats. The three of them are smartly turned out: Esme in a white lacy dress and her usual wide-brimmed straw hat, Miranda in long baggy trousers and a mauve blouse, and Simon wearing pale green chinos and a white, collared shirt. As far as Laurie can tell, Simon's beard has been combed. The three of them have a vaguely solemn air, but there is nothing remotely grave or reverent in their demeanour. Small talk is exchanged, from which Stef remains aloof and insulated behind her dark glasses.

Every so often the whispered voices of young girls leak out from behind the wall to the right of the new building. Sister Margaret makes sporadic and brief appearances from behind the wall, looking more than usually distracted. Four groomed and be-suited Indian men arrive, escorted by Sister Charity, and they too are ushered into places in the front row next to Laurie. Before taking their seats they shake hands with all the other people there, repeating what must be their names to each in turn, though no one can understand what they are saying. Three of them have thin, dapper moustaches, the other, clean-shaven, has prominent gold front teeth, and all four are bedecked with ostentatious gold watches and rings. Once settled, the men gaze stoically in front, not speaking to each other or to anyone else.

After another ten minutes or so, talk among the Europeans has dried up and there is a fidgety silence.

'Well, it seems we're just waiting for the lads, now,' Laurie murmurs, turning to the row behind. 'Any idea where they could be?' he asks Esme.

'No idea,' she answers. 'Dougie was at breakfast this morning. He said they would be here.'

Two more nuns arrive and sit down quietly at the end of the second row without meeting anyone's eyes. Then Sister Margaret reappears from behind the wall, counts the number of people present, and vanishes again. A minute or two later she re-emerges, approaches Laurie and Stef and bends down to whisper to them: 'Two people are not here.'

'It's the two boys,' Laurie tells her. 'Well, they're men really. Friends of Jake from university. Or rather, one is.'

'We cannot wait any longer.'

'Who are these people?' Stef asks, indicating the Indian men to her right.

'Two are from our local town council, two are local businessmen. May I introduce you?'

'Speculators, are they?' Stef asks. 'The ones who are going to build the hotel?'

'They are benefactors, Mrs Daniels, people who like you have generously contributed to our charitable institution.'

'Let's just get on with it, shall we?' Stef tells the nun curtly.

'Certainly, Mrs Daniels,' the nun replies.

'It's Daniel,' Stef says. 'Stephanie Daniel is my name. I wish you could get it right.'

'Daniel?' the nun repeats. She looks serious, then slightly worried.

422

'Got it!' Stef says patronisingly, before turning away to stare in front of her.

'We will start the proceedings,' Sister Margaret tells Laurie, before trotting back behind the wall. They hear her voice issuing instructions, then she returns and sits down in one of the remaining seats in the front row, just as four more nuns arrive from the direction of the yard. The two older ones manoeuvre themselves into the second row, the other two stand at the back. Both of the seated older nuns start to fan themselves with twitchy, fluttery motions.

Suddenly, a loud hiss emanates from a speaker placed on the ground a few feet in front of Laurie, causing everyone to jump. It is followed by an equally jarring drumbeat, which is soon joined by the scratchy sound of a disco tune, also at top volume. Sister Margaret leaps up, runs to the wall and shouts something, whereupon the volume is turned several notches lower. She returns more calmly to her seat and as soon as she has sat down a line of twelve girls shuffle out from behind the wall, all dressed in crimson tunics and blue leggings and trailing long yellow ribbons which they twirl enthusiastically above their heads. The girls are aged between ten and fifteen years old and are all of different heights, but each has a bright, unwavering smile fixed to her face and a large yellow flower pinned into her rigorously brushed and parted hair.

'My word!' Cynthia exclaims.

'Bravo, bravo,' cries Oliver, clapping excitedly. He stops clapping in order to unsheathe his camera with which he begins taking pictures.

Turning to face the audience, the girls launch into a frantic synchronised motion in time to the music, kicking their heels out and waving their arms with ribbons flying. They appear entirely concentrated on their routine, skipping, jumping and swaying from side to side in unison, following each phrase of the recorded music in approximately coordinated movements. Then, the tune changes, a sitar and tabla replace the dance music, and the girls slow their steps and begin a melodic chanting.

'What are the words?' asks Oliver.

'No idea,' answers Cynthia.

'They're singing "Thank you",' Miranda says. And then Laurie can hear it, the two words repeated over and over: 'Thank you, thank you, thank you...'

'Marvellous, marvellous!' he hears Oliver saying, followed by a throat clearance and more camera clicks.

The music changes again, the tempo increases, and the girls stop singing as, still smiling, they begin a new routine, this time jerking their legs to left and right and swinging their arms. As the backing track quickens, the smiling girls resume their 'thank you' chorus until, with strings and banging bass drum rising to a noisy crescendo, they lower themselves onto one knee at roughly the same time, thrust their arms into the air with yellow ribbons held aloft and freeze as the music suddenly stops. In the echoing silence that follows, the smallest girl in the group takes a couple of steps forward, stares gravely at the audience and in a quiet voice says, 'Welcome to India.'

Everyone claps, including even Stef, Laurie notices, though less zealously than anybody else and still wearing her poker face. The girls relax from their kneeling pose, pluck out the flowers from their hair and, stepping forward, present one to each member of the audience.

'Very impressive!' Oliver is saying, still clicking. 'Great discipline! And such stamina!'

'They must have been rehearsing for weeks,' Cynthia says to Esme.

The dancers file back behind the wall, leaving only the small girl who announced the welcome to India. She is now carrying in her arms an object draped in a white cloth and standing a couple of paces behind Sister Margaret who is back on her feet. 'Thank you, children,' the nun declares. 'Most commendable.' Then, with clasped hands, she turns to the assembled group. 'This performance has been devised by our pupils as a small token of our gratitude to the Jack Daniels Trust, which has made such generous donations to our school, and to all our other benefactors and facilitators.' Here, she turns and extends a smile to the four Indian men, who, inscrutably, continue to sit mute and immobile.

'Jack was a young man from England...'

'Jake!' Laurie jumps as his wife shouts out her son's name. Sister Margaret looks at them with a puzzled expression. 'His name! It's Jake. Not Jack. Get it right!'

'I'm so sorry for my mispronunciation. Jake! Of course. Jake was a young man from England who worked with us very hard. He was someone his family can be proud of, and he is remembered by us all with great fondness. He will no doubt also be remembered in the times to come by the children who use this Recreation Centre.' Her expression turns more sombre. 'At this moment, I believe that he is sitting at God's side and watching us. He will no doubt be extremely satisfied to witness the fruits of his works. And now let us all say a prayer for him together.' She bows her head, and the nuns immediately follow suit, followed by everyone else in the audience except for the Indian men, who continue to sit blank and unmoving, and, Laurie notices, Stef.

'Jake, with all our hearts we are grateful to you for your dedication and your hard work. God in His infinite wisdom has surely rewarded you by admitting you into His kingdom. May you be blessed by Him eternally, and may your parents and family also be blessed. We are a short time on this earth, and we must do all that we can with our limited resources in the service of God. We shall remember you always in our prayers. God be merciful. Amen.' She raises her head. 'We will now say together Our Lord's prayer.' She recites the prayer, accompanied loudly by the nuns and less fervently by the contingent of westerners.

When she has finished, she raises her head and whispers to the girl still standing behind her, who steps forward and hands her the object covered with white cloth. Like a conjuror revealing a wondrous manifestation, the nun deftly whips away the cloth to reveal a silver plaque, which she holds aloft. 'Ladies and gentlemen, I name this Recreation Centre the Jake Daniels Recreation Centre and I declare it open.'

The plaque, Laurie assumes, is intended to be fixed on the completed building. Then, amid the polite applause, he hears his wife mutter: 'Jesus Christ, they've named it after a bloody whisky!' With the sun glinting on it, it takes a few seconds for him to make out through squinting eyes the plaque's florid inscription, 'Jack Daniels Recreation Centre', with yesterday's date below.

Suddenly Stef is on her feet. 'Wrong!' she shouts. 'Wrong wrong wrong! This is a complete farce and a waste of time!' She pushes past Laurie and the startled Indians to march out of the yard. Laurie stares after her, rises from his seat and looks around, seeing the eyes of all on him.

'She's very upset,' he explains, embarrassed, before setting off after her.

He is close behind, calling her name, but Stef doesn't respond until finally, at the gate, she whirls round, her face hard and white with fury.

'Leave it, Laurie! Leave me alone! Go away!'

He stops a few feet from her. 'Stef... Please let me help.'

'Too late for that! It doesn't matter. Just leave it! I need to be alone. I'll see you later, probably.' Spinning back round, she is about to rush across the road when they are both startled by a blaring horn. Stef pulls back just in time as a motorbike careers past, two men astride, their faces wrapped in scarves and aviator sunglasses.

'For Christ's sake!' Stef exclaims, then shouts after them: 'Bastards!'

Once more she sets off across the road. Laurie is about to follow when he feels a hand on his arm. It is Miranda.

'Don't. Let her go, dad. You can't do any more.' She places herself in front of him. 'Come on. Let's go for a walk.' And she threads her hand under his arm, gently turns him around and leads him along the street away from the town centre, towards the fields.

'Where is she going?' he asks, as if in a daze.

'No idea,' Miranda tells him. 'Don't worry about that now.'

Laurie meekly lets himself be led, grateful to relinquish the responsibility for making any further decisions.

'It's over now,' Miranda tells him in a soothing voice.

'Yes, it's over. It could have been much worse,' Laurie admits.

'Everything's going to be good now,' Miranda says. 'Stef will go her own way, wherever that is, and everything's going to be fine.'

'Yes. Okay.'

And they walk on, arm in arm, along the pot-holed road.

Chapter 47 | Truths and lies

Filled with a burning disgust, Stef storms into the hostel's lobby and through an open door spots Dougie and Jules in the lounge. They are seated at the same table in one corner of the room where she found them the day after their arrival, and as on that occasion they seem to be locked into some kind of grim confrontation. This time, however, it appears to be a silent face off, and Stef's first impression suggests that it is even more intractable than the previous one. Her advance into the room jolts them out of their spell.

'Good morning, boys. Congratulations! You were late again and now you've completely missed the ceremony. Marvellous! Where were you?'

'We couldn't make it to the ceremony, Stef,' Dougie explains. 'Really sorry.'

'Were you *stoned*?'

Dougie looks startled. 'No! Actually, we had something to discuss.'

'An argument?'

'That's really not your business,' Jules says.

Stef turns a haughty expression on him. 'I'm just wondering how any of this is any of your business at all.' She turns to his companion. 'Listen, Douglas – Doug – there's something I need to clear up with you.' Dougie blinks up at her, looking worried, while Jules scowls suspiciously. 'It's about Jake's book.' Dougie feels himself shrivel at this unwelcome news. 'I need you to tell me the truth. No messing about, I'm serious now. What really happened? All that stuff about leaving it in a hotel – it was bullshit, wasn't it?'

'Professor Daniel,' Jules interrupts, pronouncing her academic title with a mocking edge. She turns to him impatiently. 'There's something you really need to know – in case you haven't guessed it already. There was no book.'

'No book? What do you mean? Why do you say that?'

'Jake was not writing a book. He has never written a book.'

She glares at him. 'I don't know where you got that idea. Why do you say that?'

'Everyone knows. There was no book. Trust me.'

'*Trust you?*'

Jules sighs and turns to his companion. 'Tell her, Doug.'

Stef directs her bellicose glare back onto Dougie.

'I really don't know anything,' Dougie says, feeling himself flush. 'He might have been writing a book...'

'Tell her there was no book, Doug. It's only right.'

'Stop it!' Stef barks. 'Of course he was writing a book. Esme told me...'

'She was shitting you,' Jules informs her in a quiet, level voice, his expression uncompromising. 'She told you what she thought you wanted to hear.'

'That's ridiculous!'

'Actually, it's ridiculous to think that he was capable of writing a book! *Any* book. And, by the way, Esme's not quite the saint you take her for. She made it all up!'

Rearing above them, Stef glowers down at their upturned faces. Dougie lowers his eyes, clearly embarrassed, but Jules coldly returns her derisive stare. She points an accusing finger at him, full of disdain. 'You didn't even know my son! He wouldn't have given you the time of day. And who are you anyway? What are you even doing here? You're stoned all the time. You're not contributing. You're nothing! Just go home. Go!'

'I'm just telling you the truth, Professor Daniel. I'm the only one who is!' Jules says. 'And there's something else.'

'Go on.'

'Personally, I don't think it's right that everyone else is discussing things that you seem to know nothing about. About your son.'

'Go on.'

'Well, without beating about the bush...'

'Definitely let's not beat about the bush!'

'...you asked us just now if we're stoned. And we're not. But Jake was. All the time.'

'Say again?'

'How could you not have been aware that your son was strung out on junk, Professor Daniel?'

'Junk?'

'Hard drugs. Smack. Heroin. He was high when he got on that motorbike.'

Stef's eyes narrow. 'Jake was always experimenting.'

'This was more than experimenting. He was completely gone. That's why he died.'

Stef bows her head, as if pondering. Her shoulders seem to be quivering, then they are astonished to hear a scraping sound from her. They suddenly realise it is a rasp of laughter, for her features, when she raises her head, reveal her face creased in a savage mirth.

'Do you think I'm totally stupid? What do you take me for? I'm his *mother*! I know everything about that boy! Do you think they didn't do an autopsy? I can tell you to the milligram how much of that stuff was swimming about in his bloodstream! I know everything there is to know. But it doesn't make a jot of difference. That's just data.'

The two men stare dumbly, as if they have been trumped on the last hand.

Then Jules speaks up. 'And I suppose you also knew about his gambling habit, Professor Daniel? That he owed a sackful of money? Did you know about that? Is that just data too? And by the way, did you know what a total loser everybody thought he was?' Stef stares uncomprehendingly, and Jules continues, gathering momentum as if smelling blood. 'You built him up to be a golden boy, but you don't seem to understand that actually he was a bit of a shit. He lied, he cheated, he stole people's girlfriends, stole their boyfriends. To be honest, he wasn't a great human being! Which might explain why no one was around to sort him out. Esme certainly didn't! Did you never wonder why she left him in the lurch?'

'For god's sake!' Dougie shouts, his eyes flashing anger.

'Let's have some truth around here!' Jules shouts back.

'No!' Dougie retorts.

'Just tell her the truth, Doug! You know better than me. He was evil!'

At this Stef's dry laugh crackles forth again like sandpaper scraping.

'Evil? Little boy, what do you know about evil?'

Jules stares back defiantly.

'So is that what all this is about? You're jealous! You're jealous of a dead boy whom your boyfriend fancied. Did he fuck him? Is that what all this is about?'

The two are frozen in their seats, once more speechless. Then, in a quieter voice, Jules adds: 'That's why Esme left him, Professor Daniel. Because he was rotten.'

'Esme didn't leave him,' Stef instantly returns. 'He left her, unfortunately. The biggest mistake he ever made. At least I thought it was at the time. Thanks to you I know better now. He saw through her, and it turns out he was absolutely right.'

'That's what he might have told you,' Jules says. 'But it was *she* who dumped *him*. She couldn't stand him any longer. Go ahead and ask her.'

'And why should I believe *her*, pray? You've already told me she's a liar and a worthless friend.'

'And of course everyone knows why your son thought he couldn't count on you,' Jules continues, his tone still lethal with a cold, controlled fury, 'seeing as you were always shit-faced.'

'Jules! Enough! Just shut up!' Dougie is bellowing, almost bouncing off his seat.

Stef looks more detached than ever, as if she is observing the exchange from a distance or on television. She has a vague smile on her lips as she regards her attacker, then shakes off the words with a brief shudder, and the eyes that she turns on them now display an immense fatigue.

'Oh, go away!' she waves them off. 'Grow up, and leave me alone. You're boring.'

'We're just letting you know, Professor Daniel! You have a right to know.'

'Just fuck off! *Fuck off!*' she roars now as she turns and walks out of the room. Her steps can be heard slapping rapidly up the stairs.

Dougie stares at Jules. 'I can't believe what you just did!' he says. 'In fact, you're completely unbelievable.'

'Because I told the truth?'

'Yes!' Then Dougie is on his feet and gone, too, out through the veranda door, leaving Jules scratching his head, his face puzzled, then resigned. 'Fuck!' he mutters. 'Fuck them all!'

Chapter 48 | The fall

In the bedroom, Stef locks the door and sits hunched on the bed, eyes clenched shut. She feels her heart beating hard in her chest, the sweat soaking through her clothes. She jerks to her feet and turns up the fan's speed, then returns to the bed, head bowed, fingers at her temples. Gradually her heart quietens, the sweat dries off her skin, and a feeling of resigned calm settles over her. She knows, as she has done all along, that there is no option. After all she has already made the choice when she packed her suitcase – or rather confirmed a choice she had made years before. But still she holds back. It is a teasing reluctance, a self-indulgence. Her little one will be hers. Why rush?

Eventually she gets up, shrugs off her shoes, and crosses the room to the red suitcase. She crouches over it, pulls back the zip, part-opens it and inserts a hand. She rummages inside, left and right, then her hand scrabbles about her clothes with more urgency. Finally, she fully unzips the case, and with the lid open starts to throw aside the clothes until her eyes are drilling blackly into the empty case, her face grim, her teeth grinding. It is not there. A sound escapes her, a sob and then an oath. 'The bastard!'

On her feet now, her hands are two fists at her sides, her eyes wide and her heart once more beating hard. She leaps back across the room, pulls open the door and hurries barefoot down to the lobby. There is no sign of Thomas. She shouts his name, three times, until finally he appears at the door behind his desk, his face for once betraying a hint of impatience. There is a granule of rice stuck to his chin.

'Thomas, I must have the key to my mother's room.'

'Your mother's room, madam?'

'Yes. It's urgent. It's her medicine. I need to fetch her pills.'

Thomas looks at her quizzically for an instant, smile-less, frowning, then he reaches into a drawer and extracts a key.

'Please come, madam.'

He mounts the stairs, excruciatingly slowly, Stef holding herself back two steps behind. In the corridor he stops at the door to Cynthia's and Oliver's room and turns the key. Standing aside as Stef rushes in, he watches as she wildly scans the room. Then, feeling the manager's eyes on her, she turns to him.

'Just give me a moment, will you?' she says, and ushers him firmly back into the corridor, closing the door after him.

Seeing the double bed she scowls, then she opens the cupboard, pulls open drawers, and finally searches under the bed from where she pulls out a neat, green canvas hold-all. It is not locked. Tearing it open she gazes down on the golden liquid in the plain glass bottle with its fancy yellow label: Glenmorangie.

There is also a small tartan bag in the suitcase, which she empties into the case, slipping the bottle inside before stuffing the hold-all back under the bed. Casually holding the tartan bag at her side, she opens the door to find Thomas still waiting in the corridor, his face blank.

'Thank you, Thomas,' she says, as she walks calmly along the corridor to her own room. Once inside, she locks the door and closes the shutters, throwing the room into a semi-darkness. She unscrews the bottle-top and carefully pours two inches of the whisky into the tumbler at her bedside. Then, screwing the lid back on, she places the bottle on the table and carries the glass to the seat by the window, where she sits down with a slow deliberation. She wants there to be calm and pleasure, both at once. She must savour the experience, draw it out, but then it occurs to her that she is fetishizing the moment, and perhaps subconsciously postponing it. Which is a waste of time. So she raises the glass to her lips and takes a sip. There. Her eyes relax, lose focus, and all her muscles untense. Now, at last, she has arrived.

She takes another sip, feels the heat burning inside. What she has been missing. If only she hadn't made that absurd promise to herself, all of this could have been avoided. She would have felt right from the start. No anguish, no anger.

Out of nowhere, a vision of Michael flashes up in front of her. What is he doing here? He is looking benign, his face soft like an angel's. The vision fades. If only he had known him. Stef was the vessel but his was the seed. And how she had treasured that gift! From the start, her fire was subsumed in the lava of maternal love, the love that melts all boundaries. Michael, all intellect, his emotion locked securely away in an inner vault, compromised and confused, had nevertheless granted her something she could love with all her soul, with a passion that transcended intellect. How she loved to stare at that baby's bald globe.

You will be aware of an absence, presently,
Growing beside you, like a tree,
A death tree, colour gone.

Stef drains her glass, and automatically pours a second. The heat rises to her brain, and she feels more complete now than she has done for the last two weeks.

Come,
lean to my wound; burn on, burn on.

Again, she throws back the golden contents of the glass, swallowing hard. She takes a deep breath, her eyes alight now, alive. She regards the glass's emptiness. It looks naked, and she refills it. As she raises it to her lips, she hears a light knock at the door and straightens, sitting motionless, hardly breathing. The knock comes again, slightly louder.

'Stephanie?' It is her mother's voice.

The handle turns, but the door won't open.

'Stephanie, dear?'

As Stef sits stock still, glass poised, she is aware of an enormous silence in the room which not even the clattering birdsong outside can pierce. The seconds drag past until her mother's receding footsteps can be heard. After a few more seconds, she drains her glass then immediately pours herself another measure and dispatches that one. A deep convulsion shakes her and she lurches to her feet and falls onto the bed, eyes clouded, the fast-spinning ceiling fan above her an indistinct blur.

Outside the room, through the window, she hears voices and a familiar throat-bark. Unsteadily, she gets to her feet and crosses the room. There, seated under a parasol on the lawn, are her mother and her mother's paramour. They are at a round table, a metre apart, still as statues. They are monuments to how one used to be, or how one ought to be, or how one could be. The spell breaks when one of the figures moves, putting cup to lips, and when the other waves away an insect, perhaps a fly or a bee. She sees a butterfly float past. This place is infested with insect life. Stef knows she could never bear it if she didn't know she would soon be leaving.

Her mother turns to Oliver, opens her mouth, words came out, a distant burble, too quiet for Stef to make out. Oliver turns a little, briefly looks at Cynthia, opens his mouth, and the words are more distinctive this time – Stef thinks she hears: 'Not for the first time,' or perhaps 'Not the worst time,' – or was it 'worst crime'? 'First sign'? Whatever it is, Cynthia nods briefly without shifting her gaze from the trees on the far side of the lawn.

> They do not come from the Bay of the Dead down there,
> But from another place, tropical and blue,
> We have never been to.

Immobile, Stef is lost in a dream. Then, reaching a decision, she swiftly empties her glass, put on her shoes, looks around for her hat and sunglasses, and, stopping only to rinse the glass and thrust the bottle under the mattress, sways out of the room. She creeps downstairs, past the reception desk, and heads out, ignoring her mother's querulous 'Stephanie...?' and the inquisitive looks of both.

The sun bears down cruelly, and her body shakes. It takes her a quarter of an hour to reach the Institute. As she walks, the words of Jules crowd her head, with her lips mouthing her unspoken rejoinders: *Not a saint. I never said he was a saint.... We're all tainted. That's no reason to write someone off...*

Once arrived, she goes straight into the office where she finds Sister Grace staring intently at her computer screen.

'Where is Sister Margaret?' Stef demands.

Sister Grace blinks up at her, perplexed. 'Sorry?'

'It is very important that I speak to Sister Margaret. I need to see her right now. And don't tell me she's in a meeting! Or gone to Bangla Desh!'

Gaping at her, the nun picks up her mobile phone with jittery hands, jabs at it, and talks fast in Malayalam.

'I have asked her to come,' she tells Stef. 'You must wait, please!'

Stef continues to loom over the desk as the nun turns back to the screen looking intensely uncomfortable.

'Will you sit down, Mrs Daniels?' she says finally.

'Daniel!' Stef shouts. 'It's Daniel!'

The nun looks frightened now, with eyes stealing from side to side, wondering what to do or say. Just then Sister Margaret appears at the doorway.

'Professor Daniel,' she says. 'Can I be of assistance?'

Stef whips round and glares at her.

'Where can I find Judith?'

'Judith?'

'The little girl. Judith!'

'Why do you want her, Professor Daniel?'

'I'd just like to speak to her. There's something important I need to tell her.'

'You can tell me, Professor Daniel. I will tell her.'

'No! It's something I need to tell her myself.'

'Professor Daniel, this is a school. We are doing important work. You cannot walk in here and demand to see a child. You must inform me of what it is you wish to tell her.'

'Is she in the classrooms?'

The nun regards her severely. The blood is pulsing hard in Stef's head and she feels trickles of sweat on her cheeks. She is aware of Sister Grace watching them both with alarm. 'No, she is not in the classroom,' Sister Margaret is telling her. 'She is out.'

'Out where?'

'She is with her sister.'

'When will she be back? Can you please tell me when she will be back?'

Sister Margaret consults her watch and frowns. 'Actually, they should have returned twenty minutes ago.' She breaks off to say something in Malayalam to Sister Grace who immediately picks up her phone and punches a number. She speaks a few phrases then says something to the older nun, who turns to Stef. 'Sister Clara informs us that they have not yet returned.'

Stef feels a cold hand curl around her insides.

'Is Judith alright? Why isn't she back?' The nun shrugs, opens her mouth, but Stef interrupts. 'Oh God, she might have been in an accident...'

'That is most unlikely, Professor Daniel.'

'How do you know?' A terrible vision presents itself to Stef, an image of a racing motorbike, of masked riders, of a little girl straying into its path to the deafening blast of a klaxon.

'God is looking after her.'

'God?' Stef stares at the nun as sweat streams into her eyes. 'Sometimes God is looking the other way!' And she whirls round and exits from the room.

Back outside the Institute she looks desperately up and down the street. An autorickshaw suddenly pulls up in front of her, the heavily jowled driver leaning out.

'Lift, madam?'

'No!'

'Where you want to go?'

'Nowhere!'

'I take you.'

'No!'

As she starts off in the direction of the market, the rickshaw moves with her, blocking her way.

'Lift?'

'No! Go away.'

She manages to squeeze past the three-wheeler's front wheel and walks fast along the side of the road. She is covered in a sticky film of sweat now, coating her face, neck and arms. Everything and everybody seems to be in her way: dogs, vehicles, shoe-repairers, random heaps of rubbish. A hungry-looking boy dressed only in ragged shorts places himself in front of her. He is tethered to a blind man staring vacantly in her direction, and puts his fingers to his mouth, scooping invisible food. Stef tries to get past him but he is insistent. 'Sorry, no. Sorry! Excuse me...'

As she makes a wide loop past the pair, a motorbike seems to be aiming straight for her but swerves at the last second. Two bicycles wobble past. In front, a group of people are huddled around something she can't see. She has a vision of the little girl lying on the busy road, apples and onions scattered around her, blood pooling in the dust. She pushes her way to the front of the group, but the object of the crowd's attention turns out to be a horse on its side, still shackled to a heavy cart, panting and snorting through foam-flecked lips.

Struggling back out of the crowd, head pounding, Stef continues walking, then stops to wipe the stinging sweat out of her eyes with her damp sleeve. Suddenly she is confronted by the little girl Judith, the smiling woman Elizabeth beside her. They are facing her, a few feet away.

'Judith!'

The little girl looks across to her, then up at the woman, whose customary artless smile is now tempered by a hint of uncertainty.

Rushing forwards, Stef stoops down to Judith's level and tries to embrace her, but the girl slips easily out of her arms.

'I was so worried about you!' she tells her, gazing into her impenetrable green eyes. There is no sign of comprehension. Stef turns her attention to the older woman, who continues to stare, the warmth leeching out of her smile by the second. Dressed in a patterned sari and with a gold nose-ring, she is pretty, Stef sees, though there is also something cowed in her face, something desperate. She's not much more than a girl herself, in her mid-twenties maybe. Perhaps life has not treated her so well.

'You are Elizabeth?' Stef asks. The woman nods, the half-smile frozen on her face.

'Do you know me?' Stef asks, trying to make her words slow and clear, but Elizabeth shows no sign of understanding. 'Did you know my son, Jake? Did you know Jake?' There is only the empty stare. Stef points to Judith. 'Sister? Daughter?' Still there is no response, just the quizzical look reasserting itself, replacing the ghost of her smile.

Stef turns back to the little girl.

'You can come with me!' she says. 'I will look after you! You can live with me in my house. In England. Outside London.' The girl looks back to her sister-mother, who continues to fix Stef with her dark brown eyes. 'I will arrange everything,' Stef says. 'It'll be fine. Come on!' And she takes Judith's arm and rises to her feet. 'Come on! Let's go.' But the girl resists, fear creeping into her features. 'Come on! Come on!' Stef pulls a little harder. The girl looks imploringly at Elizabeth. 'You can come too,' Stef tells the older woman. She wipes her wet brow with her sleeve again. Her ear is blocked, distorting all sound, and she is feeling a bit dizzy, a bit sick. 'We'll all go! To England! It'll be fine!'

Elizabeth's expression has turned to unconcealed consternation.

'Come on! Come on! Please! We'll go now. We'll all go!'

Elizabeth is wailing now, clearly upset. Judith is clinging to her. Somebody stops next to them, barks something at Stef.

'Come on! It'll be fine!'

A small crowd has gathered, bicycles and passers-by stopped. 'Please!' Stef is pleading now. 'We can be together!' Men are talking at Stef. An old woman with a high, cracked voice is shouting. One man's voice very close to her is saying in English: 'You must go now! Please go away!' Stef turns to explain to him: 'It's alright. Really. I can look after her, you see. I know her. She belongs to me!' The man is saying something, but Stef doesn't hear. She feels faint. When she turns back, she sees Elizabeth and Judith being led away by one of the men. The old woman is still shouting at her.

'Madam, I will bring you to a doctor,' the man next to her is saying. 'Please be calm.'

'I'm alright! Let me go!'

'Stef?' She looks around. It is Miranda. Her reassuring hand is pressed lightly on her shoulder. 'Are you okay? What's the matter?'

* * * * * * * * * *

441

Twenty minutes later, Stef and Miranda are in the hostel garden. Stef has a tall glass of water in front of her.

'Drink!' Miranda urges her. 'You're dehydrated.'

'I'm alright, Miranda!' Stef is saying. 'For God's sake! Why are you fussing?'

Miranda walks away, and Stef hears her whispering to Cynthia and Oliver. She feels a bolt of anger to see her mother wrapped in her sari.

Cynthia whispers something back, and then Miranda is speaking again. Stef hears the word 'aggressive'. Then Cynthia is standing over her. 'Stephanie, dear, you really ought to lie down.'

'I'm okay!'

'You're not okay. You look pale as a sheet. Please go to your room and lie down. Where's Laurence?'

'How should I know where he bloody is?'

'Dear, you must lie down!'

'Okay! Stop nagging!' Stef cries in exasperation, rising abruptly to her feet. She grasps the table as she feels her knees spongy and the ground treacherous beneath her.

'Oliver!' Cynthia is shouting. 'We need a hand!'

Oliver rushes over and he and Miranda take an arm each as they escort Stef through the lobby and to the stairs, Cynthia following behind with the glass and a jug of water. Stef is aware of Thomas at his desk with a severe face.

With Cynthia and Oliver on either side, Stef is eventually manoeuvred up the stairs and into her room. The shutters are closed, the light is soft and soothing. Cynthia removes Stef's shoes and, after making her finish her glass of water, gently presses her down onto the mattress. Someone is wiping her face with a cool, damp flannel. Reassuring but forceful words are uttered, then the door closes behind them and at last Stef is alone.

She closes her eyes and feels her head throbbing insistently.

With a groan she struggles back to her feet and rummages through a drawer. After swallowing a couple of Neurofens washed down with water, she lies down again. But her brain can't stop. There is no rest here after all. Beneath the mattress, her hand closes gratefully around the whisky bottle and she half rises in order to pour herself a measure. With the first sip she feels distinctly better, and she settles back down on the bed with a sigh of exhaustion, sensing the alcohol in her blood.

She feels the cliffs vanish, sees the innumerable waves spreading beneath her, hears the sea drumming in her ears. The white petals are darkened with sea water. Everything falls in a tremendous shower, dissolving her.

Out of nowhere, the memory comes back to her, of being in Cornwall. She was in her teens. Where was she? Outside a house. Oh, yes, she was at Talland House, Virginia's holiday home outside Zennor. She remembers standing at the door, talking to an irate man who had never heard of Virginia Woolf. She just wanted to see her bedroom, just for a minute or two, but the man told her to go away. She wanted to see the room where she woke every morning to the knocking of the blind in the wind, the rush of the waves in the bay below. No. No no no no no. Not possible. And she swore at him, the ignoramus, and ran away, blinded by her tears, ran past the flowering gorse. Little Stef, thwarted.

Chapter 49 | Full disclosure

It is eight o'clock. Darkness has descended and the atmosphere in the dining room is thick and airless. The room has the unsettling feel of a siege, for the walls are under attack by lashing rain, with an undertone of frequent, booming cannonades of thunder. Unperturbed, in his creased white trousers and a high-collared, gold-buttoned white jacket, Francis is quietly passing between the door to the kitchen and the tables carrying jugs and dishes.

Miranda and Esme sit at one table with an array of rice, vegetables and dal between them. Esme is staring at her plate with evident distaste.

'What's the matter with it?' Miranda asks.

'I had a look in the kitchen earlier. All the vegan dishes they've been preparing for me since we arrived – they're not vegan at all. They use ghee with everything, for a start, and eggs. Shetty assured me it was all going to be vegan-friendly. I'll eat it anyway, I just feel I've been scammed.'

'Count it as experience,' Miranda says. 'You can't afford to trust anything here. Ever since arriving in India I can't stop feeling I'm constantly being taken for a ride.'

Esme picks at her food without enthusiasm and Miranda views her own plate with renewed suspicion. During the lull in their conversation, Miranda tunes into her father's voice across the room, where he is seated at a separate table with Cynthia and Oliver.

'I don't know what she thought she was doing,' Laurie is telling them in a low voice. 'It must be the emotion. She's been building up to this for months, you know. And things haven't exactly run smoothly.'

'She does seem very highly-strung,' Oliver agrees, more volubly. 'I expect she just needs a good night's sleep.'

Despite the shutters and screens, moths are batting against the central light shade, near to which is poised an emerald-green lizard. Two of the Indians who were present at the morning's ceremony at the Institute are eating at a table in one corner of the room, not speaking to one another as their fingers expertly gather and convey to their mouths neat packages of vegetable and rice. They seem to be alert to the conversation about them, and occasionally, as they chew, they raise their heads to eye their fellow diners. There is no sign of Simon, Jules or Dougie.

'You know,' Esme tells Miranda, breaking their silence 'I keep thinking back to that period of my life, when Jake and I were together at uni.' Miranda stops chewing, lifting her eyes from her plate. She has never heard Esme speak more than a few words about her time with Jake. 'Being here has brought it all back. And the funny thing is that I've always tried to erase those memories, and now I find myself dipping back into them, almost enjoying them. He still intrigues me. Even though he was infuriating, and I was always losing my patience, at the same time it was the most...interesting period of my life.' She laughs, embarrassed. 'Maybe that's why I keep dreaming about him.'

Startled by Esme's confessional tone, Miranda struggles for something to say, then an unfamiliar urge to be equally candid comes over her. 'I never got it, actually. What you saw in him. I could never work it out. I know he could be super charming, and witty and a laugh to be with. I know all that. But he was manipulative too, and a bully. You must have known that better than anyone... And you must have seen that there was no future with him.'

'Oh, I knew *that*! That didn't matter. But, whatever it was he had, it was real. Well – fake and real at the same time. That sounds stupid, doesn't it? I can't explain it in words. If I could explain it I don't think I'd still be thinking of him. All I know is that afterwards, after we split, everything seemed so...safe. And kind of small.'

Miranda is still unsure how to respond. She feels frustrated. She can't grasp what Esme is saying, but she desperately wants to. She puts it down to her own character – 'safe', as Esme put it. She is the opposite of Jake: cautious, self-conscious, unwilling to throw herself into anything with that same recklessness that was second nature to him. That anarchic streak must somehow have resonated with Esme in a way that it never did with Miranda.

'Isn't it the same for all of us though?' she says eventually. 'Don't we all look back on our student days and early relationships with that kind of nostalgia?'

'Nostalgia?' Esme repeats. 'Is that all it is?' She is frowning, apparently unconvinced.

They continue eating, and Miranda again overhears her father above the rain's rattle: 'This wasn't at all how I planned it. It's not what I was hoping for...'

'Laurence: you've done all you can,' Cynthia tells him. 'Stop torturing yourself now. It's done. And we can leave on time tomorrow.'

'I've asked Thomas to book a taxi for the four of us,' Laurie says. 'Ten o'clock. Miranda and Simon are taking a later train.'

'What about the boys?' Cynthia asks.

'No idea what their plans are. I think they're heading north, back to Mumbai.'

Just then there is a commotion outside the door leading into the lobby. Francis hastens towards it, then swerves to avoid Stef marching in. With dishevelled hair and her shirt and trousers wrinkled and stained, she stops and casts a troubled gaze about the room as all eyes turn towards her.

'I've broken something in the hall,' she announces dramatically as she makes her way towards the table where Laurie, Cynthia and Oliver are sitting.

'Hallo, love!' Laurie says, on his feet now. 'How are you feeling?'

She stands over the table and surveys them all. 'I presume you've been discussing me.'

'Dear, are you well?' Cynthia asks.

'No. I'm not. I've got a jack-hammer headache hammering in my skull. And the thunder and rain...' Her eyes sweep across the room, settling on the table where Miranda and Esme are seated.

'Good God almighty! Are you still here?'

Esme rises and takes a few steps towards Stef.

'Stef, are you alright? Is there anything...' But she stops short as Stef points an accusing finger to her.

'Traitor! And deceiver! Don't you come near me, hypocrite. You've lied from the beginning!'

'Stephanie!' her mother sternly exclaims. 'That is completely uncalled for!'

Stef turns to her. 'That bitch deserted my son, deceived you and me and all of us, and allowed him to die. She's deceitful and a hypocrite!'

'I'm sorry, Stef,' Esme begins. 'I was...'

'Too late, Judas! Too late for apologies. Too late for asinine moralising after the event, too late for regrets. A work of fiction, I understand? Hilarious. You've stuck the knife in and dug my grave, and I will dutifully fall into it. Then you can all go to bed.'

Laurie is trying to restrain his wife now, trying to steer her back out of the room. The Indian diners are staring, shocked, and Thomas and Flowery have both appeared at the door next to Francis. All are frozen at the spectacle.

Looking frightened and upset, Esme takes another step towards Stef, who screams: 'Don't touch me! Get out! I don't want to see you!'

Esme flinches and stops. 'I'm sorry,' she says in a low voice, then turns around and walks quickly out of the room past Thomas, Flowery and Francis.

'Stef, this is completely out of order,' Laurie says, hands on hips.

'Yes!' Stef declares triumphantly, swaying slightly. 'I am completely out of order. I'm not fit company right now. At all. I'm not at all perfect. Are you perfect?' she says, turning feverish eyes to her husband. 'Are *you*?' she says to her mother.

'Stef, please. What's going on?' pleads her husband. 'There was a call from the Institute this afternoon, from Sister Margaret. She said you've been harassing her pupils.'

'Harassing them, am I? I'm so sorry. My standards are slipping. I'm not such a good girl, am I? But then who is good? Are you at all good, Laurence? Did you enjoy the ceremony? All the little girls?'

Cynthia raises her voice. 'Stephanie, are you drunk? You're making a complete exhibition of yourself!'

'I'm so sorry to be an embarrassment to you, mother. But you're not such a great model of behaviour, either, are you? Cavorting with this old fool at your age! Cohabiting! Pretending to be married to preserve your dignity!'

'Stef...' Laurie says, one hand covering his eyes as if to shield them from the vitriol.

'And you!' Stef turns back to Laurie. 'You think you know this man,' she tells her mother and Oliver, pointing at Laurie with an outstretched hand. 'But you haven't got a clue... He's a bloody stalker! I've been harassing the pupils, have I? Well, so has he! He's not on a bloody sabbatical, he's on a watch-list. Suspended pending further investigation. Following accusations of inappropriate behaviour towards his twenty-year-old female students. He's facing a charge! Are you aware of that? He's well on his way to getting himself a criminal record. End of career! He's no bloody hero, when you're aware of the facts.'

Hearing these words sends a bolt through Miranda, like a shot of electricity that has somehow burst into the room from the storm outside. She rises from her table and stares at her father, her face a composite of shock and disgust. Laurie's face looks equally pained and shocked.

'Ask *his* pupils the meaning of harassment!' Stef continues in her declamatory, grating tone. 'Let's be honest, he's a filthy lecher. You should see what I found on his laptop. I think you'd have a different opinion of darling Laurence!'

'Dad...?' Miranda says.

'Shut up!' Laurie shouts, without turning to her. 'It's rubbish. Lies! She's lying!'

'Am I? Take a look at his laptop some time, dear Miranda. Remind me to give you the password. It's not very original.'

'That's enough!' Laurie shouts. 'Enough, Stef! You're drunk and out of control. I warned you! Didn't I warn you? About your drinking? Well, I've had enough. I've been patient, but you've crossed a line. You've gone way too far this time!'

'Big bloody deal!' Stef shouts back. 'Forgive me for letting the cat out of your bag, but it's about time there was a little more honesty around here. Full disclosure! All of you, you're so moralistic, so desperate to tell me the truth, what's real and what's not – but you're all wallowing like pigs, knee-deep in sordid lies.'

She is swaying more violently now, and suddenly raises a hand to one ear. 'Shut up! I can't stand it!' She lurches towards the door. 'Excuse me, everyone!' she croaks, more softly now, then pushes her way through the mute crowd at the threshold. 'Must be going!'

The sound of her steps rushing back upstairs fades away, then the violent slamming of a door can be heard. The silence that settles on the diners is broken by Thomas marching across the

449

room to Laurie and announcing in a near hysterical tone, 'Professor Johnson, sir, this is entirely unacceptable and regrettable!'

Laurie gapes at him, then races out of the room and upstairs in pursuit of Stef. Miranda immediately runs after him. As she reaches the landing, her heart pounding against her ribs, she halts as she sees her father in the corridor, his fists banging on his bedroom door, unaware of her presence. He twists the handle to no avail, and thumps again. 'Stef! Stef, open up!' There is no response. 'Open the door immediately, Stef.' No response. He puts his ear to the door and hears nothing. 'That's it, Stef! you've played out your hand.' Silence. 'I've had enough! It's over! We're finished! Is this what you wanted? I warned you. I spelled it out. Is this what you wanted? Right! So we're done. Finished. You can go your own way. I won't be there for you any more. You're on your own!'

With that he looks about him, eyes wild, but as he catches sight of Miranda the wildness drains away and is replaced with a panicky, trapped expression. With slower, more measured steps he returns back along the corridor towards her.

'Dad?'

'Not now! Please...'

'Is it true?'

'Of course not! For god's sake! It's all lies. Excuse me, I really can't handle this...' And he quickly descends the stairs, crosses the lobby and runs headlong into the rain.

Chapter 50 | The vanquishing

Lightning erupts across the sky and the rain sheets down. As soon as Laurie finds himself outside on the grass he halts, instantly drenched. The prospect of remaining in the deluge in his shirt sleeves is absurd, yet where is there to go?

Retreating hastily back to the shelter of the covered veranda, he loiters, feeling lost, uncertain of his next move, when there is another brilliant flash of lightning and all the lights of the hostel are simultaneously extinguished. He hears the voice of Thomas inside shouting at Shibu, no doubt instructing him to fire up the emergency generator. Gradually, as his eyes grow accustomed to the blackness, he finds comfort in the intense, wet gloom, the hissing water, the anonymity of the night. He feels at one with it, enveloped and protected. Groping for a seat and lowering himself into it, with nerves still on edge, he finds himself reflecting with disbelief on what has just happened and what is now likely to happen. However, there is little solace to be had in examining the events of the day or peering into the immediate future. Rising like monsters out of the mud, dark thoughts coil around him, filling him with dread. Somehow they must all get out of here and return home. But what then? Stef is demented, further away from reality than he has ever seen her, perhaps irretrievably so. A line has indeed been crossed. His children too must be faced and secrets unravelled. The obstacles are formidable, perhaps insuperable.

Momentarily the lights flicker on, and the few seconds before the fuse is once more tripped are enough to reveal a hunched shape at the far end of the veranda. Only after darkness has once more descended does he recognise what he has seen: Esme, her back towards him, facing the rain. He hesitates, then rises to inch past the tables and chairs towards her, his wet trousers clinging to his thighs. She looks round when he is a few feet away.

'Esme, it's me – Laurie.'

'Hi, Laurie.' Her voice above the crashing rain sounds unsteady, as if she has been crying. He prays that she did not overhear Stef's rant about him. He must assume that she didn't.

'Am I disturbing you?'

'No worries.'

He refrains from sitting down, however. 'Esme, I'm so sorry for what just happened. What Stef said was unforgiveable. And frankly unfathomable.'

'She was justified,' she answers in a low monotone. 'It's true that I did tell her some lies. In the past. I didn't think they mattered.'

'To do with Jake?'

He sees her nodding.

'Stupid question,' he says. 'There *is* nothing else in her world. Only him.'

'I'm not going to excuse myself. But at the time I thought it was simplest, and harmless. I really did. But it was wrong. And I didn't do the right thing by Jake, either.'

'You know, sometimes there is no right thing to do. You just have to make instant judgements all the time.'

'How is she now?'

'She was completely out of her mind in the dining room. Unhinged. Almost definitely drunk. Now she's locked in our room. She won't talk to me.'

'I'm so sorry,' Esme says, her voice now soft and tender. 'It must be awful for you.' He senses waves of empathy flowing from her, and he feels something inside him cracking.

'I've tried. I've tried for so long. And it's come to this. You know, I told her before we left that I wouldn't tolerate her boozing any more, that it would break us. And I think it has. And now I don't know which way to turn.' He bows his head, covering his face with both hands. He hears her chair scrape back, her tongue-click of sympathy, and feels her reassuring arm on his shoulder.

'I wish I could help,' she says. Her voice and gentle touch set something off inside him, a surge of emotion that he can no longer suppress. His body is wracked and he hears himself moan in pain, and then Esme is cradling him in her arms. Dumb gratitude for her comforting presence overwhelms him, and he wraps his arms around her. For a few seconds they are rocking back and forth. Burying his face in her neck, he feels her warmth, breathes in her perfume. The hard knots of tension in his head and neck are loosening, his skin is tingling to her touch. It feels so right. He realises that he has missed this intimacy for too long. He presses against her, caresses her hair, feels her breasts on his chest and kisses her neck. He feels her body stiffen but he persists, finding her face, kissing her cheeks and finally her mouth.

Suddenly he is propelled backwards as she struggles to disentangle herself. Though it is still pitch dark, he is aware of her stepping back, senses her wide-eyed stare no doubt filled with fear and outrage. 'No! Don't do that!'

'Esme, please. I'm sorry. I need you so much.'

'What the fuck!' Then she is stumbling against the chairs and tables, pushing past them, heading for the door and disappearing into the lobby.

Stunned, Laurie lowers himself into the wicker chair, head bowed, rubbing his palms against his brow and eyes. She might not have heard Stef's accusation, but she still thinks he is shit.

For a long time, he sits alone on the veranda, the din of the rain periodically accompanied by a deep roll of thunder. His thoughts are battered by cascades of lacerating guilt. He is only roused when the hostel's lights flash unexpectedly into life, this time remaining lit. He looks about him, blinking. He feels exposed, but thankfully there is no one in sight. He has no wish to speak to or be seen by anyone, and swiftly rises to his feet, hurries into the lobby and scampers upstairs as silently as he can. He sees and hears no one. The corridor is empty. He puts his ear to his bedroom door but there is no sound within. He knocks gently, then, when there is no response, harder.

There is no alternative. He returns downstairs. Now he can hear voices behind the closed door of the dining room, but not Thomas's. He goes behind the reception desk, and raps on the door that leads to the manager's quarters. There are footsteps, then the door opens a few inches and Thomas's face appears. For the first time since Laurie has known him, he looks annoyed.

'I need a key for my room,' Laurie tells him. 'My wife must have fallen asleep. I can't get in.'

'One minute, please.' The door clicks shut again, and a few moments later Thomas reappears with a key in his hand.

'Come,' he tells Laurie, slowly ascending the stairs with Laurie following. At the bedroom door, Thomas knocks softly, waits a few seconds, then inserts the key and turns it. As soon as he has pulled open the door Laurie is inside. The room is dark, but when he finds the light switch they can both see that it is empty.

'Thank you, thank you, Thomas,' he mutters as he takes in the room's disarray. Feeling the need to say something placatory, he continues in as calm a voice as he can manage: 'Very kind. We'll be checking out tomorrow, of course, as planned.' He can see that the hostel-manager is staring at the bed a-swirl with a confusion of bedsheets and, on the bedside table, the empty bottle of whisky. Glenmorangie. Desperately wishing that Thomas would leave, Laurie pulls open the door into the bathroom and tugs on the cord to switch on the light. At first he just sees the bathtub filled to the brim with water, with wide puddles on the floor around it. On the chair next to the tub there is an empty glass and a scatter of pills.

His heart stops, and he steps back in terror. There are two knees sticking out of the water, and there, in the tub, submerged, still clothed in her pale trousers and, for some reason, her travelling jacket zipped-up to the neck, is Stef. Her hair floats around her. Her eyes and mouth are open.

With a grunt of despair Laurie grasps her arms and attempts to heave her out of the water, but at first he can't move her, can't get a grip. A second, redoubled effort enables him to force her upright, soaking himself in the process. Strangely, she has her daypack strapped on her back. And then a heavy stone falls out of a jacket pocket and he realises that her jacket and daypack are both stuffed with rocks, weighing her down. They tumble out of the jacket into the tub. He recognises them from the garden – they are the ones used to border the flower beds. He unzips the jacket and wrenches it off her, but still he can't prise her out of the water. Her body slips from his fingers and slides back lifelessly, her hair trailing like reeds in the water. She is gone.

In horror, he steps back. His head is exploding. With a soundless scream he pushes past the paralysed figure of Thomas behind him, rushes out of the bedroom and hurtles downstairs into the lobby. Flowery is there at the desk, staring with alarm as he runs back into the storm outside.

He runs and runs. Out of the hostel gates, alongside the sewer, onto the road he runs, blinded and gasping, and doesn't hear the angry trumpet blast or the engine's roar until it is too late.

Chapter 51 | Aftermath

At noon the next day the bell from the temple is tolling an irregular rhythm. The monsoon rain has ceased for now, possibly to return in the evening.

'Can that be for Stef?' Oliver asks, ear cocked at the clanging bell.

'Of course not,' Cynthia tells him peremptorily as she fans herself with a rapid, machine-like motion. 'It's some Hindu ceremony. They often do it at this time of day.'

Oliver nods and looks away. He seems to find it difficult to meet Cynthia's eye, she has noticed, as if unsure of how to act. Idly, she wonders what training accountancy gives for this kind of situation.

They are seated on the veranda, waiting for a taxi. The local police have told them to stay in the area until enquiries have been completed. In any case they must arrange for the body to be flown back, unless Laurie expresses his intention to make any alternative arrangements. It is one of the many questions that hangs in the air, and will have to remain unanswered for the foreseeable future. Thomas, who has disappeared from view, apparently completely traumatised by the recent sequence of events, has left all practical matters in the hands of Flowery, who has organised the booking of a hotel in town for the couple. The police don't care where they stay as long as they know. Of course, there is no question of them remaining at the hostel.

From the entrance gates, Cynthia sees Dougie. All the beads and scarves have gone, and he is clean-shaven and wearing a broad-brimmed cotton hat and dark glasses, the sleeves of his check shirt neatly rolled.

He approaches their table and nods grimly.

'Mind if I join you?' he asks, to Cynthia's surprise.

'Please...' she says. She has hardly spoken to him or Jules since their arrival, but now a kind of survivors' solidarity has established a bond among the hostel's guests.

He gestures towards their cases stacked just inside the lobby. 'Are you off?'

Cynthia nods. 'We're not going far – a hotel somewhere, close to the hospital. It'll be easier to visit Laurie from there.'

'How is he?'

'The doctors say it's not life-threatening. A broken collarbone. It could have been a lot worse.'

'What actually happened?'

'He was struck by a motorcycle. Apparently he rushed out into the main road after finding Stephanie. Goodness knows what he was doing, or where he was going. He has concussion too.'

'Is he awake?'

'I don't know. I'm only saying what we've heard. We'll visit him this afternoon.'

'And you?' Dougie asks Cynthia. 'How are you both feeling?'

'Utterly shocked, of course, like everyone else. We're all a bit dazed.'

'I'm very sorry,' Dougie says. His voice is sober and sincere.

'Obviously, it was the last thing we expected,' Cynthia says. 'Obviously. Anyway – what are your plans?'

'I've found a homestay in town. In a quiet street. I'll stay until the police say I can leave.'

'With Jules, I suppose.'

'He's found a place too.'

'Oh...' Cynthia raises her eyebrows.

'We've decided we need a bit of time apart.'

'I see.'

'Things are a bit difficult right now,' Dougie explains. 'In fact Jules feels he might be partly responsible for what happened.'

457

'Surely not!'

Dougie shrugs. 'Something he said to Stef. We had a sort of row. He thinks it might have tipped her over the edge.'

'Oh, dear,' Cynthia says. 'Listen, you tell him that he shouldn't feel in the least responsible. Stephanie alone is responsible for what she did. She had a sort of row with me, too. A big row, actually. And she had a row with Laurie, and Esme, and … she was very angry, you see. She was quarrelling with everyone. So please tell Jules that none of this is remotely his fault. Honestly.'

'I know that,' Dougie says. 'He knows it too, on one level. But you can't help what you feel.'

'We're all in a state of shock. The reverberations affect everyone, and they will do for a long, long time, I'm afraid. You can't forget something like this, and you can't stop that inner voice of reproach. It's very normal.'

Dougie gives a tight smile, nodding but seemingly unconvinced.

'Nothing anyone said can have provoked her into taking such a drastic step,' Oliver interjects. 'She was literally out of her mind.'

Cynthia frowns at her partner, hearing the pomposity in his voice and knowing that Dougie will have heard it too. Turning back to him, she is struck by his expression, irretrievably sad and rather lost. 'When death strikes,' Cynthia says in her most grandmotherly tone, 'there's always a tendency to think you might have been able to make a difference. We all feel that, in varying degrees. I'm sure I said the wrong thing at some point, too, or could have acted differently. But we must banish those thoughts. They really don't help.'

Gazing across the garden, Dougie keeps silent, then says: 'Well, maybe it was the end of the road for us anyway. Everything's up in the air right now. So… Well, I'd better get packing. See you later.'

He gets up and disappears indoors.

'He seems rather shaken up,' Oliver says.

'That's hardly surprising,' Cynthia responds. 'Aren't we all?' She contemplates Oliver and wonders whether he too is feeling burdened by guilt. Didn't he play his part too? And did he rise to the occasion, show his mettle, or did he disappoint expectations? As it turns out, he is, after all, quite an ordinary man, she reflects, an aging, balding pensioner in the twilight of his life. Yes, quite ordinary, whatever he might have been in the past, whatever he might have done. She still doesn't know what it was that Miranda found out about him, but it matters now even less than it did before. All his mystique has evaporated. And she no longer knows what it was she expected of him, either. He was just a fantasy of hers, a construct. She had no right, really.

As she studies him, he turns to face her then quickly looks away. She sees the uncertainty and fear in his eyes, and a strange shyness. Is there also love?

And there is something else that she now feels for Oliver, something that surprises her somewhat: distrust. Just a thin sliver of it. Perhaps it was always there after all, just that it's more visible now, to both of them. Without doing anything she can put her finger on, and without omitting to do anything, he has somehow let her down. There is nothing she can point to, but she can't help feeling that he has not after all risen to the occasion. A line from Forster occurs to her: 'One touch of regret, not the canny substitute but the true regret, from the heart, would have made him a different man.' And for the first time she makes a comparison – one that she has never allowed herself to make – between her erstwhile husband, Roger, and this temporary husband, between the one who is so self-satisfied, the other who was fundamentally self-*un*satisfied. Stephanie, she now sees, inherited this too from her father.

Her cold, critical judgement shocks her. But it is no judgement, more a plain, unsentimental analysis of the way she feels. For everything has changed now, irreparably, and she is not capable of judging herself or anyone else. People are what they are.

Jake too. Even Jake. Most of all Jake. That construct they all had, the thousand constructs, they died with Stephanie. Just a confused boy, after all, accidentally turned into a god.

For something to do, she rummages in her bag, pulls out a packet of Fishermen's Friends and pops one in her mouth. Her hands fall on something else in her bag – a postcard. She takes it out and examines it. It is from the Chola museum they went to in Chennai, just two weeks and a lifetime ago. It is an image of Shiva Nataraja performing his cosmic dance. His hair is flying within the flaming halo, his face slightly smiling, his four hands pointing symbolically – one holding a fire, another a drum – while one foot stamps down upon a dwarfish demon. Cynthia turns over the card and sees her handwritten notes there, taken from the explanatory panels in the gallery. 'Damaru – drum beating the first sounds of creation. Agni – fire of creation/destruction. Dwarf = illusion, ignorance. Nataraja = lord of dance, king of actors.'

She puts the card back in her bag. It is her souvenir. The dance is done, and her vision is cleared a little. She is free of a few illusions. She welcomes her new unclouded clarity, feels foolish to have thought that she could live any other way, as if any other way could ever be a satisfactory basis for life. Whether she can reconcile herself with the new, unadorned version of Oliver is another matter. Probably, in the long run, she can. It will be a duller life, but on a sounder foundation. She couldn't hope for anything better at her age.

A sleek white taxi pulls into the hostel gates, and the couple get to their feet. The driver alights and loads their luggage into the boot. They have already paid their bill, thanked Thomas and Flowery, tipped Francis and Shibu, and made their awkward farewells. They will no doubt see Simon, Miranda and the others presently. It only remains for them now to leave. The driver holds open the door for Cynthia and she climbs in, next to Oliver. They exchange a brief clear-eyed glance, then both stare straight ahead. Only as the taxi pulls away does she turn to look back at the hostel, knowing that that she will never set eyes on it again, but equally sure that it will stay with her, a constant presence in the short time that remains of her time on earth.

Chapter 52 | The ocean

'Wait, stop!'

The rickshaw driver glances back at Miranda and obediently pulls into the side of the road.

'I'll walk the rest,' she tells the driver, climbing out. 'Here...' and she hands him three hundred-rupee notes – twice the sum that he quoted for the ride. He nods, revs, and shoots away. Miranda crosses the road, and calls after the figure she has spotted walking towards town.

Hearing her name, Esme stops and turns. She waits for Miranda to reach her.

'I was trying to get away without anyone seeing me,' she says as Miranda draws near. 'Can't handle goodbyes.'

Yes, Miranda notes, she looks well disguised, hiding behind dark glasses, a sun-hat pulled low and a scarf wrapped around the bottom half of her face. She is loaded up with a tall rucksack, yoga mat rolled up and strapped on the bottom, plus a shoulder bag and, around her waist, an embroidered bumbag. She could be any one of the thousands of travellers on the India trail.

'You're not hanging around for the police enquiries, then?' Miranda asks.

Esme shakes her head as she loosens her scarf and carefully lowers her rucksack onto the ground. 'I don't see the point. I had nothing to do with any of it, with what happened to Stef or Laurie's accident, so how can I make any difference? And it's all going to be endless bureaucratic mumbo-jumbo, isn't it?'

Miranda can understand Esme's need to distance herself from the events at the hostel, but she is still surprised by her hasty and surreptitious exit.

Perhaps reading the gist of Miranda's thoughts, Esme says: 'I'm sorry to leave so abruptly. I just really need to get away. I hate all this. It's so tragic and meaningless. And there's really nothing I can do here. I was going to write to you later, in the next day or two.'

'Don't worry,' Miranda is saying. 'It's all very weird. I can't really believe it myself. I've just come from the hospital.'

'How is Laurie doing?'

'He's unconscious, got a couple of broken bones, but the doctors say he's okay. He'll be very traumatised, of course.'

'And Simon?'

'I left him at the hospital. He's furious with everyone. Also shocked, naturally.'

'God, what a mess.'

'An all-round disaster. Completely unreal. So are you on your way to Kanyakumari now?'

Esme shrugs. 'I don't care. I don't have a ticket. I'm just going to board the first train that stops, wherever it's headed. I can't even face talking to a rickshaw driver so I thought I'd walk to the station.' The two women contemplate each other for a minute, then embrace. 'Listen,' Esme says, pulling away, 'I'll call you in a couple of days. It feels like I'm abandoning you all, running away and leaving you with all the shit to clear up, but I honestly won't be much use here. I've had enough. Don't tell anyone you saw me go.'

'Good luck, Esme.'

'Good luck!' And Esme shoulders her rucksack once more, adjusts her scarf, and continues her steady, anonymous walk to the station. She seems somehow diminished, Miranda thinks as she watches her go. She expected something more from Esme, though she cannot think why or what that could be.

Miranda sets off on the five-minute walk that will bring her back to the hostel, her heart a whirligig of emotion. She is so dazed by the events of the last twenty-four hours, she feels she is living in a dream.

Just inside the hostel gates she finds Shibu bent over his scooter. He straightens immediately and offers her one of his disarming smiles, but not quite so dazzling this time, there is a nuance of sympathy or regret or at least some awareness of the tragedy that has befallen them all and which cannot be verbalised. She smiles back appreciatively. He suddenly seems an emblem of normality.

In no particular hurry to enter the hostel, she pauses to admire the shiny Suzuki scooter.

'Beautiful!' she tells him.

He nods and contemplates it himself, pride painted on his face. He looks up, beaming, and for once he is looking directly at her, without the usual shyness. His eyes are bright and bold.

He pats the saddle. 'You come?'

'With you?' Miranda answers, stupidly she realises. 'Where?'

He gestures vaguely northward. 'Ocean!'

She raises her eyebrows and considers his unexpected offer, taking in his eager, friendly face, his bushy hair. He is wearing a spotless violet-coloured shirt with his usual, equally pristine white dhoti and his cheap rubber sandals on his cracked leathery feet. The ocean. It's an appealing prospect. She has not seen the sea since leaving Kochi. And yes – now seems a perfect time.

On an impulse, she nods. 'Okay. Wait.' Before she can entertain any second thoughts, she rushes up to her room, changes her blouse, finds a hat, and throws some money, her phone and a costume and towel into a bag. Five minutes later she is back on the hostel's drive. With an expression of slight surprise, Shibu looks up from polishing the scooter's chrome crash-bars and smiles again – *will he ever stop smiling*? He hoists up his dhoti, mounts the scooter and presses on the ignition. It purrs instantly into life. Then he pulls down a foot-rest for Miranda and gestures for her to mount behind him. She takes this as a signal that she should ride side-saddle, Indian-style. With her bag over her shoulder, she manoeuvres into position and wraps one hand around his thin waist, clasping him lightly and holding onto her hat with the other hand. There is no one to say goodbye to, nor has she any wish to seek someone out to tell them where she is going. Like Esme, she just wants to disappear.

Undoubtedly, what they are doing must be contravening numerous social norms, and briefly she wonders how serious the consequences could be – for Shibu if not for her. But she has to trust him. It's his country and she's in his hands now. He will let her know if they are going too far. She similarly dismisses the fleeting notions that she is putting herself in danger, that she doesn't know this man, that she is stepping into the unknown. In fact, this multiple infraction gives her a frisson of delight. She feels elated, invulnerable, armed with complete faith in her own powers of self-preservation.

It is Miranda's first scooter ride in India, and the sensation of the wind in her face and hair is exhilarating. Shibu drives carefully, avoiding pot-holes, slowing right down at the speed-bumps and rarely overtaking anything bigger than a bicycle. He doesn't try to converse, leaving her free to soak up the landscape undisturbed. At her request, he stops at a bridge to allow her to take photographs of the giant, spider-like Chinese fishing nets in action, dipping into the water on either side. The usual white egrets are perched in rows on the curved shafts, ready to snatch up any small creatures that are netted together with the bigger fish.

As they set off again, a renewed feeling of freedom blows through her in the rushing air. What an excellent pace to observe the countryside: slow enough to take it all in, fast enough to escape intrusive stares! Though she is not actually driving the scooter, she feels perfectly in control. She can observe the local people get on with their business, appreciate the minutiae of life, the daily tasks, the errands, the barefoot villagers walking calmly beneath the soaring coconut palms and along the reedy water courses, the men in dhotis, the women in saris, the children in their starchy school uniforms, farmers and fisher-folk and shopkeepers and policemen, a motley crowd, most of them ignoring her. There is water everywhere, in channels and canals and lakes, alongside the road or glimpsed through the trees. It isn't exactly an untarnished landscape, this is no postcard paradise, for there are discarded plastic bags to be seen, piles of rubble and ugly, half-completed cement constructions at regular intervals – but still there is something clean and natural and spontaneous in the corrugated shacks, the rough-and-ready acres of patchwork cultivation, the clusters of palms and banana trees, the explosions of hibiscus and orchids amid the unfettered vegetation. She wonders if she has finally found 'the real India', the one that has been eluding her, but she quickly dismisses the thought. The real India does not exist, she knows that now, she herself is no longer interested and anyone seeking it is sure to be disappointed.

After a drive of thirty minutes or so, they arrive at the sea – pale green, majestic and mighty under the towering bundles of purple-grey clouds. There are few people to be seen on the broad expanses of sand, just a couple of family groups straggling along the waterline or sprawled in untidy circles in the shadows of palms. Shibu does not stop at the first beaches but continues northward up the coast to where the shops and shacks are more dispersed and the most frequent figures to be seen on the sand are fishermen. Finally he slows down and draws to a halt beneath the shade of a row of banana trees.

He half turns, gestures to her to dismount, then does the same. He pulls the scooter onto its twin stand, locks it and pockets the key. He fetches a rolled-up bundle from beneath the saddle, which Miranda assumes contains everything he needs. 'Come,' he says, and they start walking towards the water. A warm breeze blows the dust from their hair and skin. They stop a few feet from the waves and, with an expert wriggle beneath his dhoti, he slips discreetly into baggy black bathing shorts. She follows suit, wrapping her towel around her as she changes into her one-piece, though keeping her shirt on over her costume for modesty's sake, as she has seen local women do. For once she feels quite unself-conscious about displaying her fleshy thighs. Shibu turns one of his huge smiles on her, then strides dauntlessly into the waves. She follows, equally enthusiastic, feeling the syrupy water lap at her calves, then her waist. It is warm but still refreshing, a blessed relief to body and spirit.

Later, they join other couples and families at a seafood restaurant in a nearby resort village. Conversation is minimal, but they laugh a lot. Apart from a brief text Miranda sends to Ian, she has swept her mind clean of memories and responsibilities.

An hour later, after dark has fallen, they mount back onto the scooter and ride a mile or two further north. Shibu parks outside an anonymous-looking concrete block next to the beach. They climb steps to the first storey, he produces a key and they enter a simple, starkly furnished room with flaking white walls and a bare bulb and fan suspended from the ceiling, and there is an adjoining bathroom. He draws up the shutters to reveal a small balcony and waves gently crashing just a few feet away. Miranda pulls open the door to the balcony and steps out. The moon lights up the sea. She turns her face up to the flower moon, which is nearly full, and it gazes back, fat and orangey between black clouds. It seems to encompass her with the sand and the sea and the sprays of stars visible in patches, bringing them all together as one. She feels wrapped up in the shawl of night, and a sensation of unity, of kinship with the clouds and heavenly bodies, passes through her, leaving a strange freshness behind.

Shibu is standing next to her, similarly caught up in the theatrical spectacle, and she feels that he too is part of the grand unifying force. Their fingers touch, then her hand is lightly held in his.

After a few more minutes, soothed by the sizzling grate of the waves, they step back through the doors into the room. There is one large double bed covered by a clean-looking sheet. Miranda switches off her phone and hangs her hat on the single hook on the back of the door. Without any fuss or ceremony, they disrobe and enter the shower. The water splutters at first, then flows silky and warm. Afterwards they make love on the bed and fall asleep to the whispering sounds of the sea.

Early the next morning, they contemplate the now velvety-looking ocean from the balcony, then don their costumes, cross the few feet down to the water, and, hand in hand, gingerly re-enter. It is cooler now, but still soft and welcoming. Miranda feels herself merge with it. She floats and bobs and sinks and swims, and finally surfaces onto the empty sand feeling like a goddess. It won't last, she thinks. But it doesn't matter.

Printed in Poland
by Amazon Fulfillment
Poland Sp. z o.o., Wrocław

62174639R00280